CRIME IN ITALY

CRIME IN ITALY

LEWIS VAUGHT

First published by Level Best Books 2023

This novel is entirely a work of fiction. The names, characters and incidents portrayed in it are the work of the author's imagination. Any resemblance to actual persons, living or dead, events or localities is entirely coincidental.

Lewis Vaught asserts the moral right to be identified as the author of this work.

Author Photo Credit: Carol Hommel

First edition

ISBN: 978-1-68512-254-6

Cover art by Richard Hendel

This book was professionally typeset on Reedsy.
Find out more at reedsy.com

To Kim

"The man's name was MacLyle, which by
looking at you can tell wasn't his real name,
but let's say this is fiction, shall we?"

> — THEODORE STURGEON,
> "AND NOW THE NEWS…"

Chapter One

It was a perfectly ordinary meeting that Thursday evening, right up to when the gun came out.

It was a closed meeting, no visitors allowed, in theory at least. Not that being overrun with tourists is a major problem in AA. It was the Thursday night Twelve and Twelve meeting at St. Luke's Methodist, on 86th Street. Since it was the last Thursday of the month, we read a tradition from the *Twelve Steps and Twelve Traditions,* and since it was March, we read the Third Tradition, "The only requirement for AA membership is a desire to stop drinking." Counting Schwartz and me, there were eighteen men and seven women present at the beginning of the meeting at 8:00 p.m., none of us newcomers to AA, or even first-timers at that meeting.

Phil G., a former sponsee of Schwartz's, ambled into the meeting late, as usual, and took a seat back at the south end of the room, wearing also as usual a none-too-clean pair of jeans and a T-shirt too small for him, and no mask. This particular T-shirt was black with white block lettering: "I'm the Youngest, and the Rules Don't Apply to Me," which might have been cute on someone forty years younger. Certainly a ten-year-old whose gut didn't show between the shirt-tail and the top of his pants would have been considerably more charming. It had been almost a year since Phil and Schwartz had parted ways, Schwartz telling Phil he needed to get a new sponsor, one who could help him take the Fourth Step, not one who could do it for him. The separation hadn't gone particularly smoothly.

Phil sat there with his usual ominous glowering smirk, while the discussion of the Third Tradition went on. As usual, he was playing with his phone, watching either America's Funniest Home Videos or some rock video, most often the 1979 AC/DC song "Highway to Hell." He watched that video and listened to that song over and over, and he liked to tell people that was the first song he'd learned to play, and he told people that over and over as well, so that it was clear Phil had more problems than just garden-variety alcoholism, a matter which I happened to know Schwartz had discussed with Phil's mother. I had been in the room when Schwartz made the call, because he had wanted evidence of the discussion, just in case. He takes sponsorship seriously, as he assured Phil's mother, who was definitely not Ms. or Mrs. G. anymore, if she ever had been.

At least tonight, Phil had the sound turned off on his phone. It would not have been unusual for him to try to show the video to someone else after or even during the meeting, although he had been reminded any number of times that no one comes to an AA meeting to see a video. In fact, because phones are also cameras and because that "Anonymous" is important to a lot of people, it's really bad manners to have a phone out in a meeting, quite aside from the matter of paying attention to what's being said. Phil clearly considered that manners were among the things that didn't apply to him, or perhaps he simply didn't recognize manners. Identifying the source of another person's motivation is difficult and may say more about your own experience than theirs.

As usual, when it was his turn to read, Phil said he was just going to listen, not that he did so, and the turn passed to the person on his right, Tony M. What wasn't usual about Phil on this occasion was that he had laid a dark blue canvas bag on the floor by his chair, but I didn't really pay attention to the anomaly, because I had long-since ceased finding Phil interesting. My bad, mistaking unpleasant for unworthy of attention.

Tony finished the reading, then the fellow chairing, Jeff, asked who would like to begin the discussion. A longtime member across the room said, "My name's Lew, and I'm an alcoholic." People said, "Hi, Lew." Lew went on,

"I'm grateful for this tradition, in that if the requirements were any stricter, I probably wouldn't qualify." There was no sign that he had captured Phil's attention.

"You hear well-meaning, good-intentioned people talk about how their belief in God has been a crucial part of their recovery," Lew said, "and that's fine, but then some people go on to say that without belief in God, you don't have a chance at staying sober. Thanks to this program, I've been able to stay sober for over twenty-one years, and I don't believe in the supernatural in any form whatsoever."

Lew went on for a couple minutes, then he passed, and people thanked him. Lew was a tad defensive about his atheism, but everyone was used to it, and to him, and nobody was upset one way or the other. The discussion passed to Iris, a slim, nice-looking woman in her mid-thirties, on his right. In her light gray slacks, open-neck white blouse, and dark blue sweater over her shoulders, she might have walked straight to the meeting from a Land's End photoshoot.

The fact is that almost all my attention was actually on the meeting. Iris had a pleasant voice and, as usual, kept her comments relevant to the topic and serious but not solemn, then it was Julia's turn. Julia, around forty, dressed for success, so apparently still going to the office, very quietly said she was just going to listen. After Julia, it was Ashley's turn. Ashley, a bit younger than Iris and I, late twenties perhaps, in jeans and a work shirt, short-cropped hair, shared for a couple of minutes, in her pleasant, soft-spoken eastern Kentucky or West Virginia accent, with her usual insight and good sense, then passed to Paul. Paul, a tall, slightly balding, slightly heavy man in his late forties or early fifties, like Julia in office wear, agreed that inclusion was a good thing so far as he was concerned. Paul then said, wandering a bit off-topic, "My understanding is that stupid is a life sentence, but crazy they can work with." Paul went on in that vein for a minute or so, then passed.

I was next. "My name is Rainer," I said, "and I'm an alcoholic." That was when Phil stuck his phone in his hip pocket, reached down into his bag, and took out a very large, very shiny revolver. He stood up, and I shut up, and the room was suddenly very quiet.

Ignoring me and everyone else, Phil held the revolver at his side and walked directly toward where Schwartz and I were sitting. Phil was smiling except for his eyes. A few people gasped and made other soft noises of alarm as he approached Schwartz. "Leo," he said, "you dumped me, and it's time for payback, motherfucker."

Schwartz, sitting on my right, had my right wrist in his left hand, stopping my hand on its way to the back of my belt. "I've got it," he murmured. He let go of me and stood up as Phil came up to him. Phil held the gun a few inches from Schwartz's broad chest, his hand not quite steady, the muzzle of the revolver wavering but never moving away from Schwartz's center of mass. Phil squeezed the trigger.

Nothing happened. Phil looked at the big gun, shook it as if trying to get it loose from something that wasn't there. He looked back at Schwartz, repeated, "Motherfucker," and squeezed again, again without result. Over and over, he tried to fire the piece, repeating the word like a mantra, then Schwartz reached out, got his left hand around the barrel of the revolver, and forced it downward, as Phil kept on trying to shoot. With his right hand, Schwartz got hold of the butt and, with a sudden effort, twisted the revolver free of Phil's grasp.

"Now, gentlemen," Schwartz said, not very loud but quite clearly.

As if they'd rehearsed it, in a sudden rush, five of the other men got hold of Phil, and they dragged him none too gently back to his chair and sat him down on it. The room was abruptly filled with voices, Phil yelling obscenities at the guys holding him in his chair, some of them giving him some of the same back, and others just talking in a release of tension.

Schwartz snapped, "Quiet!" and the room got quiet, aside from Phil.

I'm not sure how Schwartz does that without actually being loud. I called 911 and explained the nature of our emergency. I noticed that the one person who had already been quiet was Julia, who sat weeping, her shoulders heaving, three chairs over from Phil. Iris and Ashley, on either side of her, held her, patted her shoulder, assured her everything was all right, which struck me as appropriate even if it wasn't particularly true.

Schwartz said quietly, "Just shut up, Phil," and nodded to me.

Knowing Schwartz would be thinking of the revolver as evidence, I drew my P239 and held it at my side. That got Phil's attention. Actually it got everyone's attention. Julia's sobs were still audible, but relatively subdued.

Tony and Bert stood next to Phil, each with a hand on his shoulder, and Schwartz brought a chair up close, in front of him, sat down, and began speaking to Phil, while we waited for the police to arrive. He held the revolver the way you hold a revolver, pointing the muzzle down, so Phil had two reasons to be quiet. Schwartz's voice was low, steady, utterly calm. He flicked back the gate behind the cylinder, pushed the ejector back, and a big cartridge popped out, fell on the carpet. He clicked the cylinder around a notch, ejected another bullet.

"As I explained at the time, two years ago, Phil," Schwartz said, as he went on unloading the gun, "I quit as your sponsor because, after a lot of work and a lot of thought, I finally realized I wasn't doing you any good. I told you you needed a new sponsor. A sponsor's job is to lead you, guide you, help you through the Twelve Steps, but you have to follow your sponsor's lead, and you couldn't or wouldn't or anyway didn't do that with me. We got to the Fourth Step, and you refused to do it. Remember?" Phil responded with his favorite polysyllable.

"We went over and over how to do a searching and fearless moral inventory of yourself, and you said you were going to do it, and you said you were doing it, but you weren't. You wrote nothing about your character defects, nothing about your wrongs. The only thing you wrote was a list of people you thought you should make amends to, and that's Step Eight, not Three or Four." Phil suddenly tried to get free of Tony and Bert's grip, without success. Schwartz went on. "When push came to shove, you suggested that I write your Fourth Step for you."

"You could've done it," Phil snarled. He tried again to shrug off Tony, a former Colts linebacker, and Bert, who had no particular chops that I was aware of but was clearly up to the task at hand. They pressed downward on his shoulders, and Phil stayed in his chair. And, of course, Schwartz was sitting squarely in front of him, holding the revolver.

"Forgive me for going on like this," Schwartz went on, "but the fact is that I have a certain amount of nervous tension to release, thanks to your antics, and it's either shoot you dead or talk. For some reason, I'd rather talk. You wanted me to do your Fourth Step for you, and I went over and over it with you, explaining why that wasn't going to happen. The bottom line is that you didn't want a sponsor, Phil; you wanted a free ride. Pardon the personal remark, but it seems to me that's what you want from life, and that's what you want from AA. I worked with you longer than I should have, because I didn't want to give up. But there are other alcoholics who do need and want help. I can't do the steps for you, and you're not entitled to a free ride. No one is. Nobody is, inside or outside of AA."

I'd asked Gwen to go out in the hall to direct the police, and we heard footsteps approaching the room, then Gwen's voice, "In here. It's all right now." Schwartz turned the revolver in his hand, looked at it and at the six cartridges on the floor, noted quietly but distinctly, "It was fully loaded," then he laid the gun on the carpet, under his chair. I holstered my Sig. Schwartz sat back as two police officers entered the room, Glocks drawn but at their sides. I had told the 911 operator the gun had been taken away from the assailant, but the cops knew guns didn't always stay taken away.

They were strangers to me, but Schwartz knew the older one, Olson. Schwartz took the lead in explaining the sequence of events. Olson, maybe thirty-five, gave their names to the room. There was no tilde on his partner's name tag, but Olson pronounced his partner's name correctly, of course. Olson told Peña, "This is Leo Schwartz and his man Rainer Zufahl; they're private investigators." He didn't sound overly impressed. Cops make a point of not being impressed by PIs. I was surprised he knew my name, and more surprised that he pronounced it correctly: *z* as in "pizza," rhymes with "minor you-all."

Both officers secured their sidearms. Olson took a pen from his breast pocket and used it to pick up the shiny revolver from under Schwartz's chair, showing it to Peña. Peña, who I'd guess had maybe only a year or two on the force, nodded and got the cuffs on Phil's wrists, leaning him forward to do so, and Olson asked Schwartz, "You just took this away from him while he was trying to shoot you with it?" Peña took out a notepad once he had Phil cuffed.

Schwartz was smug but trying hard not to seem so. "I could see that it was a Peacemaker-style revolver," he said, "and the hammer was down. I was actually in no real danger, unless he'd tried to hit me with it or, less likely, figured out how to fire it. It's a Ruger Super Redhawk in .44 magnum," he went on. "It's single-action, so it has to be cocked manually before every shot. Apparently, Phil didn't realize that." From the look on Phil's face, now that he'd had that explained to him, he'd like to have another try at shooting Schwartz for being a lousy sponsor, or perhaps for the public firearms instruction. He contributed four syllables to the discussion.

From the look on Schwartz's face, he had regrets too. Olson placed the Ruger in a large plastic bag he'd taken from one of the black pouches on his heavy belt, but the long barrel kept him from zipping it all the way closed. He scooped up the bullets with an index card, dumped them into a smaller bag. "Unbelievable," he said. "You were that confident, with the fucking barrel practically against your chest." I got the definite impression that Olson was now impressed. Indy cops on the job don't generally talk like that inside churches, even in AA meetings, especially around white people, which all but two of us were.

"I didn't really have much choice, you see," Schwartz said. "By the way, you'll probably get at least as many of my prints off that as you get of his." He nodded toward Phil. "The prints on the cartridges will not be mine. However, there are plenty of witnesses to what happened. But I'd exercise discretion in asking for statements; not everyone here is eager to shed their anonymity."

"Oh, naturally," Olson said, "Of course, I wouldn't want to ask for names merely because people in an AA meeting happened to witness an assault with a deadly weapon. But Jesus." He wiped his brow with his free hand, turned to Peña. "Get names of witnesses willing to give names, and for God's sake, you know the routine." Olson and Schwartz were obviously acquainted with each other.

Olson asked me why I hadn't done anything to protect my employer.

Before I could get a word out, Schwartz said, "Having assessed matters, I specifically forbade Mr. Zufahl from opposing the attacker so that I could deal with the situation myself, hoping to avoid unnecessary violence."

Olson told me, "You're armed," and I affirmed it. On request, I showed him my State of Indiana private detective's license, my CCW permit, and the Sig in the holster at the back of my belt. "Everything's in order here," he conceded. Cops can sometimes resent it when they have no reason to haul you in, especially if you happen to be a private eye, but Olson was being big about it. As I said, he knew Schwartz. He didn't ask for Schwartz's license, just the number, and Schwartz gave it to him, from memory, of course. Schwartz showed him his S&W, also 9mm. There are private detectives who go around unarmed, of course. In books.

Peña had quite a bit of contact information in his notebook, and was still getting more, while keeping an eye on Phil. I found it gratifying how many people volunteered their statements and their contact information, Iris and Ashley and, bless us, Julia included. AA is, after all, supposed to be somewhere you can be anonymous, but that didn't seem to be much of a concern with this crowd, some of whom had been seeing Schwartz and me at meetings for years and all of whom were seeing for the first time that we were carrying. Flourishing firearms during meetings in churches is not encouraged, even in a red state like Indiana. Of course, they'd all been seeing Phil for a while too.

The meeting was certainly over. Olson asked Schwartz and me to come down to the 42nd Street station to help with the processing. Bert and Tony ended up coming too, which was kind of them.

Olson and Peña led the way, with Phil between them, Peña holding Phil's right arm. Schwartz had to put up with quite a few hugs and handshakes before we could leave the church. He is not a hugger, but I was proud of the way he took it. We followed the officers and Phil out to the parking lot, got into our cars. I drove, following the black and white, and Tony and Bert followed us. We went over to College Avenue, then south to the station.

At the station, two officers took Bert and Tony aside to get their statements, and Phil used his phone call to reach out to his mother rather than to a lawyer. She said she'd call him a lawyer, Phil told the police. Then he handed the phone to Schwartz. "She wants to talk to you."

Schwartz took the phone and listened, and for whatever reason, the police just suspended operations in place, after re-cuffing Phil, while the one-sided conversation went on for a couple minutes. Then Schwartz said, "No, actually, it's not a matter of my pressing charges, Madam." He listened some more. "No, Madam, your son threatened me with a loaded firearm, albeit ineffectually, and the officers confirm that that constitutes assault with a deadly weapon, which is a felony." More listening. "No, I can't just make it go away…. No, I'm afraid not, madam. It's not merely a civil matter; it's a criminal offense—"

Finally, Schwartz sighed and handed the phone to the desk sergeant, who listened for a few moments, then broke in to tell her where Phil was and to remind her to get in touch with that lawyer. He added that the police were also interested in knowing where Phil had gotten the gun, since he said it wasn't his. He listened awhile, then hung up, and added Phil's phone to the plastic bag containing his other personal effects, not including the revolver, naturally.

"She says it's her husband's," he told us. "He keeps it in the nightstand, loaded." To Phil, "Your stepfather's, right? You realize that's theft, on top of the assault, unless he lies and claims he gave you permission? Which I didn't get the impression he was likely to do, but you never know." It didn't seem to make much of an impression on Phil, who told the cop to give him his phone back. Officer Dickens declined to do so, but gave him a face mask, which Peña secured for him, and Dickens went on with the check-in procedure, and then they took Phil back to a holding cell. They went over the information with Schwartz and me again, confirmed they had our address, phone, and so forth. Tony and Bert signed their statements, so did Schwartz and I, and we were free to go. Schwartz thanked Olson and Peña before we left, not ostentatiously.

Schwartz and I shook hands with Bert and Tony outside the station, thanked them for coming down with us, and we headed home. "Quite a meeting tonight," Schwartz said as we turned east onto 80th Street. I agreed with him.

Chapter Two

At about nine-thirty the next morning, I was dusting the room I call the office and Schwartz calls the library, when the phone rang. One of these days Schwartz's office, or library, will contain the last landline in North America. I was closer to my desk than to his, so I sat down as I picked up my phone. "Leo Schwartz's office, Rainer Zufahl speaking. How may I help you?"

A fairly familiar voice said, "Rainer, it's Iris Warner. You know, from the 12 & 12 and the Big Book meetings at St. Luke's?" I recognized her first name of course, but Warner had been news to me the night before, when she'd given her name to the police. I assumed that Zufahl had been news to her as well. I said yes, of course, I remembered her. "That was quite a meeting last night," she said.

"That's exactly how Mr. Schwartz put it, and I certainly concur," I said. "It's good to hear from you, Iris. What can we do for you? Or did you just want to make sure we made it home all right?"

"No, not at all. Well, I mean, it's not just to see…I'm not sure whether it's you and Leo I need, or just you," she said. From her voice, she was under some strain, and I didn't think it was left over from watching Schwartz disarm Phil and hold him for the police yesterday. "I don't really know how to go about this, Rainer."

People who pronounce my name correctly move to the head of the line, and she got it just right. Of course, she'd heard it from me every time I'd read or shared in a meeting at First Baptist, but I was in no mood to deduct points. I found myself unexpectedly very interested in this conversation. "Well, Iris, we can take it either way, your preference. I can make an appointment for you with Mr. Schwartz, and naturally, I'd be present too, or if you'd rather, I could meet you somewhere." Folks who need a private eye or think they might can require careful handling.

"Do you think you could—" Iris broke off. Then after a short pause, "Could you come over to the house this afternoon? I think it would be easier to talk about here, actually."

"Sure," I said. I checked the calendar to make sure, but it was just as wide open as I'd thought. "What time would be convenient?"

"Could we say two o'clock?"

"Fine," I said. "Would you like me to bring Mr. Schwartz or—"

"I think I'd rather explain it just to you," Iris said, "if that's all right. It's one of those things that …" Whatever it was would be just between us, for the time being, that is. No doubt there are operatives who keep business secrets from the boss, but I'm not one of them.

"I understand," I said, not entirely dishonestly. "Can you give me the address, please?"

"Certainly," she said. I was surprised when she told me it was in the low eighties on Morningside Drive, which was only a few blocks west and a little north from where I was sitting, albeit in Meridian Hills, the other side of College Avenue. Houses and grounds in MH tend to be several times the size of their counterparts in Windcombe, where Schwartz and I live. Schwartz's wife used to call our neighborhood the Greater Williams Creek Area, with a wide smile that made it clear how little she cared about it.

I told Iris I'd see her at her house at two o'clock, and after the usual amenities, we hung up. I finished dusting, sorted the mail, placed Schwartz's on the center of his desk blotter, and took a look at the stuff intended for my attention.

Now, I want to be straight with you, and I will report things as they happened, the way they happened, but at times it's a bit hard to decide what to put in and what to leave out. That is, sometimes I'll need to mention things that occurred, but that's for completeness, with no guarantee of relevance.

Schwartz's mail that morning, for example, included, among other things, two items that could easily be taken as portents, but shouldn't be. There was the monthly newsletter *American Fireworks News,* with its motto "He Who Hath Once Smelt the Smoke Is Ne'er Again Free," and there was the new *NAR Member Guidebook.* So I'm telling you right up front: Schwartz belongs to the Pyrotechnics Guild International and the National Association of Rocketry, but not to the NRA. He has been making fireworks and setting them off on the Fourth of July and New Year's, and he has been designing, building, and flying model rockets and high-power rockets, both since long before we met, over ten years ago. He likes to point out that amateur rocketry and pyrotechnics have nothing to do with each other. And he certainly knows guns. If I could have left all that out and stayed honest, I would have; it would have been easier, heaven knows. For what it's worth, his books on rocketry, pyrotechnics, and firearms take up about eight feet of the shelves that line all four walls of the office from floor to ceiling. All things considered, it's hardly disproportionate.

To tell you the truth, all this—telling the truth, I mean—is turning out to be harder than I expected, but I hope it will be helpful, to myself at least, in getting clear about what happened that eventful spring, the first spring of the plague.

Anyway, I was dealing with my share of the mail when Schwartz came into the office, or library, and said good morning. He was wearing a dark blue tie with a light blue broadcloth shirt and jeans, with a corduroy jacket that matched the tie. As usual, he set down his coffee cup on the coaster and took off the jacket, and hung it over the back of his chair before he sat down to the mail. He went through it, and by the time I'd dealt with the bills and letters and had given them to him for his signature, he was reading a fireworks article by Ian von Maltitz. When he finished it, he signed the letters, okayed the bills, and asked me what was new and exciting.

I told him about the call from Iris Warner, whom, of course, he remembered, and he agreed that he could manage without me for a couple hours that afternoon. "If, that is, you feel safe without a chaperone," he added.

I figured I'd go ahead and rise to the bait. Might as well, given that he pretends to think any woman under sixty is planning to disrupt our current arrangement. He and I both live in his house. My bedroom is on the second floor, down the hall from his. The bed, dresser, chairs, table, and books and pictures, and other things in my room belong to me.

I told him, "Yeah, I gave it a lot of thought before accepting her invitation. God only knows what her wiles are like on her home turf. She's certainly good-looking enough, which means she's probably married. But I reflected that, in the absence of concrete evidence one way or the other, I really have no idea about that, one way or the other." I was warming to my theme. "As I think I've heard you mention, theorizing in advance of the facts is a poor idea, and a house in Meridian Hills means an income that wouldn't be strained even by one of your most exorbitant invoices, so I decided to risk it."

"Pfui," he answered. "You know that I know you well enough to know that you would go even if you had incontrovertible evidence that she was a black widow planning to add another fly to her collection." He picked up the NAR guide, glanced inside, dropping the discussion. "I see they've dispensed with the table of contents this time."

"Yeah, that's a hell of a note," I said.

"Well, it certainly makes it harder to find what's in and where it is." I refrained from pointing out that it wasn't my fault. Listening to Schwartz comment on the world's shortcomings is about half of what he pays me for, I suspect. He picked up his current book, Daniel Kahneman's *Thinking Fast and Slow,* opened it to the leather strip he used for a bookmark, and leaned back to read. "Why rely on the address? Check with the bank about Ms. Warner's solvency. I happen to know that she used to be married to a billionaire. She could be a pauper now." That was typical Schwartz, all right. A couple times a week for at least a couple years he and I had seen Iris a couple nights a week, and we were Leo and Rainer to her, but once she looked like she might become a client to be billed, it was all business.

"Sure thing, boss," I said. He hates being called that. He long since quit trying to stop it, because he knows I only use it when he's earned it. Check on the client's ability to pay. Next he'd be telling me to wear gloves and booties at a crime scene.

I finished up the routine, got the small stack of items for the bank, and went to the garage. I hadn't driven the Prius in a while, so I took it for the errands I had to run in Nora, five blocks north and a few east. Like all three of Schwartz's cars, it's an inconspicuous gray. Also like all of Schwartz's cars, there's more under the hood than one might expect.

After I'd taken care of the deposits and had learned that Iris Warner and for that matter her former husband, Buckland Norman Warner, who was Buck to Herb Green, the assistant bank manager I spoke with, could take care of any foreseeable fee about a thousand times, I ran by Kroger with Schwartz's list of items for dinner. It was one of those blue-sky March days that says spring is here to stay this time—a lying sky. In Indiana, "weather" is just another word for "betrayal."

I finished up the shopping and took the Prius back to the house. I left it in the drive, since I'd be taking it to Iris's later. Schwartz was back with his book, and he didn't look up when I came in.

I typed up my notes for Schwartz, filed them, and emailed the file to him. It's not the most efficient system, but it gets him the information. Buck Warner had graduated Purdue with a double major in math and computer science and had within a year made his initial pile just over twenty years before, with a program that simplified collation of medical records, according to the bank manager. I gathered this allowed doctors, nurses, and other medical and insurance personnel to get their jobs done in lots less time and with lots less effort, with an extreme reduction in errors. Buck was still head of WarnerCorp, no space and no period, the company he'd founded when he had the product ready for market, and it seemed that it was still very small, about a dozen people altogether, all of whom had made out very nicely by being in from the start. It wasn't clear that they had any new products, aside from upgrades of the original program, which was called WarnerCōp, long *o*, no *e*. On the other hand, it wasn't clear that they needed any new products, since nobody in the company ever had to work again if they didn't feel like it. Or that they would give a damn about my opinion of their name for a medical-database enhancement.

Besides sending him the electronic file, I printed out the inevitable hard copy for Schwartz. His theory is that it's harder to burn paper files in a safe than to erase them from a computer. I've never really tested the idea myself.

"No additional instructions?" I asked him before leaving for Iris Warner's.

"Just the usual," he said. "We know Ms. Warner one way, as a fellow alcoholic, which may be highly relevant or totally otherwise in regard to her case, if indeed she has a case." He closed the book on his thumb. "It will be interesting to learn what she says she wants to see you about, and what she *really* wants to see you about. Remember that all is not necessarily as it seems, although sometimes things are exactly as they seem. It may or may not be related to last night's ruckus. As if you need my advice. Intelligence guided by experience. And as I've said any number of times, alcoholics are like other people, only more so." He went back to the book, muttering, "Merci, Rick."

I said I'd bear it all in mind, and I made sure the front door was locked behind me when I went out to the Prius. I could have walked over in ten or fifteen minutes, but a stranger walking without a dog in Meridian Hills is likely to upset someone with little enthusiasm for strangers.

So, not wishing to spook the natives, I drove over to the Meridian Hills address, reflecting that yesterday we hadn't had a case in a couple weeks and hoping this would turn out to be something financially worthwhile, which was more than one could say about the ruckus with Phil. As I turned from 81st onto Morningside, driving slowly among the large, heavily wooded lots and the large, heavily overbuilt houses, I reflected further that, when the time came, it could be a real pleasure to make out the bill for whatever services we might end up rendering. The branches of sycamore, oak, and cottonwood overhead were letting the first of their leaves out to catch some sun. I concentrated on nature to push away what Schwartz calls my nascent revolutionary impulses.

The Warner house was large and what Schwartz would probably call pseudo-classical, with a row of white columns along a roofed porch in front, bay windows, dormers on the third floor, and a parking area big enough for a tennis court. Unlike some of the surrounding mansions, it was set on a generous lot, so you didn't feel you were walking into a frat house. I put the Prius behind a silver Mercedes, with a Toronto Orange Corvette drawn up very close to it, top down, too close to let someone get in the driver's side of the Mercedes. I had seen the Mercedes in the parking lot at meetings, so I figured the Corvette might be Buck's, but for all I knew, it might be Iris's second car. I checked; it was a console automatic, which I filed away to mention to Schwartz. He would never buy a sports car himself, any more than he'd try to get his picture in the paper, since the last thing a detective wants to be is conspicuous, but he had very definite ideas about stick shifts, and I suspected he'd tack five or ten percent onto the bill just for that automatic transmission.

I put on my mask and admired the view of the winding road between the trees as I went up the flagstone walk, and I realized I was looking forward to seeing Iris outside the rooms of AA, in her natural element, so to speak. I wondered why as I rang the bell and heard it sound inside the house.

Iris opened the door herself. I had half-expected to be admitted by the help, but she seemed to be a regular do-it-yourselfer in her faded jeans, another white shirt open at the throat, and a pair of worn-looking zapatos on her feet. On either side of her mask, her light brown hair was gathered back in a short ponytail. "Thanks for coming, Rainer," she said. "I appreciate it."

I said I was glad she'd called. She let me in, then led the way down a hall with a spacious, well-lighted living room on the left, a slightly more formal parlor or something on the right, then a dining room and kitchen complex at left, and at right a surprisingly extensive library that looked like someone spent time there. A desk in the center held a laptop and the usual paraphernalia, and there was a pale blue sweater over the back of the leather desk chair. We proceeded to a large flagstone patio, with a pergola providing partial shade, not that it was really needed. The sun felt good. A blue ceramic pitcher and matching beakers and bowls with chunks of lemon, sugar cubes, and mint leaves graced a glass-top table between a pair of padded lawn chairs well out of the shade.

"I hope iced tea is all right?" Iris said. There was something appealing about how she made a statement sound like a question. I told her it was fine, and we sat. Iris poured iced tea, suggesting we could do without the masks while we drank it. I agreed.

I tried my tea, nodded approval. It was based on straight Lipton's or someone's oolong, brewed quite strong and chilled almost down to freezing, but with something else laid over that brisk, astringent tea, and I thought I detected hints of nuts and spices. "Hmm, there's vanilla and clove, isn't there? And almond, maybe? And something else I can't quite place. It's really very good." Truth helps with small talk.

"You got it almost exactly," Iris said. "There is also a tiny amount of caraway and a touch of pistachio. The trick is not overdoing the nuts. You just want a tiny bit of that nutty taste."

I nodded. "I'll be sure to tell Mr. Schwartz about it," I said. "I know he'll be interested."

"I'll send a Thermos home for him," Iris said. "I remember he has expressed a fondness for iced tea." I had heard her talk in AA meetings, of course, but I'd never noticed how similar her voice was to Freda's, Schwartz's late wife. I hadn't heard Freda's voice in almost three years.

Even though we'd been in meetings at the same time, we'd never been just the two of us together before, without the rest of the room. Iris was probably concerned about AA democracy, I thought. It can be an effort for alcoholics to switch over from AA to real-world mode, not that it always is, but it can be.

"He'll appreciate it," I said. I didn't recall Schwartz discussing iced tea in a meeting, but that didn't mean much. Trying to remember everything you hear in an AA meeting is a good way to go crazy. I took another drink of iced tea, then set the cup down on the table. "So, what can we do for you, Ms. Warner?"

"Oh, it's 'Ms. Warner' for the client, hmm?" She smiled. "Why don't we just drop the pretense that we don't know each other, Rainer? I'm Iris, and you've heard me share God knows how many times, and I've heard you share, and the same for Leo, but I've never talked about my marriage in the rooms. I keep that for my sponsor and just one of my sponsees. But we know each other in the way we need to. Including Leo. He's impressive.

"I feel I can trust you, like I can trust some other people in the rooms. Not everybody, but you guys, certainly." She drank some tea. "I didn't know you and Leo were detectives until about a year ago. There was something you said in a meeting that piqued my curiosity, and I looked you up. In fact, I used a firm WarnerCorp has worked with to do a little research, just to make sure I wasn't getting myself into trouble." More tea. "It was all good news. You and Leo check out just fine, it seems." She waited, and I nodded agreement. "He really makes fireworks?" she said. I nodded. "And rockets?" I nodded again. "And collects guns?" Yep.

Iris shifted gears. "I got sober at twenty-five, after seven horrible years, and I've got almost seven years; next July 14 will be seven years since my last drink."

I thought about sharing my sobriety date and so on but decided against it. The client to be was talking.

"I asked you here about my husband, or rather ex-husband," Iris said. "We split this past year, you know. It was completely amicable, really. Buck is still drinking, sometimes more than he should, but not often, really. It's not for me to say whether he's an alcoholic, but for what it's worth, I don't really think he is. It didn't bother him that I wasn't drinking with him. You know the way drinking wives and husbands sometimes get resentful about the alcoholic spouse when they get sober? Well, Buck wasn't like that at all. But the truth was that we got married too early. We were young and bright and full of confidence, financially successful, incredibly so. But ten years later we had grown apart. Maybe it's just that we hadn't grown together, if you understand what I mean?"

I hadn't a clue of course. I've never been married, but I nodded, I hoped sympathetically. "I think I know about what you mean," I said. "I've known other people it's happened to." I didn't understand them either, now or at the time.

"But I had my money, and since Buck was the one who really wanted the divorce primarily—"

"The divorce was his idea?" I have to say I found that a little hard to believe, but I hadn't met Buck Warner.

"Yes, and once I realized that he didn't want to be married to me anymore, I found I didn't really want to be married to him either. It's almost as if we slept together, had this ten-year dream, then woke up and realized it was time to go home. If that makes sense."

As much as people's later explanations for their earlier actions ever make sense, I thought, but didn't say. It was really extraordinary, the way that pale March sunlight showed the lights and darks of her hair and the faint freckling across her nose and cheekbones.

"So, anyway, we've stayed friends, or actually, I should say we've become friends, since the divorce was final, ah, ten months ago. I mean, we stay in touch better than we did when we were married, and it turns out not living together is great for both of us." She closed her eyes a moment, apparently getting ready to take the plunge.

"I'm not sure about all the details," she said, "but something is strange at WarnerCorp, and it has got Buck worried, really wrapped around the axle. There's something wrong financially, and I don't know exactly what it is. Buck was looking into it, and he said he'd gotten as far into things as he could, using internal sources of information. He said he didn't want to use our usual in-house people, because it might be one or more of them who are up to no good. Then, two days ago, Wednesday, he simply stopped talking to me about it, or anything else, really.

"It's making me crazy, not knowing whom to trust, and I think it's been making Buck crazy too, and maybe that's why he's clammed up, but I don't know that. I'd like you to find out what it is and maybe help me, help us figure out what to do about it, if you can. Find out, I mean." She was gripping that stoneware cup like she was trying to leave fingerprints on it.

"Of course, Iris," I said. I thought about people being such good friends they have each other investigated. "How do you suggest I go about it? I take it a head-on approach wouldn't be a great idea. What would you suggest?"

Iris thought a bit, but I got the impression that was for show. I suspected she'd planned this meeting out pretty thoroughly and had given a lot of thought to how to get what she wanted, but hadn't come up with good answers. I tried to help her out. "Is there some way I could get a temporary position at the company, as some kind of consultant, say? From what I've heard, it's a pretty snug, tight-knit group at WarnerCorp, not a crowd to get lost in." I didn't ask how masking and social distancing were affecting the snugness.

"Well, I had this idea. Ilona Marchand, my sister-in-law, my brother Andrew's wife, well, his widow, is Buck's right arm, officially Office Manager and Human Resources, and Ilona and I get along well, always have. I think I can say that Buck and I both trust Ilona, even if no one else." I kept quiet about some of the people I'd known other people had trusted, but something occurred to me.

"Wait a second," I said. "I thought Ilona Marchand was the widow of Ernest Marchand, who was Buck Warner's right-hand man. I read or heard a while back that he had died—" I had read it that very afternoon, but there was no reason to be overly frank with the client at this stage.

"Yes," she said, "she is. Ernest had a massive heart attack three months ago. Unlike my brother, Andrew, he went quickly, out like a light."

"It wasn't clear from the account I read—"

"No, it wasn't, Rainer, nothing about it was clear, because although Ernest's death was purely natural causes, given that he'd played football for Brown in one of their rare three-season winning streaks, he'd let himself go, and he drank too much, and he smoked too much, and in the last few years he also ate too much, and forty-nine is by no means a suspicious age for someone who does all that.

"He told me once, knowing I was an alcoholic, that he'd realized he'd started drinking dinner. Well, that wasn't news to me; it may not take one to know one, but an alcoholic can spot alcoholic behavior a mile away, even—" She laughed shortly. "Even when it isn't there.

"But it sure as hell was there with Ernest. He told me that he'd therefore taken a resolve to have a decent dinner every night. He didn't cut back on the drinking; he just made sure the last drinks of the day didn't land on an empty stomach.

"One of the curses of wealth is being able to afford everything that's bad for you, and Ernest killed himself with the very best food and drink and handmade English cigarettes of the most expensive Virginia and Turkish tobaccos. Taco Bell, Early Times, and American Blends wouldn't have hurt him any worse.

"But the thing is that Ernest died in a hotel room, and he wasn't with Ilona. It was a fairly simple matter to tidy things up, and I did most of the tidying, with our lawyer, Stan Frieden, capably backing me up. We paid off the woman and started her up in her own business back home in Windsor, Ontario, of all places to come here from. We paid off about ten percent of the hotel staff, the ten percent who could take care of the rest.

"We paid off the relevant people at the bar across from the hotel, where she and Ernest met, and the relevant people at the bar in the hotel, where she and Ernest stopped by for a nightcap on their way to his destiny and her sudden affluence and return to the bosom of her family and friends in Canada, if she had any. She struck me as bright enough to realize her best interests lay in going along, accepting a technically quite legal gift, and keeping quiet herself. Being back home can help keep anyone quiet about where one's been."

"Would that be experience talking?"

"To some extent, yes," she said. "Not that I've ever—"

"Sorry," I said. "Force of bad habit."

"Well, anyway, Ilona knows the truth, as much as she wants to know anyway, if not all the details. Of course, Ernest's death settled his estate exclusively on her. He felt Brandon, her and Andrew's son, had been adequately taken care of by Andrew."

"Really?" I asked. "What, by the way, is Brandon's last name?"

"It's Wilson. His father was my brother Andrew Wilson, and so that was my maiden name, Wilson. Anyway, Ernest left it all to Ilona."

"Backtracking a bit, when your brother died, he left it all to his wife and son?"

"Yes, pretty much. Andrew's will included token bequests, mainly art, books, personal stuff, to all of us, but the bulk of his estate went to Ilona and Brandon. She got two-thirds; he got one-third. Which in any case is a lot of money for a young man who has never worked a day in his life and seems to have graduated with few skills or abilities aside from telling people what a great football 'career' he had at Brown." I started to interrupt, but Iris nodded and said, "Yes: just like his stepfather. Do you understand how unbig a deal athletics are in the Ivy League, except to the players, of course?" I nodded in turn, to be agreeable.

"Without, I would guess, intending to, he's on the way to following in his stepfather's footsteps. What is it about old football players, anyway? In my opinion, he's a spoiled, entitled kid, and I think raising him was one of the few things Ilona can be said not to have done well. Maybe I'm too harsh, but that's my take on the matter." As if everything comes down to parenting.

"All right," I said. "Now, how do you see Ilona taking to all this? If she's the day-to-day HR and Office Manager, which I take it means she can hire and fire when necessary, she will have to know what's going on. I don't see any way around it. Am I misreading the situation, Iris?"

"You called me Iris."

"Should I revert to Ms. Warner?"

"No, not at all. As I said, I think we can trust Ilona, and if we can't, I give up. I think she will agree to the plan if she knows I think it's a good idea, and I can email and text Buck, and he can either agree or open up and object, and she can confirm that he agrees, since she sees him every day at the office and I assume they're still talking. The truth is, I haven't been going in very regularly the last couple of months. There's really not much for me to do there, and unlike others, I don't find myself inventing projects." It would have given her a good start on social distancing anyway.

"I haven't discussed this with her," Iris went on, "but I think she might be willing to hire a short-term consultant to provide some outside perspective on whatever they're thinking about now. You know, as a plausible cover story."

"So you think she'll be sympathetic to your wanting to find out what's going on?" I asked.

She seemed to bristle a bit, then clamped down on it. My insistence on clarity was straining her patience. Interesting. "Oh, yes, I'm sure. And she might be a good person to talk with about that," Iris said. "Come to think of it, why haven't I talked it over with her already? God knows we both care about the company. Why don't I call her?" She took a phone from her pocket.

I held out a hand to stop her. "Now, first, let's make sure we agree on what we want to say. Why not share your misgivings with her, and find out what she thinks? If it seems like a good idea after you've both talked a while, I could do, say, a three-day stint, maybe a whole week, at WarnerCorp, looking over the existing operation—"

"I'm not sure how much of an operation there is," Iris said. "I think it's a case of corporate coasting, as much as anything." It occurred to me that that would be a good title for my report of the job, The Case of the Coasting Corporation, but I kept it to myself. "That in itself, it seems to me, is ample excuse for Ilona to bring in a consultant."

"Well, that course I took in systems analysis a few years back will finally come in handy," I said. Sure. "Why don't you call your sister-in-law and find out what she thinks about what's bothering your former husband? I can stay here while you talk, or I could take a walk down by your fish pond." I replaced my mask, and she did the same.

"No, please stay, Rainer." She ran down the contacts list, chose Ilona's number. The March sunlight was certainly nice on her skin and hair. "Hi, Ilona? Yes. Remember I mentioned that Buck and I had some concerns about what's going on with the company? I wonder if I could ask a favor—"

Chapter Three

Friday, March 27

Back at the office, Schwartz had switched books. Kahneman was closed on a bookmark, and he had a new book open. I would have reported to him right away, but I had to wait for him to finish a paragraph. It was a pretty long paragraph. I shouldn't really complain about his attitude toward work, but it does delay my reports on occasion.

Schwartz stopped. He looked at me for a moment, as if he'd just realized I was there. Perhaps it was my expression. "I suppose you'd like to report." He slid a strip of leather into the book, laid it next to the other. "Proceed, Rainer, verbatim if you please."

After ten years of his training, I can give it to Schwartz word for word, and I did. He is a good listener, once he decides to listen. I gave him my meeting with Herb Green, the bank manager, and then the discussion with Iris, including the gist of her discussion with Ilona, as she had given it to me. When I had finished, he leaned back and sighed. It was inescapable: work was coming his way for sure, and there was no graceful way to avoid it.

"So," I said, "it's arranged with Ilona Marchand, and I'm expected at her place in Carmel at eight this evening to discuss the details. I'll probably start Monday, and God only knows how long it'll take to figure out what financial shenanigans are going on at WarnerCorp, if that's really what's happening, or how long you will have to struggle on without me. I have to say that my impression is there's something going on Iris hasn't shared with me. I mean, amicable divorces are all well and good, and I'm all for them. If you're going to get divorced, amicably is definitely the way to go—"

"Shut up," Schwartz muttered.

"Just trying to fill you in on the situation as I understand it."

"Pfui. You're trying to goad me into action, and there's no appropriate action for me to take," he said bitterly, "unless you think I should also go undercover as a consultant at WarnerCorp."

"Not at all, sir," I assured him. I glanced at his book, and saw it was one he was rereading. "I've got that handled. I just wanted you supplied with all the facts, so that while you're sitting here reading about the calamitous fourteenth century, I can proceed with the twenty-first, knowing that, intellectually, you're actually working hard at the case—"

"That's enough." He shifted gears. "What do you say to China Wok for dinner? Carry out, of course."

"Sure. I'll make the run. What sounds good to you?" We always get enough entrees and appetizers to ensure there would be leftovers. China Wok makes broccoli taste good, and they don't skimp on the shrimp, either.

I called to place the order, then made the run up College Avenue to the strip mall on the east side of the street, just north of the Seven11 at 96th. We ate in the kitchen, put the copious leftovers away, and washed up. I admit I dawdled a bit. Their roast pork fried rice is wonderful. The secret ingredient may be opium.

"You're going to be late for your appointment with Ms. Marchand if you don't get a move on," he said, and he was right, of course. I stepped into the bathroom to check that my shirt and tie were still presentable, thought about suggesting that I switch cars, lest I be refused entry at the gate, but decided Schwartz had probably had enough of me for a while.

"Any final instructions?" I asked when I came back to the office, but Schwartz had already returned to his book, and all I got was a quiet snort in reply. I headed for the car.

I drove to the address, and the gate stayed locked as the guard asked me my business. I told him Ms. Marchand was expecting me, and he didn't trust memory but consulted his pad to confirm, then let me in. It was clearly the crème de la crème of Carmel's gated communities, with high brick walls not quite hidden behind long rows of Lombardy poplars. The guards were professionals, not the usual uniformed cop-wannabes, and two watched, one noting my license-plate number, as the fellow in charge checked my identification. I was pretty sure all three guards were ex-police, and none of them looked to be of retirement age. I noted that they could get a tire-shredder up to prevent unwanted entrances and exits in both lanes, which were separated by a freestanding guardpost between the gates, which were by no means flimsy. I'd have liked to check inside to see what weaponry was available for holding off the peasant revolt, but it was important to play the part of responsible, trustworthy visitor, especially as dusk was coming on, so after getting official permission, I drove in, took the winding road to the right, and headed for the Marchand house, which was on Plantagenet Place, believe it or not. I wondered whether there was a Stuart Street and a Windsor Way.

As I took my time driving, I checked out the stone and brick palaces, most with attached three- or four-car garages, although some had separate carriage-house structures for the transportation. The trees looked to me to be about ten years along, mainly maples and sweet gum for quick growth. I suppose they're all right if you don't have to deal with those sticky gumballs personally. Not too many years ago, this had been a corn or bean field, but bulldozers can create decorative lakes and nice hills and knolls to break the monotony.

The Marchand house was surrounded by sugar maples, with nice lines of evergreens defining the backyard. As McMansions go, it wasn't bad, two stories with full attic, brick with stone corners and window borders, and decent space for visitors' cars. I admired the floral borders along both sides of the brick walk to the front door, mainly impatiens not quite in bloom, I think. There were islands of plantings around the trees in front, with here and there an inconspicuous miniature pagoda. Someone wasn't afraid to be different from the neighbors. No garden gnomes, though; there are limits, after all.

It was eight o'clock on the dot when I rang the doorbell. The door was opened by a good-sized man of about thirty, in a light gray suit and dark gray tie and white shirt and mask, and he nodded when I stated my name and let me in. I recognized him, but he didn't know me, of course. "If you will come with me, sir," he said in a voice softer and more cultivated than I'd have expected from a former linebacker whose jacket didn't quite disguise the holster under his left armpit. It really wasn't supposed to hide anything. This didn't seem to be the appropriate time to tell him I recognized him; we were both on the job. He headed into the house, which could have held two of Iris's, and I followed him into a clean, well-lighted room with a grand piano at the far end, beyond it a fireplace I could have parked the Prius in, and sofas and chairs everywhere, paintings with recognizable subjects on three walls, and an eastern exposure from a long line of french windows.

He brought me halfway across the room to where a woman wearing a blue mask and what I took to be a silk caftan was rising from a comfortable-looking chair at a low table well stocked with bottles, glasses, pitchers, and so on. "Mr. Zufahl, Ms. Marchand," he said with another nod. He was obviously announcing me, not introducing us. It was a relief they didn't make him wear livery, but perhaps that had been a matter for negotiation.

Ms. Marchand thanked him, and he asked if there would be anything else. "No, Kenneth, thank you," she said. She was closer to fifty than forty, I happened to know, but from what I could see looked ten years younger; she had had excellent raw material, and she had clearly been careful with herself, I thought. She had a nice tan, and her light-brown hair was streaked from the sunlight, but she hadn't overdone it. On a first-name basis with the help. I had watched Ken Beardsley play for the Colts a couple times, before the third and final dislocation of his knee had taken him out of the game for good. He'd had the sense not to do a Namath, as Murray Kempton had once put it, "destroying his body for a religion that to everyone else was only a game." I was glad to see there wasn't a trace of the injury when he walked.

We sat, and Ms. Marchand offered me refreshment. I took Pellegrino with lime, and she stuck with her highball. I saw that the caftan was actually a loose blouse and pants, raw silk, gathered at the wrists and ankles, with a sash of the same beige or taupe or whatever neutral shade it was. It looked very comfortable, so long as you weren't planning on anything in the way of physical work. She wasn't.

"So," she said, "Iris would like to have you in as a consultant at Warner-Corp." I got the impression she wasn't completely sold on the idea.

"Well, yes," I said, "but essentially just by way of cover. She and Mr. Warner suspect that something is amiss with the finances, as I believe you know. My understanding is that they think something serious is going on, something that they don't feel comfortable sharing with just anyone, and—"

"So are Buck's suspicions really Iris's business?" she asked.

I smiled, not overdoing it, I hoped. "Now, in my business, that's for the client to decide, Ms. Marchand, but since you are involved, of course, that's relevant too. Do you think the Warners are making too much of the situation?" I drank some water. "Or is there really a situation at all?"

"Well," Ilona said, "in the first place, it's no longer 'the Warners', although she kept her married name after the divorce. Do you mean do I think they're imagining things?"

I stayed noncommittal. Knowing when to shut up is an important part of questioning people.

"Actually, no, I don't, but like Iris, I can't quite put my finger on what's wrong. She was mistaken, by the way. Buck and I talk, but we haven't talked about whatever it is that's eating him, but something is, I can tell you. You don't work for someone for ten years without—" She stared at the table for a moment. "But I can't help the feeling that something is off somewhere. I've worked with Buck, for Buck, for years, since before the thing went turbo—"

"Beg pardon?"

"I mean, before WarnerCōp turned out to be exactly what everyone in the medical/allied health business needed. You have to understand that no one, Buck included, saw that phenomenal success coming. He thought he'd come up with something useful, but he had no idea how useful it would be. You know how it is, I'm sure: someone's software or hardware or firmware turns out to be wildly successful, and suddenly the fellow who produced it is a genius." I didn't get the impression she thought Buck Warner was actually a genius. She didn't seem hostile, just amused but trying not to show it.

"Buck was an exception, Mr. Zufahl." Ms. Marchand looked up at the spring landscape, a meadow with trees and clouds, as if she hadn't noticed it before, then she pulled down her mask and took a drink of her highball while she decided how to describe her employer. "He didn't let the success bug bite him, you see. Sure, he accepted the success of the program, which has the simplest, most user-intuitive interface on the market. Our society loves gods, you know, but Buck refused to become one. It wasn't some phony modesty, either. He just stayed off the pedestal, and he politely but firmly declined to play the fame game."

"You're speaking of him in the past tense," I said, "which, so far as I know, isn't necessary or appropriate."

She ignored me. "I'm talking about how Buck was, how he behaved, when WarnerCōp, the product, took off and WarnerCorp, the company, really got going. For one thing, there were so few of us that it was a serious struggle just to meet the initial demand, and we didn't have time to interview new people to help carry the load. Buck was never above any grunt work. If anything, he took on too much of the down-and-dirty, nitty-gritty stuff, while keeping on top of things at the same time. I think the effort almost killed him, to tell you the truth. He could do just about anything but delegate. Fortunately, everyone else in the company pitched in too. When the head guy is packing boxes up for shipping to customers, you need to be in there helping too. That's one reason Buck was so generous with employee ownership. I mean, there was absolutely no legal requirement that he hand everyone stock in the company, and the lawyers went nuts when he told them what he wanted to do, but he did it anyway. He felt he owed it to people for their contribution, and Buck is all about doing the right thing.

"Early on, there was a serious bug that—well, it was serious enough it needed fixing, and Buck not only got the fix ready, he made sure it went out free, with good instructions on how to install it, for a painless, effective fix, and he offered to indemnify anyone who'd suffered a loss because of the bug. He liked to joke that there are no bugs, just undocumented features, but when it came down to it, he came through. Not one customer asked for compensation.

"Of course, with the success came the money, and with that and the unavoidable fame, he's had to spend a fair amount on insulation from the public. We all have, but not as much as Buck." She finished her highball and poured another from the pitcher. I was wondering if that might be a virgin version. We weren't sitting close enough to smell alcohol, if any, and she was showing no trace of the effects of the drinks.

"Have you ever thought about fame, Mr. Zufahl?"

"Not much," I said. "In my business, fame is a handicap. All that stuff about great detectives in books is just hot air. You don't want your picture in the paper, and you don't want to be recognized. Suppose I asked you to name a real detective; you might be able—"

"Allan Pinkerton," she said.

"And another?"

"I can't think of one," she said, "except fictional ones, of course." At least she didn't mention them.

"Exactly. So, no, I haven't thought about fame that much, because I have no need to," I said. "But we were talking about Buck Warner."

"Yes, and he's had to distance himself," she said. "Fame means people you don't know think they know you, and of course, they don't; they only know or believe whatever they've read in magazines or heard on television. But you can't just hold an open house for each and every stranger who reads or watches TV, or pretty soon you don't have a life of your own.

"It's affected all of us in the company, you know. Buck did employee ownership from the get-go, as I said, and we all have more than we ever expected. You know, I'd really be more comfortable in a house like the one I grew up in." I kept on listening, but I recognized that she'd slid into a canned spiel she'd played so many times it just came out automatically. Personally, I wouldn't have liked to have to deal with the public thinking it had the right to impose on my time, not to mention the rest: people imagining they were somehow entitled to a cut of the pie, since they saw it as so big that a little slice wouldn't make a difference, never mind how many slices there were.

Or, and here she got back off automatic pilot, the matter of protecting kids from those who thought they were fair game, and I wondered if that had something to do with Buck's problem, if he had one.

"So here we are," Ilona Marchand said, "barricaded in our gated pseudo-community, and about the only thing we have in common with our neighbors is wealth. And that just isn't enough for a real community, but it has to do." She tossed down the last of her drink.

"And so," I said, "you're all right with Iris's idea of me coming on as a consultant next week?"

"Oh, I think so. Will you be with us long?"

"Well, of course, that depends on a lot of factors, some of which are beyond our control, even beyond our imagination. I was thinking about three days, but I suppose it could go a week. Who knows what will happen, after all?" I set my glass down in a highly professional way. "Can you provide me with a list of the staff members?"

"Sure," she said. She reached down for a navy and gray leather bag at the end of the sofa, took out a folded sheet of paper. "Should you be taking notes?"

"All in here," I said, pointing at my temple. "Working for Mr. Schwartz means developing one's memory, among other things. Many other things. I may need you to spell some names if there are any non intuitive—"

She handed me the list. "Try to remember which pocket you put it in, Mr. Zufahl." I reflected that I deserved that. "Would you think starting Monday morning would be advisable? Do you need any other information besides the staff roster? Will you use your real name?"

I nodded as I looked over the list of names and titles. I asked her how long each person had been with the company, what they really did at WarnerCorp, who reported to whom, and a bunch of other questions I would be glad to bore you with, if any of it had ended up helping, but as it turned out not long into the consultancy, Ilona and I were wasting our time and effort.

We decided I would be Charles "Chuck" Wood, on the grounds that people would think it was too corny to be phony, and that would be a distraction from possible doubts about my really being a consultant. After all, the bank manager's Herb Green was a real name. I would come with all the usual accoutrements of a hired expert, and I'd arrange interviews with each of the staff members, starting with Buck, assuming he was in, and then Ilona, and so on through the rest. We discussed questions I'd be asking people, and I did take written notes, as an aid in working up a printed form of the kind any hired expert would have.

It was well past ten by the time we had finished, and the pitcher and glasses were long empty, and our masks were back on. Ilona assured me I could call her if any further questions occurred to me, and I asked her to call me if she had more ideas. I was ready to take my leave when she leaned back on the sofa, gave a medium-heavy sigh, and said, "Now, I wonder if you might be able to help me with another matter, something confidential, but nothing to do with what we've been discussing. Something private, I mean."

"Well," I said, "I am a private investigator, employed by Leo Schwartz, also a private investigator, so perhaps you could give me some idea of what it's about, and if I can help, of course, I'd be glad to, assuming there's no conflict of interest with—"

"Oh, there's no conflict with Buck and Iris's problem," Ilona said, maybe a little hastily, a bit too emphatically. "It really has nothing to do with Iris or Buck or anyone at WarnerCorp; it's an entirely private matter of mine. Someone is trying to blackmail me."

One thing Schwartz and I are in total agreement about is blackmailers. Of course, I would report to Schwartz every last detail of everything Ms. Marchand and I discussed, but at the moment, there was no reason I could see why I should inhibit her by mentioning that now. If she had any sense, which she certainly seemed to have, she'd know that anyway.

"I'd be delighted to help you deal with a problem like that, Ms. Marchand," I said. "Tell me all about it."

"All right," she said, "although I think I would find it easier to talk about this if it were Ilona and Rainer." She sat back on the sofa, then said, "I'm going to get some more refreshment, if you don't mind. By the way, Rainer, has anyone ever told you you're a remarkably formal man, for a private eye,

I mean?"

"It's been mentioned once or twice, I think," I said. "I suppose it's an inheritance from my parents. Germans tend to be more formal than Americans. They make more of a big deal than we do of the difference between acquaintances and friends." No point in getting into a tiresome lecture on the *du/Sie* distinction. Schwartz enjoys ragging me about being pedantic. Ilona got up to pick up the tray with the pitcher and cups, and she went for the drinks. I spent a few minutes perusing the artwork in the room. There were two smaller pieces I had seen reproduced in books, both engravings, not paintings.

When she returned with a tray, I could tell that the small carafe didn't contain water, but it was, after all, her house. She poured herself a drink while I resupplied myself with iced tea. She sat back, just looking at me very frankly, very deliberately for a few moments, then she took a sip, then a bigger one, and leaned forward to set her glass down on the coffee table between us.

"It began when I was married to Andrew Wilson," she said, "before Brandon was born, and it ended about ten, twelve years later." I wasn't clear whether that was after it had begun or after her son was born, so I shut up and listened. "Andrew and I joined a group of like-minded people, all couples, who liked to keep things interesting by, well, keeping things interesting. We would meet once a month at each others' homes, taking turns, of course. There were always at least a dozen couples in the group, sometimes thirteen or fourteen, sometimes fewer, and we would get together monthly…I'm having a hard time explaining this. In some ways it's as if it happened to someone else, it's been so long…"

"There's no hurry, Ms. Marchand," I said. "Ilona," I corrected myself.

"I know, Rainer," she said, "but it's hard now, looking back on it, wondering what in God's name we thought we were doing. But at the time, of course, I had no idea there were cameras involved."

"Cameras?"

"Yes," she said. "I didn't know Andrew was filming what happened at our house. He had had a security system installed, which of course, I knew about, but what I didn't know was that he was filming, or rather videotaping, everything that went on when we hosted the gathering."

"And I take it that what went on wasn't the sort of thing most people would want recorded for posterity?"

"Correct." Ilona took another drink, a healthy one, and kept the glass this time. "You have to understand, Rainer, that we were younger, and I was certainly more trusting than..."

"So," I said, "your husband made videotapes, and someone else has come across them, and that someone is now trying to blackmail you."

"Well, so far, it's just the threat of blackmail. I haven't made contact with the blackmailer; no specific demands have been made," she said. She slid a manila envelope out from under a small stack of magazines on the table. "I'm afraid I handled the note, so fingerprints will probably not be—"

"That's no problem," I assured her. "Most blackmailers know about gloves. It might be possible to detect if he wore latex or cotton gloves, but even that's doubtful."

She handed over the envelope, which was high-quality creamy stock, large enough to hold a stack of unfolded sheets of 8½" × 11" paper. The envelope had been sealed and stamped, postmarked at the central Post Office downtown. It had been slit open at the flap end. I took out a single sheet of very nongeneric stationery. It was a heavy cream bond, but the printing was from some ordinary laser printer, twelve-point Arial. Only the paper itself would turn out to be traceable, with a little luck.

"That's my own stationery," Ilona said. "Or perhaps Iris's. I have some here, over in that desk—" She gestured over her shoulder at what looked like an antique in the corner. "And there's a supply on my desk at the office. Iris and I gave each other some, as a joke." I didn't ask for more of an explanation.

The printed message read, "I have copies of your husband's tapes. What would it be worth to you to keep them private? Call me after 10:00 p.m." Below was a ten-digit number. A local number to an untraceable burner phone, no doubt. I'd try to run a trace, legally, of course, but equally, of course, it would be a burner. As Schwartz commented once, "We only try to trace it because if we don't, the bastards could use their usual phone, and someday some S.O.B. will be smart enough and cocky enough to realize that, and he'll leave his regular phone number, and we'll nail the hubristic mother because we had the *sophrosyne* or maybe just the humility to go ahead and run the routine trace, which may or may not be adequate recompense for all the time you spent trying to trace burners, but there it is."

"When did this arrive, Ilona?"

"Tuesday."

"Have you called the number?"

"Yes," she said. "There was no answer. I got the envelope in the mail Tuesday, but I didn't look at it until after dinner. I think it was a little after nine that I read the message."

"And you assumed, and still assume, that the tapes mentioned are the ones your husband made of the group's activities?"

"Sure," she said. "What else could it possibly mean?" She shifted around on the sofa, but I didn't think it was physical discomfort.

I nodded, thinking about it for a moment. "How hard would it be for someone to get hold of a few sheets of your stationery?" I asked.

"Here at home, I think I'd be aware of anyone being here, in this room, at my desk, and that's where it all is, what I have in the house. At the office, though, someone could easily come in and take stationery from my desk. It's in the box it came in, in the upper-left drawer of my desk; anyone could pop in to leave a note or memo, take a few sheets, slip them into a notebook or file folder, and pop out again." She took a drink. "For that matter, anyone could have just as easily gotten the stationery from Iris's desk at the office, or at home."

"Still not totally paperless?"

"Oh, no, but there's a lot less waste than there used to be. Personally, when I read a book or magazine, I want to turn the pages manually; I like the feel of it in my hands, the smell of the paper and ink and glue."

"You're amazingly old-fashioned, if I'm not mistaken," I said. "I don't mean that as a criticism." Schwartz could amuse himself about Iris and me all he liked, but it occurred to me that Ilona might really make an impression on him.

"It's a pretty personal remark all the same," she said. "I don't mean that as a complaint."

I liked her better all the time.

"Well," I said, "the next questions are also going to be rather personal, but I ask it professionally: Did you stop Andrew's filming when you found out about it? And: How many tapes are there?"

"Oh," she said. She said nothing more for a couple minutes, looking as if she wished she were somewhere else, then: "I told Andrew to stop when I found out about it. It turned out that all the men knew about the tapes, and Andrew had shown them a tape he'd made of one of our sessions. With at least two cameras in every room in our house, he had a lot to work with.

"Of course, the technology back then was pretty unsophisticated, and the cameras were larger and a lot more expensive than they are today, but Andrew got them as small as possible for the time and built them right into the walls and furniture. They were motion- and sound-activated."

"How many cameras in all?"

"Sixteen, I think." She did a mental review of the house, nodded. "Right: sixteen."

"Each loaded with one videocassette."

"Correct."

"How many, ah, meetings did your husband record?"

"Five," Ilona said. "He'd already done four, and right after the fifth, I found out about it, and that was it with that." She looked like she wished she had a cigarette to stub out.

"And how did you find out?" I asked.

"It turned out that some of the other women knew about the tapes. Sharon—I'll keep her last name to myself—called, and we were talking about the meeting at our house the month before, and she mentioned something about hoping this year's tape was as good as last year's, and I had no idea what she was talking about." She glared at me, as if it were my fault, then her face softened slowly.

"I found out from Sharon," she said. "Andrew had made tapes of five of our hostings, and he'd shared an edited four-hour film with the other men and three of the women. He knew perfectly well I'd hit the ceiling. At first, I told him to destroy all the tapes—"

"All eighty or so of them," I said.

"But he promised to keep it private, but apparently, he didn't. Anyway, he stopped making tapes after that, if only because he started to get sick, and we stopped getting together with the others anyway, so that was that. Until now."

"Do you know where Andrew kept the videotapes?"

"He had a closet in an upstairs room with three gun safes in it, big enough for shotguns and rifles, and one of the safes housed the tapes." I did a little mental calculation and decided that was reasonable. Eighty videocassettes would come to something over one and a half cubic feet, so they would fit into a gun safe easily.

"And he kept the tapes?"

"Yes. We watched the one he'd shown the others, and it was interesting—" She broke off, looked at me.

"But you'd rather not share it with the rest of the world now."

"Exactly."

"Are the tapes missing?"

"I checked," she said, "and they all seem to be there."

"But someone has got his hands on at least one of them, and he's made a copy," I said. "He's sent you a note, but he's not answering the phone. Have you tried again?"

"Yes, every evening, about nine or quarter after, I've called, and there's no answer."

"This is one for the books," I said. "Usually, a blackmailer can't wait to sink the hook in, but he's sent the note, then doesn't answer when you call."

"Maybe I don't have anything to fear from someone this disorganized," she said.

"I don't think I'd count on that," I said. "Maybe he's disorganized, or maybe he's just unstable. What you don't want is public exposure of Andrew's tape, whichever one or ones we're talking about."

Ilona said, "I hope he's not creating an excuse to go public."

"Well, disorganized or unstable or whatever he is, I can't see how he'd need an excuse, but if that were the case, why send you the note?"

We discussed the situation for another quarter hour, without noticeable progress. I told her I would bring my boss up to speed, and we'd get on it. It certainly seemed to me more urgent than the case that had brought me there in the first place.

Chapter Four

Friday, March 27–Saturday, March 28

It was late when I got home, and Schwartz was getting ready to call it a day, so I told him good night, put away some things around the office, and went to bed myself.

The next morning, after the usual routine, I reported to Schwartz, and he listened to the full report, both as to the coming consultant position at WarnerCorp and the blackmail scheme someone was trying out on Ms. Marchand. I gave him all of it, word for word, with relevant descriptions, as usual. He was miffed at the idea that I would be undercover most of next week, but the blackmail twist piqued his interest. I sat in on a conversation between him and Neil Parkinson, our lawyer, in which he argued for bringing back public flogging for blackmailers, kidnappers, and certain other cold-blooded, deliberate offenders, as capital, not corporal punishment. Parkinson pointed out once that the Constitution is pretty clear about prohibiting cruel and unusual punishments, and horse-whipping would certainly qualify as unusual. Schwartz said it wouldn't be unusual after the first dozen or so. I don't think he was entirely being facetious.

Schwartz had a few questions about the consultant pose, but I had anticipated that, and we hashed out the details. About the blackmail, he really dug in, and we covered it pretty thoroughly. It had been unpleasant to see how embarrassed Ilona Marchand had been, talking about something so far back in her past that was being dredged up now, and talking about it with someone she'd never met before. Schwartz pointed out that, tough as that had been, it might well have been worse, had she and I known each other better. "It's more like reporting a crime to a police officer you don't know," he said. "Hard but not as hard as telling an old friend, perhaps." I agreed that he had a point, but I can't say I was totally convinced.

"I'll have to think about this," Schwartz said, and I thought he'd be going back to his book. "In all likelihood, the supposed blackmailer is enjoying Ms. Marchand's discomfiture, probably laughing his ass off," Schwartz said. "Dammit." He'd been working on curbing his profanity and vulgarity, since his sponsor had mentioned that its use is not the sign of spiritual growth and more especially since his grandson had gotten old enough to start talking and pick up vocabulary when and where he heard it. He hadn't had much need to watch his language while his daughter was growing up. She had arrived a month prematurely by emergency cesarean, and there'd been some problem with oxygen deprivation or something, and she'd been born deaf, and her language acquisition had been hard-earned indeed. And now his grandson was repeating everything he heard.

I suggested, not for the first time, that he institute a penalty box for himself, a can he could put, say, a dollar in every time he violated his own language rules.

"Some people decide they just don't have to sweat the small stuff, and they don't. I wonder if the blackmailer's motivation is not to extort money, but rather just to torment Ms. Marchand. That would explain the note and phone number. Every time the phone rings, and he lets it go unanswered—"

"He?"

"Or she," Schwartz said. "Although that note has a masculine odor to it, wouldn't you say?" I shrugged. I could see it either way, frankly, and I'm perhaps a bit less inclined than Schwartz to draw such conclusions. I think it may be a generational thing, but I'd be loath to tell him that.

Schwartz is fond of quoting Bertrand Russell's remark that there are two kinds of work in this world: moving parts of the earth's crust from one place to another, and directing others to do so. The first kind is the kind you get paid to do; the second is the kind you pay others to do. We went over the plans for the consultancy and what little we knew about Ilona's problem, then he went back to Kahneman until lunchtime. We sat outside at Biscuit, which had been a twenty-four-hour breakfast place and still was, although it had also become an excellent Mexican restaurant when new management came along.

We had just returned to the office after lunch when the doorbell rang, and I went to answer it without being directed to do so. Through the one-way glass, I saw the substantial form of our neighbor Ed Stroh standing on the front stoop. Ed lives a few doors down the street from us, and he and Schwartz drive together to monthly-in-warm-weather rocket launches in Muncie, where their club, the Rocketeers of Central Indiana, shares space on the Academy of Model Aeronautics flying field with the airplane enthusiasts. Schwartz says Ed has an entire room of his house full of rockets he's built. Schwartz's are hanging from the ceiling of the garage, which is about half filled with them. You know who does the actual installation of the damn things.

I opened the door to let Ed in, and he thanked me and said hello, and asked me how I was doing, as always. Ed, balding and stout, was wearing a white open-collared shirt and light brown slacks. He had a dark blue windbreaker on his arm. It was a warm day for late March, and he'd walked the block or so from his house, and he'd broken a sweat. We walked to the office together. He and Schwartz hadn't seen each other for a while, so when Ed had taken the red-leather chair in front of Schwartz's desk, they got the preliminaries out of the way, including the offer of refreshment. Ed declined, and Schwartz leaned back in his chair and asked, "What can I do for you, Ed?"

"Well," he said, "the truth is, I'm not sure. You know Eugene and Lawrence, my father-in-law and brother-in-law, live over on Delaware, in Arden?" Schwartz nodded. Arden is a neighborhood south and a bit west of our own, good-sized houses mostly dating from the 1920s and earlier, although there is a scattering of more recent ones, the original buildings having been knocked down and replacements put up over the old foundations. "They moved there about five years ago, after my mother-in-law died, to be closer to Phyllis, supposedly, although we don't really see them all that often, maybe every couple of weeks or so."

I'd met Eugene, not Gene, and Lawrence, not Larry, Abernathy a couple of times over the years, and frankly, I thought Ed and Phyllis were fortunate not to have to spend more time than that with those two cold fish. Two excellent arguments for social distancing, even without a pandemic. Eugene had been retired from some commercial bank for a couple decades, and I don't think Lawrence had ever worked a day in his life. He had moved back with his parents after school, I'd been told, to help with things around the house. Perhaps I was being unfair, but I'd never been able to carry a conversation with either or both much past the weather. Heaven knows what they did with themselves in the course of the day. During the consultation, I kept my opinion of Ed's in-laws to myself.

"But anyway, Phyl calls them every day, and we stay in touch that way. But two days ago, she called, and there was no answer. She thought something might have happened to her dad, so she went over to check on him. Well, on both of them." Ed shifted in his seat.

"The house was locked, but of course, she has a key. Neither of them was home, and she thought maybe they'd gone out, but she looked in the garage, and both cars were there. That's really unlike them, Leo. Eugene drives that ancient Mercedes, and Lawrence uses the Porsche Eugene decided he didn't like anymore, and they were both there.

"But the thing is, neither Eugene nor Lawrence was home, and Phyllis got no answer calling either of them. She went through the whole house, and they weren't there."

"Have you called the police?" I asked. Ed nodded.

Schwartz shifted in his seat. "No doubt they told you it was too soon to worry, or at any rate too soon for a missing-persons report."

"Exactly," Ed said. "The cop I spoke to suggested that they might have taken a trip, with a cab to the airport, to avoid the long-term parking charges. I mean, I admit that that would seem to make sense to someone who didn't know them, but Eugene and Lawrence aren't exactly world travelers. I doubt if either of them has a passport, frankly. Anyway, they'd never just take off like that without a word to Phyl or me. I can't imagine it anyhow." Ed was the picture of a man who's been bothering the police because his wife has been telling him to. My guess, he wasn't missing the in-laws, but he was married to Phyllis, who knew perfectly well how to wind him up.

"It certainly does seem uncharacteristic of them," Schwartz said. "Have you been to the house yourself? I assume you have a key."

"Sure I do, and when Phyl called and told me they weren't home, I went over. The beds were made, the sink was empty, the dishwasher was loaded partway. I mean, there was no indication of anything out of the ordinary, except that nobody was home and the cars were in the garage."

Ed wiped his forehead with his handkerchief. "Look, the last time those two guys went anywhere without us, it was to Phyllis's cousin's daughter's wedding in Tucson a year, year and a half ago, and the logistics were like for the Normandy invasion. Phyl and Norma have never been close, so even though she and I were invited, she sent a gift and regrets, but Eugene and Lawrence went out. You know Eugene's always been pretty close with his money, and he asked Phyllis to take them to the airport, to avoid taking a cab, and she picked them up and brought them home when they got back. I was sort of surprised they flew rather than driving, but with them, you never know." He was more upset than I'd realized earlier, wringing his handkerchief in his hands. "I suppose it's possible they'd spring for a taxi if they were going somewhere, but it's certainly not what I'd call typical behavior, you know?" Ed looked at Schwartz, then me. As if I had a clue. "And without a word to Phyllis? I can't believe it, Leo."

Schwartz nodded agreement. I did too. We were all on the same somewhat depressing page. This did not look to be a paying case, but it didn't seem to me that it would take long to find out where the missing in-laws were.

"Rainer," Schwartz said, "why don't you go to the house with Ed and see if perhaps you can turn up something he has overlooked?" Ed was straightening up, and Schwartz headed him off. "As you should know perfectly well, Ed, Rainer is trained to observe, and it's quite possible he'll notice something you may have missed, if there's something to be noticed. It's certainly no reflection on you. If he finds nothing, it should relieve your anxieties, and Phyllis's as well."

And, of course, it would get me out of the house and let him get back to the serious business of reading. Schwartz had a few unnecessary instructions for me, mostly to impress Ed Stroh that he was taking the case seriously. We agreed that I would drive both of us over, so that Ed could let us in the house and observe me observing.

It was only a five or six-minute drive to the Abernathy house. Heading south on College, I paid attention to the road. The winter had been rough on the pavement, and there were potholes to avoid if possible. Ed was pretty quiet, but he said he was sorry to put me to so much trouble. I assured him it was no trouble at all; it was the sort of thing I got paid for, which was certainly true enough. The fact is that I like the give and take with Schwartz, and if he didn't like it, he could have done something about it long ago.

Delaware Street in the low 70s is a winding, wide avenue with old-growth trees and mostly old, well-maintained, good-sized houses on generous lots, many set back on low hills well above street level. Ed told me where to turn in, and I drove up a moderately steep incline to a circle around a flower bed already planted with pansies, with a double garage door at the north side of the house. It was a three-story brick, that dark-brown weathered-looking brick with vertical scoring, and a steep, dark orange tile roof. I was glad it wasn't my job to keep it repaired. I have a problem with heights. We walked around to the front door, and Ed let us in with his key, or maybe it was Phyllis's.

Inside, I noticed that the heat was on, set at sixty-eight degrees, which didn't really tell me anything, and looking around, it seemed everything was in order. Ed explained that Lawrence took care of dusting, sweeping, and the housework generally, so that was how he helped out. It saved Eugene a few bucks, since hiring someone for a house that size would not have been cheap. We walked through the ground floor, encountering nothing untoward, then went up the staircase off the front hall.

I got the impression that it was definitely a house where a couple of men lived, especially from the upstairs bedrooms. The spare rooms, or perhaps guest rooms, had the usual furniture, pictures on the walls, mainly still-lifes and landscapes, the sort of pictures you probably wouldn't hang in your own room but couldn't sell and couldn't quite bring yourself to simply throw out. Eugene's and Lawrence's rooms ran more to portraits. I'm no expert, but they seemed to be old watercolors and oil paintings of no particular distinction; there were certainly no unsuspected Old Masters hanging in either bedroom.

Just to be thorough, I found the spring-loaded pull-down ladder to the attic in an empty guest room closet, and I went up to have a look around. Ed stayed below. The attic was empty. Fairly new pink fiberglass bats had been laid down between the joists, probably within the past few years, on top of the blow-in rock wool, which was no doubt original with the house. There were no bodies stashed up there. There was nothing at all up there besides the rafters and joists and insulation, not a single box or old lamp. I went back down and returned the ladder to the ceiling in the closet. I washed the dust from the ladder off in the bathroom sink, using a new golden ovoid cake of scented soap, honey with almonds. The faucet seemed not to have been used in a while. Neither had the slightly stiff blue towel I dried my hands with.

Ed and I went back downstairs, then we checked out the garage, which was exactly as he had described it. Both cars were there, both of them silver-gray, and the hoods were cool. Of course, I felt like an idiot checking them, but I didn't want Ed feeling there was anything cursory about the investigation. I looked around the garage. There was an automatic washer and dryer along the wall next to the house proper, with a water heater and a water softener, and a gas furnace next to them, semi-walled off from the rest of the garage, with shelves over the dryer holding a box of furnace filters. There was an assortment of ice scrapers, brooms, mops, and dustpans hung on racks screwed to the wall. The wall opposite the double doors was faced with pegboard, with an assortment of tools hung neatly from hooks and prongs and rings. On the far wall from the door to the house were half a dozen shelves filled with paint cans, brushes, rollers, tubes of caulk, jugs of antifreeze, gasoline additives, paint thinner, and so on, most of it pretty dusty. Nobody dusts the stuff on garage shelves. There was a snowblower, a rototiller, and a chipper below the shelves, with a plastic bin for storing newspapers for recycling.

I looked the whole area over, with Ed along, and I noticed that on the waist-height shelf, there was a clear space not quite two feet wide, with a rectangular area pretty much free of dust, between boxes of trash bags and a stack of plastic tarps. On a higher shelf loaded with automotive stuff, I found a narrower space with a round clean space about six inches in diameter.

Going back to the wall with the tools, I went over it more carefully, and there at the lower right, I spotted two empty hooks two or two and a half feet above the floor, between a couple carpenter's saws on the left and some coping saws on the right. I wasn't sure yet what this meant, but I had an odd feeling things were about to get dark.

We'd been through the house and garage from ground level up, so the basement was next. Given the size and age of the house, I figured the cellar would be extensive and quite likely filled with most of a century's leftover furniture, broken or just not liked, and the usual detritus you find carried down for storage. There I was surprised. We found the door to the basement off the kitchen. The whole thing had been redone sometime in the past twenty or thirty years, by the paneling and the short-nap indoor-outdoor carpet, and the acoustic hanging ceiling tile.

Aside from the remodeling, the place was bare: no sofas or chairs or stools, no bar, wet or otherwise. It looked like the rec room of a family that has decided to rec somewhere else. There was a bathroom in one corner, and inspection showed it was the place where the original coal-fired furnace had been. "So when they went from coal to natural gas, they put the new furnace in the garage, not the basement," I said.

"Eugene or Lawrence wouldn't want to have to be going downstairs all the time," Ed said. "Probably Eugene."

"That makes no sense," I said. "A gas furnace doesn't need stoking. Assuming nothing was going wrong, the only thing they'd have to worry about would be changing the filter once a month."

"Do you change your furnace filter every month?"

"No, I change Schwartz's furnace filter every month," I said. "If it was up to him to do it, it wouldn't get done." I looked around. "You know, I don't think I've ever seen an emptier basement. Or attic, for that matter. It's amazing; they don't seem to have had any squirrel tendencies at all. If they had it, it was there to be seen. Of course, some of the cabinets and desks upstairs may tell us something." While I was talking, I realized that I'd become convinced that something actually had happened to Eugene and Lawrence. Those empty spaces in the garage were bothering me.

We looked the basement over thoroughly, but there wasn't anything to spark interest, no loose carpet corners where the concrete floor had a new, still-wet patch, nothing. We went upstairs again, and I called Schwartz.

"No sign of them," I told him. "No signs of violence, either. Absolutely nothing to suggest that they haven't just gone somewhere without telling Ed."

"Aside from what's known about their usual habits," he said. "Why not come on home?"

"Okay. I think a detailed report can wait until I get there. I'll tell Ed to keep in touch with the police, but it's probably nothing at all." I paused a moment. "What will we charge him?"

"Nothing, of course. We haven't done anything for him aside from trying to allay his fears. I'll see you shortly." He hung up.

Ed didn't want to leave without learning anything much, but I finally got him to leave. We drove back without a word. I dropped him at his house, then drove home, put the car in the garage, and went in to report to Schwartz. He went back to his book.

Chapter Five

Sunday, March 29

The next morning was Sunday, which Schwartz likes to start off with a big bacon, eggs, waffles, and fried potatoes breakfast, followed by a glance at the front page of the paper, "to see what they want us to believe today," and an assault on the puzzles. After that was out of the way, we were discussing the events of the day before, when the doorbell rang. Considering what the last ring had ended up bringing us, I have to admit I hesitated a bit. I glanced at Schwartz and saw that his expression matched my feeling. "Might as well answer it, I suppose," he said after a moment. I nodded and got up, and answered the door.

I recognized the woman on the front porch as a neighbor, but I knew her only to say hello to. I had seen her walking her dog in the neighborhood between College Avenue on the west and the old Monon railroad line, which is now a biking/hiking trail, on the east, between 78th Street on the south and 83rd on the north. I'd also seen her somewhere else, but it took a while for that to surface. She was in her early to mid-thirties, I'd have guessed, with short brown hair, wearing a pale blue blouse and dark blue slacks, carrying a large shoulder bag on a strap. I introduced myself and asked her if I could help her, and she said, "I'm Viola Ketchum, Mr. Zufahl. I live a couple blocks from here, on Windcombe. I apologize for coming on a Sunday, but I think I need to see Mr. Schwartz."

It's not as if we insist on appointments, but after what Ed Stroh had brought us the day before, I thought perhaps we might want to consider a change in policy. I invited her in anyway. It would head off another digression by Schwartz, at any rate. I led the way to the office and gave her the red leather chair facing Schwartz. "Ms. Ketchum, this is Leo Schwartz. Mr. Schwartz, Viola Ketchum, a neighbor of ours, over on Windcombe. She walks a wire-haired terrier named Oscar." Ms. Ketchum gave me what I thought was a puzzled look, but I figured I was imagining it. I wasn't.

I got seated and moved a pad over to take notes. I like to think my memory is good, as I've mentioned, and most of the time it is, but it would help to have a written record if and when I got around to writing up the case report. You never know in advance which cases will need one. And, as I was to find out, you never know when your memory is letting you down without telling you so.

"What can I help you with, Ms. Ketchum?" Schwartz asked. "But perhaps some tea or coffee would be welcome?"

"No, I'm fine," she said. "It's about my Uncle Jim's will."

Schwartz kept his face straight. The last time a case had involved a will, it had ended up with a very unhappy client, no fault of ours, and an uncollectable fee, no good to us. "Is there a problem with the will?" he asked, taking the trouble to make it sound reasonably courteous.

"Well, not exactly," she said. "Uncle Jim died just over two months ago, on January 13. He was widowed, and he and Aunt Cynthia had no children. Both his brother, my three cousins' father, and his sister, my mother, predeceased him." She was looking for something in her bag, so she missed the look on Schwartz's face at the word 'predeceased', a sure sign she'd been talking to lawyers recently, or at least listening to them. She took a manila envelope out of the bag. "He left each of my cousins ten thousand dollars, and he left me this envelope—"

Schwartz interrupted, gently. "Excuse me, but did your uncle and your cousins live here in town?"

"Uncle Jim lived in Broad Ripple," she said, "on 64th Street and Guilford"—about a mile and a half from where we were sitting—"and my cousins grew up in Kansas, although now they're grown and married, they live in

New Mexico, Texas, and Kansas."

"Their names and ages?"

"Harriett Anderson is forty-four, I think, and she and her husband are in Albuquerque; Kelley Ellenbogen kept her name, is thirty-nine or forty, and lives with her husband in Austin; and John Ellenbogen is my age, thirty-five, born in the same month, and he and Jessica live in Wichita."

"And your parents?"

"My mother and father were killed in a traffic accident on the way back from my Uncle Alexander's funeral four years ago. There was an accident up ahead on the Interstate, and traffic was backed up, and a tractor-trailer hit them from behind, and they were—"

"You weren't in the car?" Schwartz asked.

"No, I was in Europe at the time, and Mom and Dad had told me not to come home for—"

"Of course." Schwartz was trying to avoid letting the client get emotional, but I thought he could have used some pointers. "Now, when your Uncle Jim died, Harriett, Kelley, and John each received ten thousand dollars, and you got that envelope, is that correct?"

"Yes," Viola said.

"What was their reaction to this disparity?"

"What do you mean?"

"Well, they got a substantial amount each, and you got an envelope, which I assume did not contain a hundred hundred-dollar bills. Were any or all of your cousins upset? Did anyone raise objections?"

"Well, no," she said. "They didn't actually come back for the reading. The lawyer, Mr. Parkinson, sent each of them certified copies of the will, along with the checks, and I came to his office." That explained how she had made her way to our door. Neil Parkinson is one of the few lawyers Schwartz trusts and likes, and he'd known how to get rid of her questions efficiently.

"When was the will read?" Schwartz asked.

"Yesterday afternoon." No time wasted. "Here's the envelope, and what it contained," Viola said, leaning forward and handing the evidence to Schwartz.

I got up and went over to his desk to see. He opened the flap and shook out a twice-folded sheet of good-quality rag bond and a square photograph. The photo was an ordinary Polaroid, which you don't see a lot of lately, showing a fireplace and the walls on either side. To the left was a brown door with some sort of herbal chart on it, and a bulging bag hanging from the middle hinge of the door. "That's his bag of grocery sacks that he kept for the dog, you know, to clean up after her when they went for a walk," she said, pointing, in response to Schwartz's unspoken question.

To the right side of the photo were bookshelves crammed full, with a saltwater taffy box atop the books on the third shelf up and a Whitman's Sampler box two shelves higher. In the center of the picture was a used-brick fireplace with a rough-hewn wood mantelpiece crowded with candles, photos, a couple of trophies, an incense burner, and miscellaneous litter. Above the mantel hung a double gun rack holding a pair of Kentucky rifles, and above that a ceramic name plate with "Ellenbogen" in fancy blue script. Below the mantel were the glass doors of the fireplace, reflecting the flash used to take the photo, and a fireplace set with poker, shovel, tongs, and brush. A popcorn popper and some skewers hung from the wood mantel on the left, a bellows, and a big leather fireplace glove on the right.

Schwartz laid down the Polaroid and, picked up the sheet of paper, unfolded it. A double column of capital letters was printed down the center of the sheet:

IM
DB
TC
KM
VK
AE
TS
MI
JS
BT
RR

TR

CG

WH

JT

MR

AP

RB

DS

BS

RC

FP

PP

TH

LR

JT

JC

DF

MG

CJ

MJ

SK

JM

VS

WW

"Ten-point Times Roman," Schwartz muttered, "printed on a laser-jet printer. Not particularly recently, either." Like Schwartz, I could see that the type was slightly degraded, as if the page had been moved from one place to another over a period of time. He turned the sheet over. The back was blank.

Schwartz looked up at Viola Ketchum. "I take it you have no idea what this means?"

"No, that was what Mr. Parkinson thought you could help me with. Look,

I'm not independently wealthy or anything, but if you're willing to work on a contingency basis, I could—"

Schwartz loves moments like this, if only to put it to me. "Let me assure you, Ms. Ketchum, that if I am not the worst businessman on earth, some poor soul is in a world of hurt. Of course, we'll take the case. Damn the money." He paused. "Damn," he repeated, thinking of his grandson again. He leaned back, laid the sheet of paper on the desk in front of him, stared at it. "How well did you know your uncle, Ms. Ketchum?"

"Could you make it Viola, Mr. Schwartz?" She took a moment to choose her words. "I suppose I knew him pretty well, up to a point. He was just over seventy when he died. I went over to the house every week to see him, make sure he was getting along all right, and we talked on the phone every evening, so—"

"So it would be safe to say you were closer to him than your cousins were? I don't mean just geographically, but emotionally as well. You saw him weekly, talked with him daily, made sure he was safe and in good health. I dare say you ran errands for him on occasion, perhaps provided transportation when he didn't feel like driving, now and then cooked a meal for him?"

"Well, yes, that's true," she said.

"Did your cousins stay in touch with him?"

"Oh, I doubt they did, aside from Christmas cards or whatever. After all, the distance and—"

"Precisely," Schwartz said. "So we can assume, I think, that this cryptic list is no joke, cutting you off with a sheet of paper after your years of devotion."

"Oh, come on," she said, "I'm no martyr. It's just that, after Mom and Dad died, Uncle Jim was about all the real family I had left besides my cousins. So I kept in touch with him, and I wasn't expecting anything from him. To be honest, I was surprised his estate amounted to as much as it did, besides the house and the bequests and—" She pulled herself together. "He lived quietly, I think I'd even say modestly, and he had friends, but he never gave the impression of being terribly well off."

"So you didn't have great expectations from his will? He never told you, or even hinted, that you would 'be taken care of,' as the expression goes, when he died?"

"No, not at all. It never occurred to me, frankly, that I'd get anything at all. But I wasn't expecting something like this—" She gestured at the paper.

"What sort of man was your uncle?" Schwartz leaned back in his chair, closed his eyes, opened them, shifted to the client. "What did he do for a living? What were his interests? Who did he know? Tell me about him."

"Well—" That got her started, and if any of what she told us about Uncle Jim had been any help at all, I'd happily share it with you, but in fact, most of it would do you as little good as it did us, and you aren't trying to earn a fee, so I'll spare you most of the chaff.

What we found out that mattered was that he had been a puzzle fan, subscribed to the daily and Sunday newspapers because he did the sudoku, the word jumble, the crossword, and the crypto-quip each and every day with his morning two cups of coffee. He liked puzzles of all kinds. So far, he reminded me of Schwartz. Unlike Schwartz, however, he also liked devising them, and he'd had a number of crosswords and other sorts of puzzles published in books and magazines, Viola said.

He had been an accountant with a software firm downtown for the last twenty years of his career, had retired at sixty-five and a half, and he'd been a Mason, a Presbyterian, and a Republican, all without any noticeable excessive zeal. He'd been lax about lodge meetings for ten years, about attending church for fifteen, and about the GOP for at least thirty, Viola thought. "He thought the church had gotten too liberal and the party had gotten too conservative," she said. "I don't know what he thought about the Masons, but he hadn't been to meetings in a long time, although they did send two men to the funeral. I think he paid dues and things like that, but you know how it is when people get old; they sometimes get...."

"Cranky?" Schwartz suggested. "God knows I feel it coming on myself. Be that as it may, your Uncle Jim was a puzzler, which I think is probably our best clue to this little conundrum." He picked it up, turned to me. "Does it suggest anything to you, Rainer?"

I took it from him, looked down the double column of letters. "People's initials?" I suggested. "But whose?"

"Exactly," Schwartz said. He glared at the sheet balefully. "Imelda Marcos," he said. "Isaac Mizrahi. Isaac McKneely." I stared, astonished that he knew either name. He couldn't care less about fashion, and I doubt he's ever read a sports page. "Ike Mindy. Ira Madison."

I jerked my head up. "Ilona Marchand," I said.

"Ilona Marchand," Schwartz repeated quietly.

"Who's Ilona Marchand?" Viola asked.

"Someone we know," Schwartz said. He went back to the sheet, tapping his phone to summon Google. "Ilona Massey," he continued. "Ilona Mitrecey, Ilona Marino, Ilona Margolis, Ilona McCrea, … Who the hell knew there were so many Ilonas with last names beginning in *M*? Good Lord. Iris Murdoch. Iris what's-her-name?"

"Warner," I said. "Don't tell me it's an upside-down *M*."

"Right. This is no way to proceed."

"Maybe the letters read vertically," I suggested.

Schwartz frowned, then read letters that way: "IDTKV … pfui. MBCMK … more nuts. Or from the bottom, WVJSM…WSMKJ…. No, that makes no more sense, either, that I can see."

He leaned back in his chair. "I think, Ms. Ketchum, you should hang on to your inheritance for now, but if you'll permit it, Mr. Zufahl will scan the document and photo, and we will see if perhaps we can tease some meaning out of them."

Viola nodded, and I took the exhibits over to my desk. "And the envelope," Schwartz added. It made no less sense to me. I scanned the photo and the sheet with the initials or letters or whatever they were, then returned the originals to Viola. She didn't seem in a hurry to leave, but after a while, we ran out of small talk, and she went. I sat at my desk trying to make something of the initials, if that's what they were, and trying to see some good reason for the photo, without success in either case. When I looked up, I saw that Schwartz had departed.

Looking around, I saw him out in the eight-sided gazebo in the backyard, which he calls a summerhouse, since it has walls and a door with a lock. It's centered in the backyard and is remotely heated via an underground duct from the house, so that there are no hot elements in the gazebo itself. Since this is where Schwartz makes fireworks, that's eminently sensible. I went out to see what he was up to.

He looked up as I came in. Neither of us felt the need to say anything. I watched him weigh chemicals, some of which he ran through a blender before depositing them in a mixing bowl. He put the lid on the bowl and began shaking it. After a while, he spread brown paper on the counter, placed a wood-framed screen on it, and emptied the mixing bowl onto the screen. With gloved hands, he ran his fingers through the mixture, sifting it through the screen until it was all definitely finer than forty-mesh and well combined. He poured the mix into another, larger bowl, then took a plastic jar from the bottom shelf, weighed out an amount of gray metal, then stirred that into the mix.

"What are you making?" I asked him, just to break the silence.

"Zinc stars," he said. "Ian von Maltitz says their blue-green color is unlike any other, and I want to see for myself. 'Ian von Maltitz': another IM name. Good Lord. Rainer, I think I may be losing my hold on what little sanity I have left." He put a lid on the mixture bowl. "The thing is, the zinc is so much denser than other metals used in stars that it takes extra boost to get the shells to the proper height, and I'm just a bit trepidatious about that. So I'm doing a trial batch, just to see."

"Not something you could just go buy, I suppose."

"No, not really. The commercially available consumer fireworks naturally are designed to appeal to as wide an audience as possible, so this is really the only way to find out what they'll look like. Assuming I can get them lit."

"I'm willing to bet you can."

"With the right primer, I will," he said. I watched him shake the powdered zinc and the mixture of chemicals. Of course, I knew, because he'd explained it to me, that you never screen metals, any large particles of which would only get caught in the screen and would be a real pain to remove. He got the zinc mixed in to his satisfaction, took off the lid, gave the bowl a spray from a bottle of diluted rubbing alcohol, stirred it, sprayed again, stirred, sprayed, then scooped the dampened mass out, shaped it into a patty, and laid it on a cutting board covered with waxed paper.

He laid a couple wood strips left and right of the dampened star mix, then laid waxed paper over it and began to flatten it with a rolling pin. When he had it down to the thickness of the wood strips, he took another jar, labeled Primer #3, from the shelf. He spooned primer over the flattened star mix, patted it gently, then with a long, thin kitchen knife began slicing the mix into quarter-inch strips, which he flipped over, unprimed side up, one by one. When he had all the strips cut, he sprinkled more prime on them, then cut them into quarter-inch squares.

Schwartz spooned more prime into a pan, spread it around, then transferred the squares into the pan of prime. He shook the pan to get all the damp sides coated, then put a drying screen on the brown paper and emptied half the contents of the pan onto it. He gave the screen a light shake so that all the loose primer would fall through onto the paper, then he put the screen into his drying box. He filled a second drying screen with the rest of the squares, shook it, and stacked it on top of the first screen in the box.

He emptied the loose primer back into a jar, cleaned up the counter, and went to the door to flip the remote switch that would circulate air through the drying box, set it for four hours. "I checked all the fire extinguishers," he said, "and they're all good." There were four extinguishers mounted on alternate posts of the gazebo. He closed the window slats, since it would be chilly that night. "Enough of that for today," he said. We went back to the house.

Chapter Six

Sunday, March 29

The rest of Sunday was pretty quiet. In the evening, Schwartz's daughter, Gina McIntosh, came over with her son, Josh, who was four and, unlike his mother, hearing. I'd known her since her bedroom was the one between Schwartz's and mine, and I'd picked up a little ASL, but not really much. My signing is slow and short on vocabulary, basically what Schwartz calls Primitive Signed English. The ASL grammar, according to him, is very different from English grammar, verbs at the end, adjectives following nouns, no definite article, and so on. A great way to feel inadequate is to know and like a deaf person, pardon me, a Deaf person, and to wish you could keep up with the signing.

Schwartz says she continues to razz him about his signing, and he's been at it for thirty-some years. "If you're going to learn another language, don't wait till it's as hard as possible," he says. When he's around Josh, he talks and signs simultaneously, on the theory that he needs all the stimulation he can get. This evening, however, Schwartz had drifted into a new topic.

"Needless to say, it pales to insignificance, compared to the sheer enormity of Nazism, or Naziism, with a double *i*, as real obsessives spell it, the crimes against humanity, the war crimes, the peace crimes—all the demented war on civilians and erstwhile civilians who failed to conform to that twisted, demonic vision of what the future of Germany and German-dominated Europe and eventually the world would be could be should be—compared to everything else, it's trivial, but I don't think that means we have to let the bastard off the hook on the grounds that he gets a free pass on the small stuff since his other crimes were on such an appalling scale…." He looked around to make sure Josh wasn't within earshot.

"What the hell are you talking about?" I had to ask, since the boy was off in the kitchen with his mother, who was warming up something she'd brought over, on the theory that without her, Schwartz and I would slowly starve. Neither of us objects; she learned to cook from her mother, and she learned well. Schwartz took a planning pad, quarter-inch squares with blue lines, from a desk drawer. He took a soft-lead pencil and shaded seventeen squares in a five-by-five square. "The Nazis ruined the swastika," he said, "and I realize it comes off as petty, all things considered, but have you ever tried to work up a fretwork border—"

"No, I haven't," I said.

"—and suddenly noticed that the pattern has unexpectedly developed a sinister aspect? Well, it happens, or anyway, it has happened, to me, and it's a pain in the—" Schwartz's grandson toddled into the workshop— "in the back of the lap," Schwartz finished. He picked the boy up and leaned back to make lap room. "Look who just turned four last Wednesday," he said, "and who's going to become a big brother in a couple months, isn't he?"

Josh nodded. "Going to have a little sister," he affirmed. He squirmed down, announced that he had to use the bathroom, and took off on that errand. Schwartz took his hand off the pencil sketch, pulled the sheet loose, crumpled it, tossed it into the wastebasket.

"Have you had any flashes of insight into Ms. Ketchum's conundrum?" he asked.

"No," I said, "and I think we both know that flashes of insight are your department, not mine. I also think you only asked because you wanted to say 'Ketchum's conundrum'. I have to admit, it has a nice sound to it. If I were writing this up, it would make a good title. Better than 'The Case of the Coasting Corporation,' anyway. But that would mean using her real name, which I doubt she'd appreciate, so I suppose that's out."

"They're two separate cases," Schwartz objected.

"Yes, and have you noticed that we've now got three distinct cases just four days after we had nothing at all for two weeks?"

"Not to mention that escapade with Phil," he pointed out. "That's going to mean showing up to testify for sure."

"Maybe they'll work out a mutually agreeable settlement," I said.

"Maybe, but let's not count on it. And please don't waste any time dreaming up titles for that and the blackmail case." I already had, but kept it to myself.

Josh returned to the room and climbed back on Schwartz's lap. He began to color in squares on the pad with the soft pencil. "Why spoil the beauty of a thing with legalities?" Schwartz quoted, more or less rhetorically. "Actually, though, I'd rather you didn't write up our cases. There are so many legal pitfalls to avoid, and I don't think people would really care to read about real detective work. Better to leave crime writing to the folks with the imagination to dream up interesting stories. Just one man's opinion."

Gina came in and signed to him, and he signed back high, over Josh's head. They conversed, and I missed almost all of it except Gina's smile at me as she gathered Josh up for departure. "Beef stew in the oven," Schwartz translated, "Swedish meatballs and noodles in the freezer, and it was nice to see us both."

I signed, "Good to see you too," to Gina, then Schwartz got up from his chair, carrying Josh, to go out to her car. I stayed put.

When he returned to the office, we discussed the next day's plan, and since there were a few details to iron out about my consultant role at WarnerCorp, I called Ilona Marchand. I decided not to mention that we had found what might be her initials at the head of a list brought in by another client. When we had the preliminaries out of the way, I asked what time I should show up, who to report to, and all that sort of thing. We agreed on the stage directions and the general tenor of the script, and when I could think of no more questions to ask, we wrapped it up, and I rang off.

I spent a couple hours working up forms to use as part of my cover, and I printed out a few in a reasonably businesslike, up-to-date format, including a few minor typographic errors to give the nitpickers something to criticize. With any luck, the superficialities would distract sufficiently from the realities so that I could spend three days asking questions without arousing suspicions about what was actually going on. Sooner or later, someone would let me know I should mind my own business, but I hoped that would just end one line of inquiry, not cut off the whole thing. We would see, I told myself as I hit the print button and let the deskjet start spitting the sheets out.

Schwartz was finishing Kahneman while I took care of that business, and the office phone rang just as he closed the book, and the last sheet fell into the hopper. I answered, "Rainer Zufahl," since it was Sunday. I'd have said, "Leo Schwartz's office, Rainer Zufahl speaking," Monday through Friday, on the landline. I let Schwartz know who it was: "Oh, hello, Iris."

She said, "Rainer, I've been thinking, and I'm really not sure we're doing the right thing here. I wonder if we should call it off, or at least postpone it—"

"Iris, you know the Starbucks in Nora, the freestanding one?"

"Sure, but—"

"I'll meet you there in ten minutes," I said. I covered the microphone with my leg, told Schwartz, "Client's getting cold feet."

"Bring her here," he said. I held the phone down for a moment, couldn't think of a good reason to object, and then told her, "Scratch that, Iris. Can you come to Mr. Schwartz's office? Yes, now." She asked for the address, which of course, she had on my business card, but it probably wasn't to hand. "That's right across College from Meridian Hills, best to take 81st across, then follow it when it curves around, and...yes, that's right. See you in a bit." I hung up.

Schwartz gave me the look that is supposed to make me feel guilty about forcing him to get to work. "No deal," I told him. "You heard me offer to meet her at Starbucks, and she could have asked me over if she'd wanted. Apparently, she's decided she has to see you."

His expression had changed, and then I got it. "No. That's not it at all," I said. I could barely keep my voice under control. "No, you've decided you have to see her on your home turf, not in an AA meeting, not as a fellow alcoholic, but to assess her as a potential threat to our domestic if all-male bliss. You really think this designing woman has got her—"

"Shut up, Rainer." He took the Kahneman book to the shelves, found a good spot for it. It was a keeper. Easily half his books end up being donated to the library after he reads them, but even so the shelves are crowded beyond all reason. "You should find time for this one," he said as he shelved it. He got Richard Dawkins's latest from the table and brought it back to his desk. It would be interesting to see how this one fared. He keeps most but not all of them.

He had settled in nicely with it when the doorbell rang, and I went to let Iris in. I saw she'd driven the Corvette. She was wearing a crisp white blouse, very pale yellow slacks, and comfortable-looking black shoes. She had a black-leather shoulder bag that could have held dinner for three but probably didn't; it was devoid of impressive lettering. We said hello, then I led the way down the hall to the office.

Like most people, the first time they come into the office, Iris stopped dead as she came in the door. You just don't see that many books every day, unless you're a librarian. The office had been two fair-sized rooms once, but now it was one good-sized room, completely lined, floor to ceiling, with bookshelves. Schwartz stood and gave her a nod as she took in the books.

Iris sat in the red leather chair, looked around again, and said, "I don't know what I was expecting, Leo, but this is amazing. I might have expected you to be a book collector."

"It's actually a symptom," he said, sitting down again, "of an overweening need to possess, to own, to have, and I suspect it's not unrelated to the disease the three of us have in common. I don't really collect books; I accumulate them. But would you care for refreshment?"

Without waiting for an answer, he turned to me. "Rainer, I washed Iris's Thermos, and there's a fresh pitcher of tea in the refrigerator, if you wouldn't mind." I wouldn't. I saw what he'd been up to that morning, after finishing off the Thermos Iris had sent Friday. I assembled the pitcher, glasses, ice bucket, and so on on a tray, put the empty Thermos and cap in a bag, and I brought it all into the office as Schwartz was saying, "—was really excellent, and I've taken the liberty of trying to duplicate it myself, with one small additional ingredient that I hope will not ruin what was already a marvelous concoction.

"Are you familiar with the Japanese tea ceremony?" he asked Iris as I poured and passed the glasses. It was clear that either Iris had won him over or he wanted her, and me, to think she had done so. "It's remarkably interesting, complex, and crucial to a culture that goes back, despite many political changes, many centuries."

As a matter of fact, Iris knew about the tea ceremony, and the two of them got along great discussing it as we sipped our tea, and I listened. Tea is fine, and I like it, but I was having a hard time seeing the connection to the WarnerCorp case, probably because there wasn't any. Schwartz was having a good time shooting the breeze with someone other than me, his employee, and he liked talking with someone who could keep up.

A few minutes into the conversation, Iris held her glass out, as if reading the ice cubes, and she said, "All the ingredients I told Rainer about are there, although I think you've left the caraway understated a bit, but there's something else, isn't there, Leo?"

Schwartz nodded, clearly pleased. "I was afraid the caraway would be overwhelming," he said.

"It can be, but straining it out after infusion keeps it calmed down. Now, what is that something else?" Iris seemed to be having as good a time as Schwartz. She took another healthy sip, held it in her mouth a moment, then swallowed. "Sesame," she said.

"Excellent!" Schwartz said. He reached over the desk and extended a fist. Iris reached out, and they bumped knuckles.

"I hope you don't feel I've meddled with a masterpiece," he said.

"Oh, please," Iris said. "You've added something to it, and I would never have thought sesame would blend so well with the other ingredients. Did you steep whole seeds or crush them first?"

"I crushed them quickly but not thoroughly—"

"So the infusion gets whole and crushed seeds…. Interesting." She took another sip. "You must show me how you made yours. I have to admit, it's a real improvement." She stopped short of batting her eyes at him. Schwartz was absolutely beaming. She nodded decisively. "A real improvement, no doubt about it—"

"Well, with inspiration like the tea you sent me, I had to see if I could duplicate it, and I came close." That definitely was what he'd been doing when I called Saturday. I had expected him to have finished the Kahneman book sooner than he had. He'd been brewing small batches of iced tea, probably considering some of those raspberries and blackberries in the fridge, and finally coming up with the sesame idea.

"You fellows really know your tea," Iris said, politely and half-correctly. She set down her glass on the wooden coaster. Schwartz and I set ours down too. "But I'm really here on Buck's behalf, even if it's without his knowledge or permission. But Ilona agrees, and that will have to do." She glanced from Schwartz to me, then: "Ilona is very concerned about keeping things discreet, since if word gets out, one way or the other, that there's some sort of problem with the business, it could be disastrous.

"As you know, the company is almost totally identified with Buck, and so is WarnerCorp. The software is fine; we're sure of that. It's constantly under revision, updates are regularly issued, and, as I suppose you know, the pricing structure is designed so that any medical/allied-health entity, no matter how small or how large, can afford it and use it in perfect harmony with any and all other software and any and all hardware they could possibly be using.

"And so far as I can tell," she went on, "the people at WarnerCorp are all in fine shape too. To tell you the truth, after going over the matter, I find it hard to believe what a good, solid crew he's got. They've all been with the company from the start, and he hasn't lost anyone to the competition, because there's really no company in the field that can offer really brilliant people what WarnerCorp does. And of course, being based here makes a huge difference in cost of living, compared to either coast or Texas, for that matter.

"I mean, do you know of any other company that explicitly tells people to go ahead and help other companies interface with their software, and that pays them very generously for doing that? You know what customer service is like, for the most part, in the United States today. Well, if you pick up the phone and call the number that's printed on every piece of documentation we supply, you're connected to someone who knows the software inside and out, who can refer back to old versions that haven't been updated, who can answer the customer's questions and take care of problems, usually in less time than it would take to write a letter of complaint, much less get it into snail-mail." I noticed that "we" in reference to WarnerCorp.

"And," Iris went on, "the person you speak with will be fluent from birth in the English language—"

"Language acquisition can be said to begin at birth," Schwartz interrupted, "although, in fact, the infant will not actively produce language until—"

"They all speak American English," I put in, trying to get us back to business.

"And three, counting myself, speak Spanish, three, counting myself, speak French, one speaks Mandarin, and one Arabic."

"Making seven in all," Schwartz said.

She did a quick count in her head. "Yes, although I haven't been going in on a regular basis since Buck and I divorced."

"Yet you referred to the company as 'we,'" Schwartz said. "You consider yourself part of the company, after all, even after you and Mr. Warner ended your marriage. So I take it that your concerns about him are both personal and professional. Professional in the sense of having to do with the company's welfare as well as his."

Iris nodded, then said, "The next question would be why I turned to a detective rather than an accountant.

"The fact is, I don't think it's a financial problem at all. I think Buck is worried about something external to himself or as external to himself as anything at WarnerCorp can be. We've stayed close, and in many ways, we've grown closer as friends than we were when we were married. He's concerned as all hell about something, but he suddenly slammed the gate closed, and I haven't a clue what's getting to him, and whenever I try to ask him, the wall goes up and stays up."

Gates or walls, Schwartz kept his face straight. "When did you first suspect something was bothering Mr. Warner?" he asked.

"About three months ago. Quarter closing is always an intense time, and end of year all the more so, but I could tell something wasn't okay with him this time. It wasn't the usual level of intensity, and when I tried to raise the matter, he deflected the entire subject."

"So the silence has gone on longer than a week?" Schwartz seemed to consider the possibilities. "Perhaps it's a romantic involvement, which obviously he might not wish to—"

"No, not at all," Iris said positively. "He was in a relationship with Christine Leland, an old friend from school, and everything seemed all right with them." She brushed the hair back out of her eyes, even though her hair had not been in her eyes. "As far as I knew. I don't really ask, of course, since it's really none of my business, after all. But Christine told me a couple weeks ago it is over between them."

"Yet you are worried about him, as well as about the company," Schwartz said. "Why? I mean, what have you observed that leads you to believe the problem, if there, in fact, is one, is beyond Mr. Warner's ability to identify and correct? What makes you think something is, in fact, wrong at all?"

"Well," Iris said, "I'm not the only one who's worried. In December, Buck told me he's onto something that's going on, and at first, he even asked for my help, yet he's keeping secrets himself," Iris said. "From me, from Ilona, from everyone at WarnerCorp. I have stayed in touch with everyone; after all, it's a small group of people who have worked together for a decade."

It occurred to me that this was also technically an accurate description of Schwartz and me, but I just kept on listening.

"No one wants to come out and say it, but everyone really is concerned about Buck. He sits through business meetings without a word to anyone, on any subject. He calls meetings to discuss completely irrelevant issues, political stuff, articles he's read that have nothing to do with the business. People are worried. About Buck, and about WarnerCorp."

If you have the impression that the conference had run out of steam, then you've kept up. Schwartz tried to pin Iris down, and I contributed a bit, but she had nothing more definite than her flat assertions that she knew her ex well enough to know something was eating him and that other people in the company agreed with her, which seemed a bit unusual if this had already been going on for three months or so. But as for concrete realities, there was nothing. Schwartz knows when they aren't biting, and he decided to call it an evening.

"Mr. Zufahl, er, Rainer, will start tomorrow morning as a consultant reporting to Ms. Marchand," he said, "studying the company in an effort to suggest new directions, new opportunities, new…. Well, I needn't rehearse the play for you. I hope you will be at the office while he is consulting. If there is something to be found, I expect he will find it, probably well before the end of the week."

"And if he doesn't?" Iris's arms were folded across her chest.

"If he doesn't find anything, that will be a fair indication that there is nothing to be found." Schwartz turned over a hand. "We appreciate your confidence in asking for our help, Iris. We truly do. But you must recognize that that must be based on our ability to detect things that really exist."

Iris was clearly ready to tell him what to do with his suspicions that she was imagining everything, but she got hold of herself, picked up her handbag from the floor, and set it on her lap. "I tried to discuss the fee with Rainer last week, but he was, shall we say, evasive about the amount."

"Let's leave that alone for the moment," Schwartz said. "I'm sure we will be able to agree on a reasonable amount when the time comes."

"A hell of a way to do business," Iris said. I rose with her to see her to the door.

The social temperature had dropped a few degrees, but I didn't let on I'd noticed. As I let her out, I told her I'd be in touch tomorrow evening after my first day at WarnerCorp, and she said that would be fine, then she turned to me as I held the door open. "Do you think it's all in my head, Rainer? Tell me the truth."

"No," I said, "I don't, and neither does Mr. Schwartz. But he has to cover all the bases, and it's not impossible that—"

"It's not impossible that I'm out of my mind hiring you," she said. "It's not impossible that I'm imagining everything. But I'm sure I'm not."

I was experiencing an almost irresistible impulse, but one thing I've gotten from years of AA is practice at resisting almost irresistible impulses. Mostly they involve liquids, and sometimes they involve words or actions. "Restraint of tongue and pen" is the catchword. The thing is, I was also experiencing the certainty that Iris was fully aware of my mental state and that she wasn't rooting for restraint. Schwartz likes to say that most alcoholics have an infallible moral compass, the problem being that the needle points due south rather than north. All you have to do is recognize that what you want to do is the direct opposite of what you should do. Iris and I looked into each other's eyes for a very long moment, then she nodded. "I'll look forward to seeing you," she said, "tomorrow." She went to her car.

Back in the office, Schwartz was immersed in Dawkins. "Did I mention the Corvette?" I asked him, knowing I had. "She drove it here. Automatic transmission."

He didn't look up. "Triple her bill," he said. He turned a page. "Letting me muck with her tea recipe, which was already as close to perfection as one could expect. That woman will bear watching."

"Yes, indeed," I said, but I couldn't get a rise. I was ready to bet that Dawkins book would end up a keeper.

Chapter Seven

Monday, March 30

Monday was interesting. I drove the Camry to the WarnerCorp offices, half a block south of 96th Street just off Keystone, almost but not quite over the line into Hamilton County. They had the top floor of a gleaming, reflective nine-story steel and glass hive, which I'd bet killed a hundred birds a year. I had my shoulder bag/briefcase, and unlike the people I was going to meet with, I was wearing a lightweight gray suit and a maroon and gray striped tie. Ilona had told me they were full-time office casual, but a hired consultant has to dress the part.

Ilona was waiting to welcome me when I came out of the elevator, and she led the way to what would be my office for a few days, a room almost as big as Schwartz's library, but with more windows and far fewer books, by a few thousand or so. The paintings on the wall were corporate abstract, which an artist of my acquaintance had once described as "better than you could do, but only by two art classes, and utterly inoffensive." There was a spacious, empty desk with a chair and a conference table that could seat eight easily, ten in a pinch: there were three armchairs along each side and one at each end, and the two extras were at the far end of the room. The interior windows had shades in case anyone broke down in tears during the interrogation.

Ilona went to the coffee service on a low table on the narrow wall near the door. "Cream? Sugar?" I asked for cream, no sugar, wondering why she was making me coffee. She sat in the armchair facing the desk, and I sat across from her.

"Well, I have to say you look the part," she said.

"The part?" I asked.

"The part of an outside expert."

"You know, Mr. Schwartz once quoted a definition of expert," I said. "'A damn fool with a briefcase and a collection of jargon, five miles from home.'" She smiled, but didn't respond.

I told her, "I've got some forms that you might want to look over, make sure I'm not stepping on any corporate toes." I took them out, handed them to her, got my laptop set up on the desk while she looked them over.

"These aren't half bad," Ilona said, "for a damn fool. We might actually get something worthwhile out of your consultancy."

"Well, perhaps they could serve as a starting point to discussion," I said. "For now, I think they might be a starting point for finding out what, if anything, is happening."

"That shouldn't be happening," she said.

"Yes." I took a planning pad from my bag, uncapped a pen. Ilona filled me in on the office assignments as I sketched the layout and filled in names and titles. The floor was a rectangle, almost a square, with the elevator, stairs, kitchen/lunchroom, restrooms, and two utility rooms in the middle, surrounded by a wide corridor and offices all around. Everybody had at least one wall of windows, how democratic, and the four corner offices had two. I wondered to what extent some would be more equal than others.

"By my count, there are fourteen offices, and we've filled them all in except for the corner rooms," I said.

"The northwest and northeast are conference rooms," she said. "Southwest, this one, is an open office/conference room." She pronounced the slash. "The southeast is sort of combination short-term storage, supplies, and informal meeting room. Sometimes you want to talk, but not in a conference room and not in someone's office."

I wrote "Storage/conspiracy" in the southeast rectangle. I assured her this was just to get things clear, which putting it on paper did for my visual memory. I flicked on the shredder next to the desk, and my map of the floor went in, the first contribution to the bin.

"What's the monthly rent on a whole floor of this building?" I asked her, not that it mattered or I really cared. She was a good conversationalist, and I found myself glad that the consultant pose let us spend time together before she unleashed me on the troops.

"There's no rent; WarnerCorp owns the building," Ilona said. "Buck bought it five, six years ago, when northside real estate was really saturated all of a sudden. I could find out how much he paid, but I'm pretty sure that it made more sense for him to simply pay cash and be done with it. WarnerCorp pays an outside company, Aztec Management, to manage the lower floors, not to mention keep things shipshape on this one. It's the corporate equivalent of hiring a maid."

"Okay," I said. "I wish Mr. Schwartz would think about doing that. Hiring a maid, I mean." I was drifting from the business at hand. "So, according to the chart I just disposed of, from left to right, Buck Warner, CEO, and you, Office Manager and Human Resources, have the offices on the north end of the floor, then the offices along the west side, from north to south, are those of Geoff Parsons, CFO, Keith Benedict, Head Programmer, and George Kearney, Primary Programmer. On the east side, north to south, are Clare Thomason, COO, Lara Collins, Chief Programmer, and Jean Stevens, Top Programmer. At the south end are Henry Appleby, Chief Assistant, and Iris Warner, title iffy, when she's in."

"Iris's title is Vice President," Ilona said.

"I can't help noticing that the women are all on the east side and the men all on the west side. I mean, is this happenstance? I couldn't tell you the odds—"

"Less than one and a half percent," Ilona said. "Would you like to know how the offices were assigned, Chuck?"

"I'd be fascinated," I said, "and I bet I'm about to learn something about men and women."

Ilona sat back in her chair. "We got together in front of the elevators and drew poker chips from a basket, white ones that Iris had numbered one to ten. The central areas and the four corner rooms had all been assigned by Buck and me, so for the regular offices, Buck held the basket, offered it around, and in no particular order, we each drew a chip. I got eight, and I don't remember exactly who else got what. But number one choice was Laura Collins, and she picked the center east office. Then was Clare, I think. Anyway, with precedent determined by chance, we freely chose this layout."

"Well, that certainly tells me something very important about Warner-Corp," I said

"and I really wish I knew what it was. We all know what century we're living in, and you are all working in an industry where keeping ahead of the present is pretty much mandatory, and you've voluntarily segregated your offices by gender. It will sure give me something to bring up in case conversation lags. Speaking of which—"

Ilona had glanced at her phone to find out the time and at her wristwatch for dramatic effect. I was pretty sure that watch cost more than I made in a year. "It's eleven, time to present you to the staff," she said. "Let's head for the northwest conference room."

I left my stuff in my temporary office and headed north with Ilona.

The conference room was already populated when we arrived. They had left two chairs at one end of the conference table for us. "Well," Ilona said, "word has gotten around that we have invited Charles Wood to meet with each and all of us and perhaps come up with some suggestions the company might take—" She went on with the presentation or introduction, and I kept a nice neutral but not overdone smile on my face as I beamed my way around the table. At Ilona's prompting, they went around the table, giving their names and job titles. Every single one of them, Buck included, said "and Customer Service Representative" after the title I'd been given. Damned if they weren't sitting exactly the same way the offices were arranged, aside from Ilona and me. Iris was cool; she gave no indication she'd ever set eyes on me before. Henry Appleby was on Ilona's left, and the table ran up that side with George Kearney, Keith Benedict, and Buck Warner at the end, and on my right was Jean Stevens, with Lara Collins and Clare Thomason farther along. Ilona turned to me, and I gave the short speech about myself, some of which was actually true, like my year of graduation. Any of them who got suspicious could find out Chuck Wood was absent from some places he should have been present, and letting them have a look at my honest blue eyes, I wouldn't have been in the least surprised to learn that every person in the room knew perfectly well that I was a plant. They had all worked together so long that they knew each other better than they realized they knew each other. Whatever motivated that office arrangement, it was probably not going to be relevant to finding out what was getting at Buck or what, if anything, was going on under the table at WarnerCorp.

I said I'd like to arrange a meeting with each of them, and they sent me their schedules for the week, and inside of five minutes, I had a full dance card, as Schwartz would say. Frankly, I don't know what that means and don't really care to find out. Doubtless there was some significance to the sequence, but it wasn't for me to discern:

12:00 noon Monday, March 30 Lunch
1:00 p.m. Monday, March 30 Buck Warner
2:00 p.m. Monday, March 30 Jean Stevens
3:00 p.m. Monday, March 30 Henry Appleby
4:00 p.m. Monday, March 30 Keith Benedict
9:00 a.m. Tuesday, March 31 Clare Thomason
10:00 a.m. Tuesday, March 31 George Kearney
11:00 a.m. Tuesday, March 31 Iris Warner
12:00 noon Tuesday, March 31 Lunch
1:00 p.m. Tuesday, March 31 Geoff Parsons
2:00 p.m. Tuesday, March 31 Lara Collins
3:00 p.m. Tuesday, March 31 Ilona Marchand
4:00 p.m. Tuesday, March 31 Interim Summary Presentation to Staff
Wednesday, April 1 Further Discussion as Needed
Thursday, April 2 Final Summary Presentation to Staff, time TBA

The rest of the hour was spent in ordinary chitchat, and before we knew it, it was lunchtime. People began to disperse. Buck said welcome again, told me he was eating at his desk without issuing an invitation to join him, and he said he would be expecting me in his office at one o'clock. I conferred with Ilona and ended up popping out for a sub sandwich and a quick call to Schwartz, if only to tell him I was pretty sure it was common knowledge I was a ringer, although no one had said or done anything to confirm that idea. Certainly no one had questioned, much less objected to my presence. He remarked that you can be paranoid even if they're really out to get you and hung up.

Chapter Eight

While I was impersonating a consultant at WarnerCorp that afternoon, Ed Stroh returned to Schwartz's office, dissatisfied with our investigation so far. Schwartz filled me in when I got back that evening, after dinner, from Ed's knock on the door at noon, as he was sitting down to lunch, to their visit to the Abernathy house, to their return to the office later in the afternoon.

Schwartz got to spend most of the morning reading. Ed told Schwartz he'd called the police again earlier, but they said it still didn't look to them like a missing persons case. Schwartz told me, "So I asked him, why not wait another day, when the time would be fulfilled, but he was too antsy for anything like reason, much less patience. I fixed him some lunch, and after we ate, we headed over to the house.

"You had been over the house and garage, attic and basement, and I want to say I think you did a really good job of looking and also reporting back to me. I felt almost as if I'd been there. The garage was arranged exactly as you said. By the way, since both cars were unlocked, I popped the trunks and checked, which I don't recall you mentioning." He always goes formal in his language when he's making a point he wants me to remember. I had thought about the cars, but the absence of smell had let me just forget about searching them beyond a glance at front and back seats. "There was nothing in the trunk of either car besides first-aid kits, flares, that sort of thing. The hanging tools and the shelves were just as you described. I think there's a can of Bondo or J B Weld and some trash bags or tarps missing, and a couple of saws, as you said."

"I don't think J B Weld comes in cans," I said. "I could check, but I believe it comes in tubes, pairs. Like epoxy."

"I believe you're right. Unless I'm mistaken, it actually is an epoxy. But please check. You realize, of course, that it will probably be a recently used can of paint and not yet replaced painter's tarp. Of course, I looked for something in the house that would account for the paint or whatever, but there was nothing obvious."

I could tell he was holding something back. Sure as hell, this was leading up to some dramatic conclusion. I knew better than to try to rush him.

"So we went through the house again, and everything looked perfectly innocent upstairs and downstairs, and I don't mind telling you that the place gave me the creeps. It was obsessively clean and obsessively neat. I hope I never find myself that organized, that compulsively orderly, and hygienic. If I show signs of that, please understand that it could only be the result of a stroke, and call 911. No wonder the spaces for the can and the box and the saws jumped out at you."

I thought he was laying it on pretty thick at this point, but I kept quiet. If I prodded him, it would only extend the agony.

"We went through every room, and I looked in every closet, under every bed, behind the sofas and beds against the walls. I've never seen a house that I knew had been lived in and that I thought had never known a dust bunny.

"Then I started looking at the undersides of tables and chairs, counters and shelves, and I found something." He paused, making me play my role in his own compulsive or obsessive game. Being Schwartz, he left the end of the sentence, "you missed," unspoken. It didn't help, of course.

"What did you find, Mr. Schwartz?" I asked, keeping my teeth from clamping with some effort. "What did I miss, and where was it?"

He shifted in his chair, drank iced tea, and said, "It was a small splash of dried blood, or something that looked like dried blood, and it was on the underside of the dining room table." He showed me the photos he'd taken with his phone, with and without a flashlight beam. It looked like a splash of dark liquid on pale, unpolished wood, not more than three inches long and wide, beginning an inch or so from the edge of the table. Each image kept the edge of the table in view. "I took a sample, certainly well under ten percent, and we dropped it off at Dr. Marvell's office on the way back. He will analyze it to determine whether it's blood, not that I don't know damned well that it is, and so do you.

"Especially," he went on, after another, self-congratulatory slug of tea, "since I found another, similar splash on the underside of the small table on the wall near the table." He showed me more photos. The wood was a little lighter in color, so the dark splotch stood out more clearly.

"Geesh," I said. It was depressing, for any number of reasons.

"Indeed," Schwartz said. "Understand, Rainer, I'm not criticizing your search of the place. Or the thoroughness of your search. You had no good reason to be sure there'd been any violence at all—"

"No," I said, "except that Ed was convinced something had happened, and now it's obvious that it has happened, and I missed it—"

"Spilt milk," he said. "I took a sample of the second splash, naturally, and Dr. Marvell has both of them, so we can wait for him to confirm that—"

The phone rang, and I started. I knew, somehow, that that would be Dr. Andrew Marvell's confirmation that the matter Schwartz had handed him was, in fact, blood, as neatly as the phone call in any TV series. I answered the phone on Schwartz's desk. Might as well do something useful. It was Marvell. I told Schwartz who it was and handed him the receiver.

"Yes, Doctor; good evening…. It is indeed blood. Human…. Both O positive…. Yes, of course, I realize that. Yes, it's for a case. No, I believe we'll be able to interest the police, and they can…. Please send the bill here, or bring it by if that's more convenient…." They chatted further for a few moments, then Schwartz thanked Marvell again and hung up.

"Well, now we know what we thought we knew. It's human blood, and it's less than a week old. From the places it was found, assuming it wasn't placed there deliberately but was overlooked during the cleanup, I think we can safely add support to Ed's missing-persons report." He leaned back, glanced at the clock. It was almost half past nine. "My father used to say that, if the phone rang before nine in the morning or after nine in the evening, someone had better be dead. How times have changed."

"Someone almost certainly is dead," I said. "Eugene and Lawrence would be my guess, and it's better than a guess now, isn't it?" I thought I owed him a chance to lecture me. I could have looked under the goddam table, even if I'd have felt like a damn fool doing it. This business is not based on looking dignified. Or on missing clues.

Schwartz said nothing. He wasn't in that kind of mood, it seemed. "Shall I call the cops?" I asked.

"No, not now," he said. "Tomorrow morning will do. I'd like to have a look around the house before we notify Inspector Mercer. The police have been rather positive with Ed Stroh, although I suppose they get tired of civilian false alarms. Still, if they'd taken him more seriously—"

"Even though so short a time had elapsed," I began.

"Let's not let them off the hook so readily," Schwartz said.

I sighed. He clearly had something else entirely he wanted to talk about, and I was his captive audience. I wish I knew what it was that kept him apparently distracted from business, even while that's exactly what his mind is working on. I really wish he wouldn't go off like that, as he sometimes does, in front of clients. At least Ed Stroh, Iris Warner, and Ilona Marchand weren't present. He wanted to discuss tea, and he did so. After fifteen minutes on the pros and cons of sesame and other additives, I'd had enough. "Perhaps I could interest you in my day?" I asked.

From his expression, you'd have thought I'd asked if I could interest him in shares in an imaginary uranium mine, then his face shifted over to the real world. "Of course. Pardon the digression; it could have waited."

"No problem, sir." I briefly savored the apology. "I met with Ilona when I arrived, and then there was a staff meeting, all hands present and on deck."

"Everyone was there?"

"Including Iris Warner," I said. "Ilona introduced me, or rather introduced Chuck Wood, to the assembled multitude, and they introduced themselves to me, with titles, and—"

"Yes, about those titles," Schwartz interrupted. I had texted him the layout. "Have you ever seen a more eccentric way of defining responsibilities? 'Head Programmer,' 'Chief Programmer,' 'Top Programmer,' 'Primary Programmer.' How many chiefs can the tribe support? It's ridiculous, amateurish. And this is an incredibly successful company. I find it hard to believe they aren't just having us on." He looked totally disgusted.

"Well," I said, "if they're having us on, they're having the rest of the world on too. I collected business cards from holders on every desk, and those are the titles, as far as they go, but you haven't got to the best part." I fished the four cards from my breast pocket and spread them on his blotter. "And they all add the same thing on, just like on the cards: 'and CSR.' Everyone at WarnerCorp, from the CEO down to the Chief Assistant, who, by the way, is the only Assistant, so I guess he might as well be the Chief, is also a Customer Service Representative."

"That is insane," Schwartz said. "As well as inane."

"Oh, I'm not disagreeing," I said, "but it also seems to be real. I spent an hour each with the CEO, the Top Programmer, the Chief Assistant, and the Head Programmer, and every one of them except Appleby took a customer call while I was with them. Appleby took four calls, passed each one on to a different person, so we could continue our conversation. I've never seen anything like it."

"Well, we do like a mystery," he said, "and this is certainly one. I wonder who came up with this."

"Actually, I think I know. If Buck was being straight with me—"

"Why on earth would he be straight with you?"

"Well, unless he's an idiot, and he's not, he knows damn well I'm a private detective looking for enough skeletons to haul out of the closet to justify a decent fee, so he might as well just play it straight, keeping the usual secrets to himself."

"All right," he said. "Please report, highlights only, trusting your intelligent judgment guided by experience."

"Right. After lunch, I met with Buck Warner, Chief Executive Officer and

Customer Service Rep. His office is exactly the same size as everyone else's, and I doubt you could pick it out from the others if the nameplate were removed, aside from those subtle clues that distinguish a man's office from a woman's. Seriously, he has a nice desk and a nice carpet, and the rest of the furniture is nice, but—for a company of WarnerCorp's stature—there's just none of the ostentation you'd expect. Aside from a painting that I'm pretty sure is a genuine Dufy."

"Raoul or Jean?"

"Raoul, I think. A still life that isn't exactly in focus. Anyway, it's certainly a spiffier office than this one, but then they all are. You'd find them a bit short on books, aside from what seems to be a standardized binder system. Paper hasn't quite gone away, even at WarnerCorp. Buck Warner is forty-five, physically in great shape, quite good-looking, dark brown hair with just a touch of gray at the temples. He wore a golf shirt and jeans, which is pretty close to a company uniform. If you ask me, the guys are trying to dress to look like Buck without looking like they're trying to look like Buck.

"He was downright chatty for a CEO who knows his ex is wondering about him, and he told me everything I could possibly want to know about the history of the company, from its inception as a simple interface between insurance companies and doctors' offices and hospitals, right up to yesterday. He filled me in on how the package, which is what he calls WarnerCōp, has grown up to the present day. He wasn't shy about mentioning money, either. I've got enough information in my notes to do a financial analysis of the company.

"As I understand it, it facilitates the communication between the different entities that use it, and unlike its early competition, it has always been good at helping while staying out of the way. Buck compared it to an OR nurse who supplies the surgeon with what is needed, anticipating but never dictating."

"Good Lord," Schwartz contributed.

"Yeah, there's no shortage of hubris at WarnerCorp, but it's not just the CEO. Warner is downright voluble about ideas for things WarnerCōp could be expanded to do. Most of it went over my head, frankly. After an hour with him, I have to admit the man has all the signs of brilliance, but there's something missing that I can't quite put my finger on.

"Drink? Drugs? Women? Boys? What's his jones?"

"I don't think there's anything like that in his makeup. It's not so much a what's-missing puzzle as an is-something-missing puzzle. I want to see if we can get him here, maybe Wednesday, after I've interviewed everyone and we can take the lid off the consultant thing."

"No, that would defeat the purpose," Schwartz said. "You're looking for what's eating the man, not what's going on with the company. Damn the company. This was supposed to be highlights."

"I have to say Warner is an interesting person," I said. "I think he's more complicated than the run-of-the-mill computer-world genius zillionaire. He told me some of the things that the company does with its preposterous profits—his phrase, by the way—and that he personally does with his share, and it's a long list of things I'd never heard about. He's more than publicity-shy, but on the other hand, he's not secretive. It's almost as if he's trying to be good and to do good without being seen to be or do good."

"There's got to be a name for that," Schwartz said. "Silent philanthropy. Quiet benefaction. Who knows?"

"Well, anyway, he's an interesting person, all right. If there is anything gnawing at his soul, I certainly got absolutely no whiff of it."

"That's a mixed metaphor."

"Yes, sir. After Warner, I met with Top Programmer and CSR Jean Stevens. She's forty-two or -three, depending on when her birthday is, a little on the thin side, and her version of the company uniform is jeans and a short-sleeved light orange blouse, no pocket or pocket-protector or anything so cliched. They really work hard at being different in the same way. She is married, two kids in college, and unless I miss my mark, she has a thing for the boss. She's one of the Francophones, incidentally."

"'French speaker' would be less pretentious," he said. "Unhappily married?"

"Not judging by the family photos on the desk and shelf. I think I spotted a small Utrillo on the wall where she can see it. God knows what one goes for. No, I think she just thinks of Buck Warner as what she'd go for if she weren't already committed. She confirmed most of what he told me, just covering the same ground. She came up with some ideas for future versions of the package, but I think it was mostly a matter of improving existing features rather than anything new. Of course, I took notes, and I'll include all that in my written report, when I get to it. I started on it after the last session this afternoon."

"And next was Henry Appleby?"

"Yes, Henry Appleby. Forty years old, single, not bad looking, but seems to be something of a loner. That's just an impression. No photos in his office, and no clutter on the desk or shelves. Spartan, if you will. And he's not just Chief Assistant and CSR, although he's all of that. He's also Security, or I'm ready to take up mahjong, not that he outright admitted it. He's CSR in that all calls come to his phone, and about half the time, he says, he can either tell the caller what to do next, or he can refer them to the right place in the documentation and walk them through to the solution. The rest of the time, he transfers the call to the right person.

"Appleby also takes care of routine trafficking of mail, express, hardware and network problems, and all that sort of thing. But there's only routine office reproductions on his walls, no really valuable art. He's the only man in the office wearing a jacket, which would seem odd if he weren't carrying."

Schwartz's eyebrows went up. "Indeed. You're sure?"

"Specifically, an S&W 9mm under his left armpit, and I'm pretty sure a backup piece on his right ankle. He crossed his legs at one point, very carefully, not showing off, just being comfortable. He's obviously computer-competent, in spades, and his office is adjacent to Iris's, for whatever reason."

"Is he a recent hire?"

"Not at all. Every last one of them has been with the company from the get-go. I don't know exactly how things developed, but he's the guy who replaces anything that needs replacing, and he's only one office away from the supply/conspiracy room. If I were guessing, the whole office is bugged, and I'd be willing to bet next month's salary Henry has the AV for anything and everything that happens at WarnerCorp. I also bet they don't erase tapes every week to save money."

"Why would they? Save money, I mean. Do you think Appleby might be behind that problem Ms. Marchand wants help with?"

"It's certainly a possibility," I said. "Of course, Henry isn't the only one competent to keep tabs on things in other people's offices, and they have access to the sort of spyware that you don't order from the back pages of a magazine, and you don't find with a garden-variety sweep. But if I were choosing the person most likely to have his finger on the pulse of WarnerCorp, he'd be my pick. He's a busy guy, all right. But I noticed that every time I tried to steer the conversation back to my supposed subject, the future of WarnerCorp, he'd take it back to generalities.

"I think Henry Appleby's vision for the future of the company is the present of the company. It's not just ordinary human resistance to change; he likes things the way they are and sees no reason to fix what ain't broke."

"From his perspective."

"Right. The last meeting was with Keith Benedict. He's Head Programmer and, of course, CSR, forty-nine, widowed, four kids by the photos all over his desk, a bit heavier than he ought to be, which explains the treadmill in his office, and he was crunching raw carrots and celery the whole time we met. When he got the customer-service call, he had to swallow a mouthful of crudites. He mentioned all sorts of things they could do with the software to increase its usefulness, but if I understood him at all correctly, they were the same stuff Warner was talking about. Unless I'm wrong, he's the guy closest to Buck, from a friendship standpoint, I mean.

"I got the impression that Benedict could have any title at all, and he'd live up to it. The customer call he took during our meeting was about ten minutes long, and I could hear the person's voice practically shouting at him at the beginning. Benedict didn't have to look at a single manual—unlike the others, aside from Appleby—while he talked to whoever it was. He has a very deep, soothing voice, really pleasant to listen to. Reassuring, basically. Someone at a doctor's office, or it might have been a hospital. Anyway, the other voice got quieter pretty early, and by the end of the discussion, he was telling them, 'You're welcome. Not at all. We're glad we can help. Really, you're quite welcome. Please feel free to call any time, and just ask for Keith. Yes.' It was impressive."

I sat back, stretched, checked the clock. Eleven fifteen. "I noticed that by the time I was starting with Benedict, never mind finishing, people were calling it a day. Not clock-watchers, clock-ignorers. They seem to just come and go when they please."

"Would you expect anything different?"

"I suppose not," I admitted. "When I wrapped it up with Keith, I went back to that southwest office and conference room to get the briefcase and laptop, and Ilona came by. She said there was something she wanted to talk to me about, but then she said it would keep till tomorrow. So I thought I'd try to arrive early enough to see her, before I meet with the others. I've got Clare Thomason, COO, George Kearney, Primary Programmer, and Iris Warner, VP, if she even shows up, in the morning. After lunch, I'll see Geoff Parsons, CFO, Lara Collins, Chief Programmer, and Ilona Marchand, Office Manager/Human Resources. It promises to be a grueling day, all right."

"Mine should be interesting too," Schwartz said. "I'll call Inspector Mercer in the morning, and if a couple of blood splashes on the underside of the furniture don't pique his interest, I'd be surprised. In fact, I think I'll pick up Ed and call from the house. I can pick up the tested samples from Dr. Marvell on the way. It will be pleasant to hand Inspector Mercer a case. I've grown tired of his conviction that I interfere in cases where I don't belong. He can't name a single occasion when I got in his way on a felony investigation, but his general distaste for private operatives poisons our relationship. You'd think a seasoned police officer would be able to distinguish prejudice from experienced judgment."

I couldn't disagree. I understand why the cops aren't fond of private detectives, but we always went way out of our way to stay scrupulously legal and scrupulously considerate. Schwartz has never had his picture in the paper, and we've tried hard to soft-pedal mentions of his name or mine in the press. The only newspaper person he ever talks to is Helen O'Connell, an old friend of his at the Indianapolis *Times,* which is what passes for a "liberal" Democratic paper in town. She trades information with Schwartz and, on occasion, even with me; she is a regular at Wednesday-night poker with me, Paul Surcutt, Frank Kinder, and Sonny Weinstein, who are three operatives Schwartz hires, in that order, when we need help.

Helen O'Connell works at the *Times,* but I have no idea what her job title might be. I wonder if she knows herself. Schwartz talks to no other journalists, and Mercer knows it. If Schwartz doesn't actually resent Mercer's attitude, he certainly deplores it. He works at getting along with the police, which any private operative who wants to stay in business does, and he works harder than most. But as he says, success breeds jealousy, however unreasonable.

I was drifting. Schwartz said, "It's too late to phone now. Call Ms. Warner as early as feasible tomorrow, and ask her to be there in time for your interview. If we're to make a success of her investigation, she should be willing to help out to that extent. What?"

He'd caught the expression on my face, I suppose. I said, "Okay, boss, I'll call her from WarnerCorp when I get there, and I'll text her right now, just to let her know we mean it."

Schwartz went on: "Before you leave tomorrow morning, call Paul, Frank, and Sonny. I have an errand for Paul, and I'd like Frank and Sonny to accompany me and Ed to the Abernathy house in the afternoon. Paul can come after nine, and the other two at one."

Paul Surcutt is in his early forties, generically unremarkable and unimpressive in appearance, which just goes to show you what first impressions can do to complicate your life. If Paul is tailing you, you stay tailed, and you'll never notice he's there. He can disappear in a crowd or all by himself, and he'll never lose sight of you, on foot downtown or wherever you drive. I once watched him getting off a Red Line bus, helping an elderly woman with her two huge shopping bags, and I found out later that she never knew until she was told that Paul wasn't just a kind stranger; he was her hired bodyguard.

Frank Kinder, rhymes with "cinder" not "binder," is younger, late thirties, almost as good-looking as he thinks he is, which is a bit of a challenge in the detective business, where being noticed is not an advantage. Frank is very good at his work, though not in Paul's class, and he has the sense to know that, and without mentioning it, he studies Paul's technique carefully. I don't think it's something that can be learned; it's innate. Frank also thinks he could do my job, but in my opinion he wouldn't last a week. He could never take Schwartz's endless digressions on extraneous subjects, just for starters. Those aren't shared with Paul, Frank, and Sonny, for some reason. It's a personality thing; trust me, he wouldn't last. He could do my job, but not for Schwartz.

Sonny Weinstein is Frank's age, married, unlike Paul and Frank, with two girls, about as good-looking as he thinks he is, not very. He's a few pounds heavier than a doctor would recommend for a man his age, but there's more muscle than fat in there. Sonny isn't hard to get along with, and he's as good as Frank at tailing, research, and surveillance, but he undervalues himself. Schwartz does not take advantage of that fact, to his credit, paying Sonny what he's worth, not what Sonny thinks he's worth. He is one of those people that people open up to. If you find yourself telling the story of your life to a balding, slightly overweight male stranger in Indianapolis, his name might well be Sonny Weinstein. He likes to explain to new acquaintances that his grandfather decided not to translate the name into English when he found out it would be "Cream of Tartar." Thinking that's funny is one of Sonny's few character defects.

I could imagine the scene tomorrow at the Abernathy house, with Schwartz flanked by Frank and Sonny, inviting the police in to check out the house. I'd bet he'd save the blood until after they'd looked around, give them a chance to make the same discovery he had. It occurred to me that this might not be taken in the spirit it was intended. It didn't occur to me that it wouldn't happen tomorrow at all.

Chapter Nine

Tuesday, March 31

First thing the next morning, I called the crew from the office, and while I was at it, I gave Iris Warner a ring. I had to leave a message with Cynthia, whoever she was, but she said she'd let Ms. Warner know I had called. I wondered briefly how much of the message would be conveyed, but that was clearly not something I could do anything about, so I checked to make sure the briefcase was properly stuffed, and my tie was straight, and I left for WarnerCorp.

When I walked out of the elevator at seven fifty-eight, the cold hit me like a wall. The air was icy. The office looked and felt deserted, but I saw that Henry Appleby was on the job already, which was not surprising. He said something had gone wrong with the air conditioning, and he was fixing it now. I suppressed the urge to strike up a chat with him about the relative merits of SIG Sauer and Smith & Wesson. It wasn't difficult. I was sure Henry knew the whole consultancy thing was a ruse. I was just as sure that we were as well off leaving things tacitly understood.

I got out my laptop and the forms and other impedimenta, and by quarter after eight, had a fair imitation of work spread out, so I went to get a cup of coffee. The kitchen was nicely supplied with a variety of straight and decaf coffees, teas, cocoas, and herbal preparations, and I felt vaguely unappreciative sticking to coffee, although the pitcher of cream from the fridge was a pleasant touch. There were no paper or plastic cups. I found the china in the top left cabinet. I'm no expert, but it obviously was not cheap crockery. I wondered who did the washing up. The cabinets also disclosed containers of white, light brown, and dark brown sugar, three kinds of honey, and a wide variety of jellies and jams, some sugar-free, some not. There was a basket with oranges, lemons, and limes to the left of the imposing samovar on the counter. Either someone at WarnerCorp liked their tea Russian-style, or they wanted to be ready for someone who did. I thought about trying some later in the day and about asking Henry Appleby about the cleaning service.

With my coffee, I headed toward Ilona Marchand's office, on the off chance she had come in early. I knocked at her open door, leaned in, then saw something and stepped inside. I stepped outside again and yelled, "Henry, have you seen Ilona this morning?" It wasn't a very nice thing to do, but I couldn't help it under the circumstances. I glanced at my watch. It was just past 8:22.

I heard Appleby answer, "No, why?" as I set my coffee cup on the nearest plant stand outside the door. I stepped back into Ilona's office and approached her desk, checking to make sure I was stepping on nothing but clean carpet, touching nothing. The first thing that came to my mind as I took my phone out was that now I'd probably never know what she'd wanted to talk about.

She lay on her front on the floor behind her desk. She was wearing light brown slacks, a long-sleeved, high-necked, ruffle-front white blouse, pulled out in back, navy canvas loafers, and a yard of stout cord tied tightly around her neck. Her face was turned to the right, toward me, unrecognizable, swollen, a shade of purple never seen on a living person, even aside from the protruding eyes and tongue. A pale green sphere, polished jade, I thought, lay a few feet to her left. I went back to the doorway, stepped out into the hall, yelled for Henry to please come quick. Thinking it over, I stepped back into the doorway, blocking the entrance to the crime scene.

My hands were steady as I dialed 911, but I had to clear my throat before I told the operator, "My name is Rainer Zufahl, I'm a licensed private detective, and I have to report a homicide." By this time, Henry had come up, obviously wondering what was going on. I nodded to him, as if that mattered. There was a click on the phone, and I was switched to an Officer Marley, to whom I repeated my name and reason for calling, and gave the address, and identified myself as a private detective. Henry started and stared at me when he heard that, but, to his considerable credit, he didn't try to go through me into Ilona's office.

Marley said he'd heard of me, told me I worked for Leo Schwartz, which I affirmed. I assured him that I would stay put and would not interfere with the body in any way or permit others to do so. He said officers would be right over, and I told him Security would meet the officers at the elevator. I thanked him and hung up. How you conduct yourself at a crime scene can make a big difference in how you get treated by the police. Sometimes.

"You heard," I told Appleby. He nodded. "Don't go in," I said. I stepped aside to let him glance in and confirm my account of the situation. He leaned in past my shoulder, saw as much as he needed to, and stepped farther back in the hall.

"Jesus," he said. I agreed. He said he'd better meet people at the elevator and ask them to go directly to their offices and wait there. I said tell them, don't ask them. He nodded and headed off.

While we waited for the cops to arrive, I phoned Schwartz to let him know things had changed. He cursed without apology or regrets, gave me the usual unnecessary instructions, then said, "Just what we needed, a dead client."

"I'm not sure she quite qualified as a client," I said. I hung up. I had liked Ilona, and now she was dead, and we'd never have that conversation about whatever the hell it was we were going to have a conversation about. From the sounds of the sirens approaching, we'd have company soon enough.

Two uniforms were the first to arrive, and Henry sent them to me. I was glad we hadn't had to deal with WarnerCorp employees before the cops arrived. The black and white in the parking lot would let them know something was up. An Officer Harrington and his partner Officer Jenson came up, and I stood aside to let them go in. They commented on the cold, and I told them it was being worked on.

Harrington came out again and asked who had discovered the body. I said I had, at 8:22. It was now 8:37, and I wondered, pointlessly, how fifteen minutes had gone by so quickly. Discovering a dead body is not a method I'd recommend for clearing the mind. I realized I had picked up that cup of coffee and was still holding it. I drank it down. It was almost room temperature.

Harrington sent Jenson to help Henry at the elevator, and he got on the phone himself. I stood there with my empty cup.

People were arriving, and I told Harrington I would help Jenson and Appleby with the employees, and he told me to go ahead but not to leave the premises. As if. Benedict was the first to arrive, and I walked with him to his office, said the police were in charge, and would he please stay in his office and talk to no one. He didn't like it, but he went and sat down at his desk. I closed the door to his office and returned to the elevator.

Jean Stevens and Lara Collins arrived together, got a quick briefing from Jenson and Appleby, who turned them over to me. I escorted them to their offices, gave them the same instructions, and closed their doors on them.

Geoff Parsons was next, alone, and he got the same. When I got back to the elevator, Jenson and Appleby were greeting George Kearney, and I took him to his office.

Buck Warner and Clare Thomason came out of the elevator, and got the same welcome as everyone else had. Buck wanted to know why the hell it was so cold and what the hell was going on, announced that as CEO, he had a right to be informed what was going on at his company, and I told him to shut the hell up if he didn't want Officer Jenson to place him under arrest. Appleby told Warner and Thomason to please go with me and to please follow my instructions, and that there would be an explanation as soon as possible. Warner didn't like it, but he was smart enough to go along with it. We went with Clare Thomason to her office, I asked her to stay there and talk to nobody, and we'd get back to her as soon as possible, then I took Buck to his office. We had to pass by the open door of Ilona's office, where uniformed and plainclothes police officers were coming and going. I saw a couple scientists go in. I steered Warner past the door and brought him to his own.

Just inside, he stopped and turned to me and said, "What the hell is going on, Wood? Why are the police here?" It occurred to me that he'd had time to think things over, and apparently, he'd decided to play along with the idea that I was just a consultant. Or perhaps he was among the few who simply didn't know what was really going on.

I told him, "You'll find out soon enough, Mr. Warner. My name isn't Charles Wood; it's Rainer Zufahl. I'm a detective, and I work for Leo Schwartz."

"Leo Schwartz? What's going on?"

"Ilona Marchand has been murdered," I told him. His eyes went wide, and he stepped back as if I'd slapped him. His face registered shock, dismay, horror, disbelief.

No matter how long you've been in the detective business, you keep on trying to spot guilty people by their reactions, and that's especially true of murder suspects. Even though experience tells you it's impossible, you keep looking for some telltale sign of guilt or innocence. I looked at Warner, couldn't discern a thing. "An officer will come to ask you questions before long," I said. "Please stay in your office and discuss this with no one until then. I think it would be a good idea to sit down, but don't call anyone. Please." I shut the door.

I headed back toward the elevator, where Jenson and Appleby were greeting Iris Warner. I thought I would take her to her office, but Jenson told me I was wanted in the situation room, which was the southwest room where I had been based. Appleby took Iris away, and I figured he would fill her in if he thought it was appropriate. Jenson thought he was going to take me by the elbow for the short trip to meet those in charge, but I quickened my pace and made it to the door on my own steam. I saw that my bag and computer had been moved to a side table.

Seated at the conference table was an old acquaintance, Augustus Mercer, Gus to nobody except perhaps his wife, Inspector Mercer to me, and everybody else. Another chair was occupied by a plainclothes cop I didn't know, and one of the guys in white lab coats was sitting at the desk with a laptop. Standing with his back to the inside wall was Sergeant Steve Ripley, who never sits when he can stand, because that makes him ready for action. Steve really isn't a bad fellow at all, aside from his attitude toward private detectives. He's one of those old-school types who you'd think had all been left in the twentieth century where they belonged. To take one example, he calls private investigators private dicks. Who is that insensitive these days? I've even heard him refer to Bonita Dahler, one of the best female P.I.s in town, as a dick. Really.

Mercer regarded me with a noticeable lack of enthusiasm. "So, Zufahl, it will be interesting to learn how you just happened to wander up to the ninth floor of a building you don't belong in, on the premises of a multimillion-dollar corporation that thinks it's hired a consultant named Chuck Wood." He gestured sarcastically to a chair across the table, and if you think it's not possible to express sarcasm with a gesture, you should have been there.

Steve Ripley snorted.

Clearly, Mercer and Ripley had had time to chat with my pal Henry Appleby. I took the seat Mercer indicated, made myself comfortable for the long haul. "Sure, Inspector," I said helpfully, "I'll be glad to answer any questions you might have." I'd been kept pretty busy in the time since I'd found Ilona's body, and that had kept me distracted, and I knew the distraction was going to wear off very shortly, and I'd be dealing with the mental impact of finding the body of a woman who I'd been talking with the day before and who I'd been looking forward to talking with some more. It was going to hit me hard, and I might as well be sitting down when the reaction came. I started talking, and the plainclothes cop I hadn't been introduced to took notes on a laptop. I knew they were recording as well. Even if they hadn't been, I figured that Henry's spyware would be capturing everything.

Then I realized that, if the place was that thoroughly wired, not that wires are actually used, there'd be a nice clear record of the murder, and we wouldn't all be sitting here. "So, Inspector, can I assume that some unknown person has sabotaged the surveillance? Probably the same person who set the air-conditioning on 'meat locker.'"

"What the hell do you know about surveillance?" Mercer wanted to know.

"Oh, come on," I said. "As you so astutely pointed out, this is a multimillion-dollar company, and just for starters, there's enough art on some of these walls to start a small but select museum, never mind whatever else they don't want people walking off with. I had to have a special key for the elevator, and I bet the ground-floor stairway doors don't open without one from the stair side. The hardware and software they use to keep things running are all here on this floor.

"I haven't discussed the matter with Mr. Appleby, but if he's not on top of the security here, my name really is Charles Wood." Ripley snorted again, even less pleasantly. "My guess is that the audio-visual records of this place since quitting time yesterday have disappeared, and they disappeared in a way that didn't set off any alarms, or Appleby would have been right on top of the problem.

"Not only that," I went on, taking the time to stretch out those muscles that would eventually be tensing up, especially with the godawful cold air, "but you have nine seasoned staff members who are as familiar with computer hardware and software as you'll find this side of Silicon Valley, and they know the workings of this company, including the security system, not to mention the climate control, as well as they know their own families. Better, in all likelihood. Any one of them, or two or more in concert, could have deep-sixed the security tapes or disks or whatever they were, without leaving a trace.

"Any of nine people could have come in here any time since five yesterday afternoon, met with Ilona Marchand, waited for an opportunity, and killed her. I bet that paperweight on the floor next to her was in her office, and I further bet that cord around her neck was cut from the blinds in her office. Then they went to the utility room or wherever the security system was physically located, and they performed a lobotomy on it, dropped the temperature to confuse the matter of time of death, and went home."

Ripley said, "That almost sounds like a confession, Zufahl."

I didn't bother to look over my shoulder at him. "No, it doesn't, Steve, and even you must have noticed that I called it in, which would have been a pretty nervy thing to do, all things considered. What, do you think I arranged an appointment with Ms. Marchand on my magic self-erasing phone, managed to erase the record of the call from her phone as well, not to mention from the cloud or wherever Big Brother stores that stuff these days? Then I disabled the security system without leaving a trace and, after I hit her on the head with that jade ball or whatever it is, I cut a few feet of handy cord from her blinds and strangled her with it, and on my way out I turned on the AC and set it to Arctic? Thanks for the compliment, Steve. I had no idea you thought I was such a genius."

Mercer glanced at a paper, one of a stack in front of him. "Preliminary exam shows she was hit from behind with some heavy blunt instrument, probably that jade ball on the floor. She had a few rocks, what are they called, geodes, and some petrified wood in her office; apparently, she appreciated geology or something. God knows. They're testing the contents of the office now." So at least the police weren't seriously entertaining the idea that I'd killed Ilona, or that item would have been kept private. Mercer clearly was not looking forward to grilling a line of multimillionaires to find out which of them had murdered one of their own. I couldn't blame him, frankly.

"So I take it, I'm free to go?" I said, rising from my chair.

"You're free to sit your ass down and explain why the hell you're here," he said.

At times it can be a real pleasure to show off, but this wasn't one of those times. For one thing, the reality that someone I'd met and liked had been murdered was sinking in. For another, I had no idea what, if anything, Schwartz was doing. It was ten minutes to eleven, and, for all I know, his visit to Eugene and Lawrence's house was still on. But there was nothing I could do about that, or much of anything else, so I just spilled it all.

I gave them a high-points account of my meetings with Iris at her house, with Ilona at hers, including the part about blackmail, and Iris's visit to Schwartz's office. Once the stage was properly set, I gave it to them verbatim from my arrival at WarnerCorp on Monday, which suddenly didn't feel like just the day before.

I included every last detail of my conference with Ilona in the morning, the full-staff session following, and the interviews with Buck Warner, Jean Stevens, Henry Appleby, and Keith Benedict that afternoon. I went through my discussion the night before with Schwartz, keeping nothing back. There seemed no reason to keep anything back.

"So this whole rigamarole about you being a consultant all boils down to Warner's ex-wife's suspicions that something was eating at her husband? Ex-husband," Mercer summarized.

"Yes, but there was also the business Ilona had mentioned about being blackmailed, and we thought I could look into that at the same time," I said.

"Killing two birds," Mercer said, then stopped. I almost thought he was blushing with embarrassment, then I realized it was high blood pressure.

"Of course," he went on, "Iris Warner will confirm your story in every particular."

"Well, I don't know that for sure," I said. "You may have noticed, Inspector, that witnesses sometimes shade things a bit in their own favor. Especially witnesses of a socio-economic class that isn't particularly used to being given the third degree by the police." I had thought of saying "cossacks" but decided against it.

"Yeah, well, we had sort of taken that into account," he said. "No doubt they've all called lawyers by now anyway. But the former Ms. Warner is the one who can confirm your story—or not."

"That's still her name," I said. "I don't know how I can convince you that I don't tell stories, Inspector. I'd think by now you'd have come to know my reputation for scrupulous honesty, particularly when there are so many witnesses to catch me up if I lied. And I'd have appreciated some thanks for my initiative in sequestering those witnesses in their offices so that they can't collude in fixing up a misleading account of events, but you don't seem inclined toward gratitude this morning—"

Mercer slammed a big hand down on the table, hard. The guy taking notes looked up, plainly startled. "Get the hell out of here, Zufahl, but by God stay available, or I'll have your license, and your boss's too. Get out of my sight, and let me get on with these witnesses."

He nodded at a uniformed officer just inside the door, and they all watched as I collected my briefcase and laptop from the table, slung the strap over my shoulder, and accompanied the uniform to the elevator. He rode the elevator down with me, went out through the lobby with me, watched me unlock my car, stow my stuff on the passenger seat, and drive off. They weren't missing a beat there.

Chapter Ten

Tuesday, March 31

I called Schwartz before heading back, in case he wanted me to collect some evidence to bring home with me, but he just told me to return to the office and drive carefully while doing so. I went to the kitchen for a glass of water before I went in to report. He was at his desk, and he asked how I was doing, and he was actually quite considerate about things, and gradually I calmed down to something like normal. Before long I was giving him the crop, from getting to WarnerCorp before the morning rush, to finding Ilona's body, to the arrival of the police, to my session with Inspector Mercer and company.

It's remarkable how much a person can remember, with the proper training, which I'd had, and the proper questioning, which Schwartz was providing now. Not that there were any epiphanies, but I found I could come up with the verbal description to get the whole morning across to him, from my own point of view. He had some background questions after I'd given him the narration, for example, about the surveillance equipment and its location, how long it had taken Henry Appleby to discover the system had been trashed, how the police had reacted to that news, what they seemed to think had happened, and who they seemed to be focusing on, and about forty other points he wanted to know about. He finished up, more or less predictably, by asking if I'd had time to eat lunch, which I hadn't. I hadn't realized it was that late. The police had certainly kept things moving, and me busy.

The phone rang as we finished up the discussion of the office layout. It was Mercer, and Schwartz was on it. He said no, I wouldn't like to come down to 42nd Street for a talk; he, Mercer, had sent me home in no uncertain terms, and that was where I was going to be for the foreseeable future. He suggested that Mercer and Ripley might like to come by his office on their way to the station. The conversation dragged on for a while, as it tends to do when two people are too stubborn to be reasonable. Finally, it was decided that, if Mercer felt like coming by, we would let him in.

Of course, I realized that Schwartz was irked because he'd been looking forward to presenting Mercer and the IMPD with solid evidence that Eugene and Lawrence Abernathy were missing and quite possibly dead, and now there seemed but little chance that he'd be able to do that today.

Schwartz hung up the phone, then said, "I called Frank and Sonny to cancel our visit to the Abernathy house, of course, but Paul had a productive morning at the Ellenbogen residence. Perhaps I can fill you in before Inspector Mercer arrives."

"Sure," I said. I hadn't given a lot of thought to Viola Ketchum and her Uncle Jim recently. Funny how finding corpses can shake a person up. It's really not as common an occurrence for a detective as fiction would have you believe. But at least I didn't feel like a drink would be a good idea.

"I asked Paul to come by for instructions, and I gave him a copy of the Polaroid photo that was included with that preposterous list of initials, and I sent him to Ms. Ketchum's for the key to the Ellenbogen residence. I solved the list, by the way, and I suppose you have, too."

"No, sir," I said, "I apologize, but I've been somewhat preoccupied recently. However, if you like, I'll get right on it."

"Self-pity is never an attractive characteristic, Rainer," Schwartz said, "and insincere, sarcastic self-pity is especially irritating."

"Good to know it's working."

"Right." He took a deep breath, blew it out, dismissed the distraction, and went on. "At my suggestion, Paul invited Ms. Ketchum to accompany him, which turned out to be a good thing. They went to Mr. Ellenbogen's house, and Paul used the Polaroid to get the proper perspective, and he took a photograph of the same scene, as precisely as he could."

"That would be good enough for us," I said.

He nodded, "Indeed. Of course, it was like those puzzles with two almost identical pictures, where the idea is to identify a stated number of differences. As I said, having figured out the initials, I knew what to look for, although it's possible I would have been able to find it without the rather heavy-handed clue."

Now, you've probably figured out the meaning of the damn list for yourself, so you know exactly what he was talking about, and you are almost certainly thinking I'm totally thick, but I hadn't, and I didn't. The truth is, Schwartz was having a good time with this, and he probably thought he was being helpful, distracting me from the morning's events. Maybe he was right. But my point is that he liked explaining things in his own way, in his own time. He pays me, but it's not really always enough.

"Yes, sir," I said. "I'm sure you would have spotted the difference even without the clue you so cleverly figured out. All those word jumbles, crosswords, sudokus, crypto quizzes, and other puzzles you do in the paper every morning have really paid off here."

"Someday, Rainer," Schwartz said, staring at the far edge of his desk, "you will go too far, and you'll be standing on skis in mid-air, wondering where the snow went.

"I noticed that the rifles over the fireplace had been switched." He handed me the Polaroid Viola had brought and a hard copy of another photo, the one Paul had taken. Paul had emailed or texted the photo to him, and he'd managed to print it without help from me. He was bursting with pride, and I saw no reason he shouldn't be. Living in the twenty-first century with the rest of us.

Since he'd laid it out for me, it was easy to see what was what. The same two rifles were in both pictures, but they weren't identical. In the Polaroid, the rifle with the lighter stock was above the one with the darker stock. In the second photo, the darker was above the lighter. It wouldn't have been obvious to me, frankly.

"With Ms. Ketchum's permission, Paul took more photographs, for documentation purposes, and I asked him to bring both rifles here, along with anything else that a close search of the house would bring to light."

"So that's why you wanted Viola at the house with Paul, to keep the search legal."

"Well, it would have been legal in any case, but if some observant and public-spirited neighbor had called the police, it would have helped avoid misunderstanding."

"So those Kentucky rifles are here?"

"Not yet, but they soon will be. I asked Paul to phone me when they had finished looking through the house and were on their way here. I haven't heard yet, but it really shouldn't be too long now." We both looked at the landline, as if we could make it ring on cue, like in the movies. "Frankly, I have no idea what Paul and Ms. Ketchum might be looking for, but he is trained, and she seems intelligent, so whether they find anything or not, it won't be a complete waste of time."

"Client participation can be a good thing," I said, "with the right client and the right case."

"If there is anything helpful to be found, I expect they will find it."

The phone rang, and I answered it at my desk. It was Paul, of course.

I told him he was calling too late, and we didn't want any, and he came back, "That's good, because we don't have any, except for a couple of old Kentucky rifles, and frankly, I wouldn't trust you with a dangerous firearm, even a rusty old muzzle-loader."

Schwartz picked up his phone. "I take it there was nothing else of interest, Paul?"

"That's right," Paul said. "Of interest, maybe, but not really relevant to the case. Viola and I will be there in ten minutes, with the guns."

"Excellent. See you shortly." Schwartz and I hung up.

Schwartz took a magnifying glass from his middle desk drawer, pointed to the Polaroid with the tip of a pencil. "It's difficult to see in such a small picture," he said, "even with the glass, but if you look carefully, you'll notice that the rifle with the lighter stain is a percussion lock, and the one with the darker stain is a flintlock." With the glass, I could just barely see the difference. Not only the size of the photo, but also the lighting, made it hard.

"So you asked Paul to bring both of them for some reason?"

"Yes, and the reason was that I don't know whether the clue from the list of initials referred to the Polaroid or to the way the rifles were hung. Choosing one way or the other guarantees a fifty-percent chance of error; bringing both eliminates chance altogether."

"So," I said, "spill it. What's with the rifles, or with one of them?"

"I have no idea," he said.

"You know perfectly well how infuriating you're being, don't you?"

"Of course. Have another look at the list." He handed it to me. "I'm willing to bet you'll get it before Paul and Viola arrive. You think puzzles are a waste of time, but in fact, you're not bad at them. It's just that you don't enjoy them." He started clearing things off his desk to make room for the rifles, and I turned to the initials.

Now, as I have said, I realize you've long since got it, but I had been distracted. Still, it was only a couple minutes before I saw it. Schwartz was laying a folded white bath towel along the far side of his desk when the dime dropped.

"Okay, I get it," I told him, and the doorbell rang.

Chapter Eleven

Tuesday, March 31

I let them in. Viola came in, followed by Paul with a cased rifle in each hand. He handed me the one in his right hand, which I took with my left, and we touched fists. We trooped down the hall to the office and went in. When we reached Schwartz's desk, Paul and Schwartz greeted each other and Schwartz and Viola said hello, then Paul carefully eased his rifle out of the open end of the case and laid it on the folded towel, leaving space for mine. His was the lighter colored percussion-lock gun. I slid the dark-stocked flintlock out of its case, got it balanced in my hand, and laid it alongside the other gun. Paul, Viola, and I were standing, lined up facing Schwartz, across his desk. The rifles were lying on their left sides, muzzles to Schwartz's right, our left, both lock side up.

Viola was doing a pretty good job of holding it in, but I could see she was wondering what was up. Schwartz told her, "I should explain about the list of initials, Ms. Ketchum. But perhaps you, too, have figured out the puzzle." He handed her a copy of the list, and she took a good look at it.

"Well, maybe I'm just dense, Mr. Schwartz, but the truth is I have no idea what's going on here. Why did you have Paul bring the guns from Uncle Jim's house? Does that have something to do with the list of letters? I don't get it, to tell you the truth, and I'd appreciate an explanation, if you can provide one."

Schwartz would rather deal with anyone than an upset woman, so he tried to tell it clearly and straightforwardly. "The list was not hard to figure out," he said, "once I realized that the first two pairs of letters had been separated to fit the other pairs, that the first four letters belonged together."

"IMDB," she said. "It's the International Movie Database."

Schwartz's eyebrows went up, although I don't think Viola noticed. He said, "I suppose they know 'database' is one word. Anyway, it is, and if you'll—"

Viola was catching up fast. "TC, Tom Cruise," she said. "KM, Kelly McGillis. VK, Val Kilmer."

Schwartz dislikes stolen thunder, especially his own. He slid a sheet out from under a stack on the small table behind his desk, handed it to her. Paul and I looked over her shoulders. It was in his neat, small handwriting, in black ink, annotated in red:

Internet Movie
Data Base
Tom Cruise
Kelly McGillis
Val Kilmer
Anthony Edwards
Tom Skerritt
Michael Ironside
John Stockwell
Barry Tubb
Rick Rossovich
Tim Robbins
Clarence Gilyard (omitting "Jr.")
Whip Hubley
James Tolkan
Meg Ryan
Adrian Pasdar
Randall Brady
Duke Stroud
Brian Sheehan

Ron Clark
Frank Pesce
Pete Pettigrew
Troy Hunter
Linda Rae } (splitting and
Jurgens T. } running names
C. Cassidy } together)
Debi Fares
Mark Gadbois
Chase Jazzborne
Monty Jordan
Scott Krambeck
John Morgan (omitting the "C." and "Sr.")
Victor Spadaro
Wendy Wells-Gunkel (lopping off the second element of the last name)

"And of course, from this, it's obvious what is intended," Schwartz said. "It's the IMDB cast listing of a film," he said. "It's not one I've seen, as a matter of fact, but it made a big enough splash in 1982 to—"

"*Top Gun!*" Viola said, "I've seen that movie!" I had to give Schwartz credit for self-control. He nodded, taking it like a gentleman.

"So the point of the list was to draw attention either to the top gun in the photo or to the top gun hanging over Mr. Ellenbogen's fireplace." He looked up at the client.

Viola repeated, "*Top Gun.* The top gun." She looked like she'd just had the meaning of life explained to her. "That's amazing, Mr. Schwartz, just amazing."

Schwartz was gratified. "Doubtless you would have figured it out yourself in time, Ms. Ketchum."

"In a year, maybe," she said. She looked doubtful.

"Why don't you all sit?" Schwartz said. We took chairs, Viola between Paul and me.

"So which gun is the top gun?" she asked.

"Let us see," Schwartz said. "Was it the top gun in the picture or the top gun in reality? If I were guessing, I would guess the flintlock, but fortunately, that's not necessary. We have both, so let's take a look at them." He took a small mirror and a penlight from the items on the small table, handed them to me. He took hold of the dark-stocked flintlock, which was closer to him, let it rest on its butt and muzzle as he lifted the part where the barrel ended, and the wood bent. He eased the muzzle past the edge of the desk.

"The first thing is to make sure it's unloaded," Schwartz said. "Too many people have been killed by guns they assumed weren't loaded." To Viola, "Your Uncle Jim would have to be an idiot to hang a loaded gun over the fireplace, but he was human, and we know how they behave. Rainer, use the mirror to focus the light down the barrel without getting your hands directly in front of the bore." He took hold of the rifle just above the trigger and guard, with the other prepared to pull the cock back. "It's on half cock now, so let's see what's in the pan." There was a loud click as he raised the cock all the way back. He turned up the steel frizzen, the part the flint strikes sparks from, and exposed the pan and the tiny touch hole that would communicate fire to the charge at the rear of the barrel, if there was a charge. "No priming powder in the pan," he said, "so in any case we're really quite safe. Let's make sure there's no powder or ball rammed down the barrel. Light, please."

I held the little mirror at an angle, keeping my hand out of the way, and I shone the light on it, shifting the light and mirror angle until the light beam was reflected into the barrel. Schwartz said, "Do you see that gleam in the touch hole?"

As a matter of fact, I did, and Paul and Viola took a look and agreed with Schwartz and me. "Very well, we know the flintlock is empty. How about the percussion?" He let the flintlock down, and Paul and I switched it with the other. Schwartz got the piece upright and raised the hammer. "There's no cap on the nipple, so it's technically safe, but let's make sure. Shine the light directly into the nipple, Rainer."

"Jeez," Viola said. "I had no idea guns were so erotic."

That stopped Schwartz cold. He just looked at her.

"Well," she said, "cocks, balls, nipples...."

Schwartz nodded slowly, then said, "Light, please." I shined the light into the nipple, and Schwartz held the mirror at the muzzle. Paul and Viola said they could see a gleam of light.

"Well, that's good," Schwartz said. "If you can see through a tube, it's either empty or full of something transparent, which black powder, lead balls, and patches aren't. We might as well confirm our observations the other way as well." He pulled the ramrod from the loops beneath the barrel, ran it down the barrel, marked the point even with the muzzle with his thumb, then pulled the rod out, laid it alongside the outside of the barrel. The end came within half an inch of the blunt end of the octagonal barrel. "Good," he said.

We went back to the flintlock, and he pulled the ramrod, went through the same procedure, and got the same confirmation. "All right, we now know both guns are safe," Schwartz said.

Viola looked perplexed. "So the rifles aren't loaded," she said. "I don't understand what that tells us."

Schwartz said, "It tells us that it's safe to examine both guns to see what they can tell us. I don't mean to be tedious about it, but there's nothing more dangerous than an 'unloaded' gun." You could hear the quote marks the way he said it.

"Now, the clue from the list tells us to look at the top gun, either the one in the photo that was enclosed with the list, or the one in reality. Let's see what we can find. The obvious place to look is the patch box." He got a thumbnail under the tip of the rectangular brass door set in the ornate brass box inlaid in the butt of the gun, opened it with a soft click. He tilted the rifle, and a number of small objects fell out onto the towel: a square flint, the edges sharply angled, half a dozen dull gray balls, a few inch-square patches, and a red-orange, black-tipped plastic object a couple inches or so long, less than an inch wide, less than half an inch thick.

"A thumb drive?" Viola said. "Why would anyone put a thumb drive in an old rifle—" She suddenly went red. "Of course: where better to hide a thumb drive than in an antique, where....."

Schwartz nodded. "Rather ingenious, isn't it?" he said. "Why would anyone check the patch box of a Kentucky rifle?" He replaced the flint, patches, and lead balls in the patch box. He went over the rifle from one end to the other, found nothing else interesting. "Of course, we could take the rifle apart, and we will if it becomes necessary, but I very much doubt it would be worth it." He set the flintlock down.

He raised the percussion rifle and pried at the patch box, which was oval rather than rectangular like the flintlock's. It stuck a bit at first, then the door opened, and he shook out more patches, more lead balls, a small plastic capsule with a dozen or so copper percussion caps in it, and another thumb drive, apparently identical to the first. He picked up the thumb drive, and with a felt marker printed a *P* on one side. He marked the other one with an *F.* He replaced the caps, patches, and balls in the box, snapped it shut. He laid the rifle down as if it had lost all interest for him.

"So," Schwartz said. "Two thumb drives, apparently identical, one hidden in one rifle, the other in the other." He looked up at me. Would you mind putting these somewhere out of the way?"

I picked up the flintlock, slid it into one of the gun cases, and Paul did the same with the other. I went to the standing cabinets in the corner, unlocked the door of the one on the left, and stood the rifle inside, with Schwartz's other long guns. Paul put the percussion rifle beside it. They were so long they barely fit inside the cabinet. I locked them up, and we returned to our seats. Schwartz had taken the towel off his desk and laid it on a chair. He replaced the lamp and other things he'd removed to make room.

"Are they identical?" Schwartz asked. "Let's see what's on them, shall we?"

At that moment, the doorbell rang, and I stepped into the hall to see. "Mercer, with Ripley in tow," I told Schwartz.

He had already opened his desk drawer and had swept the thumb drives into it, out of sight. "Ms. Ketchum, would you like to become better acquainted with the Indianapolis Metropolitan Police Department?"

Viola was pretty cool about it. "Not particularly," she said.

"I thought not," Schwartz said drily. "Paul, would you be so kind as to see Ms. Ketchum home discreetly?"

"It would be a pleasure, sir," Paul said. He and Viola rose, and I took them to the back door, leading out to the walled backyard, or back garden as Schwartz calls it. At the far end, beyond the pagoda, is what looks superficially like a simple wood gate but is actually a very sturdy steel door that opens from the inside only without a key. Paul led Viola down the brick path. I heard the doorbell ring again as I watched them go out the gate to the narrow pathway on the other side. It would take Paul about two minutes to circle around for the car and pick Viola up. I relocked the back door. I permitted myself a smile at how well they'd hit it off; for a guy who looks like nobody, he's loaded with charm. I wiped my face straight as I headed for the front door to admit the law.

I opened the door, greeted Mercer and Ripley warmly, but they just brushed past me rudely and headed for the office. Steve was standing just inside the door, and I passed between him and Inspector Mercer as I went to my desk. Mercer was in front of the big leather chair, his face above his mask almost as red as the chair, and he was jabbing a finger emphatically at Schwartz. "So we get a call this morning, reporting a murder, and it came from your man Zufahl, who's there under false pretenses, and by God if he doesn't—"

"Shut up!" Schwartz roared suddenly, and Mercer, astonished, shut up. Schwartz didn't pass up the opening. "Inspector, I will not be berated without cause in my own office, and if you cannot behave in a civil manner, I'll ask you to leave. Despite the best efforts of the hooligans in charge, this country is not yet entirely a police state, and if you have no good reason for doing so, you have no right to invade my privacy uninvited. Now, either sit down and act like a civilized adult human being, or leave my house." He loves it when he can get away with it, and today there was no reason he couldn't.

Mercer looked like he was deciding whether to have a heart attack or a stroke. He stood there for ten seconds, by my count, before he got himself under control enough to sit down. "Can I offer you and Mr. Ripley refreshment?" Schwartz inquired courteously. He can walk that psychological tightrope perfectly. "Some iced tea, perhaps? I've recently come across a recipe I think you'll enjoy."

Mercer took a deep breath. He reached into his shirt pocket for a cigarette, let his hand drop. He gave them up years ago but still misses them. "No," he said, just above a snarl. "Oh, hell, yes, I will at that." He half turned toward Steve. "Take a seat, Ripley; we're probably going to be here awhile." I went to the kitchen for a tray, glasses, and ice. There was a fresh pitcher of what I was sure was Iris's blend in the fridge. I brought the tray to the office, set it on the corner of Schwartz's desk that had recently held the butts of a couple antique rifles, and served ice tea for the four of us.

Mercer can't give up his conviction that Leo Schwartz is out to make a monkey of him, despite all evidence to the contrary. Granted, with the state's not exactly rigorous standards when it comes to P.I. licenses, not to mention CCW permits, I could understand why he and the rest of the department didn't appreciate outside interference, but it wasn't as if we had embarked on an investigation with the intention of horning in on a murder case. Schwartz explained as much to our guests, and he ran down the sequence of events, from the first call from Iris Warner to the moment I had called him, after not before I had called IMPD about Ilona's dead body in her office. He anticipated Mercer's questions perfectly, emptying the bag completely, leaving him nothing to ask.

By the time Schwartz was recounting his discussion of tea with Iris, Mercer was nodding, understanding what Schwartz had been doing, if not precisely applauding his performance. Since we are totally honest when there's no compelling reason not to be, Schwartz's account of the case agreed perfectly with mine.

Mercer went to take another drink of tea, saw that he'd already finished, and set the glass down on the coaster. "What did Ms. Marchand tell you about blackmail?" he asked me, not offensively.

I looked at Schwartz, not really for his approval, but to get across to Mercer and Ripley the idea that I thought I needed to get. Schwartz nodded, and I said, "She told me that she and her late husband had once belonged to a small, private club, a group of people who got together once a month for interpersonal interaction—"

"A sex club?" Mercer asked.

"So I gathered," I said.

Mercer frowned. "You would think," he said, "that people of a certain social status would have the good sense—"

"Pfui," Schwartz said. I love it when he speaks German to the police. "You know perfectly well, Inspector, that in this country 'social status' means 'financial standing,' no more, no less, regardless of what the self-anointed elite may think and may want the rest of us to think. Do you seriously imagine that wealth connotes intelligence or even discretion? With all the evidence to the contrary? I repeat: pfui."

Mercer looked uncomfortable. He'd certainly heard this line from Schwartz before, if not as often as I had. I suspect he worries that Schwartz is going to radicalize Ripley or something. He said, "I just mean that simple self-preservation would keep people out of messes like this. Did Ms. Marchand tell you anything more specific, Zufahl?"

It's 'Rainer' when he's in a good mood. I wasn't surprised that he wasn't. "From what she said," I told him, "I gathered that they used to get together once a month, and the men would draw a number from a box or a hat or whatever, and the women would draw a number, and they'd pair off, and that would be the arrangement for that particular get-together."

"'Get-together,'" Mercer snorted.

Ripley asked, "Suppose a married couple drew each other?"

"I don't know," I said. "She didn't go into the details. I suppose they could have redrawn numbers or something. Maybe they—"

"Oh, for the love of...." Mercer said. "Who cares what they did? The point is they had this sex club, and somebody found out about it somehow, and they were putting the pressure on Ms. Marchand, am I right?"

"That was the gist of it, Inspector. She had gotten a letter marked Personal, on nice-quality stationery, and her secretary had passed it on to her unopened, and she'd opened it, and inside was a letter, no heading, date, or greeting, and of course no signature, asking her to think about what it would be worth to her to keep the history of the Mid-month Nature-study Club secret. It was neatly printed, one paragraph, probably from a laser printer."

"'The Mid-month Nature-study Club', for Pete's sake," Mercer said. "She keep the letter and envelope? Not that they'd probably help much. Tracing a laser printer is easy in the movies and on TV."

"Apparently, that's what they called it," I said. "And, of course, I asked. She said she'd shredded the letter and the envelope too." I kept my face straight. Schwartz knew I was departing from the facts, but he had given me strict instructions to that effect.

"So they met in the middle of the month?" Ripley asked.

"She said they got together on the Saturday night on or after the fifteenth of the month," I said.

"Suppose one or more of the women had her—"

"Forget it, Steve," Mercer told his subordinate. "We don't give a damn about the logistics of their sex club. We don't care what they were up to, whoever they were or wherever they were. We're concerned with blackmail here, which is a crime, by the way, not screwing around or being stupid, which isn't, thank God, or we wouldn't have time for anything else." He went for another cigarette, let his hand fall again. "Did our murder victim tell you when this club was active?"

"She wasn't overly specific," I said. "That is, I don't know when it started, but she said she and her husband went to the get-togethers until six months before his death, when his health began to decline."

"So they were going to their club right up to eight years and two months ago," Mercer said. He knew exactly when Andrew Wilson had died. I saw the look in Schwartz's eye, the slight nod of his head. He always approves of people doing their homework thoroughly, even the police. He would probably say, especially the police.

"I guess so," I said, as casually as possible.

"And we have only your word for it that this blackmail attempt ever happened, or that this conversation with Ms. Marchand ever happened, either." If Mercer had tried, he couldn't have come up with a quicker way of changing the expression on Schwartz's face.

Schwartz snapped, "Do you accuse Mr. Zufahl of spinning a yarn, Inspector? What possible reason could he have had for making up such a tale? Do you imagine that he is such a witling as to complicate a murder case by slandering the victim?" He snorted. "Or that I am colluding with him on the slander?" He shifted in his chair, warming to his subject. "How long have you known me, Inspector? And Mr. Zufahl?"

"No, I'd have to retract that," Mercer said. To me, "You're a lot of things, Zufahl, but you're not a—" He refused to parrot Schwartz. "You're not an idiot. I admit you wouldn't make up crap like that just for the hell of it, and I can't see what advantage you'd get from a story like that about a murder victim. I suppose I really ought to be surprised that you mentioned it at all." He shook his head almost ruefully, turned back to me.

"So, you really were at WarnerCorp, pretending to be a consultant of some kind, hired by Iris Warner, to investigate what it was that her ex-husband, who happens to be worth northwards of a billion dollars, was worried about? Plus this side job about blackmail for Ilona Marchand?"

"That's about the size of it, Inspector," I said as earnestly as I could.

"Zufahl, you're checking into the mental health of a billionaire at his ex-wife's behest and chasing a blackmailer at the same time. It's a wonder nobody killed you," he said unkindly.

"Well," I said, "I suspected that the cat was out of the bag about the consultancy pose. I got only part way through the interviews yesterday, but from those four, which you have my notes of, as well as casual conversation with others in the office, I got the impression, just vibes, no hard evidence, not even any specific comments, that at least some people at WarnerCorp thought something was up with Buck Warner."

"Well, great," Mercer said. "You're getting vibes. Wonderful." He stood up. "Come on, Steve. Let's get out of here. Vibes may be contagious." He stomped out to the hall, turned right. Ripley gave a quick shrug of his beefy shoulders, apparently to Schwartz and me, and followed the Inspector out of the office.

Since an event a couple years ago when I assumed Mercer had left the premises only to find out he hadn't, I went to the hall, ready to help them get on the outside of the front door, but this time they managed it on their own.

Chapter Twelve

Tuesday, March 31–Wednesday, April 1

I returned to my desk in the office. "Well, that took care of the consultancy business," I said.

"Oh, I don't know," Schwartz said. "The pose, yes. But we still have a client, who is perfectly capable of paying us to find out what's bothering Buck Warner."

"True," I said. "And then there's still the Stroh case. What should I do about that?"

"I did a little checking myself today," Schwartz said. "I called the Halls of Records at the City-County Building, and after being transferred around a few times, I learned that the house was built in 1926, and that neighborhood was annexed by the city of Indianapolis in June 1957. According to the records department, or rather according to the person I spoke with, Sarah with an *h* Brown with no *e*, the street was excavated for city sanitary and storm sewers that summer. That side of the street was connected to the sanitary sewer the second week of October 1957."

"Okay," I said, "but what does that tell us?"

"It tells us there's probably a disused septic tank on the property," he said, "since, although it's possible that the tank was removed and the hole filled in with fill dirt, it's fairly unusual for the homeowner to go to the expense, when all you really have to do is leave the thing alone and just forget about it. The owner is most likely fully occupied with the long mound of sand

and clay from the house to the street, where the new sewer line has been laid. The Department of Sanitation doesn't care about your landscaping, and as I recall it, it's the owner's responsibility to get the hump leveled with the rest of the yard." He looked at the clock over the door.

"It's late. There's no pressing reason to return to WarnerCorp tomorrow morning, so instead go back to the Abernathy house, with Ed Stroh. We may as well include him, since he's the main spark. Look around the outside of the house and see if you notice anything amiss."

"Okay, boss," I said, and we packed it in for the night.

At nine o'clock Wednesday morning, I rang Ed Stroh. I told him Schwartz wanted me to look around outside. He was enthusiastic, so I picked him up at home, and we drove down to Arden. We walked all the way around the house, noting the pergola with grapevines all over it, most of the vines out of reach without a ladder, a paved patio, a rather run-down wood deck at one end, with a railing that looked totally untrustworthy, and an elaborate brick barbecue pit with chimney. There was a good-sized shed, or barn, in the northwest corner, way past the driveway turn-around.

Ed stayed inside the house as I walked around the front yard. Looking into the foundation plantings south of the door, I found nothing, but north of the door, I spotted the modern white PVC access point, which from the dirt and dust, hadn't been disturbed in decades. It was a four-inch plug screwed into the main line, well camouflaged with ivy, yew, and hemlock close to the house, with hostas and myrtle in front of the shrubbery. A few daffodils were still hanging in there, and some tulips were almost ready to bloom. I saw a neighbor across the street clipping some shrubs and watching us.

From the access point, the sewer line would almost certainly run straight out to the street, and the septic tank, if it was still there, would probably be fairly close, on one side or the other of the line. The grass was a bit high, but it didn't take long to spot the access to the septic tank, a miniature manhole cover, dark brown with corrosion. I called Schwartz. "There's a septic tank in the front yard, and it looks to me like the manhole cover or lid or whatever it is has recently been tampered with. There's some kind of shiny weld or solder or something showing around the joint between the lid and the base it fits into."

"I'll be right there," he said and hung up.

I went back in the house to tell Ed that Schwartz was on his way. He was sitting in the kitchen, making a cup of coffee with a Keurig. He made one for me, Columbian, without asking, and I took it, with powdered creamer from the counter. We sat down at the breakfast nook off the kitchen, facing each other across the small table, and drank our coffee. "I can't help the feeling that they're gone," he said, staring at the cup in front of him. "For good, I mean." He looked up and said, "I don't mean that it's good that they're—"

"I know what you mean, Ed," I said. "I'm not sure, but I think that's the way Mr. Schwartz is thinking too."

"All these years, and you still call him Mr. Schwartz," Ed remarked.

"Old-fashioned German upbringing," I said. I finished my coffee, set the cup in the sink, and ran water into it. Schwartz was taking his time getting there. "I'll go out to meet him." Ed ran water into his cup and joined me as I went out to the septic tank opening.

As I knelt to take a closer look, Schwartz pulled into the driveway, driving the Camry. Sometimes he's fine, sitting at home while I'm out doing the legwork, but once in a while he gets itchy, and this had certainly been a week to rile a person up. Ed came over to see what I was doing, but I waited until Schwartz got there, and reported to him, Ed listening. While I was talking, Schwartz reached in his jacket pocket and tossed me a small tape measure. I put it to use and found that the manhole cover was about thirteen and a half inches in diameter. I so informed Schwartz. Mentally I multiplied by two and a half; it was about thirty-three and a half or maybe thirty-three and a third centimeters. I could think of no possible significance to that fact. I doubted that the International System would be a factor in the case, and I turned out to be right about that.

From the same pocket, Schwartz took a small roll of yellow tape and some golf tees. He used the tape and half a dozen of the tees to surround the septic tank opening and me in a circle about twelve feet across. He and Stroh stayed outside the yellow tape. I stayed where I was.

"Here's what I find disturbing," I said, pointing with a pen at the seam, where the round lid sat in the base. "See this thin silver line squished out a tiny bit between the lid and the base? That's definitely new. Bondo or J B Weld or something."

"Yes," Schwartz said. He took out his phone, ran down the contacts list, fingered a number. "Hello," he said. "This is Leo Schwartz, calling for Inspector Mercer." Pause. "Then perhaps I could speak to Sergeant Stephen Ripley. Yes, I'll hold."

Schwartz held the phone at his side. "Rainer, when you were in the garage, did you happen to notice a sturdy chisel and a hammer, a small sledge, perhaps? Not the kind of chisel for wood, the kind for splitting things that don't want to be split." I said I had.

Schwartz said to Stroh, "Do you think you could bring them, Ed?"

"Sure," he said. "You want a cold chisel and a small sledgehammer. Right?"

"Right, a cold chisel." I had forgotten the term. "And a heavy hammer, please. There's no telling how hard it will be to get this thing off."

Schwartz's phone squawked, and he replied, telling someone where we were and what we'd found. It didn't take long for Ed to find a one-inch chisel and a small sledgehammer and return with them to the front yard. The neighbor had joined Schwartz and Stroh, nodding a greeting, not chatting, just present. Schwartz was talking to Ripley. "No, Sergeant, I am not trying to waste your time or Inspector Mercer's. I know we just saw you at my office yesterday. As I said, I am no longer at my office; I am at…. What's the address, Ed?" Ed gave it, and Schwartz passed it on to Steve Ripley. "I have reason to believe that bodies of the missing persons Mr. Stroh reported to your department last week are about to be found, and I thought that, as a matter of professional courtesy, not to mention the responsibility of a citizen and taxpayer to assist the police in the investigation of a crime, I should report the matter to you." Ripley had something to say, and Schwartz listened to it.

"Very well, we will await your arrival then, Sergeant. No, we will touch nothing. Of course. Thank you." Schwartz hung up. "They'll be here in a few minutes," he said, as a general announcement. Then, to the neighbor,

"Have you seen or heard anything out of the ordinary the past week?"

The neighbor said no, he hadn't, but he didn't really keep an eye on the place or anything. Schwartz requested his name, and I wrote it down, Jared Fleuve, and got his phone number and street number. I knelt again, still not touching the little manhole, of course, and inspected the joint between cover and base. From above, the shiny material showed only in a couple places, from about one-thirty to four-thirty and about seven to ten, with the street side as noon and the house side as six. When I got down close to the lawn, I could see more of the silvery stuff, but it was a very thin line.

"Bondo, do you think?" Schwartz asked.

"That would be my guess," I said. "There's generally a rubber gasket sealing these things, you know, originally to prevent unpleasant odors from escaping the septic tank, no doubt. I'd bet they cleaned off the metal as best they could, in the dark certainly, and then used the Bondo to seal the lid permanently."

I was still kneeling there, and I noticed a dent in the lawn about a foot from the manhole cover, with a sprinkling of rust particles next to it. I was pointing that out to Schwartz when the unmarked police car, a Crown Victoria, pulled in the drive and parked behind his Camry. Inspector Mercer and Sergeant Steve Ripley got out and headed our way. A black and white pulled in after the CV, and Officers Olson and Peña got out. I resisted the temptation to wave.

Inspector Mercer had grown no fonder of Schwartz and me than he had been twelve hours or so earlier, but he's known Schwartz long enough to expect him to behave professionally in front of witnesses. He asked what was happening, and Schwartz gave him an account of events, not stressing the lack of action by the police, but word for word, and then he reached in his pocket and handed Mercer the two blood samples. "So you think they're in the septic tank," Mercer summarized. "Good of you to wait for us to arrive. Steve, go inside and confirm that the blood stains are there; take a uniform with you. I see you have the tools ready, Schwartz, so I'll just have to take your word you haven't taken a look already."

I was startled when Jared Fleuve spoke up, loud and clear: "That's absolutely untrue, Inspector. I've been here the whole time, and these men have waited for you to arrive. They haven't opened anything." In a couple minutes Ripley came back with Olson, told Mercer the blood was there, although how it had gotten there was still an open question.

Mercer made it clear to Mr. Fleuve and everyone else that he didn't really think we'd gone ahead without him and the other officers, then he told me to get the hell out of the way, and he motioned Peña over. "Let's see how hard it is to get that lid off," he said. "Hit it easy the first time, then harder if you need to." Olson, meanwhile, had taken the usual documenting photos of the scene, including everyone.

Peña knelt right where I'd been, and he fitted the edge of the cold chisel in the narrow groove around the rusted manhole cover. He adjusted the chisel's angle, then gave it a fairly soft whack with the small sledge. That was enough. The Bondo, or perhaps the rust it was trying to grip, came loose, and the round plate jumped off the base and flipped onto the grass on the far side of the hole. Peña laid down the hammer and chisel and shone a flashlight into the septic tank.

"Looks like plastic tarp," he said. "Lots of blue plastic and yellow bags, I think. Do we have a gripper?"

I had seen one in the garage, and I said so, and I went to fetch it. Schwartz, Stroh, Fleuve, and I watched, and I covertly filmed with my phone as Peña reached in with the gripper and pulled out part of a painter's plastic tarp, then Ripley helped him lift it all the way out. Ripley laid it on the lawn, down toward the street. Sergeants are versatile. Peña continued to look into the hole. "Jesus, I don't like the looks of this a bit," he said, and he leaned in with the gripper, reaching for something. At last he got hold of it, and he reached in to steady it with his left hand as he brought it out of the hole. It was a package made up of a yellow heavy-duty leaf bag, closed with a plastic tie, with the free end of the bag wrapped around the package, folded under, and sealed with a strip of shipping tape wrapped completely around the package. "There looks to be a dozen of these down there," Peña said. He handed the yellow package to Ripley, who set it on a new sheet of heavy clear plastic Olson had brought up from the cruiser.

"Let's see what's inside the first one before we drag all the others out," Mercer said. It was a good idea, of course. Had it turned out to be nothing more than carefully wrapped garbage, it would have saved a lot of effort.

It wasn't garbage. It was a male human pelvis, detached from the legs and most of the spine, reduced to an object small enough, turned sideways, to pass through that narrow opening. It was fairly ripe. Mr. Fleuve walked a few yards toward the street, bent sharply, and vomited. By now, Ripley was on the phone, giving someone instructions on what to bring, while Peña groped around, trying to, then succeeding in getting hold of another package within reach. The second contained a thigh. It wasn't clear whether it belonged to the pelvis. Mercer told the cops to rewrap the packages and not to open anymore; leave it for the M.E.

There was no question of witness identification while we waited for the longer reacher/grabber and other equipment to arrive, so Mercer went over what he called our story again from the beginning. Mr. Fleuve was back, sitting on the front step, looking very pale indeed. Ed Stroh, pretty pale himself, was sitting beside him, assuring him that it was all going to be all right. God knows what made him do that, or say that, or believe it in the first place. Ed looked like he needed somebody to reassure him. It was pretty clear that nothing was going to be all right with Eugene or Lawrence ever again.

Sirens announced the arrival of more vehicles, and people were stepping out front doors and peering out windows on either side and across the street. Officials emerged and approached our group.

Given the age of the house, Schwartz said, it was almost certain the tank was concrete, sides, bottom, and top. The police van had brought men with drills, sledges, and a jackhammer, and by early afternoon there was a three-foot opening in the septic tank, and a man in a hazmat suit was passing up packages and other things that probably hadn't been there a week earlier. We stuck around for the whole operation, not by request.

There were twenty-four sealed yellow packages, counting the two Peña had fished out. There were two wadded-up plastic tarps stuffed into an unsealed trash bag, besides the loose one he'd brought out first. There were two saber saws, one a bit larger than the other. There was a cardboard box with the tail end of a roll of yellow plastic bags. There was a partially used can of Bondo compound, which when mixed properly with a setting agent hardens to the touch in an hour. It's very useful in repairing dings and small dents in automotive bodies, or in sealing up septic-tank openings until someone comes along with a hammer and chisel.

They helped the man in the hazmat suit out again, and he took off the hood and the rest. He said that was it; the old contents of the tank had long since solidified, and everything that had been dumped in recently was out. Four uniforms carried up a heavy steel plate and placed it over the hole. The packages and saws and plastic and Bondo had been tagged and bagged and taken away by the time they had the area marked with police taped and the house sealed as a crime scene. Schwartz asked Mercer if we were needed further. Fortunately, Schwartz's grandson wasn't around to hear the answer, but it came down to no, but stay available, as if.

Schwartz drove Ed home, and I drove back alone. I put the Prius in the garage and waited for Schwartz to get home with the Camry. We hadn't had lunch, for obvious reasons. We went to the Golden Dragon for dinner, where we dawdled a bit, discussing the day's events. We agreed that we were pretty much out of the Abernathy case now, with the cops all over it, and of course, the WarnerCorp investigation was out, but even so, we were only a couple minutes late for the meeting at Union Chapel United Methodist Church.

Chapter Thirteen

Thursday, April 2

The next morning, after I'd dusted and sorted the mail and so on, I got Viola's two thumb drives from the safe, and plugged them into my laptop, made copies in two new directories, and returned the drives to the safe. Not that that antique would have slowed down a real safe-cracker who was living in the same century as the rest of us.

I was busy with the files when Schwartz came in, said good morning, sat, picked up the bills and other mail I had placed on his desk blotter, crushed them into a ball in his hands, and dropped the whole mess into the wastebasket. It was just pique. He knew perfectly well that I'd fish it all out and return it for his attention.

"Those flash drives," he said. "What is on them?"

"I thought you might be interested," I said, "so I'm taking a look right now." I got the printout of the file list of the F flash drive and handed it to him. On my screen, the P flash drive's file list was identical to the other:

What's Wrong with AA	12kb
On Horseshit	11kb
The End of All Things	9kb
Miscellaneous Detritus	22kb

With the times and dates of composition all identical, deleted here, and all four identified as Open Document files, ditto. I couldn't see anything to distinguish between the two.

Schwartz waited until I had printed out the second list and handed it to him. "They appear to be identical," he said. "If so, what was the point of specifying the top gun, whichever one was meant, the one in the picture or the one in reality?"

"I don't know," I said, realizing that that wasn't very helpful. Might as well anticipate the inevitable, so I asked, "Shall I check the contents to confirm that they're really the same?"

Schwartz didn't look enthusiastic, but he nodded. "No one is expecting Charles Wood at WarnerCorp, and heaven knows we're not needed or wanted down at the Abernathy house." I realized he was really upset. Trashing the mail was nothing all that unusual, but it wasn't like him to repeat the obvious.

"By now, who knows how many more blood stains they've found?"

"I don't think this is a case that will require artificial insemination," Schwartz said, using his euphemism for police-supplied evidence where there's not quite enough of the naturally occurring kind. "The two splashes should be enough to show where the killings occurred. Did you see anything in the collection from the septic tank that looked like it could cause those splashes?"

"No, sir. If I were guessing, I'd suggest Eugene and Lawrence were incapacitated somehow, and they were laid out on a tarp, still alive, and worked over until the killers—"

"Plural. So we're agreed that there were at least two killers."

"Yes, sir. Eugene and Lawrence may not have been formidable, but just in terms of keeping two adult males in line, it seems to me at least overwhelmingly likely that there must have been at least two, maybe three or more assailants."

"Very well. Neither of us is on the witness stand, and with any luck, we won't be. So the assailants got their victims trussed, I would imagine, and interrogated them until they either got the information they wanted or they decided they didn't know anything."

"Or Eugene and Lawrence died from the interrogation," I said.

"Not both," Schwartz said. "If we assume that the victims were supine on the tarp, then in all likelihood, those splashes were made when a throat or throats were cut. Blood spurted upward almost three feet to make those splashes under the tables. The forensics will tell whether they came from one person or two."

"Eugene had to have been at least sixty. I don't know how far blood would spurt if his throat was cut."

"But after an energetic interrogation…. Oh, damn the sugared language…. After perhaps hours of torture, even an old heart, stressed beyond human endurance…. I'm betting on blood from both of them, one toward the side table, one toward the dining table. God, what a ghastly way to die."

"Yes, sir, it's depressing, and it doesn't help that we didn't particularly like them."

"No, in an odd sort of way, it even makes it worse, you know? Our minds are strange, Rainer. Because they were not our favorite people, we are struck with a misplaced sense of guilt as we contemplate their horrible suffering. It makes no logical sense at all, yet there it is." Schwartz made a fist on his desk. "Who would do such a thing to the Abernathys, and why on earth?"

"I don't suppose the cops will feel like sharing their evidence with us," I said. "By now, the scientists will be busy examining those two dozen chunks, fitting them together like a couple jigsaw puzzles, and they'll know what happened, in terms of trauma to the bodies while they were intact. Maybe there will be fingerprints, with all that blood."

"I doubt it," Schwartz said. "I didn't see any gloves, disposable or otherwise, in the materials taken from the septic tank."

"No, they were smart enough not to leave their fingerprints inside latex gloves. What gets me is the way they went to such lengths to keep things tidy, with the tarp and all. Were they just trying to hide the fact that Eugene and Lawrence were murdered? That's also the only reason I can think of for stashing the remains in the septic tank. It took a lot of time to cut the bodies up into pieces small enough to fit the septic tank and to wrap the pieces in the trash bags. Also, they must have put everything in and sealed the lid at night."

"Certainly. It would take a fair amount of daring, or at least desperation, to open the tank, carry the body fragments and other stuff out the front door, without lights, and put everything in, then seal the lid. The Bondo, at least, would have required some light. Let's drive past the house tonight after dark and see how things look from the street, how much light the streetlights provide or, more likely even in that neighborhood, fail to provide. I suppose they could have brought the lid inside the house, for light, applied the Bondo, and then carried it out again and set the lid in place."

"Good idea," I said. "You realize, of course, what all this points to, vis à vis the killers' familiarity with the house and grounds."

"Of course. They knew the place well. That septic tank did not suddenly present itself as a hiding place. They knew it was there; they knew where it was; they had perhaps hidden something in it before. I wonder what it was that brought them to use it, as I think we can tentatively assume, again."

I pondered that question but came up with nothing. Schwartz went on: "If you were using a septic tank to hide something you wanted to retrieve, would you just take the lid off and toss it in?" He muttered something that might have been Pfui.

"Well, no, of course not," I said. "It would have to be a bag or something that would fit, obviously, and you wouldn't want to fish around for it; you'd want to be able to haul it out easily when you came for it."

"When we next hear from Inspector Mercer, let's ask him if they found a nonstandard hook or bracket or other attached device that a bundle could be suspended from. My money is on a spike driven into the wall of the tank a few inches below the hole, perhaps just out of sight a few inches to one side."

"Makes sense to me," I said. I was still trying to postpone the examination of those files, but then it occurred to me that I had a file-comparison program already waiting on my computer. At least, whatever those files were, it wouldn't take long to find out whether they were exactly the same and, if not, where the differences lay and what they were.

Schwartz was still on the Abernathy case. "I wonder whether there's any evidence that the lid was left loose or was stuck down before. Well, the police are on it and probably in no mood to share. And so far as that goes, they're investigating Ms. Marchand's murder as well. I don't think we've handed three corpses to the police in so short a time period before."

"Or ever," I pointed out. "Not that breaking that record is likely to endear us to them."

"No," Schwartz said, "we will have to earn their affection." He allowed himself a smile. "Please do take a look at those thumb drives, Rainer. We can't go back to WarnerCorp without an invitation from the client, and Ed Stroh's got no real standing in the Abernathy murders even though it was originally his missing-persons report that led to the discovery of the bodies. Frankly, I can see the point of view of the police on this. They don't want us trampling their ground, and legally they are completely in the right. Morally is another matter, but it has no legal standing. Let's see what's on the drives."

I went to the directories with the copies of the files and fired up the comparison program. I noticed Schwartz had turned to the Extra section of the *Star*. He was busy with the Jumble, crossword, Sudoku, and Cryptoquip while I went through the file comparison.

All four files seemed to be the same size, but even as I watched the lines flash by, the program building an extensive list of differences between each pair of files, I began to suspect what the difference really was. It took a while, mainly because I'd never run the program before and was being careful to follow the instructions step by tiresome, but doubtless crucial step.

I took a look at the results of the comparison, and knowing Schwartz's hangup about paper, I printed out the four reports, which the program had allowed me to format in the form I found most convenient, two columns labeled Drive F and Drive P, with page and line numbers at the left for easy reference, listing the words that differed from one file to the other. The software let me add headings to each page: "What's Wrong with AA," "On Horseshit," "The End of All Things," and "Miscellaneous Detritus."

Frankly, I was pretty pleased with the result. The words under the heading "Drive F" were consistently misspelled; the ones under "Drive P" were spelled correctly. I handed the four single-spaced sheets to Schwartz just as he finished the Cryptoquip. Sometimes he has a comment about the quality of the pun in that puzzle, often as not comparing it unfavorably to his own all-time favorite, "If musician Monk played only solos, it would be true that one is Thelonious' number," as if I haven't heard it a hundred times before. I leave the puzzles in the newspaper alone. Schwartz leaves the rest of the paper alone, for the most part. His reaction to the front page is "What do they want me to believe today?" And I'd be willing to bet a week's pay he's never read a sports page.

Schwartz looked through the four sheets carefully but quickly. "What do you make of it, Rainer?"

"Well, for some reason, Uncle Jim left Viola two sets of files, one with spelling mistakes left in and one with the spelling corrected. So it seems the movie title meant the top gun in the Polaroid." I stopped. It's been my experience with Schwartz that generalizations about people older than thirty-five are not always welcome. "I suppose it's just possible that when Uncle Jim put the thumb drives in the rifles' patch boxes, he accidentally hung the flintlock above the percussion lock."

"It's possible," Schwartz agreed, "but it strikes me as unlikely. He wouldn't have to take the rifles down from the rack just to put the drives in the patch boxes; all he needed to do was flip them open and stick them in."

"Wouldn't the other stuff fall out?" I asked.

"Perhaps. We have the rifles. Let's try it." He got an old thumb drive from his middle drawer. We went to the gun cabinet, I unlocked it, and I took out one of the gun cases. It was the one with the flintlock inside it. I took out the piece and held it horizontally, the muzzle to Schwartz's right, the butt with patch box to his right, and the lock toward him. He opened the lid of the patch box with his left hand, caught lead balls with his right, tilted the top of the rifle toward me, dropped in the bullets and the thumb drive. I re-cased the flintlock, and we repeated the experiment with the percussion rifle, with similar results. In both cases Schwartz needed to tilt the rifle so that those lead balls and the thumb drive would stay in while the door was open. I locked the weapons back in the cabinet.

Schwartz was looking at the photos again. "With that kind of gun rack, he could just lift the rear end of the rifle, slide it about a foot rearwards, and he could get it tilted to keep the balls in while he shut the door. Then he'd just slide it back in place. It's hard to tell from the photo, but I almost think he could do it with the rifle left in place, just rotate it back. The left-hand support holds each rifle just behind the loop of the trigger guard. I think it would be possible to—" He stopped talking abruptly, nodded to himself a couple times. "Why are we speculating? Do you have Ms. Ketchum's phone number? I want to take a look at Uncle Jim's house myself."

Did I have her phone number? The thing is, Schwartz didn't even realize the question was insulting. He's right about his head for business: he doesn't have one.

I called Viola. She said she was with a client but could be free by two that afternoon, and she'd be glad to let us in Uncle Jim's house. She asked if we'd made any progress, and I assured her we had, but didn't get specific. She gave me the Broad Ripple address, again and unnecessarily, but if that's the worst thing you can say about a client in this business, you're doing okay. I asked Schwartz if he had anything further to say, but he didn't. I told her, "We'll see you at the house at two," and hung up.

"Which gives us time to read the manuscripts," Schwartz said. "I take it that, since the P files have been proofread or at least spell-checked, the percussion rifle, the top gun in the Polaroid, tells us to read the corrected version. Would you print out a paper copy for me? Oh, and could you email me a copy of the results of the file comparison? That's quite a handsome table, and I'd like to have another look at it."

And he'd done so well working all that scary electronic equipment before, but after all, he's the boss, and I'm the leg-man. I offered to email it to him on his laptop, but he said he would rather have a hard copy with no formatting or other changes to it, exactly as it was on the drive, insofar as possible. Okay.

As the pages came off the printer, I took a look at them. There was no header or footer, or page numbers. I asked Schwartz if he'd like me to add page numbers by hand, in red, say, to help keep them straight, but he said not to bother. He meant not to bother him and Dawkins, of course. After printing the fifty-four manuscript pages, some pretty dense text, some with lots of space, all four documents, I collected the sheets.

I squared the sides and foot, laid the stack on the corner of his desk, and he laid down his book and took up the manuscript. I had it on my laptop's screen, of course. The top of the first page was titled "What's Wrong with AA." Okay, I thought, it's either a screed by someone who has invented a sobriety program that borrows the Steps, probably modified, and other aspects of Alcoholics Anonymous, or it's a garden-variety AA bitch session, in which latter case, I deduced, Uncle Jim was an alcoholic, because AA doesn't actually piss off anyone but alcoholics and, presumably, the competition. As Schwartz once remarked, AA was founded by a stock-market speculator and a proctologist, so how pretty should we expect it to be?

One of the continuing bewilderments of AA is how little AA means to the rest of the world. We continue to overestimate our importance to the world at large.

I scanned that first document, all twelve pages of it, and frankly, it seemed to me to be lacking in originality. Of course, just getting things down on paper is a good way to get them out of your system, so Uncle Jim may have thought it was good therapy for him to write the piece. And, also from Schwartz, anyone who reads AA literature looking for literary elegance and captivating felicity of expression is barking up the wrong tree, to use a cliché Bill Wilson would have liked, with his fleeing alcohol as from the plague and removing hands from a hot flame. I've always wondered about that hot flame. I've never seen a cold one.

Anyway, the first essay, or whatever it was, was unoriginal but not really outrageous. God knows I've encountered crazier ideas than Uncle Jim's in AA meetings, even without counting Phil's misguided efforts. So, I thought, the real question is why Jim thought Viola, or anyone else, for that matter, needed his thoughts about Alcoholics Anonymous. He was complaining about various, not necessarily connected, things that he didn't like about AA. As Schwartz has explained to me, the bad news is that the world isn't always going to go your way, and the good news is that you don't have to like it.

Just accept it.

Then I started the second piece, "On Horseshit," which had quotations and even several footnotes. Jim seemed to be basing the essay on a book by Harry M. Frankfurt, *On Bullshit,* and all I could make out was that he was proposing a distinction between bullshit and horseshit. If I understood it right, he was accepting Frankfurt's definition of bullshit as the rhetorical stuff one shovels to others, which is intended to absolve the person shoveling it of responsibility, regardless of the facts of the matter. And he was proposing to call horseshit the stuff we shovel to ourselves so that the world seems more amenable to our hopes and dreams and wishes than it really is. The piece seemed unfinished, to me anyhow, and I thought Uncle Jim was leaning pretty heavily on Mr. Frankfurt in places. It wasn't plagiarism, but it was repeating with attribution what might have been cited, since he'd introduced footnotes anyway. I had given those pages a quick scan and was rereading more slowly, maybe halfway through, when Schwartz exploded.

"Uncle Jim is quoting me, for God's sake! Unbelievable!" His face was red, he sat bolt-upright, and he shook the sheaf of papers in his hand.

"Quoting you?" I said as I jumped up and came over. I thought he might need CPR. He realized why I was standing next to him, and he carefully laid the papers, which he had convulsively bent into a slight twist, on the blotter. He laid his hands together on the desk, and he started muttering the Serenity Prayer quietly. I whispered along with him, and on Amen I went back to my chair.

Schwartz leaned back, calm now. "It's interesting what Voltaire said about God's all-seeing omnipotence, that He is so great that it is not even necessary that He exist for His power to be made known." He took in half a bushel of air, let it out again. "That was a hell of a shock, frankly. I take it you're not in the Miscellaneous Detritus section yet. You'd have yelled as loud as I did."

It didn't seem wise to debate that point. "Could you tell me where to look—"

"He quotes me on 'facetiously', which as you know—"

"Which as I know," I said.

He took the hint, glanced down the page, turned to the next one. "He quotes me again, this time on typography, for Pete's sake."

"I'm glad Josh isn't here," I said.

"So am I," Schwartz said. "He'd probably think Grandpa was going to stroke." He kept scanning, and then he said, "That's eleven times he quoted me. I know I repeat myself, but this is incredible. How the hell could Uncle Jim have heard me say all this stuff?"

I had gone down to the start of "Miscellaneous Detritus" on my screen, and I ran a search-and-replace on the file for "schw" without checking Match Case. I went through slowly enough to read the passages Uncle Jim had quoted. My count was the same as Schwartz's, eleven quotations.

I was pretty clear on the matter, right from the get-go, because I had heard Schwartz say most, if not all, of it around tables at Starbucks and other venues before and after AA meetings. I even recalled the two Keats comments about the Cortez/Balboa confusion and the "sublime."

Well, I'd already figured, and I assumed Schwartz had too, that Uncle Jim had been a member of AA, seeing as how the only requirement for membership is a desire to quit drinking and nobody else cares enough about AA to bitch about it.

I said as much to Schwartz, and he nodded. "Of course. I can't think of a Jim or a James who has recently passed, but the truth is that I know more alcoholics than I can keep track of. But he was someone you and I have sat at a table with. Can you place him?"

"No, sir," I said. "I can think of at least three Jims we know in the Program, but they're all still alive. And I know two Jameses, both still kicking, the last I heard. Maybe there'll be a clue at his house this afternoon."

"Maybe," Schwartz said. "I certainly hope so. If we've been close enough to talk, I'd like to be able to remember him. What do you say to Biscuits for lunch?"

"Same here, about remembering him," I said. "Biscuits will be fine with me." The enchiladas are exquisite. We went back to the documents,

Schwartz smoothing his out and circling each quotation of himself in red marker.

"I'm not so sure what to think," I said. "In some of these longer quotations, I think he's paraphrasing you from memory."

"Yes, you're right. Here's a turn of phrase I'd never use, just because I don't much care for it. It's not wrong; I just don't say it that way."

"Which one?"

"'Neither assertion 1 nor 2 is true,'" he said. "I think I'd be more likely to supply the elided word in a neither/nor situation: 'Neither assertion 1 nor assertion 2 is true.'"

"Could be," I said, "but in general, I think he has a pretty good ear for your speech, and a good memory too. What was it Viola said Uncle Jim died of? And when exactly?"

"I don't think we asked her," Schwartz said. "We let ourselves get so distracted by the photo and the list of IMDB initials that the interview got sidetracked. I'm supposed to be in charge of a detective agency, and I let an important piece of information just slide. I'm going to have to practice for Josh; they're planning to come by sometime next week."

"Well, we can ask Viola in a couple hours," I said, going back to "On Horseshit." I finished it, and I was almost done with my first scan of the astrophysical musings in "The End of All Things," some or maybe most of which I had trouble understanding, and I was going through the quotations, which were certainly an eclectic collection, to put it politely, when Schwartz pointed out that it was time to leave for lunch. He got his jacket from the back of his chair, folded the stack of pages the long way, and stuck it in his left side pocket.

I drove the Prius, listening to Schwartz lament the loss of Broad Ripple's raffish bohemianism. "The last feminist bookstore in town closed before your time. Now it's just another head shop. God, I miss it. I used to take Gina there on Saturdays, when she was little, to give Freda a break. 'Dreams and Swords' it was called. I think Gina misses it too, but I could be wrong about that."

I had to admit it sounded like quite a place for a man to take his daughter, although my mind was really on those shredded-beef enchiladas with the mushroom cream sauce.

Chapter Fourteen

Thursday, April 2

I took College to 62nd, then headed east, then south into the parking lot shared by a couple rows of restaurants, a nail salon, a check-cashing place, and other pillars of society. "My favorite restaurants are in strip malls," Schwartz remarked as I parked out in front of Biscuits. As we walked to the entrance, his cell rang. "Yes, Inspector," he said. I interacted with the greeter, and we took a booth along the far wall. Schwartz was doing more listening than talking. That was not necessarily a good sign by any means.

The waitress came for our order, and Schwartz said, "Excuse me a second" to the phone, and he asked for the tamale dinner, with one cheese, one chicken, one beef. I went for those enchiladas. Schwartz was back, listening to Inspector Mercer. I was having a hard time imagining what it was that needed so much explaining. The expression on Schwartz's face was hard to read, but I suspected his respect for the good judgment of the IMPD had taken a hit. He rang off just as the food arrived.

"Thanks for leaving me some," he said. I had eaten about half the chips and salsa while he had been on the phone. He took a chip and, scooped up refried beans, ate. "The police have arrested Ed Stroh for the murder of Eugene and Lawrence Abernathy," he said.

I stared. "Apparently, they decided you, and I had nothing to do with it," he went on bitterly. "Even for a department driven by desperation, this is an extraordinarily witless move. They think, or they pretend to think, that Ed had hired help for the murders." He tucked into his tamales, and I kept at my enchiladas. "What eludes understanding is why the police are so anxious to make an arrest that they go for the one person who insisted that something was amiss in the first place. There is no public outcry in the matter. The news reports have been, shall we say, muted, considering that it's a case involving two dozen well-wrapped packages of human meat. No one is howling for the police to make an arrest, so naturally, they decide to arrest the one person who is manifestly innocent of the crime."

He said that Mercer had hinted without exactly saying so that there was pressure from on high, but it wasn't clear why. "For some reason, Inspector Mercer was extremely anxious to make sure I understood that it wasn't his idea to arrest Ed Stroh. Granted, Eugene and Lawrence were respectable tax-paying citizens, but they were hardly movers and shakers among the power elite of Marion County." He likes to remind me that, while he may be my employer, we are no movers and shakers ourselves. It's interesting to work as gofer for someone who quotes Marx, and it may be Karl, and it may be Groucho, or as Schwartz likes to put it, Karl Heinrich or Julius Henry.

"Why the hell would anyone insist on an immediate arrest, however mistaken, in a case like this?" he asked, not rhetorically. "There are aspects to this that we're missing, Rainer, and I think we'd better find out what's really going on, PDQ. Something is goading someone, and that someone is passing it along to Inspector Mercer.

"According to him, Ed Stroh drove over to the house this morning, and parked in the driveway. Of course, the front and back doors had been sealed off by the police, and the police were keeping the house under discrete observation from across the street, in the home of that neighbor, what was his name?" He knew damn well what the name was, but I indulged him.

"Jared Fleuve," I said.

"Yes. Apparently, there has been a uniformed police officer watching the Abernathy house from Mr. Fleuve's front window, and he spotted Ed in the very act of walking up to the front door, then going over to look at the cordoned-off septic tank. The police swarmed, and rather than admit to wasted effort, they have charged our client with murder. Good Lord." With a chip, he scooped up the last of his beans and rice, ate it.

We paid and went to the car. Per Viola's instructions, Uncle Jim's house was only a couple blocks north and one or two west of the lot, but midday Broad Ripple traffic was jammed, and it took us ten minutes to drive there. Schwartz filled me in on the rest of what he'd heard from Mercer, but it didn't really amount to much. "With the right lawyer, he could end up with a tidy sum for false arrest," Schwartz said as I pulled in next to a dark blue TransAm.

The house was a typical Old Broad Ripple single-story crackerbox, blue with white trim and shutters. The porch was going to need replacement in a few years. There was a flagpole with the Stars and Stripes flying above a flag I didn't recognize, yellow with a black double-headed eagle with red claws and beaks. "Holy Roman Empire," Schwartz told me. As I reached for the doorbell, he announced, "I am an idiot." I looked at him, waited. "I just realized why Ed was arrested," he said.

"Please feel free to share your insight at your convenience," I said. I pressed the button. There was no sound I could hear. Schwartz knocked, and in a few moments Viola Ketchum came to the door and let us in.

We went to the entrance to the living room, where we had a view of the fireplace and the gun rack. After some discussion, we'd decided to leave the muzzle loaders in the cabinet at the office, where there was little chance they would wander off.

Schwartz took the Polaroid out of his pocket and compared it to reality as we saw it. Except for the two old rifles that weren't hanging over the fireplace, the scene seemed unchanged from when the picture was taken. He asked Viola where the bathroom was and went there.

The client and I walked through the house, which looked like a house a man had lived in alone. There were books in every room, nothing on the scale of Schwartz's office, of course, but more than you'd probably find in most people's homes. Schwartz joined us in a few minutes, calling my attention to the art on the walls, mostly oil paintings but also a couple of watercolors, and small prints, woodcuts, and engravings, filling in the spaces between the larger pictures.

Schwartz asked Viola, "Do you know if your Uncle Jim kept a photo album? I'd like to see what he looked like. And by the way, how did he die? We neglected to ask initially."

"An album, no," she said. "He tossed the prints in the top drawer of the dresser over there." She went to a chest of drawers in a corner of the living room, to the right and outside the frame of the Polaroid, pulled the drawer out, and went hunting through piles of photographic prints. "Here's a good one of him," she said, "taken last year, at Thanksgiving."

She handed the print to Schwartz, and I recognized the face at the same time he did. I let him say it: "Seamus E."

Well, that explained that. Judging by the expression on Schwartz's face, we felt equally foolish. Both of us had been trying without success to think of a Jim or a James in the Program who had recently died. "Neither of us," Schwartz said, "thought to ask, 'What can "Jim" be short for?' So we kept racking what we are pleased to call our minds for a dead Jim or James. Pfui. On top of the business about Ed's arrest, I should be thinking about hanging it up. Unbelievably dense."

"Well, you know Seamus wasn't much of a talker, after all. I'm not sure I'd have remembered his last initial. I know I'd never heard him mention his last name." It was not easy meeting his eyes.

"No, we'd have remembered Seamus Ellenbogen, all right. Actually, I'm not sure I recall his mentioning the initial more than once. Still, we knew him, and he was often part of the post-meeting fellowship."

It's funny how you get used to strange vocabulary after a while in AA. "Fellowship" isn't all that common in most people's chat, but it's hard to come up with a substitute when you need a word for what we get from AA outside the rooms. Seamus was used to being part of the background. He would come to Starbucks and listen, much as he listened in meetings.

When there was a reading to share, Seamus would take his turn, and he read well, if rather slower than most people when reading aloud. He wasn't one of those guys who try to make it dramatic, nor was he one to read flatly; he read for sense, clearly and distinctly, without jazzing it up. His voice was pleasant enough, but nothing to get excited about.

At Starbucks or IHOP he would be there, but he was never on stage. He would listen, nodding in agreement on occasion, but he seldom said a word that wasn't really necessary. At the same time, we'd known him to take a newcomer aside on occasion, and the two of them would sit at a table across the room, talking, mostly the new guy talking and Seamus listening. Once in a while, he'd put in a word, and often as not you'd see the newcomer nodding emphatically. One thing I'd heard him say more than once was "Everybody in this room knows how I feel. It doesn't matter how we are different; what's important is what we have in common. We all thought we could pour happiness out of a bottle."

"That's where I recognized Ms. Ketchum from," Schwartz said. "We went to his memorial service at the funeral home here in BR. There was a bigger crowd than I had expected."

"Yes, I remember now," I said. "We both spoke with her before the service. What a line that was."

"Yes, you never know who will turn out. I recall her face was very drawn, and it was clear she'd done a lot of crying."

"She looks better now."

All this time, Viola had been trying to appear as if she weren't overhearing our talk, but she said, "I remembered you both from the line, and I was surprised when I came to your office that you didn't remember me. Of course, it was such a different circumstance, you know? Uncle Jim was getting on in years, of course, and he had treated his body pretty badly with alcohol for years, although he died fourteen years sober. He still smoked cigarettes, although he wasn't supposed to. His wife had died years before, you know."

"No, I didn't," Schwartz said.

"When he flipped his car, coming off the interstate too fast, coming back from Chicago. He hit the exit ramp at the split going at least fifty-five, the police said, and the car went off the road and rolled down the slope. He'd been drinking, but someone screwed up the test records, or the tests themselves, and there wasn't enough evidence to convict him. I think the court thought losing his wife was punishment enough."

"Possibly," Schwartz said, "although—"

"He kept on drinking for a dozen years after that," she said. "Then he stopped cold, no fancy detox facility, no spin-dry rehab. He called me up and told me he was going to quit drinking. It was New Year's Eve, and he'd decided to quit, on his own.

"I was afraid he'd get D.T.s, of course. I went to his house, and he agreed to let me stay with him, and I did. Actually, I was surprised that he got through the detox without the really violent, hallucinogenic stuff. He did a lot of sweating and shaking, the tremens part, but if there was delirium, I didn't see it.

"I was living in an apartment south of BR at the time, going to Butler. After the new year began and classes started again, I went to class and brought my books to his house, and at times I'd read aloud from whatever the assigned reading was. Well, that was a memorable time." I got the impression that "fondly" wouldn't be the right word for how she remembered it.

"And how did he die?" Schwartz asked. "I don't recall having been told."

"Heart attack, during the night," she said. "I had talked with him the evening before, and when I called him the next evening, there was no answer. I went over, but I think I really knew what I'd find. I called the EMTs, even though he was dead. The doctor said it must have hit him hard and killed him quick. He just looked asleep lying there, only with no rise and fall of his chest."

"Are you a nurse, Ms. Ketchum?" Schwartz asked.

"No, I'm a graphic designer at Greason & Krohn, Mr. Schwartz. Why do you ask?"

"That's a remarkable achievement, Ms. Ketchum, helping your uncle through his sobering up, and you both survived. It would be remarkable if you were a nurse. It's all the more so, given that you're not. You seem to know the right thing to do, and you do it. I am very glad indeed to have such a person as a client."

"Wouldn't it sweeten the deal if I were wealthy?"

"Of course, but let's not cross bridges prematurely. And Seamus Ellenbogen stayed sober fourteen years. Commendable."

I wasn't sure why Schwartz was taking this tack with Viola. But it wasn't the first time, or the last, that I hadn't understood why he was doing what he was doing. I only hoped he had some idea why we'd spent our morning reading criticism of Alcoholics Anonymous, musings about the distinction between bullshit and horseshit, metaphorically speaking, that incomprehensible stuff about worlds of one, two, and three spatial dimensions, and a long list of what seemed to be random quotes, including eleven from Schwartz himself.

We looked around awhile, but the place was pretty bare of clutter, aside from the books and the art, which Viola said had been done by her Aunt Cynthia, Uncle Jim's wife, who he had killed while driving drunk. She said he had had most of the drawings, prints, and paintings framed after her death, in the years when he was still drinking. There was a noticeable lack of knickknacks, except for the mantelpiece and the shelves to the right of them. That fireplace wall seemed to have been where everything loose ended up.

At a big roll-top desk in the back corner of the living room, we found all the puzzle supplies, neatly isolated from everything else. A shelf above the desk held books, tools, and other impedimenta. A computer on the desk was easily fired up, although it was so old it took a while to work itself to life. Yes, Uncle Jim had gone digital in his puzzle preparation, and it was easy to see how much work the software saved. The glue, paste, pens and so on were dusty with disuse. The pigeonholes and drawers of the desk held folder after folder of puzzle files, pamphlets, booklets, and so on. While the antique computer was warming up, we checked the garage.

There was a workshop area, and it was far less neatly arranged than the Abernathy garage. The tools were hung, laid, placed, left here and there, but we could see that this was where Uncle Jim had done his woodworking and other physical crafts. Schwartz pointed out the strong contrast between the neatness of the house and the clutter of the garage. There was no car there, but the empty space with the oil blob showed where it had been. We went back in the house.

Schwartz and Viola watched as I brought up the four files, sitting in their own private directory, and opened them: all four had been cleaned up, and the spelling was good.

My cell rang. It was Inspector Mercer, wondering where Schwartz was. Of course, since his call to my phone had gone through, he knew where my phone was, and since I'd answered, he knew where I was. I didn't cover the phone when I told Schwartz it was Mercer and would he like to talk to him, and Schwartz said no, that was why he'd turned his phone off in the first place. I told him that Mercer sounded very upset about something and that it might perhaps be advisable to help him find some reason to calm down, perhaps by talking to him.

Schwartz took my phone and wandered off toward the bedroom. Viola and I stood there and made small talk. In only a couple of minutes, Schwartz returned from the bedroom, still talking, and he asked, "By the way, Inspector, may I ask whether your men found a nonstandard hook or spike driven into the wall of the septic tank, a few inches below the opening? They did? Which, a hook or a spike? A hook. I see. Oh, just an inspired guess, I suppose you could—" Apparently, the conversation had ended. He handed me my phone, took his out and turned it back on. "Inspector Mercer is upset, as you put it, because a journalist known to us is planning an article on arbitrary misuse of power by the police force, for example arresting and jailing a person known to be innocent in hopes that the real guilty parties will be lulled into a false sense of security. He suspects that you or I or both of us have set Helen O'Connell on him and the entire IMPD. Imagine that, Rainer: he believes you would be a party to such underhanded doings. He also believes we have the power to set Helen O'Connell on him. I wouldn't undertake to tell Helen what to do about anything."

"Nuts," I said. "I shouldn't say this in front of the client, sir, but I don't want her to think I'm an idiot. That's what you were doing in the bathroom. After you said what you said out on the stoop, I figured it the same way you did. The cops arrested Ed to make the real killers think they were getting away with it. Very convenient for them from a tactical standpoint, if a little rough on Ed. So you called Helen, and I bet you even mentioned civil liberties, and—"

"And she said she bet the cops talked Ed into the whole charade, and he's probably 'incarcerated' in very safe, very well-fed comfort."

"Is Ed really that big a sap?" I asked. "You know him better than I do, after all. Would he actually play along with a plan like that? Two steps above being live bait."

"He might," Schwartz said, "he just might, if he thought he could play the hero when they make a movie of it." He snorted, not respectfully. "I wonder whether the police even bothered asking him if he would participate voluntarily. That's what Helen is really trying to get at. She is not at all interested in a series on shady practices in the IMPD. They had one just last year, and all the wounds have yet to heal."

Viola was trying to follow the discussion. Schwartz told her, "Yes, Ms. Ketchum, this is how Mr. Zufahl and I talk about clients in their absence: honestly and frankly, without hypocritical pretense. I think you should return with us to my office, lest we be tempted to say things about you behind your back."

She was smiling now. "Of course, Mr. Schwartz; I'm in your hands. Didn't you say there was something you wanted to show me?"

Viola drove her own car. On our way back home, Schwartz called Neil Parkinson and asked him to see about Ed Stroh's arrest, and he told him there was another matter they needed to discuss, but it could wait. Ed's case came first. She got to the house first, and she parked off to the side, not blocking the garage door.

Chapter Fifteen

Thursday, April 2

Back in the office, Schwartz offered Viola iced tea and went to get it himself. Viola stood, looking at books on the shelves while we waited. When the tea came, Schwartz played host, and once we were all supplied, he asked me to print four numbered hard copies of the four corrected documents, which he referred to as the Ellenbogen manuscripts, if I could number them without changing the page formatting otherwise. I set the printer to put a large red page number, preceded by the letter F, in the upper right corner of each page. I checked to make sure that left the layout as it had been, and it did. Schwartz and Viola discussed Richard Dawkins's works while I was busy.

That was taken care of, and the pages were printed, and I was ready to rejoin the conversation, when he asked me to print out a similar set of four copies of the four unedited documents. I said I assumed he wanted the page numbers preceded by a P, and he said yes, and I asked if he'd like the P page numbers in blue rather than red, and he said yes, thanked me, and turned back to Viola.

I had no idea what he was up to, but that's never new, so I printed out a few dozen more pages and staggered the four sets for Schwartz. Just for grins, I put Post-It notes on the top of each of the four first pages of the articles, if that's what they were. Schwartz used the heavy-duty desk stapler to bind a set of F copies and a set of P copies for each of us, and he handed me the extra F and P sets and asked me to put them in the safe. I complied, laying the stacks on the shelf, with the two thumb drives on top of them.

"So," Schwartz said, "we each have an F set and a P set of the Ellenbogen manuscripts, one with typos and one edited. Ms. Ketchum, I suggest that you read your sets of the documents—"

"All right," she said, "although I don't really see the point of all this, to be honest."

Schwartz said, "Your Uncle Jim, or Seamus Ellenbogen, left ten thousand dollars each to your cousins, whom he had not seen in, I believe, four years. He left you an enigmatic list of initials and a photograph, which led us to examine the antique rifles over the fireplace—"

"You know," I said, "I don't think they're really antiques at all; I think they're reproductions of—"

"Of course, you're right; I stand corrected." He sighed. "Which led us to examine the muzzle-loading reproduction rifles over the fireplace and find two thumb drives hidden in their patch boxes.

"I find it difficult to believe that Seamus left the one relative who had stayed in close contact with him, who looked after him without imposing unwanted restrictions on him, with nothing but a bad joke. I think, Ms. Ketchum, that these documents have meaning, and I intend to figure it out. Mr. Zufahl and I have read these, shall we say, very individualistic documents, without, I believe, a glimmer of a clue...." He looked at me.

"Without a shadow of a glimmer," I admitted, to both of them.

"It seems to me," Schwartz went on, "only fair to let you, Ms. Ketcchum, the client and the presumed beneficiary of Seamus's will, have a crack at the puzzle yourself. Neither Mr. Zufahl nor I have any desire to dazzle you with specious miracles; we are not magicians. So, if you will, take these documents, which Rainer has helpfully numbered F1–F53 and P1–P53, and see what you can make of them. You knew your Uncle Jim much better than we knew Seamus Ellenbogen, and it seems to me quite likely that you might recognize some item of information that would mean nothing to us."

"I suppose that's possible," the client and presumed beneficiary said, "in the same sense that it's possible that you'll start calling me Viola rather than

Ms. Ketchum." She smiled, judging by her eyes. "Of course, I'll read them, if you think it's a good idea. Should I start right now?"

"Not necessarily," he said. "But at your leisure, please go through them carefully, aware that a puzzle-maker like your uncle might use any item that would be meaningful to you and him but not to outsiders, such as Mr.—" His eyes smiled too. "Such as Rainer or myself, Viola. We will certainly do our best, but when trying to unravel a conundrum like this, it would be preposterous not to include the one person who knew the conundrum-maker best.

"There is, however, one formality that would help us a great deal," he said. He fished out a sheet from a labeled folder and handed it to her. "If you would read this over and sign it and date it, please. It authorizes the bearer to act as your representative in regard to the investigation of your inheritance."

She gave it a quick run-through, then used her purse to back up the sheet while she signed and dated it and handed it back to Schwartz. "Is there anything else?" she asked.

"Yes," he said, "would you get in touch with Mr. Parkinson?" He handed her a memo outlining what he wanted. He had clearly been busy while I was running routine errands.

"Certainly," the client said.

"Thank you."

"So I'll just take the uncorrected document home with me and have a good close read," she said.

"Yes, please."

"Can I leave by the front door this time?"

Schwartz laughed. "Of course. Rainer?"

I escorted her out, watched her drive off in the blue TransAm. I couldn't think of a single good reason for what had just transpired. That stuff about it being only fair to include the client was really laying it on pretty thick, when I considered all the times he had kept me in the dark just for the hell of it. And the business about authorizing someone, apparently not Schwartz or me, to act as her representative left me completely at a loss. Before she left I had told the client we'd be in touch if there were any developments, and she said she'd let us know if she got any sudden insights from her reading.

I went back to the office, half-expecting Schwartz to be engrossed in the Ellenbogen manuscripts, but he was reading Dawkins. I told him I'd like to tear myself away from the reading and check in with the other client who was still at large, Iris Warner. He nodded, and I left him there, slaving away.

I called Iris to make sure she was at home and in a position to receive a visitor, and she was. She sounded pretty tense, which wasn't surprising, since she'd lost a sister-in-law, or a former sister-in-law yesterday. I said I'd be right over if that was all right, and she said it was.

The drive took less than five minutes, and I parked next to her Corvette. She met me at the front door, invited me in, and we headed back toward the patio. She was wearing bleached jeans and a dark gray blouse, with navy deck shoes. When we reached the back of the house, she stood in the doorway for a moment, and I saw that she was trembling, all over, a really bad case of shakes.

She got it stopped, then turned to me and said, "If I'm responsible for getting Ilona killed, tell me straight. I had to find out what was worrying Buck, and I had to send you there, undercover. If I'd just left things alone, she would still be alive, and I wouldn't be—"

She was crying now, and the shakes were back, and I was afraid they'd turn into something else, something worse. I reached out for her arm, and suddenly she was pressed against me, hard, and I put my arms around her, held her tight as the sobs came. She was letting it all out now, and it took a while, but after a few minutes, the sounds trailed off, and the shaking stopped, and we were standing there holding each other close, and I brushed her hair with my face, wondering how to get out of this clinch with the client, and then we let go of each other at the same time, stepped back from each other just a bit.

Iris took my handkerchief and used it to good effect, stuck it in her pocket. She smiled ruefully, gestured toward the chairs on the patio and the table set with iced tea. We went onto the patio but didn't sit down yet. "Thanks, Rainer," she said. "I don't know what I'd have done if—"

I interrupted. "Iris, I'm certain your inquiry into your former husband's difficulties had nothing to do with Ilona's death. You can forget that right now. It happened, but it's not your fault. Under the circumstances I think I can tell you what she and I discussed when I went to her home." I poured tea for her and for myself while she made apologetic sounds.

"The fact is Ilona was being blackmailed. Or rather, she said she was being threatened with blackmail. Now, if you were to go to the police with what I'm about to tell you, it could put me and Mr. Schwartz in a lot of trouble, since we have withheld certain information, certain evidence, that we consider irrelevant to solving her murder." I paused, looked at her straight. "You realize, I hope, that I'm trusting you, because I'm convinced you had nothing to do with Ilona's killing. God help me if I'm wrong, but if I'm wrong I need to be in a different line of work. Street sweeper maybe."

"Mr. Schwartz and I frequently disagree about matters great and small, but there's one thing we definitely see the same way. Blackmail is one of the nastiest crimes there is. It's cold-blooded, cruel, and calculating. It's always deliberate. There's no such thing as blackmail committed in the heat of the moment.

"We will do anything we can to get a blackmailer, but the tricky part is always bringing a blackmailer to justice without exposing the victim as well. For whatever reason, when I spoke to Ilona about your problem, and we discussed my going undercover to learn what it was that Buck was stewing over, she decided to trust us with her own problem. She gave me the letter from the blackmailer and the envelope it came in. We have those items in the office safe right now, and they are going to stay there as long as necessary.

"But the thing is, we've lied to the police about that. I told a police inspector and a detective sergeant that Ilona had told me someone had written to her, threatening to expose her secret. I even told him, in very general terms, what her secret amounted to. I really had no choice about that. But I didn't tell them we had the letter and envelopes. I said Ilona had told me she'd destroyed them, shredded them, and burned the shreds.

"It's been pretty hectic lately, and we are working two other cases, but we intend to try to identify the source of the stationery, which was not your garden-variety, buy-anywhere stock." There was no reason to be more definite than that about the paper. "Tracing the printer is probably hopeless, although it might be possible to verify what machine was used if we had the machine, but we don't and almost certainly never will have."

I shut up. Iris said, "I didn't know about the blackmail, but I think I know what secret she was being blackmailed over. Was it that sex club she and Andrew belonged to?"

Well, well. So Ilona's secret was anything but. "So you know about that," I said.

"Yes, I did. When Andrew got sick, I tried to help out, giving Ilona a break once in a while, and he and I talked, and she and I talked, and the odd thing about it was that for both of them, it was as if they were discussing someone else they'd known once upon a time. I think Andrew knew, deep down, how serious his illness was, and he wanted to get it all off his chest. I hadn't been all that close to Ilona before that, but caring for Andrew brought us together somehow.

"It scarcely seemed real to me, to be perfectly honest. They told me about the arrangements and all that, but it just didn't seem to me like something either of them, much less both of them, would be involved with, you know? It wasn't like them, if you know what I mean." She took a tissue from the box on the table, blew her nose again.

"All right," I said, "you knew about the club, but you didn't know Ilona had gotten a letter. I think that may help explain why she was willing to ask me for help. Psychologically she was drafting behind your investigation, just a minor add-on."

"You have an easy face to trust," Iris said.

"So do all successful con artists."

"And I can see why Ilona thought tagging along on my case would be safer than—" Her voice broke.

"Easy there," I said. "It wasn't your fault, and it wasn't hers either. Except for putting her correspondence in the safe, we had done exactly nothing about the blackmail, and I'd spent only one day at WarnerCorp, so I'd feel pretty doubtful about assuming anything I did, which is only, by extension, something you did, caused her murder.

"Despite what you'd think from books, movies, and TV, private detectives do not investigate murders, Iris. The police are in charge of the case, and I'd be surprised if it took them very long to come up with a suspect." I thought it unnecessary to mention Ed Stroh at this point. "They are really very good at investigating this sort of crime, and let's be honest, they don't tend to give up easily on a high-profile case like this one."

"You mean when a rich person is murdered?" Iris looked faintly offended.

"I'm not saying that's a requirement, you understand, but it sure doesn't scare them off. You know as well as I do that some people are more equal than others. In this case, it means it's very likely that justice will be done for Ilona; her murderer will almost certainly be caught.

"However, and I feel a bit guilty for mentioning this—" I wished I hadn't said 'guilty'. "—we've made very little progress on the original purpose of the investigation. We don't know what has been bothering your ex-husband."

"Surely that can wait," she said.

"Well, we're not investigating the murder, so I'll discuss it with Mr. Schwartz. But I do have to ask you whether you want us to continue." I felt how thin the limb was that I was crawling out on. How likely was it, after all, that there was no significant connection between Buck's problem and Ilona's murder?

"Oh, of course," she said. "Of course, you have to ask that." She looked at the wadded tissue in her hands. "Yes, please. Please find out what's going on with Buck."

I stayed a little longer, to make sure she was completely on her feet. After a little while, I said goodbye and drove back home.

Chapter Sixteen

Thursday, April 2–Friday, April 3

When I got back to the office, Schwartz had called it a night. I finished locking up and called it a night myself.

The next morning he was in the office, and there was a cup of coffee waiting on my desk when I came down. He had his copy of the Ellenbogen manuscripts on his desk, and he was noting things with a red pen in the margin. We said good morning, and I tackled the mail. At least he was doing something connected to the case, which was a nice change.

About ten, the land line rang, and Schwartz answered it himself. "Hello," he said. "Oh, Mr. Parkinson, yes…. Yes, of course there's no bail for murder, but can't it be argued that in this case there's insufficient…. Yes, I see." They talked a while longer, but that was all there was about Ed Stroh. I would report the rest of Schwartz's end of the conversation, but then he said, "Mais certainement," and continued from there en français much faster than I could keep up with, as if it would have helped much, had he slowed down. They talked in French for another ten or twelve minutes, until Schwartz said something I could understand: "Au revoir," and he hung up.

Damned if I'd give him the satisfaction of asking. I brought him the one invoice and two other letters, laid them on his desk, and went back to my copy of the Ellenbogen articles, reading slowly. A couple times, I thought I was onto some code, some connection from one article to another, but it never seemed to pan out. I finally decided that I was following trails of breadcrumbs left by Seamus Ellenbogen's style; all four pieces, even the quotations collection, seemed to have been written by the same person, not that there was any reason to think otherwise, so there were resemblances and reflections that meant no more than identity of authorship.

At one point in that rather pointless morning, Schwartz asked if I'd noticed any misquotations in the collection. "You mean aside from where he's quoting, or maybe paraphrasing you?" I said.

"Aside from that, yes," he said. "For example, the quotation from *Penrod*, that chapter opening, is wrong. I looked it up, and the book reads 'and one of them is that he has taken to drink', whereas Ellenbogen has 'and the other one is that he has taken to drink', which I happen to think is funnier than the original, but it's not accurate.

"There are other lapses like that, here and there. I could go to the public library for a while to check as many as I can find, but there seems to be no real point to it."

"That implies that any report from memory must be—"

"There's a difference between a verbatim report of a conversation by a person who has been rigorously trained to record every word and nuance, on the one hand, and an ordinary person's recollection of a passage they've read. Harmless and not-so-harmless variations creep in.

"And there are authorial variations as well. To take an example that Seamus did not quote, Walt Whitman was constantly revising and reworking *Leaves of Grass* from original publication until he died. There were seven or eight editions published during his lifetime, I believe, and he made significant changes in every one of them, and sometimes he put in, sometimes he took out, and sometimes he put back in or took back out. So, if you were quoting from *Leaves of Grass,* not that you would do so, Rainer, which edition would you want to quote from?"

"The last one published in his lifetime, I suppose," I said.

"Perhaps. Unless what you really wanted to quote was something that existed only in an earlier edition."

"Do you really think it's something so subtle?"

"I doubt it, frankly," he said. "Seamus E. was a puzzler, not really a serious scholar. That business about so-and-so being 'an independent scholar,' i.e., a scholar without an academic affiliation, is all well and good if the scholar in question can make a living on their writings or whatever, but most of the time it just means so-and-so is a bad-tempered, irascible, pain-in-the-ass bastard.

"Somewhere or other, Edward Shils, I think it was, points out that the history of the twentieth century would have been very different if Karl Marx had been a more easy-going, collegial fellow who could have gotten an academic appointment, where he'd have had colleagues to talk with, and one of them might have pointed out flaws in his theory.

"Hey, Karl," Schwartz said, "I have been reading your latest article in the *Rheinische Zeitung,* and I think you've got this backwards: pearls aren't valuable because men dive for them; men dive for them because they are valuable. Frankly, Karl, your surplus-value theory is all just Italian sausage of a large caliber and mild flavor."

I smiled in spite of myself. "Baloney," I said. He really shouldn't be encouraged, but at times I can't help it.

"There are still some interesting questions to ask about the manuscripts," Schwartz said, back to reality. "You noticed that the uncorrected and the corrected versions had the same date and time in the log."

"Well, yes, I did. But that was actually the date and time at last saves, and there were minor differences in the times."

"Right, and in each case, the save times are within a minute of each other, and they alternate. 'What's Wrong with AA' was saved corrected about thirty seconds after it was saved uncorrected."

"Which makes sense," I said.

"Yes, so it seems to make less sense than 'On Horseshit,' and I'm getting tired of that title, to tell you the honest to God truth, was saved corrected about half a minute *before* being saved uncorrected."

"What?"

"Yes, but when we look at 'The End of All Things,' it was saved uncorrected, then corrected a half minute later, like 'What's Wrong with AA.' But again, 'Miscellaneous Detritus' was saved, corrected, then uncorrected. What does that suggest to you?"

"Not a lot," I said. "Maybe that the corrected versions were all done earlier, and the save times we have represent just when our copies were made, that is, when the files were saved to the thumb drives." I thought about it. "But that's not the way people do things, in the real world, I mean. You don't keep an old version around after you've fixed what's wrong with it. At least I don't."

"Neither do I, and I fail to see why anyone would do so, if they were correcting a faulty file in the usual way.

"Another question for us to ask ourselves," he went on, "is why we were presented with both the edited and the unedited versions. Why did Seamus make and hide two different versions on two separate thumb drives? I have the unpleasant feeling that we're overlooking something vital, something so obvious we can't see it."

"A sort of purloined letter," I said.

"Exactly. I suspect Seamus has hidden something in plain sight, and it's so big and clear and obvious that we're looking right through it."

If I'd known at that moment that he had already managed to focus on the invisible "obvious" clue, I'd probably have gone looking for a septic tank to put his body in, but fortunately, as it turned out, I didn't. I turned back to the screen, promising myself that I would grasp that bullshit-horseshit distinction before I was done, but I was less confident about the physics in that third piece.

"And why are the articles listed in that order?" Schwartz asked, rhetorically, I assumed. Wrong again, Zufahl, but I didn't know it then.

We heard nothing from the police or anyone else connected with the cases that day, although there were a couple other calls, one from a sponsee of Schwartz's who was having a bad day, which seemed to me a good time to take a walk, which I did, and one from a fellow pyrotechnicist who wanted to make dragon's eggs and wondered if Schwartz had any extra bismuth trioxide or bismuth subcarbonate he'd be willing to sell, and of course, he had and would. They talked a while about quantity and price, and Schwartz asked me to check the chemical-supplies list for both, since he would have had to turn on his laptop to do it himself.

Finally, they came to an agreement, which I could have predicted, since I knew Schwartz had bought a large batch of both, far more than he needed, and Carlson, the guy who wanted to buy some, said he'd be over within the hour. I knew I wouldn't be needed, since Schwartz likes to show off the neatly stocked shelves in the gazebo, but I went out to make sure there was a stepladder conveniently available, since alphabetical order puts the bismuth compounds up high, after the barium and before the calcium compounds. It was okay, and I went back to trying to make sense of the Ellenbogen stuff.

I had covered a dozen sheets of note paper with unsuccessful attempts at connections between passages by the time dinner loomed. Carlson had come, had been given the tour of Schwartz's pyro summerhouse, and had doubtless been suitably impressed. Schwartz admitted when I asked that he'd just given Carlson a pound of each bismuth chemical, and I suspected he'd also given him a pound or so of unwanted and unneeded advice as well, so Carlson had paid, if not in cash.

At seven o'clock, Schwartz said he'd been thinking about fried chicken all afternoon and asked if I'd object to Hollyhock Hill for dinner. Since it's only a few minutes away and since it's so good it ruins you for the fast-food kind, I said it was fine with me, so we spent a pleasant hour and a half with the best fried chicken in town, not to mention salad with oil and vinegar dressing, hot rolls, mashed potatoes, gravy, green beans, whole-kernel corn, and vanilla ice cream with the choice of chocolate, butterscotch, and mint syrup. Schwartz always goes with the mint, and I joined him that time, although I'm usually partial to butterscotch.

The conversation at dinner was completely off the topic of murder, blackmail, and torture, thankfully. At the time, I wasn't actually all that thankful, but in retrospect, it was clear that I'd simply been standing too close to the manuscripts.

"Etymology is interesting, sometimes in unexpected ways," Schwartz began. "Take the word *clock,* for instance. You know that a lot of people think 'Big Ben' is the name of that big clock in London. (Never mind that some people apparently think that the tall structure that houses Big Ben is the Tower of London. We probably can't help them.) Of course that's just an example of the common confusion, or confounding, of clocks and bells. Once mechanical timekeepers had become familiar, it was easy to muddle the distinction between the thing that kept the time and the thing that announced it. Big Ben is a bell, but plenty of folks think of the clock rather than the bell as 'Big Ben,' and it's hard to see what harm that does.

"The German word *Glocke* means 'bell,' as you, of course, know, and it's related to the English word *clock,* and English speakers probably see or hear it most often in 'glockenspiel', not that that's relevant here. What is relevant is that the word *clock* is related to the word *cloak,* not from any functional connection, but from the visual resemblance that a person wearing a full-length, all-around cape has to a tall, cylindrical bell. So once upon a time, the same word referred to a timekeeper or to a bell, and that word, with some change over time, also came to refer to a garment. You see that the causal connection is visual, not linguistic; it's the effect, not the cause, that has to do with language."

"Could you pass the gravy, sir?" I contributed.

"Certainly," he said.

"Thank you."

"You're welcome. In English translations of Aristotle's *Metaphysics,* books 6 and 7, aka Zeta and Eta, there is a lot of bewildering blather about essence and so on, made no clearer by a discussion of a cloak made of bronze. The bewilderment isn't, for the most part, at least, Aristotle's fault, but rather than of dimwitted translators, in my not particularly scholarly opinion. If one gives it a bit of thought, one is faced with two choices. Either one believes, on the one hand, that one of the greatest thinkers the world has ever known thought it made sense to make clothes out of metal, and we're not talking about armor here; we're discussing protection against wind and weather, or, on the other hand, that the same thing happened in ancient Greek that happened centuries later in English. Unless Aristotle was a knuckle-dragging moron, he's talking about a bell made of bronze, not a cloak.

"The consensus among Greek scholars, since apparently no form of the word used in the sense of 'bell' has survived the centuries, is a monument to resistance to common sense, not to mention any other kind not preserved in manuscripts and books. Ask a scholar of ancient Greek about this, and you'll get blown off with some vague bushwa to the effect that, 'well, Aristotle did this all the time.' Ask for examples, and the expert will adduce beds made of wood and men colored white. The problem is, of course, that even today, bed frames are commonly made of wood, and it's still not unusual to refer to persons with beige, buff, or tan skin as 'white,' even though 'pale' or even 'pink' would make a lot more sense. Just as we refer to persons of primarily or even partially African descent as 'black' even though their skin is brown, so we refer to those of European descent as 'white' even though their skin is merely a lighter shade than other people's.

"Even with a heaping helping of anachronism, introducing plate or mail armor a few centuries before it historically appeared, 'bronze cloak' makes absolutely no sense, and 'bronze bell' is attested physically as well as linguistically. The resistance to sense is nothing new, and certainly nothing to brag about in a species that likes to call itself *Homo sapiens.*"

Schwartz went on in this vein through the end of dinner, but it had no more to do with any of our cases than the fried chicken did.

We had no AA meeting on our schedule that evening, so we hadn't missed anything by going out to eat, but when we returned home, we found Viola waiting on the front stoop.

Schwartz got out to let her in the front door while I put the car in the garage, and I went to join them in the office. They weren't there, but I heard voices from the kitchen. Viola was sitting on the stool while Schwartz brewed tea. The kettle was on, and the cups and saucers were out, and he was scooping black pekoe and other ingredients into a muslin drawstring bag. "Trying Iris's iced-tea recipe hot?" I contributed.

"Exactly," Schwartz said, as if he were getting ready to discover the secret of eternal youth. The kettle whistled, and he poured boiling water into a distinctly unwarmed teapot, holding the string carefully outside the pot. He let it steep, lifting the bag a few times and dipping it back in, to get the water flowing around and through the tea. When he decided the tea was dark enough or something, he pulled the bag out, let it drain into the teapot awhile, then scooped it up with a spare saucer. He put the teapot on the tray with the mugs and carried the tray to the office. I thought it odd he'd chosen mugs rather than cups and saucers.

When we were all seated, and we had our tea, he asked Viola what he could do for her. She said, "You'll think I'm crazy, Mr. Schwartz, but I went back to Uncle Jim's house this afternoon, and I went through his desk thoroughly. I couldn't get over the feeling that there was a clue we'd overlooked. We found the files on his computer corresponding to the files on the thumb drives, as you know. But I looked around and found a compressed file called ms." She pronounced it em-ess.

"I opened it up, and it was the same four files that are on the thumb drives, all run together as a single file. But it wasn't the edited file; it was the unedited version, with the spelling mistakes left in."

"Of course it was," Schwartz said, trying to keep the smugness out of his voice and off his face. "When we found the drives and the files on them, the question that seemed to present itself was this: Why did your Uncle Jim leave both versions, fair and foul as they used to say in the book business, for us to find?

"The only answer I could think of was that he wanted us to compare the two versions. No other explanation seems to me to cover all the facts as we have them. Mr.—" He coughed gently. "Rainer ran a file-comparison program on the contents of the two thumb drives that made it clear that one set was correctly spelled and one set was replete with misspellings.

"Now, the next question was a bit less obvious, and I doubt that it occurred to you. It certainly doesn't seem to have occurred to Rainer, who is a trained investigator." Schwartz looked my way, inviting comment.

"Sorry, sir, but I'm as in the dark as anyone, waiting for enlightenment." The trick with him is to keep the sarcasm ostensibly civil. "I'd greatly appreciate any light you can throw on the problem."

"As I thought," he said, returning to the client. "It's getting ahead of things a bit, but I had a phone call this morning from our trusted attorney, Mr. Neil Parkinson. He was calling from Switzerland. It was late afternoon his time. He called to report on one case we are involved with, which an associate of his is handling perfectly adequately, since nothing can be done. In that case, another client of mine has been arrested on a murder charge that will never stand up, since he can be proven to have nothing to do with the crime, but knowing the depth of my concern for a client, any client, Mr. Parkinson wished to report on the situation, which is at least no worse than it was.

"However, the main reason for his call was to report that my deductions about your Uncle Jim's files were correct." Schwartz sat back a bit, his back straight. The office suddenly was very quiet. "Ms. Ketchum, your uncle left you a Polaroid photo and a list of initials that led to the thumb drives that contained files that conveyed a message that led to my dispatching Mr. Parkinson to Switzerland."

"What? To Switzerland?" Viola almost dropped her tea.

"As I am sure you know, Swiss banking includes a system of unnumbered bank accounts, the security—and the anonymity—of which is unrivaled. This security comes at a cost, as those have learned who have attempted to track down Nazi loot that was deposited in the second quarter of the last century, in order to restore property to its rightful owners."

I admit I was staring at Schwartz. So was Viola. So would you have been, if I hadn't already handed it to you so you could figure it out for yourself. You're welcome, by the way. I could have gone on and on about our clever analysis of the documents, and you'd just have had to take my word for it.

By now, of course, you're all caught up, but remember that you were given the thing without interference from the Buck Warner investigation, the Ilona Marchand blackmail and murder, and the Abernathy case.

Schwartz went on, "Armed with the appropriate credentials, Mr. Parkinson went to the bank your uncle told you about—"

"But my uncle never—" Viola gestured with her empty mug.

Schwartz's voice rose a bit. He'd played nice about her guessing *Top Gun,* but if you make a habit of letting clients get away with that sort of thing, you'll have to put up with it forever. "Your uncle gave you the clues to the files, and the files conveyed a message, and the message is why I sent Mr.

Parkinson to Switzerland."

Schwartz was enjoying himself immensely, of course. He had pulled off that conversation with Neil Parkinson as casually as if he were still in his office downtown, and Ed Stroh's incarceration was all they had to talk about, and they'd switched to French purely out of boredom. I had to hand it to him; I'd watched him make that notation on his pad with no more show of excitement than if he'd been writing down an address or a phone number. Well, as they say, merde.

Schwartz went on, "Ms. Ketchum, Viola, the message from your uncle sent Mr. Parkinson as your representative, through me, to Geneva, to the Swiss Private Bank of Industry, and to an account with a safe-deposit box that contains at least—"

He picked up that notepad and read, "—that contains at least €18,955,452 and change. A shade under twenty-three million dollars."

Viola's mug hit the carpet, bounced without breaking.

Chapter Seventeen

Saturday, April 4

The next morning, Saturday, with the usual chores taken care of, I was transcribing some pages from my notebook. It had been a while since we'd had so many cases, supposedly, but since Iris Warner's curiosity about her former husband and her former sister-in-law's blackmail had been turned into a police case by Ilona's murder, that lightened the load, from a legal standpoint anyway, but the notes needed transcription. And since Ed Stroh's missing persons case had turned into a double murder, which again was now police business, not ours, we were pretty free to concentrate on Viola Ketchum's bequest. She had calmed down after Schwartz explained that, in all likelihood, she'd end up with just some fraction of the twenty-three million, almost certainly not all of it. Still, it would have to be a pretty small fraction to be trivial.

Neil Parkinson had called early this morning, later in the day for him in Geneva, and he and Schwartz had at least kept it in English. Schwartz asked me to listen in, so I did, without contributing to the discussion. It seemed Schwartz was done pulling rabbits out of hats, at least with that case. Parkinson reported on two meetings, one with Interpol and the Swiss Private Bank of Industry and one just with the bank, which apparently had involved higher officials. He said that, since the bank account had been opened only twelve years before, whereas it was believed that the money had been illicitly acquired, not by the account holder, over thirty years ago, the interval was sufficient to keep things relatively calm with the financial and the criminal authorities, especially given our assurances of full cooperation with the authorities and solid proof that we had no connection with the perpetrators of the original crime. There was direct evidence to connect the money in the bank with the robbery of an armored car in Chicago, Parkinson said, after a conversation with the Chicago police, the FBI, the U.S. Treasury Department, and Interpol, it was clear that was where the loot had come from in the first place. Everyone at Parkinson's end of the conversation was very grateful to Mr. Schwartz for helping shed light on, et cetera, and so forth.

Parkinson reported that most of the safe-deposit box, a large one, had been taken up by twelve thousand one-thousand-dollar bills, in bundles four and a half inches thick. Atop this stash was a large envelope containing negotiable securities with a face value amounting to something over eleven million dollars, or about nine million euros.

After he and Parkinson had hung up, Schwartz talked about how effectively single or multiple removes could sanitize the proceeds of a crime. "Even one intermediate step can work wonders," he said. "Removing the connection, or merely hiding it from view, lets bygones be bygones, except, of course, for the plundered victim. If Mr. Parkinson's understanding of the matter is at all correct, the money had already lost its taint before it reached Seamus Ellenbogen's hands. By the way, we'd best get moving."

Schwartz continued the discussion on our way to Ilona's funeral at Flanner and Buchanan in Broad Ripple.

"Once Mr. Parkinson had the contents of the Swiss bank's safe-deposit box, he was able to send sample numbers from the cash and securities to the appropriate authorities, and of course, that got immediate results. The cash consisted of bundles of thousand-dollar bills destined to be returned to the U.S. Treasury, decades after denominations over one hundred dollars were discontinued in 1969. It's not clear why so long a period had passed, but that's the information we have now. The securities, of course, bonds, and so on, were much more compact. How the thieves intended to profit from such identifiable bills, I can't imagine."

"Maybe they weren't financial geniuses," I offered. Arriving at the funeral home, I found a full parking lot, and we had to walk quite a ways, with supplemental seating in a side room, almost SRO. The service was simple and restrained, and the casket was closed. The minister, who had known Ilona as a neighbor but not as a parishioner, recounted conversations they had had over the years, and in conclusion, he explained that Ilona's written instructions specified that, if any of her family or friends wished to share personal reminiscences, they should save them for later rather than inflict them on a captive audience. Schwartz wasn't the only person who had to try to stifle a laugh. We joined the long line of cars in the procession to Crown Hill. After the burial service, Schwartz and I waited in the long line of people who wanted to express condolences to Ilona's family. As he said, you always feel better after doing the right thing.

On the way home, Schwartz picked up the discussion. "I think," he said, "I'd like to know how Uncle Jim came to have his hands on the loot in the first place. And I truly hope I'm not the only one who wonders how it is that we're facing money problems in each and every case.

"Iris Warner is worried about her former husband's mental state and its effect on the financial health of the company, not that she put it so bluntly. It's more tactful to be concerned about what outside thing is bothering him than to ask what exactly is going on inside his head. And it's more acceptable to ask for help for him than to ask for help keeping WarnerCorp healthy. Have you ever seen a company rely so thoroughly on momentum, in terms of product? Yet they seem to take customer service far more seriously than is usual today. They haven't farmed it out to the Indian Subcontinent or Latin America; the customer has a phone number and an email address and even—in this day and age, mirabile dictu—a street address to turn to for help. Unless your report was completely subjective, Rainer, your interviews with the people at WarnerCorp were frequently interrupted by outside calls, which invariably received real, personal attention from those truly familiar with the software and hardware. That's unique in my experience, at least since the mid-80s. The lesson here is so obvious we can't help seeing it.

"The people who killed Eugene and Lawrence Abernathy were after something, and it wasn't cherished family heirlooms. It was something that could be hidden in that abandoned septic tank and retrieved when needed. You don't torture and murder people like them for the fun of it; you want information about something financially substantial and yet readily portable. Something that fits through a thirteen-inch round opening. I think that's worth some deeper investigation, and I think we should have a wider look at their known associates, friends, family, everyone, and that, of course, includes Ed Stroh. By the way, surely by now, the police are beginning to realize that arresting Ed was a mistake. The ploy of flushing out the killers has not worked, so far as we know. It was reckless and irresponsible to try it in the first place. I want to know more about the Abernathys and their house and grounds. By this time, the police will have examined every inch of the property, and I'm reasonably sure we'd have heard if they'd found anything.

"And the one case we've put on the back burner, ever since it became moot with her murder, the question of who was blackmailing Ilona Marchand, or trying to do so. We think we have the substance of the blackmail, but we have no idea of who was applying the pressure. We can forget about finding traces of the printer, but that stationery is worth looking into.

"Call Paul, Frank, and Sonny, and ask them to come today, as soon as feasible."

"Yes, sir. Should I tell them what this is in reference to?"

"No, I'll take care of that. Now, back to Ilona Marchand. She was married to Ms. Warner's brother, who died, correct? Having outlived him, she then married Mr. Marchand, who has also since died, I believe. Ms. Marchand seems to have been extraordinarily unlucky in that respect."

"Yes, sir. I'd ask her about that if she were still available," I said. "Marchand had a heart attack about three months ago, as I reported to you, a messy situation, involving a hotel room and a woman, not Ms. Marchand."

"How deplorable," Schwartz said. I could see that he was handling the shock just fine. For a private detective, that's a professional danger, becoming inured to the moral failings of your fellow beings. "You might inquire discreetly among your contacts as to how thoroughly the matter was hushed up. Is there idle gossip about the late Mr. Marchand, or has the family been successful at closeting the skeleton? You know how to go about that. And call back at the City-County Building about the Abernathy house, and find out what you can about Seamus Ellenbogen's life, liberty, and property, too."

"Yes, sir," I said.

"And I think I will give Inspector Mercer a call as well, to ask about Ed Stroh," Schwartz said. "And we'll see what else comes floating to the surface once we're talking. You never know what such an impetuous man may say or do. He's an interesting person, after all, and he consciously tries to avoid becoming a cliché, which is interesting in itself."

Schwartz could call Mercer impetuous if he wanted to, but it always seemed to me that he reacted to Schwartz rather predictably. He didn't trust him, but he couldn't explain why, since Schwartz was so far off the charts that he couldn't be placed in any of the usual convenient pigeonholes.

As it turned out, Schwartz didn't need to call Mercer. The doorbell rang, and there was the Inspector and Sergeant Ripley at the front door. They came in, and even acknowledged my greeting, so it was going to be a friendly meeting, at least at the start. Mercer took the red leather chair as always, and Ripley stood by the door. Schwartz offered them refreshment, and they accepted, and when I'd passed the glasses, we were like one big happy family.

"You ought to know," Mercer began, affably, "that Ed Stroh is being turned loose, thanks to a lawyer you hired, even though Stroh was in custody purely voluntarily. In fact, he was ... well, it doesn't matter now. He's free, and I expect you'll hear from him pretty soon."

Schwartz was playing his part too. "That's very gratifying, Inspector. As you know, Mr. Williams is a member of Mr. Parkinson's firm, and I enlisted his help in freeing my client. Thank you for letting me know his efforts were successful."

Mercer said, "You'll be interested to know the M.E. has made progress on the remains taken from the septic tank."

"Indeed," Schwartz said. We could have been discussing the weather.

"First of all, yes, the bodies were those of Eugene Abernathy and Lawrence Abernathy. Ed Stroh identified them from the heads, which was no pleasure for him, but he did okay. Second, from cuts and stab wounds, totaling—" He turned to Steve Ripley. "How many was it, Steve?"

Ripley consulted his pocket notebook. "Seventy-five on Eugene Abernathy that they're sure of, and ninety-three on Lawrence, that they're sure of, although the dismemberment may have concealed some pre-mortem wounds."

"From the wounds inflicted prior to death, yes, both of them were tortured. There were ligature marks on the wrists and ankles, and one still had a couple feet of clothesline-type cord around an ankle. This was a really nasty one, Schwartz."

Schwartz nodded. "And they were finished off with their throats cut, I believe, which caused the splashes?"

"Right. God knows how long the bastards worked on them."

"And we believe neither Eugene nor Lawrence knew anything about what the killers wanted." Mercer nodded agreement.

"You might also be interested in some other developments at the Abernathy house," he continued.

"I would appreciate any information you might share with me," Schwartz said. Butter wouldn't melt.

"We went over the place, and you know we know how to do that. One of the men had the idea that there might be some sort of hiding place, so we measured every room up and down, side to side, and there isn't a cubic inch unaccounted for. There's no secret rooms in that house, we're certain."

"Commendable," Schwartz commented. "A possibility has been eliminated."

"Yeah," Mercer said. "Then we went over to the outside of the house, and one of the boys, a fellow named—" He stopped.

"Ralston," Steve Ripley supplied the name.

"Yeah, Ralston, brighter than average, noticed something. If you recall, the back yard had one of those arbor things, with vines growing on it, and a well-built brick barbecue grill, and everything was built to last forever.

Except, as Ralston pointed out, the deck at the end of the patio. It was pretty old, and in very bad shape. It was made of one-by-sixes, ordinary untreated lumber, not painted or stained or sealed, and some of the boards were partly sprung, and a couple were actually broken."

"Yes, Mr. Zufahl mentioned the run-down deck, and I saw it. It did not, in fact, seem to be of the same quality of workmanship as its surroundings. So this deck provoked thought, Inspector?"

"It did, and under the circumstances, since we'd taken two bodies out of the septic tank in neatly wrapped hunks, it seemed worthwhile to have a look at the deck. It was in such bad shape that taking it out would be doing the owner a favor. We asked Ed Stroh's permission, anyway—"

"Is Mr. Stroh legally empowered to grant permission?"

"So far as we can tell," Mercer said, "he will inherit the house, but anyway, for this, he's close enough. As I said, the deck was in bad enough shape that tearing it down was an improvement. Most of the boards split when the boys got the crowbars on them—"

"You used crowbars?" Schwartz seemed surprised.

"Sure," Mercer said. "The boards weren't screwed down; they were nailed. Like I say, it wasn't much of a deck in the first place, and it was all but falling apart. It had to be twenty, twenty-five years old, easy. Anyway, they got the deck torn up, and we brought a dog in, and he was very interested, and about four feet down, we found the skeleton of a man, with rotted clothes, change, a Timex wristwatch, a pair of glasses, and a wallet that had almost completely rotted away."

"Very interesting indeed," Schwartz said. "Did the wallet contain any identification?"

"No, it didn't, as a matter of fact. It wasn't in the hip pocket of the pants, but was on the other side, at the front of the body, which was lying on its right side. So far, the experts are estimating that the body is that of a man at least fifty years old, and it's been in the ground about twenty years, minimum. It could be longer."

Schwartz said nothing. He waited for Mercer to continue. Mercer drank tea, set his glass down on the coaster, reached for a Salem Gold 100 that wasn't there, and nodded. "Well, the forensics team is going over the body now, but I was wondering whether you have any suggestions who he might be."

Schwartz nodded in acknowledgment of the invitation to participate in the investigation. No matter what you've read in detective fiction, in the real world, this just doesn't happen every day. Schwartz was also acknowledging the trust Mercer was showing him, knowing that he wouldn't be calling up Helen O'Connell to give her a story. He sighed, then said, "I have no idea, but I think the answer might lie at the City-County Building. A short time ago, I asked Mr. Zufahl to go to investigate the ownership of that house and lot, as I am sure has occurred to you as well."

"Yeah," Mercer said, "we're looking into it." His hand started for his breast pocket again, but he caught it and picked up his iced tea instead. "This is really good," he said, and I poured him and Ripley and Schwartz, and myself a fill-up.

"I could speculate," Schwartz said, "but that would almost certainly be pointless. It might be the previous owner of the house. It might also—" He drank tea. "—be one of the gang who captured an armored truck in Chicago about thirty years ago. I'm sure you remember the case, Inspector.

"One June day, an armored car, or rather truck, was captured by a gang of four men wearing uniforms of the same company, who arrived in a stolen car just as the legitimate crew had taken on a shipment intended for the U.S. Treasury. The guards were overpowered with teargas, two of them being blasted outside the truck, and the two inside the truck were forced outside."

"Yeah, I remember. The perpetrators blasted a hole through the bullet-proof glass with a single round of armor-piercing fifty-cal, ran a hose in, and gassed them really heavily. They didn't really have a choice. In fact, that's what led to the overall redesign of armored cars afterward." Cops have long memories. "Two of the perps disabled the four gassed guards, then all four drove off in the armored car."

"The truck was found in a disused warehouse in Whiting, Indiana, two days later, with the four phony uniforms all that was left of its cargo. Almost twenty million dollars in used cash, along with a considerable sum in bearer bonds and other securities, had been taken. A sizable sum in readily traceable cash was left in the truck.

"The investigation, as usual, relied to a great extent on informants, and one of the gang, who claimed that he had been assured there would be no violence, got a reduced sentence for his testimony against the other perpetrators, but he did not live out his sentence. How he was killed in a federal prison was never made public, but you know as well as I do that many things happen in prisons that are never reported in embarrassing detail. Somehow someone got to the informer, and he was found hanging in his cell only a few months after entering it. It's hard to understand how a person in that position could imagine he would survive after betraying his fellows."

"You got that right," Mercer said. "Sure, I remember the case. The thing was, the perps were identified, and the trial was straightforward, but the loot was never found. There was something really strange about what was stolen, I think. God knows they looked, and no doubt the usual pressure was exerted, but nada." He drank iced tea. "I'm sure you won't be shocked to learn that not all implied promises made to suspects are necessarily kept. Some conversations out of the earshot of lawyers, for example, or things that nobody ever got around to putting down on paper, well—"

"Indeed," Schwartz said. "It's not particularly shocking, no. I may already have suspected as much in fact." He shook his head sadly, no doubt at human perfidy.

"I suggest," he went on, "that the real brains behind the operation never came near the courtroom, much less prison. In all likelihood, the betrayal of the gang who performed the actual theft was part of the plan from the beginning. You don't have to posit a Napoleon of crime to know that those who plan crimes are often adept at keeping their hands clean."

"Of course. Anybody smart enough to avoid getting mixed up in crime realizes that patsies are often useful, and once the loose ends have been tied up, the real criminal, the mastermind of the operation, rakes in the proceeds while the fall guys rot in prison, or worse."

"I'd like to know more about the previous ownership of that house,

Inspector, but I would guess, if I were given to guessing, that the body your men have just found is that of a loose end. I hope Officer Ralston's perspicacity receives the recognition it deserves."

"He'll be gunning for your job one day, Inspector," Ripley put in.

"He can have it any time he wants it," Mercer said like he meant it.

"I would also like to know," Schwartz went on, "whether the men who were convicted of the theft are still in prison or whether, as I suspect, they may have served out their sentences and have been released."

"Steve?" Mercer said. It wasn't a question, but Mercer made it sound like one. Ripley was already dialing as he stepped out into the hall. "Is there anything else you'd like to know?" Mercer asked Schwartz, more pleasantly than one might have expected.

Schwartz said, "There are countless things I would like to know, Inspector, but it would be pointless to pester you about them."

Mercer drained his glass and set it down. "That's damn good tea," he said, getting to his feet. He paused at the door. "We'll get back to you about those bastards," he said. "Much obliged for the tea."

I followed them to the front door, and Ripley, still on the phone, even told me to have a good day as they left. I was touched, sort of.

When I returned to the office, Schwartz failed to surprise me when he said, "If you would, go ahead and ask Paul, Frank, and Sonny to come in. We shouldn't wait for the police to supply our deficiencies."

I cleared the tea things, ran water into the glasses, then went to my desk to have someplace to sit while I called the help. When that was done, Schwartz did surprise me.

"Thanks," he said. "Now, while the men are here tomorrow, I would like you to run a very important errand for me." At first, I thought he just wanted me out of the way while he readied the troops, but as he explained the instructions he was planning to give them, and what he wanted me to do, I caught on.

Chapter Eighteen

Tuesday, April 7

Three days later, exactly nothing further had transpired with the WarnerCorp case, so far as we'd heard from the police or anyone else. I'd started to phone Iris half a dozen times, but each time the thought of pumping the client for information about the case made me stop. You have to maintain some standards, after all.

At five-thirty Tuesday afternoon, Viola was in Schwartz's office with Schwartz and me and Neil Parkinson, who had gotten back from Geneva the day before. As the client, Viola rated the red leather chair, so I'd brought in one of the deep yellow armchairs from the front room and put it to the left of Schwartz's desk.

Parkinson is one of those lawyers who cultivate an old-fashioned courtliness. Unlike a lot of other people's manners, his aren't put on for the occasion; so far as I've been able to tell, they go all the way to the bone. Schwartz introduced him to Viola and, of course, vice versa, adding, "who, as you know, has been working for you for about a week now."

Viola shook hands with Parkinson and said, "A fact for which I am very grateful, Mr. Parkinson." Schwartz's formality isn't universally contagious, but with Viola, it seemed to be catching.

"Neil, please," Parkinson said, holding on to her hand a second or two longer than absolutely necessary. He's never married; as he says, he's never met the lucky woman, but it's certainly not for lack of looking. He may be the most eligible bachelor on the north side of town. Viola didn't appear to mind his hand at all. Those piercing blue eyes, black hair with a touch of gray at the temples, and that tall, lean frame were impressive. And it was far from the first time I'd met him. I silently wished her luck.

Parkinson had, as a matter of course, submitted a written report, emailed to Schwartz with a copy to me the previous evening, and we'd read it. Schwartz being Schwartz, he asked Parkinson for an oral report—he hates 'verbal' for 'oral' since any use of words is verbal, and Parkinson being Parkinson, he obliged, addressing Viola throughout, since she hadn't received a word in writing.

"As Mr. Schwartz has explained, Ms. Ketchum—"

"Oh, Viola, please," she said.

"Yes, of course. As Mr. Schwartz has explained, Viola, the Bank Suisse Privée de l-Industrie account, and the associated safe-deposit box together contain well over eighteen million Euros, although that may well be a considerable underestimate, because some of the securities in the box are not included in that total."

"You mean to say it's *more?*"

"Oh, definitely," he said. He didn't reach out and pat her knee, but he could have.

"Good Lord," she said. Something had suddenly cleaned up her language.

"Indeed. I wouldn't want to be held accountable for it, but if I were hazarding a wild guess, I'd say the final tally might well come to over twenty million."

"Twenty million dollars?" She looked at Schwartz. "But last Friday, I thought you told me—"

"Twenty million Euros, or about twenty-four million dollars," Neil said to Viola.

As a matter of fact, we learned about a month later that it came to just over twenty-one million Euros, north of twenty-five million dollars. But we didn't know that that evening, so there was still a considerable air of the unreal about those sums.

Schwartz asked Parkinson about the meetings with the bank people and with Interpol.

He smiled and said, "You know, they're used to dealing with much greater sums of money, but they're not used to American lawyers showing up after a couple phone calls. The first meeting, on Tuesday morning, was, shall we say, quite tentative, while they did their own checking of my bona fides and the origin and history of the account. I'd have to say it was done quite efficiently.

"By Wednesday afternoon, when we met for the second time, they were ready to lay their cards on the table. As you surmised, Mr. Schwartz, the number was actually two numbers."

"Yes, and for that, I am culpable," Schwartz said. "When I checked the document's 'errors,' I overlooked an omitted space. What's worse, it was caught by Mr. Zufahl's file-comparison program, and I missed it there. To be perfectly frank, I didn't overlook it; I dismissed it as an error on Seamus Ellenbogen's part.

"Of course, I underestimated Uncle Jim," he told Viola before turning back to Parkinson. "The space separated the bank-account number from the number of the safe-deposit box."

"Well, it was a fortunate mistake, at that," the lawyer said. "It gave the people at the bank something to clear up, and psychologically it helped. And, of course, it helped that Interpol was present and involved in the discussion. Otherwise, they'd have had very little to do to justify their existence."

"A problem shared by many of us at times," Schwartz said. "So the bankers clarified the numbers."

"Yes, and that went smoothly enough. Seamus Ellenbogen opened the account in person twelve years ago last October, and he obtained the safe-deposit box at the same time. He visited the box on that occasion and according to the bank's records, never returned. The bank account was interest-bearing, of course, and aside from the interest accrual, the only other activity was the annual charge to the account for the box. Nothing was added or subtracted otherwise.

"Regular reports were sent by the bank to Mr. Ellenbogen, and when the bank sent the usual suggestions to make the reports paperless, he agreed, so the reports from then on were emailed to him. He never contacted the bank about anything, and the box stayed as it was, and the account grew slowly."

"And Ms. Ketchum's title to the account and the contents of the box?" Schwartz asked.

"Well, as you know, the number is the crucial matter when it comes to Swiss bank accounts, and with the will and other documentation, since both the account and the box belonged to Seamus Ellenbogen, there really was no difficulty.

"Of course, it helped that I wasn't there to empty the account and box, but merely to establish Ms. Ketchum's claim to them."

"Just so," Schwartz said. He turned to the client. "You'll forgive my formality, Ms. Ketchum," he said with a smile, "with a client whose wealth so greatly exceeds my own. I hope events as reported so far have met with your approval."

"Good Lord, yes," Viola said. "But from what you've said, that money isn't really mine at all."

"You're quite correct," Schwartz said. "However, while it doesn't belong to you, it is de facto in your possession. Mr. Parkinson?"

Parkinson seemed glad Schwartz wasn't trying to speak for him. God knows he can do that perfectly well himself. He smiled. "It's really perfectly clear, which isn't as common in wills as it should be. The late Mr. Talbot did an admirable job of drawing up the will, heading off ambiguities very effectively. Mr. Ellenbogen states that he is leaving the stated sums to his other, listed relatives and the institutions mentioned, and he says that, aside from those specifically mentioned sums, he is leaving you, Viola, the envelope and its contents, and all worldly goods in his possession, including but not limited to what the envelope and its contents may lead you to. He goes on to state that any and all of his worldly goods not specifically mentioned are left to you.

"So, for example, you own his house, which is free and clear. He had lived there for fifteen years, and he paid off the mortgage within three years of taking possession, which is interesting timing in itself, isn't it, Mr. Schwartz?"

"It certainly is, Mr. Parkinson." Schwartz leaned back in his chair, looking up, his right forefinger tracing a circle on the arm of the chair. I could tell Viola was, if anything, more lost than I was. God knows what understanding Schwartz and Parkinson had come to, but it wasn't for me to make her feel left out.

"That just means he's thinking," I told her. "It may not look like it, but he's working hard on your case."

Viola nodded, probably just to let me know she appreciated being included in the discussion. Parkinson let Schwartz go on thinking for a minute, then he cleared his throat.

Schwartz looked mildly startled. "Yes," he said. "You also met with Interpol, I believe."

"Indeed I did," Parkinson said. "I made the appointment at the same time I called the bank, and I think it helped smooth things at Bank Suisse Privee de l'Industrie that I was able to inform them at the start that I would be meeting with Interpol and, of course, also the Swiss federal officials later in the week. I'm sure the bankers would have been happy to arrange the meetings, but they would perhaps have been less cordial under those circumstances than they, in fact, were.

"Frankly, my experience, previously and in this case, puts the lie to the common view of the Swiss as cold and grasping. I can't imagine where people get such an idea. It's like any other generalization about an entire nation." I was wondering where this was coming from. "Everyone was very helpful, in every way. The Interpol people have begun their investigation, and they've already reported that conversations with the Chicago police and the feds—our feds, I mean—have made it almost certain that Seamus Ellenbogen's deposits in Switzerland are entirely proceeds from the Chicago National Bank job thirty years ago. The cash amounts jibe fairly well, and of course, once they trace the bonds and other securities, it will confirm—or disconfirm, if that's the case, but I doubt it—that the Ellenbogen fortune is the haul from Chicago National.

"God knows where the perpetrators are," Parkinson summed up. "Long gone, no doubt."

"That may, in fact, not be the case," Schwartz said.

"Really?" Parkinson said.

"They had, in fact, been here in Indianapolis, searching for their loot. If you recall, the perpetrators were originally captured as they tried to leave; in fact, they were physically taken off a plane that was about to depart for Atlanta."

"Yes, I remember now. There was quite a scuffle when the agents arrested the men on the plane, and a couple of passengers were slightly injured, if I recall correctly."

"Exactly. One of the newspaper accounts compared it to a scene from a B movie: plainclothes police officers and federal marshals cuffing the criminals and physically dragging them from their seats, in some cases right over innocent passengers, guns pointed at the perps, all that sort of thing. One for the books."

"Or the movies," Schwartz said. "At any rate, it was a colorful capture, and fortunately, no innocent bystanders were seriously harmed. The general belief was that the thieves had hidden the loot somewhere here in town, but nothing was ever found.

"For a couple of days now, I have had three men busy searching for some specific connection between the men who stole an armored car in Chicago and someone or someplace in Indianapolis. So far, nothing has turned up, but we persevere."

"Well," Parkinson said, "I certainly wish you luck with that. However, Ms. Ketchum, I don't believe it will be necessary to find the perpetrators in order to establish your title to the Swiss funds. There is a great deal of paperwork, of course, and that's one reason I'm involved. Please rest assured I'll do my best to expedite the process."

If I'm a competent observer, Viola was ready to trust Neil Parkinson with anything and everything. It was fascinating to watch and listen. Parkinson wasn't operating in that sense at all; he was just being himself, and the shining armor wasn't necessary at all. Viola was in emotional free-fall. Of course, it isn't every week of your life you find out there's a few million dollars sitting in a Swiss bank's vaults, in your name, and you probably won't have to give quite all of it back.

"You know," she said, "I have no idea what to do with the money." She looked from Parkinson to Schwartz to me. None of us came up with a suggestion. I was busy keeping my face blank.

"Fortunately," Schwartz said, "that's not a decision you have to make at the moment, Ms. Ketchum." She didn't ask to be called Viola. The money had hit her hard, no doubt about it. "And as Mr. Parkinson has said, it's not at all clear at present how much of it, if indeed any, will finally be yours. So I would advise against castles in the air."

"Castles?"

"Fantastic plans incapable of realization."

"Don't get your hopes up," I translated.

"Oh, of course," Viola said. She turned to Parkinson. "You must think I'm being really silly about this."

"Not at all, Ms. Ketchum," he assured her.

"Furthermore," Schwartz said, "I advise you, in the strongest terms possible, not to return to your uncle's house if at all possible. In fact, I would like to ask you to leave the key with us. If you must go there for some reason, please call me or Mr. Zufahl, and he or I or both of us will accompany you there."

"You think it would be dangerous?"

"I am sure of it. The criminals responsible for theft and murder want the money they consider theirs, which they could not find in their chosen hiding place. Your uncle found it, somehow, and if they manage to discover that, they might look for it in his house. I wouldn't want you in their hands for any reason. So—if you please—avoid the house in Broad Ripple."

There was more discussion, but nothing worth worrying about, Viola handed me the key and took my handwritten receipt for it, and neither Schwartz nor I was surprised when Parkinson offered to drop Viola off on his way home, and they left together.

I came back from letting them out, and I said to Schwartz, "Jazz Kitchen or Yat's?"

"Your choices for dinner? I thought we could—"

"No, I mean Parkinson and the client. Or do you think he'll suggest something fancier, maybe Ambrosia or—"

"You, Rainer, are an incorrigible matchmaker. You are an incurable romantic, and you project your feelings about people onto them, which only leads to disappointment when they fail to behave as you think they should. You should recall the definition of 'expectations': 'resentments under construction.'"

"Yes, sir," I said in my most earnest voice. "But I have eyes and ears, and they were all working fine this evening. Parkinson has them too, and I could tell he was appreciative of some of the finer qualities of our client, and the same could be said of her. I wouldn't be at all surprised if she turned out to be the one he's been looking for, not at all."

"Nevertheless," Schwartz said, "she is currently sitting on a fortune, and even if most of it devolves to its rightful owner, a ten-percent reward for restoring it would still be a decent amount. Neil Parkinson is too much the gentleman, in the original, not the corrupted modern sense, to stoop to fortune-hunting."

"Oh, for heaven's sake. He wouldn't give a fat rat's ass about the money, and in his sleep, he could write up a legal document to ensure it stays hers; you know that as well as I do. God, you'd have to be blind and, excuse the expression, deaf not to have noticed the, what's the word I want? Between them," I finished lamely.

"Of course, there was attraction between them," he said.

"That wasn't the word I was looking for."

"Our client is an attractive woman," he said, "and Mr. Parkinson is by no means immune to the charms of attractive women, and he is himself handsome, well-mannered, and possessed of a charm of his own. But I would still advise you to keep your expectations to a minimum. If you want my further advice—"

"I don't, really."

"Be that as it may, I have noticed that you yourself are not immune to the attractions of Ms. Ketchum and, while we're discussing your feelings, the attractions of Ms. Warner as well."

"Oh, for God's sake," I said, "Viola is looking at, what do you suppose, two or three million smackers, at least before the tax man gets his cut, and Iris is already in the financial stratosphere. I'd have to be an idiot to think about either of them that way."

"Being an idiot is not beyond the reach of many of us," Schwartz pointed out. He glanced at the clock over the door. "Speaking of which, we can just make the meeting at Orchard Park if we get a move on. I don't know about you, but I could certainly use a meeting. Shall we?"

I thought for about half a second. "Sure. God knows I need one. I'll drive."

"I'll call the men on the way," Schwartz said. "I'll ask them to come at ten."

We headed out for Orchard Park Presbyterian Church in Carmel. Iris wasn't present at the meeting, not that that was our concern.

Chapter Nineteen

Wednesday, April 8

Paul, Frank, and Sonny showed up promptly, as always, at ten the next morning. Schwartz hadn't seen them for a while, and he asked each of them how they were. "Of course, we're merely following where the police have already trod," Schwartz said, "but since they're holding their cards close, we have to do what we can. Have you turned up anything new and interesting?"

Paul spoke first, as usual. "Well, we have a list of the Chicago heist perps, with notes, and as you said, the survivors were released three weeks ago. There were four men involved that we know about, although I think the police were right about there being a ringleader who remains unknown."

"Professor Moriarty," Frank put in. He laughed to show he was kidding. Sonny snickered. Paul smiled.

"Pfui," Schwartz said. "It's not news to any of us that many crimes are organized by persons who remain in the background, with minimal risk to themselves, and who have no compunction about tying off loose ends as necessary."

"Well, one loose end was Keiran Furnish, thirty-one at the time of the heist," Paul said. He spelled the first name. "He's the one who got the reduced sentence by ratting on his partners, not that it worked out for him in the end."

"It's enough to make you think criminals aren't too bright," Frank said.

"If he thought being in a different prison from the others would keep him safe, he was mistaken. I don't believe that hanging was suicide."

"Neither do I," Schwartz said, "and neither does anyone else."

"The others," Paul said, "were Evan Blessing, twenty-six when they pulled the job, Richard Medsker, twenty-seven at the time, and Terence Reynolds, thirty-four." He spelled names. "Reynolds died in prison about nine years ago, apparently of pneumonia that went undiagnosed until it was too late. The autopsy notes are not terribly thorough or complete, but it seems the prison medical staff, such as it was, maybe is, thought it was flu and prescribed accordingly, and by the time Reynolds was sick enough to catch their attention, it was too late. He died three days after he was transferred to the prison hospital ward. If it had been caught earlier, he might well have survived. Or not. The documentation is sketchy, to put it mildly.

"Blessing and Medsker served their thirty years, no time off for good behavior, no add-ons either. They weren't model prisoners or serious problem ones either, just a couple of run-of-the-mill cons. They were released three weeks ago last Friday."

"And then?" Schwartz asked.

"And then they walked out of official sight. No one has seen or heard of them since."

"Thirty years is a long time. Did either Blessing or Medsker have family? Friends? Enemies?"

"Frank can address that," Paul said.

Frank nodded. "I've been through the public records till hell won't have it, Mr. Schwartz, and it looks to me like we're high and dry. Neither of them was married at the time of the heist; Blessing was single and apparently liked it that way, and Medsker had been divorced two years. So far as I've found, there were no kids. I tracked down his ex-wife, who had remarried and divorced again, and has now been married for the third time for going on eleven years. She would just as soon not have to think or talk about Medsker at all, and she's doing pretty well at it."

"Parents? Other family?"

"No, sir, not living, for either Medsker or Blessing. No known associates of either one still alive and available. In fact, Furnish and Reynolds were almost the only names that I found in connection to either of the two surviving perps, aside from Medsker's ex."

"Her information is in your report?" Schwartz asked. He knew it was unnecessary, but it was part of the dance with Frank.

"Yes, sir. Venetia Siebert now." He spelled it. "It was Venetia Ferguson until she and Arnold Ferguson split after two years. She's fifty-three now, and they live in Chapel Hill, North Carolina. Her husband, Bernard Siebert, teaches—"

"I think we can explore that path later, if necessary." Schwartz frowned, not at Frank, but at the prospect of hard work. "What do we know about Blessing's and Medsker's movements after they were released?"

"Virtually nothing," Paul said, "which is odd. They were on the street in Joliet, and they took a bus to Chicago, and the trail ends cold at the Chicago bus terminal." He looked almost as unhappy as Schwartz. "However, Sonny has found something interesting, actually more than something." He turned to Sonny, who needn't be as diffident as he habitually is, but there's something about the walls of books in Schwartz's office that intimidates him.

"Yes, sir," Sonny said. "I went to the records office, and they helped a lot with the research. It was like they'd been waiting for years for someone to show interest. Anyway, the Abernathy house was bought by Eugene Abernathy eleven years ago, when it was put up for sale by the owner, Seamus Ellenbogen." He pronounced the name see-muss.

"Jesus H. Christ," Schwartz said. He involuntarily checked for Josh's presence, was reassured, and relaxed. "Seamus Ellenbogen owned the house and sold it to Eugene Abernathy. Good Lord."

Sonny was glad to have made a hit. "Yes, sir, he did, and he did. You asked for any possible connections, and I thought this one was—"

"Excellent, Sonny," Schwartz said. He leaned back, looked up at the ceiling. The four of us waited while he mulled over the blockbuster. I wondered how Sonny had managed to wait his turn, with a hand like this to play. Sonny doesn't have an inferiority complex, or any other kind of complex, it seems to me, but he sure underestimates himself sometimes. Even most times. I've heard him express misgivings about why Schwartz hires him. Granted, any of us could have turned up that information, but Sonny had done it.

"Very nice," Schwartz went on, to Sonny. "Seamus sold Eugene the house eleven years ago. How long had Seamus owned it?"

Sonny was a bit embarrassed by Schwartz's reaction to his news. "Well, he bought it fifteen years before, when the bank repossessed it when the mortgage payments stopped, and the property taxes hadn't been paid for a couple years, more or less. The previous owner had died intestate, you know, without a will, and there was no family that would inherit. So—"

"Who was the previous owner?" Schwartz was patient. He knew Sonny well enough to understand how he was dealing with the distinction of bringing the turkey to the table.

"That was a Mrs. Janet Jonson, no *h,* who died, aged sixty, of cancer, and left no will or anything to say who the house would go to." Sonny clearly felt the anti-climax. "She had owned the place for...." He checked his notes. "For thirteen years, inherited it from her parents, who died—"

"This takes us back well before the Chicago job," Schwartz pointed out, "by about a decade. I think we can rest easy about her parents."

"Yes, sir."

"Is there any connection between Ms. Jonson and the four perpetrators?"

"Not that I've found," Sonny said.

Schwartz surveyed the crew. Paul and Frank shook their heads. "Well, I have to think there must be something, however tenuous, that connects her to Furnish, Reynolds, Blessing, or Medsker. She owned the house when the armored car was stolen and robbed."

He leaned forward. "You know how to go about this, of course. The object is clear: some link between the very late Janet Jonson and any or all of the four—" He caught himself. "Nonsense. Between her and any one of the four. It would be fruitless to try for multiple connections when we have yet to discover a single one. Go to it, and divide your efforts as you yourselves see fit."

He tapped his desk blotter with a forefinger. "This is really excellent. We now know that Seamus Ellenbogen owned the house, and it's virtually certain that at some point, he came across the haul from the armored-car job. I hadn't been so sanguine as to expect so much, and now we need more: some link between any one of the original thieves to Ms. Jonson. Gentlemen, you have your assignment. May your efforts be crowned with success." He gets effusive in a good mood. You could almost see Sonny filing away "tenuous" and "sanguine" for future reference, along with how to pronounce Seamus. Frank wouldn't bother, and Paul didn't need to. "That's good news," Schwartz summed up, and I had to agree with him on that score. Sonny had brought home a huge slab of bacon indeed.

After a few more amenities, the men departed. Schwartz leaned back, searching the ceiling for further leads, and I kept busy with a bit of housekeeping, transcribing notes.

"Rainer," he said suddenly, "perhaps you might want to touch base with Ms. Warner about her case. It's been a while since we turned our attention in that way."

"Sure, boss," I said. "I don't suppose you'd like me to help out the boys in tracing Ms. Jonson to the bank robbers?"

"Not at all. If there is a connection, and there must be, they—or one of them—will find it. They are quite competent to follow that trail." He turned a hand over. "Somehow, the Chicago loot got to the Jonson house, which we now refer to as the Abernathy house, in fact, almost certainly got into the septic tank to await later retrieval. How, we have no idea. How Seamus found it, we don't know, but it's morally certain that he did, whether we can prove it or not, and we don't have to. Would you mind getting iced tea?"

"No problem."

When that emergency had been attended to, he went on. "Call Ms. Warner and arrange to meet her, here or at her house or at some neutral location. If that leads to another conversation with Buck Warner, that could be helpful. Her original questions about his concerns can hardly have been allayed by events. Find out what her real interest—" He brought his fist down on the desk, emphatically but not particularly violently. "Do I need to tell you how to proceed? Of course not; I'm losing it. Only *to* proceed. Please do so as soon as possible." He picked up the Dawkins book.

I gave it some thought, then went to the back yard, where the sun was shining with spring promise rather than the usual drizzle that time of year. No reason to disturb Schwartz's reading with my conversation. Of course, he was concerned about Iris, but not only about her. I called Iris and asked if she would be interested in a cup of coffee and some of the best pastry in town, at the Hellas Cafe. Of course, she would, and could she pick me up on the way? Sure. I met her out by the street, climbed into the Corvette, and we headed over to College, up to 86th, over to Westfield Boulevard, and down to the Hellas.

Half an hour later, we were finishing our baklava and starting a second cup of Turkish coffee. The Hellas was ecumenical, since the owners, Demetrios and Suleyia Andropolos, had originally come from Cyprus. He was born Greek, and she was born Turkish, and they were both American and glad of it. In Cyprus, they would have had a harder time than most married couples, since most married couples' families do not consider their in-laws fair game, literally. Iris said, "I could eat every meal here for the rest of my life, which wouldn't be long, because I'd finish every one with baklava, and that would finish me."

I refrained from personal remarks about how many pounds she could afford to put on before it bothered me or anyone else. "They do a great tiramisu, too," I said. Neither of us knew how soon the Hellas would be just a memory, just one among many victims of the pandemic.

Iris nodded agreement, gave a small stretch. "Now, I don't really think this meeting is about dessert or coffee, and I doubt you're terribly worried about my sobriety. Not that you're unconcerned, of course. What's eating you?" She was giving me a direct stare that was supposed to see all the way into my mind.

"Well, it's interesting that you put it that way," I said. "We all seem to have something eating us about what's eating someone else. I'm concerned about your concern about your former husband's concerns, and you're concerned about my concern about—"

Iris reached out and put a finger on my lips. "I'm still worried about Buck, but the approach we tried got derailed by Ilona's murder, and I forgot to mention, we were touched that you and Mr. Schwartz attended the funeral."

"Of course," I said, "although I'm surprised we were noticed, given the size of the crowd. Ilona was very well loved, wasn't she?"

"She will be a real loss to many people," Iris said. "She was so good to so many who needed someone to stand up for them."

"Yes, and it wasn't just a duty for her, was it? She was really personally, actively engaged in so many worthwhile causes, and my impression is that it was always a human thing with her. She really engaged with people on a fundamental level."

"Absolutely." Iris stirred the cup of thick black near-liquid coffee, then drank it off in one swallow.

"So why was she killed?" I asked myself and her. "I'm sure the police have been treading lightly, since that's the way they tread in a case like this, but they've been treading plenty, and we've hardly heard a peep from you. As you know, we don't investigate murders, since the police are sensitive about interference, which is what they call help from private eyes. But from our standpoint, the silence has been deafening.

"Look, Iris, I'll lay it out for you. We've got a couple other cases on hand, but one of them is a missing persons that turned out to be a double murder, so we have to watch very carefully where we put our feet down. But, as I shared with you after she was killed, Ilona had asked me, in effect Mr. Schwartz and me, to look into a blackmail threat. It concerned that sex club we discussed. You knew about it, and you knew both your brother and your sister-in-law participated. Tell me, did Ernest know about it?"

I watched her face. No matter how much experience teaches us otherwise, we still believe that somehow a person's facial expression will betray a lie. I know adults who step over cracks in the sidewalk and check their daily horoscope. We know better, but we just can't help ourselves.

"I don't know," she said, "but I suspect he did. He and I weren't particularly close, but Ilona, bless her soul, was a great one for honesty. It always seemed strange to me that she and Andrew belonged to a group like that

that depended so much on discretion.

"Don't misunderstand me: Ilona could be discreet, and she was when it mattered. But it wasn't her default mode. I doubt she ever mentioned the club to anyone else who wasn't a member, and by the time they told me, it was in their past. Andrew was sick, and that was that. It was over. But I can believe she told Ernest about it, before they were married. She wouldn't have saved it. If she told him, it was up front."

"But someone thought she would submit to blackmail over it," I said.

"Well, yes, but only because the scandal, if you want to call it that, would reflect on her work with various good causes. It's illogical, of course, since we assume that people have sex lives, but even a perfectly legal but unconventional activity like that could blight her association with any or all of those causes. It's not a matter of legality or—"

"Of course, I get it," I said. "And so far, we have no idea who was trying to put the screws to her. She gave me the letter and envelope, but so far, we haven't—"

Iris laughed incongruously, given the topic of conversation. She saw my expression and tried to stop, then she just let it out, then said, "He didn't tell you?" She shook her head. "I swear to God, I couldn't work for that man."

"What man?"

"Leo, you idiot," she said, and she laughed again, shortly. "Remember when I was at your office, talking with you and Leo, and you went to get the tea? While you were out of the room, he got the stationery, the letter, and the envelope from the safe and showed them to me, and he asked if I'd ever seen paper like this. Of course, I had, and I told him so. It's my stationery, Rainer, and it's Ilona's too. And he hasn't told you. Good God. If we're as sick as our secrets, Leo Schwartz needs a trip to the doctor. I can't believe he didn't tell you, except that I can definitely imagine that Leo would keep that from you merely because he could."

I could definitely imagine Schwartz deciding not to burden me with such information. It wouldn't be the first time, heaven knows, that he has withheld something from me just for the pure hell of it.

I admit I was a bit emphatic about the matter, but I got calmed down. It was nothing new, and it probably wouldn't be the last time, either. "Come to think of it," I said, "using the victim's own stationery is interesting. It limits our suspects to those who had access to Ilona's house."

"Or to mine," Iris said, "or to either of our offices, so there's at least a dozen possibilities. I know I keep a box in my desk, and Ilona did as well. Our birthdays are both in May, and a couple years ago, we both happened to give each other the identical set of stationery as birthday presents. Everybody in the family knew about it, it seems such a joke. You know, formal writing papers in the age of email, texting, Facebook, Twitter, and all that. Fortunate in a way that we didn't give each other goose quills and iron-gall ink horns."

"I don't know about 'fortunate,'" I said.

"Well, it does limit the suspects to those who knew," she said. "Plus anyone else who shopped at Bartleby's."

"The pen shop at Keystone at the Crossing?"

"Yes. They have an incredible selection of writing materials, tools, papers, all that stuff, for the half dozen people in central Indiana who can still write cursive. It's something of an anomaly, after all, people sending formal correspondence in this century."

"But who—"

"Exactly," she said. "Who indeed?"

"Do the police seem to have a suspect in mind?"

"If they have, they aren't sharing with me."

"With me, either." I thought about it a moment, came up dry. Nothing. "Now," I said, "about Buck...."

"Before we go back to that," Iris said, "have you spoken with Brandon, Ilona, and Andrew's son?"

"I haven't, but I intend to."

"You should, but be careful. He comes off as cool and collected, even cold, and he was eerily calm at the funeral."

"I noticed," I said. I had. Even from where we'd sat, I'd seen him greeting people, paying their respects as calmly as if it were a garden party, and they were discussing how nice the flowers looked. He was a year out of Brown, and he looked young, strong, and arrogant. I had reminded myself that college athletes might not be my favorite people, and perhaps I needed to make allowances. Sure.

"Underneath, in my opinion," Iris said, "he's very insecure, and he tries to keep up a front. I don't think he's half the tower of strength he tries to pretend to be."

"I'll bear that in mind when I talk with him." I gave her a direct look, held it a moment. "Now, about your concern about Buck...."

Chapter Twenty

Wednesday, April 8

I discussed with Schwartz my upcoming interview with Brandon Wilson, son of Andrew Wilson and Ilona Wilson, later Marchand, after I had reported on my rather sketchy talk with Iris about the young man. Schwartz just gave me the usual instruction to use intelligence guided by experience. I didn't have much recent experience with fellows like Brandon, but I can't say I particularly regretted the fact.

"The truth is," Schwartz said, "you're making assumptions about him, and that can lead you astray as easily in one direction as another. Iris Warner is his aunt, and she has good judgment, all things considered. Let him talk as much as possible, and try to keep your own prejudices—if any—under control."

"Certainly," I said. "I admit that some people rub me the wrong way, so I'll—"

"Rainer," he said, "the worst mistake we can make is to assume that we don't make assumptions. Of course, we do. Being human, we have inherited quick thinking, the ability to size up situations and people quickly, from our ancestors, who were the people who were good enough at quick thinking to live to procreate.

"The problem, of course, is that our quick thinking relies on our ability to classify, to judge others by their apparent characteristics. That means, among other things, it relies on prejudgments based on externals, appearances, group memberships. It's not only one of the bases for our survival in a hostile world, it's also the basis for racism, sexism, ageism, religious bigotry, homophobia, and all the other things we really have no use for in today's world. As the man said, 'Nobody likes rich people', but you've known enough rich people to understand that judging people by economic status makes no more sense than doing so by race, gender, color, or ZIP code. And poverty is no guarantee of virtue."

"Sure," I said. He's at his most irritating when he's right. I've noticed that that's true of lots of people, which probably says more about me than about them.

I called and made an appointment with Brandon. He suggested we meet at five o'clock at the Admiral's Head, an upscale bar north of the Marion-Hamilton County line, that is, in Carmel. It's upscale in the sense that there's no television tuned to Sports Center, or anything else. I drove up Meridian to the turnoff to 106th Street, then took Pennsylvania north a few blocks to the row of boutiques and bars on the west side of the street, and the cluster of hotels on both sides, where the Admiral's Head was doing a brisk afternoon business.

Brandon was already there when I arrived and told the hostess I was expecting to meet a young man and began to describe him, but she said, "He's already seated. Please follow me, sir." Not to be judgmental, but I think she had done some judging herself and had come to an erroneous conclusion. No problem.

And no problem meeting in a bar to discuss Brandon's murdered mother. I followed the hostess to his table. He was sitting on the bench that ran along the far side of the barroom, facing the entrance. There was a dark drink, half gone, in an old-fashioned glass on the table. I started to take the chair across from him, but he told the hostess we'd like to move to a couple of the armchairs in the private bar.

The private bar had shelves lined with books bought by the yard, and there were four groups of four comfortable low armchairs set with leather-topped tables between them. No one else was in the room. We took two chairs in the far corner, and I snagged one with a good view of the entryway.

I didn't feel a need to have my back to the wall, but I wanted to let him know he couldn't maneuver me into sitting with my back to the door. He sat down in a chair to my right, not across from me. I got the impression that the proximity was intentional, but I had no idea what he intended.

Brandon told the hostess he was ready for another Rob Roy, and while she explained that our server would be here shortly, I wondered where he'd learned to drink that. When the server came, he said he'd have another, and she asked him what the current drink was. He was surprised she didn't know, but he told her, "Rob Roy, please." I ordered a raspberry iced tea, since that was the only tea they had, heaven knows why. Brandon had definitely gotten started before he got to the Admiral's Head.

"The thing is, Richard," Brandon said, "my parents were really unusual in a number of ways, and my mom still is. I mean, since my dad died, I've tried to be her support, emotionally. And the same again, since Ernest died too. I liked Ernest, because he never tried to be my stepfather. He told me before he and Mom got married, 'You had a father, and I'm not him. I'm going to be your mother's husband. If you need anything from me, just let me know, but I'm not trying to take the place of your father.'

"Financially, she's doing fine, still working at the family business even though she doesn't have to." I didn't correct him about my name. He wasn't worried about that. Or a lot else. Still, there were topics I wasn't going to introduce into the conversation. I needn't have worried.

"So I understand," I said. The drinks arrived. The iced tea wasn't bad at all.

"But I was telling you that they were unusual. They were, very."

Brandon talked. I mainly listened. I wasn't quite sure what he wanted. I was beginning to suspect he didn't either, but then he said, "I just need to talk to someone about this, but it's not easy to find someone who can hear stuff like this without passing judgment." And, I realized, someone whose opinion you don't care about might be just the person you're looking for.

Brandon leaned over his drink like a drunk at the bar. He was more lit than I had realized. He went on, "This is weird, you know, talking about this, but I really feel like I have to. My parents belonged to this study group that met at various places, once a week, for twenty years." Oh, God, I thought. He thinks it really was a study group. Another assumption. And he thought they had met weekly rather than monthly. But what did I really know?

"Only it wasn't a study group, Richard." I left it. "It was a group of couples that got it on together once a week, and they were seriously kinky about it too." I suddenly definitely did not wish to hear this, particularly from a drunk college kid about his parents.

"Look, Brandon," I said, "we know about the club, all right? You don't have to go over this with me."

He ignored the interruption. He was going to share this with me whether I liked it or not. I was pretty sure he would have shared it with the hostess if I hadn't been there and she hadn't been busy. He said, "Sixteen or so couples got together once a week, and the women drew lots, and the men drew numbers, and the woman who got the red ball, or whatever it was, would take on the men in the order drawn, and the women who had gotten the white balls or whatever assisted in preparing and securing her for the gangbang. It is no small thing for a woman to take on sixteen men."

"I'm sure it's not," I said. No joke.

"They had some sort of complicated system with the balls, but I don't really understand that very well. It was designed to even things out, I think. There were tiles in a box with the women's names on them, and each week another set of the names of all the women present was added to the box. After a woman's name had been chosen and she had serviced the sixteen men, all the tiles with her name were removed from the box. The longer a woman went without being chosen, the more tiles with her name on them were in the box, so eventually, for sure, she would be chosen. But on average, a woman could expect to be chosen over three times per year, roughly every sixteen weeks. And not only that, but people within the group—"

"Brandon," I interrupted. "I really am not clear why you need to tell me about your parents' sex life. Lots of people have belonged to sex clubs—"

"Lots of people aren't my parents," he said, "and now they're dead, and the police say someone was trying to blackmail Mom about the goddam sex club, and it was all over and done with years ago—" He threw his old-fashioned glass and the ice across the room, where the heavy glass bounced against the paneling, scattering the ice.

"Jesus," he said, "I guess I'm really hammered." Right. He fumbled with his wallet and credit card, but he got his signature down on the slip, which I noticed included a fee for damages. I doubted this was a first. He put a hand on my shoulder as we left. I asked him for his keys, and he handed them over. I clicked his black Porsche to lock it up, gave the keys back to him once he was seated, and belted in in the passenger seat of the Prius. I knew the way to his mother's house, now probably his house, not that I'd been invited to the reading of the will.

The guards waved us, that is, Brandon into the compound. I drove up as close to the front entrance as I could, hoping I could get him inside without carrying him. No worry: his hand on my shoulder up the flagstone walk kept him pretty steady, although he needed a bit of help on the steps. He said, "Door's kept locked, and I—" He had his keys out, but a gray-haired man I didn't recognize, fifty-some but trim and sharp-looking in a black suit, white shirt, black tie, and dark gray waistcoat, opened the door before Brandon could use it. They'd been watching for him. Brandon thanked the man by name, Cornwell, and introduced me to him and him to me, no more accurately than before.

Since Cornwell and I were both hired help, I corrected Brandon about my name, and Cornwell said, "A pleasure to meet you, Mr. Zufahl. Will you be staying?"

"No," I said, "I just wanted to make sure Mr. Wilson got home all right." I told him where the Porsche was. Somehow Cornwell had acquired the keys from Brandon, I noticed.

Cornwell thanked me for taking care of Brandon and told him someone would go bring it home presently, and then he said, like an incantation, "Perhaps you'd like to shower and change, Mr. Wilson?" It was clearly a familiar routine. I wondered about Brandon's driving habits as I returned to the Prius. I wondered even more about Brandon's conversation as I drove home. It would be interesting to watch Schwartz's face when I reported that conversation, but I wasn't sure it would be enjoyable.

I certainly hoped it wouldn't set off a speech about child-rearing, or anything else, for that matter. Brandon was rolling in unearned inherited wealth, and he didn't seem ready for the experience of trying to handle it, much less himself. And if there's one thing cops can focus on, it's *cui bono?* To whose good? To whose profit? And inheriting a ton of money puts you right under their microscope, and they are very good indeed when it comes to microscopes. Even microscopes that require delicate handling.

And they had several days' lead on us.

When I got back to the office, Schwartz was on the phone with a sponsee. I got only his end of the conversation, of course, but it was pretty clear what was going on.

"No, Henry, it is not your responsibility, or your right, either. It doesn't matter what he thinks about God; it's none of your business. Your job, as his sponsor, is to take him through the Twelve Steps of AA. Yes, okay: to guide him or lead him….Through the Steps, not into your revival tent…."

Henry had a lot to say.

"No, Henry, it is absolutely not okay for you to correct his beliefs. It is okay for you to help him through the Steps, period. Look, freedom of conscience, freedom of religion, is one of those two-edged swords you hear so much about. It cuts two ways…. Yes, everyone, you included, has the right to their own opinions, beliefs, convictions, whatever. On the one hand, nobody has the right to tell you what to believe about God. Right. Absolutely… .

"But on the other hand, Henry, since everyone has the right to their own beliefs, you have no right to tell anyone what to believe, either. No, his beliefs are not for you to fix, to correct. I don't give a fat rat's ass what you believe, Henry, and I've never told you what to believe or think about religion, have I? Henry, where do you get the idea that he should listen to you, anyway? What are your qualifications to preach and teach? Hmm?" Long pause. I brought Schwartz a glass of iced tea, and he nodded thanks while he listened to Henry.

"Henry, you've made a mistake here. Yes, it's true that everyone has the right to their own opinion. But it does not follow from that, it is not true that that means any old opinion is just as good as any other opinion. I know you've heard me say this before, Henry: a well-informed, intelligent, carefully considered opinion might just possibly be better than an ignorant, stupid, careless opinion....

"Henry, you want to preach and teach, but where do you get off doing that? What the hell do you know about religion, Henry? ...

"Right, you believe every word in the Bible is true, it's an infallible guide to.... Okay, Henry, what do you know about the Bible? I'm willing to bet you haven't read it, Henry. Oh, really? You don't have to read it to know it's all true.... You claim it's all true without knowing what it says. Henry, saying that is like signing a blank check. No.... No."

Schwartz was ready to throw something, but Henry wasn't present to receive. "No, Henry, you should stop trying to correct Ron's beliefs; they are simply none of your business. No, that's not witnessing; that's trying to impose your own opinions on someone else, who has the right to—"

He covered the receiver. I could hear Henry's voice all the same. He seemed to be shouting. Schwartz said, "He's on the edge, goddammit. He thinks carrying the good news is all that's keeping him sober. Jesus H. Christ. He needs a Step workshop himself, in my opinion, which, God knows, I'm entitled to." For someone who says he doesn't believe in God, Schwartz certainly brings Him into the conversation a lot. It doesn't actually mean anything.

Schwartz had had enough. He interrupted the stream of emotion from his sponsee. "How long has it been since you've been to a meeting, Henry? Oh, they did, did they? I find that hard to believe, Henry. Nobody has the right to throw you out of a meeting because of your beliefs.... Because you wouldn't stop talking about your beliefs? No, because you wouldn't stop talking, period. You have no right to monopolize the discussion, Henry; other people need to share just as much as you do." He held up his empty glass, and I went to get him a refill.

When I returned, Schwartz was down to brass tacks with Henry. "So, what are your qualifications, Henry? What are the twelve classic religions? You don't know. How many religions are being practiced right now in this world? I mean, how many different systems of belief are there at present…. You don't know. What languages was the Bible written in, Henry? Yes, that's right, for the Old Testament, mostly. How about the New Testament? No, that's not right…. You could google it, Henry. Google 'new testament language' and learn something. What language did Jesus of Nazareth speak, Henry? No, he didn't; by his time, Hebrew was essentially a liturgical language.

"Okay, according to Genesis, Henry, from what tree did the fruit come that Eve gave to Adam? No, it wasn't an apple. From what tree was God afraid Adam and Eve would eat, so that He expelled them from the Garden of Eden? No, the Bible is very clear about these matters. If you had ever read it, you'd remember it, surely. Well, go find a Bible and read the first few chapters of Genesis and…. No, it's not a matter of opinion, Henry; it's a matter of fact.

"Why did Cain kill Abel? You don't know. How many people were in Noah's ark, and who were they? No, it's quite clear…. Henry, who was responsible for Lot's incest with his two daughters, according to Genesis? Well, that's not what Genesis says.

"Okay, Henry, let's leave Genesis alone for now. At the other end, what's the last book of the Bible called? No, that's wrong. It's Revelation, not Revelations, singular, not plural…. Well, if you think that's a trivial distinction, how many people are you married to? One or more than one? Yes, it is an important difference, you see. Henry, I'm just about done with this, and by God, I'm just about done with you, but who were the four horsemen of the Apocalypse, and what color were their horses?

"No, Henry, I'm not an expert, but I can read. You want to teach your sponsees something you know nothing about, Henry…. Look, Henry, that's no excuse. You have time to watch television, but you don't have time to read the Bible, yet…. Henry, as Dilbert says, ignorance is not a point of view. No, you—"

Schwartz frowned, looked at his phone, clicked off. "Son of a bitch hung up on me for some reason," he said. "I swear, that dim bulb is just looking for a reason to drink, and if he can't tell people what to do…. Why the hell do people insist on sharing their ignorance as if it's a gift? I don't understand it."

I let him come down from the talk with Henry. I'd heard Henry in plenty of meetings, and he always came across as a person convinced he was entitled to three times as much time as anyone else, because what he had to say was so much more important than anyone else's share. But it came down to nothing more than personal opinions, and he often had to be steered by the chair away from politics, religion, and sex, not to mention his tendency to hog the floor. I didn't like Henry, and I doubted he liked me. I doubted that Schwartz liked him either, but you don't have to like a sponsee.

What I couldn't figure out, as I gave Schwartz the report on the meeting with Brandon, was why on earth Henry had asked Schwartz to sponsor him. I didn't think I should ask, though.

Schwartz sat quietly for a moment or two after I wrapped up the report. "How fortunate Brandon Wilson is to have a Cornwell taking care of him."

"I think he probably knows it," I said.

"Imagine trying to resist all that temptation," Schwartz said. "But then, imagine trying to live with that awareness about your parents. 'Troubling' doesn't begin to describe it. I don't suppose Brandon is a candidate for the Program?"

"No, sir. As you know, it's for people who want it, not people who need it, and I doubt Brandon wants much of anything right now."

"No, I suppose not. It's certainly a nasty situation he's in."

"Yes, sir," I said, although I wasn't sure where this was heading.

"Mr. Wilson doesn't seem to be holding up well. Of course, even though the police are being tactful in every way, it has to be obvious to him that he's a prime suspect in his mother's murder, unless and until a better choice is available. I'm sure they are desperate to find an innocuous candidate for the position. Do you suppose he has the technical expertise to trick that alarm system? I doubt it somehow."

He picked up his phone. "Let's see if Inspector Mercer feels like trading information," he said.

"What information do we have to trade?"

"Very little," he said, "if any. I suppose they know by now that Seamus sold Eugene that house."

"Probably," I said, "but possibly not. I don't see any easy way to find out without handing them the information ourselves."

"Or any hard way either." He touched the autodial.

Chapter Twenty-One

Wednesday, April 8–Thursday, April 9

Not too surprisingly, that phone call did not result in Mercer and Ripley coming by to spill the beans. In fact, as Schwartz remarked, all we learned was that the police were not farther along than we were, if at all. The high point of the day was the eight o'clock meeting at St. Luke's. Henry was not in attendance.

The next morning I was giving the office a dusting when the phone rang. It was Paul, and he sounded excited, for Paul. "Rainer," he said, "suppose I could tell you which of the Chicago perps had a mother whose maiden name was Jonson, with no *h*. Would you be interested?"

I tried to keep my voice neutral. "Oh, I don't know. I'm not sure we care, to be honest. Was there only one?"

"Damn right, there was only one," he said. "Do you want to pass it on to Mr. Schwartz?"

"No," I said. "I think you should do it yourself. Where are you right now? How about Frank and Sonny?"

"Well, it was Frank who came across the marriage license. I had found Janet Jonson's birth certificate, and then when we compared notes, we realized we had a meld. I think this is what—"

"Of course, it is," I interrupted. "What time can you all be here? Mr. Schwartz needs to hear all about it, and you may as well fill me in at the same time."

"Eleven okay?"

"Sure. I'll let him know you all are coming. Congratulations." We hung up, and when Schwartz came in and got settled with a new book, with the Dawkins now on the bookshelf, I told him the troops would be coming by before lunch. I could have mentioned what Paul had told me, but he already knew there was something worthwhile coming, or the men wouldn't be coming by, and why should I upstage Paul?

When Schwartz came in from the summerhouse, where he had said he would be coating rice hulls with meal powder, he was carrying his rather worse-for-wear copy of the Ellenbogen manuscripts. "You know that fellow down the street we see in meetings now and then, older man with gray hair, usually in a ponytail, always wears a hat and long sleeves?"

"Sure," I said. "Lew something. Lew V., I think. I see him walking his dog when I'm out sometimes. Pretty brown-haired border collie, very shy but friendly dog."

"Right. So's Lew, as I recall. Friendly, I mean. Well, if it's the same person, damned if Seamus doesn't quote him too. You'd think he'd brought a recorder to meetings."

"Come to think of it, stranger things have happened in meetings. Remember that guy who showed up at Orchard Park a couple years ago, had recorded some schtick and wanted to play it in the meeting, then got pissed because Pat M., chairing, told him we were there to share from the heart, not to play pre-recorded stuff?"

"Yes, of course. How could I forget it? Try as I might. Anyway, according to Seamus, our neighbor's full name is Daniel Lewis Vaught, if it's the same person, which, together with my last name, seems to me to be playing holy hell with anonymity."

"So tell Seamus when you see him," I said.

"Nice," Schwartz said. "Someday, Rainer, you will dance off a cliff, and—"

"Well, so what if Seamus did use your names? It's not as if it's going to be published, after all. It was just there to carry the message."

"'To carry the message,'" Schwartz said. "You're on a roll here, Rainer."

"Actually, that was accidental, sir."

Schwartz was looking at the page he had turned to. "Funny initials," he said.

"Sir?"

"DLV. Roman numerals for 500, 50, and 5, or 555."

"Oh, really?" I couldn't see what he was getting at, if anything. Sometimes his digressions lead somewhere interesting, but mostly it's nowhere in particular, and this one really didn't seem particularly fruitful.

"That would be eighty-three and a third percent of the Mark of the Beast. Or maybe the Mark of Eighty-three and a Third Percent of the Beast. I have been searching the manuscript for other people we know who Seamus quoted, but so far, nothing. I can't think why he would focus on Lew and me."

"Well, that's all very interesting," I lied, "but maybe he just thought you were both quotable. Anyway, Paul called a while ago, and the boys will be in at eleven." It was almost twenty till.

"So, they found something," he said unnecessarily. "A link between Janet Jonson and the Chicago criminals?"

"Why should I spoil the surprise?"

"Why pass up a chance to tantalize your employer?" he said, laying down the manuscript and picking up the paper. He was almost done with the Crypto-Quip when the doorbell rang, and I went to let Paul, Frank, and Sonny in.

They got seated. We'd seen them a couple days before, so Schwartz didn't rise, but he offered refreshment, which as usual, they declined. "So, there have been results?" Schwartz said

Paul said, "Frank and I turned up a couple items. I got onto Janet Jonson's background, the salient feature of which is that she had a sister, two years younger, named Margaret Jonson, who Frank learned got married at—" He checked his notes. "At twenty-two to one Lloyd Blessing, then in the service of his country, infantry, rank—"

"Blessing," Schwartz said. "And they had children? Or a child?"

"Two: a daughter, Elizabeth Blessing, born here in Indianapolis after Lloyd had returned to civilian life, now Elizabeth Blessing-Hardesty, still married, a retired social studies teacher, and a son, Evan Lloyd Blessing, also born in Indianapolis, last seen leaving the main bus terminal in Chicago some weeks ago."

Schwartz leaned back, looked at the ceiling for perhaps ten seconds, then returned to earth. "So Janet Jonson was Evan Blessing's aunt, and he knew her address, which was a fair distance from Chicago, but reachable by car or, thirty years ago, passenger train, in half a day. This is very satisfactory, gentlemen, very satisfactory indeed."

Frank was, of course, glad to be in on this. "Lloyd and Margaret are both deceased, sir. They died in a house fire caused by faulty wiring, the investigation concluded, thirty years ago—"

"Before or after the Chicago job? Where?" Schwartz asked.

"About a month after it," Frank said. "Here in town. Lloyd had done well in the insurance business, and they had just built a house on North Penn. They were planning to sell the old house, but that went south after the fire, and Janet inherited the house in Arden."

"I wonder about that faulty wiring," Schwartz said. "The timing seems remarkably convenient, doesn't it?"

"I'll look into it," Frank said. He wrote in his notebook.

Paul put in: "So far as we can tell, sir, the police haven't uncovered any of this. I doubt they're looking that far back, to be honest."

"Very satisfactory indeed," Schwartz said. "I wonder how Inspector Mercer will express his gratitude when we deliver this news to him...." He leaned forward. "Now, let's review the probable chain of events:

"Furnish, Blessing, Medsker, and Reynolds, with who knows what direction and assistance from the background, assault but do not kill four armed guards as they attack and steal the armored car. They hide the vehicle in a disused warehouse, remove everything that's not immediately traceable, and abandon the vehicle, leaving traceable cash behind.

"Blessing either has arranged a visit to his aunt in Indianapolis, or he and the others simply head for her house without invitation, and she willingly or otherwise provides them a hiding place. Blessing is familiar with the house and grounds, doubtless from a previous visit or visits with his parents."

Frank said, "With the garage and basement and that barn out back, they could have stayed there a few days without her ever knowing they were there."

"Possibly," Schwartz said.

"From what Frank turned up," Paul said, "Ms. Jonson was seriously incapacitated but still living at the time of the Chicago heist. She may have welcomed a visit from her nephew, although how she really felt about his three friends, or about him, for that matter, or even whether she knew he or they were there, we'll probably never know."

"At any rate," Schwartz said, "the gang arrives by train or car, conceivably but improbably by air, from Chicago, I'm inclined to think by car, and they hole up in Ms. Jonson's house, with or without her permission. And I think we agree, possibly even without her knowledge."

"From what we've learned, sir," Frank said, "she might not have been in a position to object. They could have taken the phone, and—" He stopped. "That's all speculation, though."

"Correct," Schwartz said. "At some point, then, it occurs to Blessing that the disused septic tank would make an excellent hiding place for the loot, and he installs that hook to support the container, probably a long duffel that could easily be retrieved at leisure."

Sonny got inspired: "Or they could have run a rope to the duffel and hooked that to…." He realized it didn't really matter.

Schwartz let it go. "After a longer or shorter time, they decide that the police might trace them to that house, since the trail was fresher then than today. They decide to leave, so…. Did Ms. Jonson own a car?"

Paul said, "She had a Lincoln Town Car, but she hadn't renewed her license. It was still in the garage when she died."

"So the crooks had the sense not to take a car that could readily be traced to that address. But by this time, the authorities were searching for them, their names were known, and in fact, they were captured within two weeks of the robbery, I believe."

"Yes, sir," Frank said. "The damn fools tried to take a plane to Atlanta, and from there they intended to go on to Venezuela, for God's sake, but they were caught here at the airport."

"And Furnish peached, as they say, on his partners, but claimed to know nothing about where the loot was hidden. Doubtless he was hoping that, having served a reduced sentence, he could return, retrieve it, and escape to some country without extradition treaties with the U.S., whether Venezuela or elsewhere. But that, of course, didn't work out for him."

Schwartz surveyed the crew. "And Ms. Jonson died, knowing little or nothing about the fortune stowed in her front yard."

"Even if she had known about it," Sonny said, "she was in no shape to get it out." He suddenly realized that this, too, was no great insight. "I mean—"

Schwartz can tolerate statements of the obvious when he's in the right mood, and he was positively overflowing with benevolence at the moment. "Indeed, Sonny, she was in no shape to get it out. She died, leaving nothing to her imprisoned nephew Evan Blessing, or to her sister, for whatever reason."

Paul said, "I learned that Janet and Margaret hadn't spoken for years. Margaret had written off her son Evan, and so Janet's will left almost everything to various charities. There was one bequest to a friend of hers, one Charley Lawson, who apparently was something more than just a friend, but he had taken off years before and couldn't be found. Whatever was left over after the foreclosure went to the good causes, not to the family."

"Which left the stage ready for Seamus to buy the house, doubtless at a steep discount, and at some point, Seamus decided, for whatever reason, to have a look at the old septic tank. Apparently, it's not at all unusual for people to use them to dispose of unwanted pesticides, herbicides, and other garden chemicals. No doubt, it seems safe and harmless. God knows what he thought when he found a bag full of cash and negotiable securities inside it." Schwartz shook his head. It was all I could do not to join in. The troops waited while he considered the vagaries of fortune.

"Gentlemen," he said, "we have filled in some of the gaps in the story of what happened some years ago, and from this, we can extrapolate to current events: Blessing and Medsker came to reclaim the loot, doubtless without intending to notify the current owner of the house, and if we can imagine Seamus's astonishment at finding the trove, who knows how or why, we can also imagine their chagrin at finding the hiding place empty. A fruitless nocturnal visit to the septic tank led, inevitably but futilely, to home invasion and the interrogation, torture, and murder of Eugene and Lawrence, who, of course, knew nothing of the buried treasure.

"My God, that's a ghastly fact, and I can't really feel that Seamus Ellenbogen is quite clean-handed here. He finds a sack of loot hidden in the old septic tank. Does he really think no one will ever come looking for it? No, impossible. The whole point of hiding money is to be able to return to the hiding place and recover it. No one buries treasure, hoping that someone else will come across it. What went through Seamus's mind as he put the house on the market and sold it to Eugene and Lawrence? Did it ever occur to him to mention, 'Oh, by the way, I found a fortune in the septic tank a while back. If the people who left it come by, just send them to me; I'll keep it safe for them until then'?

"I can't help wondering whether Seamus deliberately left the Abernathys holding the bag—or, rather, *not* holding the bag—until the thieves returned to collect it, or whether he simply failed, or refused, to think of it. No, whether it cost him sleep or not, he had a lot to answer for." He looked as unhappy as I'd seen him in a while. He had a point. It was unsettling to realize we'd sat in meetings with a guy who had found that obviously stolen money and had then left Eugene and Lawrence to face the music when he sold the house and got away from it safely himself. Not that when you sit in meetings you are under the impression that you're in the company of angels, but still.

Schwartz went on, "Be that as it may be, we have work to do. I must inform the police of the connection you have found, and if you wish to be present—"

Paul wasn't concerned one way or the other, but Frank and Sonny had reasons to prefer that Schwartz handle the informing. It was so agreed. "Now, this will focus the attention of the authorities on Blessing and Medsker. The police have already considered them suspects in the Abernathy murders, so this information will reinforce that line of inquiry.

This will lead them further in the right direction, and the evidence you have uncovered will put them firmly in our debt."

Sonny grinned. "I like the idea of the cops owing us one," he said. Paul and Frank clearly felt the same way.

Schwartz nodded. "I don't mind telling you, gentlemen, that Rainer and I have felt more than a little shunted aside in this case. We started out with missing persons, which the police ignored until we discovered the bodies, then, once it was obviously murder, the police made it clear we were in the way." He laid a hand on the desk.

"In another case, a corporate investigation, with an ancillary and quite possibly related case of blackmail, in the course of which Rainer discovered the body of a murder victim—who was also the person threatened with blackmail—and faultlessly performed his duties as a citizen and as a licensed private detective, we have been deliberately excluded from the scene, making it impossible to continue the original investigations." He turned the hand over.

"Very well," he said. "Let us see how Inspector Mercer reacts to this new evidence. I seriously doubt that the police have made this connection, and we may decide to enlist the help of the press in correcting the notion that private investigators play no role in establishing justice. We will see. This is very gratifying, gentlemen." He looked from Paul to Frank to Sonny. "Very gratifying indeed. Are you sure you wouldn't like to reconsider handing the information to Inspector Mercer personally, here in this office?"

There were no takers, but they were certainly pleased when I got their pay from the safe and distributed it. "Mr. Schwartz, it's always a pleasure," Frank said, through his mask, offering a fist. Schwartz hit knuckles with him and the others, and they went.

Chapter Twenty-Two

Thursday, April 9

When the three had departed, Schwartz sat thinking for twenty minutes or so. I cleared the glasses and other things away, got things soaking in the sink, and returned to the office. I considered asking him if he'd like me to call Mercer or if he'd prefer to do it himself, but it didn't seem to me like he needed interrupting.

He returned to earth abruptly. "If we can't join the police in a murder investigation, any murder investigation, then surely there can be no objection to our continuing to look into the problems we were hired for in the first place. Mr. Warner is still perturbed, so far as we know, and Ms. Marchand was being threatened with blackmail. Well, perhaps we can goad Inspector Mercer in the direction of rational inquiry. Please call him or, failing him, Sergeant Ripley, and let them know we have evidence that may be relevant to the Abernathy murders."

I got on the phone. I had no luck with Mercer, but Steve Ripley answered on the first ring. "Sergeant," I said, "Mr. Schwartz has asked me to inquire, as a tax-paying citizen, whether you've got a suspect in the Abernathy killings, now that Ed Stroh is again at large." Ripley's reply was emphatic and not particularly respectful of tax-payers and citizens in general. It was obvious they were still looking, and there was no suggestion that they'd made any real progress at all.

"Well," I said, "if you and Inspector Mercer would care to come by the office sometime at your convenience, we might be able to help out with that." I felt it was the right time to dig a bit. "Of course, as mere private detectives, we know our place, so we hesitate to interfere in an important murder case, but on the other hand, as licensed P.I.s, we would feel compunction about withholding evidence relevant to an ongoing criminal investigation, even one that doesn't seem to be going much of anywhere."

Ripley said there was no such thing as an unimportant murder case and suggested I could tell him what we knew over the phone.

"Well, if it were up to me, Steve," I said, "I'd gladly tell you everything and let you take it to your boss as if you'd found it out yourself, but I'm following instructions. I just want to let you and the inspector know our door will be open, figuratively but not literally speaking, should you feel like coming by." He had some comments about open doors, but said he'd pass on the invitation, and we could expect to see them when we saw them. We rang off together.

When the doorbell rang a short time later, I got up to check that our visitors were who we expected, and I let in Inspector Mercer and Sergeant Ripley. Mercer strode to the space right in front of Schwartz's desk and demanded, "What's so important you can't say it over the phone?"

Schwartz leaned back. "You ask that question while towering over me in my own office, after being invited here so I might share information with you that may well help in capturing a pair of killers. Why should I feel any obligation to you, Inspector? If you can't behave in a civilized manner, I regret issuing the invitation. I am legally required to share any evidence in my possession with the police, but there are other police officers who would do just—"

Mercer gave up and sat down in the red leather chair. Ripley stayed on his feet, by the door. "All right," Mercer said. "You say you have information. About the Abernathy killings?" He looked like he was about ready to stroke. His normally red face was headed for mauve, and his neck seemed big for his collar.

"You'll recall," Schwartz said, "my suggestion that there might be a connection to the armored-car heist in Chicago two decades ago."

"Sure, but it didn't pan out," Mercer said. He leaned forward, and his face got a shade darker. "Why, have you found something?"

"Certainly," Schwartz said. "But first, you're sure you haven't?"

"Hell, yes, I'm sure. To the best of my knowledge, there's absolutely no connection between that robbery and the Abernathy killings." He suddenly looked suspicious. "Schwartz, if you've got something, say so."

"How about the fact that Janet Jonson owned that house at the time of the armored-car robbery?"

"Yeah, big deal. And there's no connection—"

"And the fact that Janet Jonson was Evan Blessing's aunt, his mother's sister."

Mercer sat up straight so fast he almost left the chair. Ripley bounced forward off the wall he'd been leaning on. "You're putting me on," Mercer snapped.

"Not at all," Schwartz said. He was a model of calm.

"Steve," Mercer said.

"On it," Ripley said, stepping out into the hall as he pulled his phone from his pocket.

"How the hell did you—"

Schwartz cut Mercer off. "Hard work," he said, "prompted by the conviction that that job was the one case that answered all the questions raised by the septic tank." He was trying not to be overtly obnoxious now. Ripley put away his phone as he stepped back into the office. Schwartz nodded toward one of the yellow chairs, and Steve pulled out his notebook as he took a seat to his inspector's right.

When Schwartz wants to, he can give a verbatim report with all the trimmings, and he felt like it that time. Ripley was taking notes the whole time, and I watched him flip to a new page eight times. Mercer can be a good listener when he puts his mind to it, and he sat and listened from start to finish. A couple times, he wanted to ask a question, but each time Schwartz said, "Later," and by the time Schwartz was finished, all the questions had been answered.

"So Surcutt, Kinder, and Weinstein dug up the connection you suspected was there," the Inspector said. "I don't suppose you'd…. No, that wouldn't be your style, I have to admit."

"You don't suppose I'd manufactured evidence, I suppose you mean," Schwartz said. "How? By creating an aunt for Evan Blessing out of whole cloth? Or by retroactively making her the owner of the house? Please, Inspector." He looked as deeply offended as he sounded.

"No, of course not, Schwartz. I'm just feeling blindsided." If Ripley's face was anything to go by, there would be some number of police investigators newly acquainted with the woodshed before the day was done. He liked getting information from P.I.s about as much as Mercer did, just as he liked owing them.

Schwartz said, "Thanks to the perseverance and doggedness of Paul and Frank, and for that matter, Sonny, you now have a clear connection between the Chicago job and the Abernathy murders. Further, I have reason to believe that the loot has been found, after all these years." He gave them the overview of Viola's inheritance from her Uncle Jim, who it turned out was also a past owner of the house on Delaware Street, and Ripley got seven or maybe it was eight more pages of his notebook filled.

He showed the cops the Ellenbogen Manuscripts, as he referred to them, with his red-pen markup, and he got from there to the decoded message, with the bank's name and address and the account and safe-deposit-box numbers, in about three sentences, and Mercer asked, politely, if he could have a copy of the red-penned manuscript, so I scanned it for him as Schwartz filled them in on Parkinson's Switzerland meetings with the bank and Interpol. Mercer actually smiled when Schwartz described Viola's reaction to the news about the money in the account and the securities in the box, and he smiled again when he heard about Parkinson taking Viola home.

"So," Mercer finally said, when Schwartz was done, "we've got the original four at the house after the armored-car job. They had to have driven down here; that much hot luggage would be too dangerous on the train, unless they were just crazy." He sat back, tried to take a cigarette out of his breast pocket, cursed softly.

"There's one other thing," Mercer said. "That body we found under that crappy deck behind the house. Who the hell was that? We've got Furnish and Reynolds dead and accounted for, and Blessing and Medsker still in the wind. So who was under the deck?"

"You'll recall," Schwartz said, "that Janet Jonson's will left almost everything to charities, aside from a bequest to a handyman and friend, Charles Lawson. I suspect that Mr. Lawson's departure, since he couldn't be found after Ms. Jonson died, occurred at the time she was visited by her nephew and his friends. Perhaps Mr. Lawson objected to their staying at the house. Perhaps he saw something he shouldn't have, like the nocturnal deposit of a duffel bag in the septic tank. At any rate, if he was present, and it sounds as if he was on sufficiently intimate terms with Ms. Jonson to be in the house, he could have been a problem for the gang. I doubt very much that they would have hesitated to put Mr. Lawson out of the way. I also doubt that anything less urgent would have inspired the completion of that deck, which I suspect Mr. Lawson was building, and—"

"Why wouldn't they bury the loot under the deck and put Lawson in the septic tank?" Ripley asked. "Or cut him up and put him in with the loot?"

"An excellent question, Sergeant," Schwartz said. "Perhaps the money had already been sealed up in the septic tank. They may have used Bondo then, as they did in disposing of the Abernathys' bodies. I have no idea why they did what they did."

"Good luck getting DNA on the body under the deck," Mercer said, "but we might do better if we can locate dental records. Steve—" But Ripley was already reaching for his phone and heading for the hall. He's not secretive, just polite, in that one small way.

Inspector Mercer was also on his feet. "Look, Schwartz, I'm much obliged for the information," he said.

"Of course, Inspector," Schwartz said blandly. "With the resources available to you, you should have little trouble confirming the identity of the body under the deck, and I expect that, now that you can be reasonably sure that Blessing and Medsker are responsible for Eugene and Lawrence Abernathy's deaths, you will be able to lay hands on them shortly. Mr.

Zufahl and I wish you well on your quest." I kept my face straight.

"Perhaps you would not object to our resuming our own investigation into Buck Warner's situation, if we can do so without interfering in the investigation into Ilona Marchand's murder," Schwartz said. "And there was the matter of the blackmail threat against Ms. Marchand as well."

"You won't be too shocked," Mercer said, "to learn that we think the blackmail threat and her murder may well be connected. We don't know if she confronted her blackmailer and refused to knuckle under, or maybe she was murdered for some reason completely unrelated to—" He caught himself. "Nuts. Stay out of the way of our murder investigation, but if you can figure out who was blackmailing our vic, please don't hesitate to let us know. You know as well as I do what you can and can't do, not that I think you always give a damn one way or the other. Go ahead with your investigation, and if you can figure out what makes Buck Warner tick, not to mention what's biting his ass, I'd like to know myself. He's a strange piece of work, but what genius isn't? If they were normal, they wouldn't be who they are. Just don't horn in on murder."

"Perish the thought," Schwartz said.

"Right," Mercer said, reverting to rudeness. "Come on, Ripley."

I followed them to the door, watched them leave, and damned if Steve didn't wink at me on the way out. Apparently, he was glad to get the lead anyhow.

Chapter Twenty-Three

When I returned to the office, Schwartz was reading the marked-up Ellenbogen Manuscript, for whatever reason. I worked on transcribing my handwritten notes for a while, and when he finally came back to reality, I was making good progress. He asked whether I was at a good stopping-off point, which was unusual.

"I ask," he said, "because I'd like to know your opinion about the Buck Warner matter. You have already met with Buck Warner, Jean Stevens, Henry Appleby, and Keith Benedict. Your interviews were interrupted by your discovery of Ms. Marchand's body. I suggest that, discarding your consultant role, you continue the interviews with Clare Thomason, George Kearney, Geoffrey Parsons, and Lara Collins. And, as seems appropriate, with Iris Warner."

"Sure, I'll just reintroduce myself, let them know there's a suspicion that the CEO is losing his grip or whatever it is, and we'll sit down and chat. Sounds really cozy."

"By now," he went on, ignoring my comment, "they must be thoroughly exhausted by the police inquiry, the endless questioning, the cross-examination, that whole inquisitorial process.

"You, however, Rainer, are not a policeman. By now, in such a close-knit organization, everyone will be aware that Ms. Marchand was being threatened with blackmail, and they will almost certainly know about the nature-study club, if they didn't already. Without overt mention of Mr. Warner's mental state, it should be possible to learn more about that aspect of things while you openly continue to look into the blackmail. Among those four people you have not yet spoken with, someone may wittingly or otherwise possess some clue to either problem."

It looked like a pretty bleak prospect to me, but he calls the shots, so we went over some ideas on how to approach them, and of course, one big question was how to get into the office in the first place. We'd killed the better part of an hour, looking at it this way, then that way, and I was suggesting that we call up Buck Warner and ask him to please order everyone to cooperate with me, when the landline rang.

Schwartz picked it up, and I glared at him. "Leo Schwartz's office," he said. "Leo Schwartz speaking…. Oh, hello, Mr. Warner, how are you? I'm glad to hear it. Fine, thank you, I'm doing well. What can we do for you?" He signaled me to pick up.

"Well, Schwartz, the police have been harassing me and everyone else at WarnerCorp since Ilona's murder, and they don't even try to hide the fact that they think one of us did it. As you can imagine, this is terrible for all of us, and I'll be frank to say it's beginning to take a toll on productivity." I wondered what productivity he was talking about. Maybe he meant morale.

"I'm sorry to hear that," Schwartz said blandly. "What can I do to help?"

"Well, I wonder if you could get your man Wood, no, I mean Zufahl, back here to look into things. The police haven't given up, but I don't get the impression that they're making much progress at finding the killer, and I think you might be able to shine some light on—well, on everything.

"I know Iris hired you in the first place," he went on, "and I know what for. I think a frank discussion at this point could clear up a lot of the mystery, so that you could get to the real question, who killed Ilona?" Buck was trying to sound casual, but there was a tightness to his voice that was anything but.

"So, as the head of the company, you would authorize Mr. Zufahl's return, under his own name, to continue to look into things?"

"Exactly. And I'd like to start by sitting down with him myself. I wasn't completely frank with him earlier, and I'd appreciate a chance to set the record straight."

"Certainly, Mr. Warner. Would tomorrow morning do? For Mr. Zufahl's return to your offices, I mean."

"Sure," Warner said, "but I thought maybe I could come to your office today, and you could ask me anything you wanted, right now."

"Let me check my appointment calendar," Schwartz said. He covered the phone, looked a question at me. I shrugged my shoulders, whispered, "Why not?" and looked at my receiver. Schwartz went back to Warner. "Shall we say eight o'clock this evening, Mr. Warner? That should give us a chance to decide on how best to facilitate Mr. Zufahl's return."

Warner wanted to come immediately, but Schwartz had mentioned to me earlier that he felt he hadn't been to the Hellas Cafe in too long, so he put Buck off till eight. They signed off.

"So," Schwartz said, "we'll see Mr. Warner this evening." He got up from his chair, said, "I think I'll make another batch of iced tea." I said fine, and he held a finger to his lips and beckoned me to come with him. We went to the hall, and he led the way out the back door. When we had both gotten seated in lawn chairs out back, he said, "You and I were discussing how best you might go about insinuating yourself in Mr. Warner's company when the phone rang, and it was Mr. Warner, inviting you back in." He rubbed his nose, which he does only before broaching a distasteful subject. "Rainer, that may well be a coincidence, Warner calling at exactly that moment, but it seems just a little bit too neat. I know that you have developed an appreciation for Iris Warner's personality and her character, but she is the only person from WarnerCorp who has been inside this office."

"And you're trying to tactfully point out that she's the only person who could have planted a bug," I said. "Never mind my personal feelings about Iris; you know as well as I do that there are walls that don't get climbed, and there's sure as hell a high one there. But let's be realistic here. We haven't been camped out in the office since she hired us. And the office security isn't all that formidable. Anyone good enough at that sort of thing could have gotten in the front door while we were both out, planted a bug, and disappeared, all in, say, three minutes."

I thought for a moment. "We used Hermes Security for the main system, but an operator as skilled as Colin at Hermes could disarm the system temporarily, enter, bug, depart, and leave the system looking like everything was A-okay."

"You know this how?" Schwartz asked.

"Colin told me so himself when he was installing our current system. I'll call Colin and ask him for a sweep; we should do that anyway, now and then."

"Very well. I suppose we'll need to update the system to ensure against this sort of thing."

"Sure," I said. "But any system that can be set up by one man can be defeated by another, unless the first one builds in some serious traps for the unwary. It'd cost a bundle, but I really think we should at least consider it, and with any luck, we'll be able to afford it with Buck Warner's help."

"Certainly," Schwartz said. "For now, however, let's get Colin here to find the bugs, if any." He looked grim. "I suppose the Hellas Cafe can wait."

"I'll get carry-out," I said. "Instead of calling, why don't I just drive down to Hermes Security right now? I can get Colin on the case; I know he'd love to find a bug to prove you need to update the system."

"Very well," he said. "And if you would, call Ms. Warner and make sure Mr. Warner's version of events is accurate. We can't take his word for it that she has told him everything."

"Will do."

"I'll stay here until you return, and we'll eat in the kitchen."

"You would be perfectly safe in the office," I said. "It's not as if a bug will bite you."

"No," he said, "I will await your return here. I don't want to go back there if someone is listening to everything we say." He glanced at the gazebo. "I have some go-getters to make." Go-getters are little things that spin around shooting fire when launched with a mortar or rocket.

"All right. I'll go get Colin. I should probably call him on my cell while I'm on my way. It's only fifteen, twenty minutes to get down there. What do you want from the Hellas?"

"Dolmathes, with the potatoes not rice, side of hummus with pine nuts and peppers, and a tiramisu."

"Okay," I said. "No baklava? Sure? Big mistake. See you in an hour or less." I left.

That was an interesting four hours. I called Colin at Hermes Security as I pulled onto College. Hermes is on 46th Street on Compton, so I took Kessler over to Keystone, then down. I told Colin I needed him on something I didn't want to discuss on the phone, and of course, that got his attention. He was waiting for me at the front door when I arrived. He's a bit shy of thirty, one of those short guys who are wiry and just a touch aggressive in manner. As always, he was dressed in black. At the moment, he was wearing a Hermes badge, which is carefully designed to clearly be such without in any way resembling a law-enforcement badge. For starters, it's pink, a supposedly proprietary shade taken from the movies that Hermes refers to internally, Colin has told me, as Panther Pink. I followed Colin into his office, and he closed the door for privacy. "What's up?" he said.

"We may or may not be bugged, in the office, I mean. We were talking about a certain matter and a certain person, and he called just at the right moment," I told him.

"Oh, well," Colin said, "that sort of thing happens all the time, you know. Of course, it mostly happens on television and in the movies, but now and then, you get a real, live coincidence in real life." He smiled. "Myself, I'd bet against it. So you want a whole building sweep?"

"I think the office, mainly, but it can't hurt to see if there's anything else going on," I said. "And Mr. Schwartz is, at last, convinced it's time to go for better overall security, like you described to me recently, something that wouldn't be all that simple for even a professional such as yourself to defeat.

"We have a guest coming at eight, so it might be best to see if there's anything in the office, then proceed from there. And I have to say I'd feel better if you came back afterward and worked up a proposal, estimate, you know, for a new system."

"No problemo," he said. "If it's all right, I'll just drive up, and I'll check your records before I go."

"Sounds good." I got up. "You want to let me out?"

"Sure," he said.

I swung by Hellas after phoning the order as I pulled onto Keystone. I ordered an extra baklava for Schwartz. No sense expecting him to watch me eat mine, tiramisu, or no tiramisu. I was getting used to the hands-free car phone, although I still felt slightly distracted from traffic. I called Iris Warner, told her Buck had called and was coming, and she confirmed that she had filled him in on why she'd hired us in the first place, although she still had no idea what it was under his skin. "What a waste of money that's turned out to be," she said. I suppressed the urge to point out we hadn't billed her yet and that she could afford it anyway, but I told her I'd bear that in mind when I made out the bill.

Colin arrived at the same time I did, and I left him in the office while I took the food to the kitchen and let Schwartz know I was back. We ate, in no hurry, and Colin finished the office sweep and came into the kitchen to check it with his electronic devices, of which he mainly seemed to be using three, from the various pouches of the leather apron he'd put on. Schwartz insisted on splitting his tiramisu with me, and he thanked me for the baklava.

An hour before Buck Warner was expected, Colin reported to Schwartz, with me present, that there was absolutely no clandestine electronic device on the ground floor. "It really pains me to say this," he said, "but I found nothing, absolutely nothing." He wasn't exactly crestfallen, but he was less cocky than usual. "However, that doesn't mean you don't need an upgrade, meaning a whole new system, which will head off any bug anxieties in advance."

Schwartz didn't ask him how else anxieties might be headed off. He thanked Colin, expressed gratitude for Hermes's services so far, and asked for an estimate for the system he would recommend. Colin said he would put together a proposal so effective "that if you do get robbed, you'll know it was me." Schwartz told him that was exactly what he needed; it would make life so much simpler.

"So Warner's call was a simple coincidence, Rainer," Schwartz said.

CHAPTER TWENTY-THREE

"Yes, but you know, it still feels wrong."

"Of course it does. But we have evolved with a set of instincts much better suited to the African savannah than to the American cityscape. We have created an unsuitable environment for ourselves. There's nothing new about this." We discussed evolution for a while, or rather Schwartz did.

"We just have to make the best of it," he said. "By the way, if I should say that Mr. Warner should be coming by soon—"

"I shouldn't be surprised to see him at the front door." The doorbell rang. "And there he is." I went to let Buck Warner in.

In the office, I steered him to the red leather chair, introduced him to Schwartz, who asked if he'd care for tea or coffee. Buck was a coffee man. I went for the setting, ground some arabica, made the coffee, and brought it to the office. Schwartz and Warner were talking about popular music since the turn of the century, for some reason, but the discussion ran down as cream and sugar got used.

"So, Mr. Warner," Schwartz began, "you are aware that we were hired by your former wife, and why."

"Well, yes," Buck said, "but that's crap. I'm not going crazy or anything. I know why she might think so, but it's not true, although I realize that asking you to take my word for it must seem a bit much."

"Can you tell me why you think she was worried about you? In what way has your behavior led her to be concerned about you?"

"I think so," he said. "I've been worried about—I should say I was worried about Ilona. She told me about the blackmail threat, after I'd asked her—look, this goes back a couple of months.

"I realize now that I should have waited longer than I did, but I'd been thinking about her for a long time, and a month or maybe five, six weeks after her husband died, I told Ilona how I felt about her, and she—"

"You're saying you told Ms. Marchand you had feelings for her?" Schwartz was keeping his voice neutral. I knew there'd be commentary when our guest was gone. I wasn't looking forward to it.

"Yes, I did. It was too soon, I realize now. Hell, I realized it at the time; I just couldn't seem to stop myself."

"And her reaction was—"

"About what a reasonable person might expect," Warner said. "She said it was too soon after Ernest's death. I mean, there were circumstances that…."

Schwartz looked at me, inviting me into the conversation. "The circumstances involved another woman, a hotel room, and a lot of hush money," I said. Warner knew what the medicine tasted like, so I didn't sugar-coat it.

"And it was a lot of trouble heading off a media circus," he said. "It took some doing, as a matter of fact. Then, after I came in, showing my feelings to Ilona, of course, she wasn't ready for any of that. I'd not realized how deeply she was still in love with Ernest, despite everything."

"Ms. Marchand was aware of her husband's activities?" Schwartz asked.

"Oh, yes, of course. It's not as if he bothered much with discretion, God knows. I mean, he never made a scene or anything when he was sober, but past a certain point, he just didn't think about anything but the here and now. He was a good husband, for the most part, but then he'd hit a bar, and he'd drink more than he could handle, and he'd make a new female friend, and once things got rolling, there was no stopping him, short of calling the police. I mean, the Carmel PD knew Ernest about as well as we did.

"He really couldn't help himself, and he really couldn't bring himself to get help. Hell, he never remembered anything that happened after the third or fourth drink. He got robbed who knows how many times, but he never stopped carrying cash."

"But Ms. Marchand's feelings for him survived all this behavior," Schwartz said.

"Absolutely, and they survived him, and I simply didn't realize it, and when I talked to her, I saw I'd put my foot in it, but I backed off once I understood how she felt." He drank coffee, although it had cooled off by then. "And I think I backed away in time. She was a bit upset, but I hadn't pressed it so far, or so fast, that—"

It was easy, now, to see why Iris had been concerned. Warner was thoroughly wrapped around the axle over Ilona, and I wouldn't have trusted him to walk the dog, if I'd had one. He went on about her, and his feelings for her, and what he thought her feelings for him had been, and what he thought her feelings for him might have become, had she lived, but you get the picture, and giving it to you verbatim wouldn't tell you any more than it told us, except that our client hadn't been imagining things. He said that he'd begun to settle down and had resigned himself to wait until the time was right, when Ilona had come to him with the blackmail letter.

This was the first indication that Ilona had shared that with anyone but us. Schwartz asked him, "What did you advise Ms. Marchand to do?"

"Well, obviously, it needed delicate handling. Something like this, with all her charitable work, would really throw a wrench in the works, but on the other hand, you can't pay blackmailers; they'll only keep coming back for more, of course."

"Was this the first you'd heard of her and Andrew Wilson's activities?"

"Well, yes, it was. I'd known Andrew, of course, since he was Iris's brother. In fact, I met Iris at their wedding. Then, later, when Ilona showed me the letter, she explained to me about the nature-study club, which I thought was, well, pretty strange. I'd never have pictured either of them as, well, partiers in that sense."

"Our understanding," Schwartz said, "is that the club met weekly, Mr. Warner, and that there was a lottery system...."

"No," Warner said, "it was monthly." Something to ask young Mr. Wilson about the next time I babysat him.

"Right. Ilona told me about it, and I can tell you, I was startled."

"Did this information change your feelings for Ms. Marchand?"

Warner looked as if the question had never occurred to him. "No, Mr. Schwartz, it didn't. I mean, I'm in no position to judge people who want to do things I wouldn't want to."

I thought that sounded a bit off. Apparently, so did Schwartz.

"Really, Mr. Warner? You weren't taken aback, even a little bit, to find that the woman you had expressed love for had engaged in these activities? Granted, it's a fairly common pornographic fantasy, but reality has a way of differing sharply from fantasy."

"Well, I certainly knew Ilona had been around," he said, "and frankly, that's something I found interesting about her. So what if, once a month, she and her husband had gotten together with others who liked a little variety? Pairing off with someone you aren't married to isn't the end of the world, and if both the husband and the wife are in favor of it, well—" He trailed off. Schwartz waited.

"So she and Andrew got together with other couples, and they traded partners for the evening, so what, Mr. Schwartz? But it was private, and it was discrete, and—"

"I wonder," Schwartz said, "exactly how the blackmail was intended to work. When you think about it, simply claiming that So-and-so belonged to a gangbang club would hardly be sufficient to cause the victim to pay." He was being deliberately offensive. "A simple, straightforward denial—"

"Wait a minute, what do you mean, a gangbang club?" Warner protested. "It wasn't that, for crap's sake."

"That is the information we have from one source," Schwartz said.

"No, no," Warner said. "They just drew numbers and paired off. If a woman drew her own husband, they'd put the number back in the box and draw again. Ilona described it to me, I mean, not in great detail, but she said they'd go to separate rooms for the evening, then gather again downstairs, when the evening was over, and they'd go home, just like after any other party."

"Are you saying they met in each others' homes?" Schwartz was trying to get clear about Warner's understanding of the matter, and I was keeping quiet. "I realize that some people's homes have many bedrooms, but there can't be many that would accommodate sixteen couples."

"Sixteen?" Warner was incredulous. "No, there were half a dozen couples, all people who knew each other and lived fairly close to each other, and they just … What the hell do you mean, gangbang?" He looked from Schwartz to me and back. "Who the hell have you been talking to, anyway, Schwartz?" It was interesting, the way his manners turned on and off.

"Perhaps we've been talking to someone whose information needs checking," Schwartz said. "Meanwhile, have you anything to add to what you've told us?"

He didn't, but he didn't want to let go. I liked the way he'd accepted the idea that Ilona and her husband had gotten together with a few other couples for some friendly spouse trading, but he was ready to defend her against the charge she'd participated in larger-scale serial sex, whether as spectator or participant apparently didn't matter. He repeated that he had no idea who had tried to blackmail Ilona or who had killed her, but he said he'd welcome me back to the office in an effort to find out. Schwartz gave him the facts of life about private eyes and murder investigations.

Before he finally left, just before ten, he said that it seemed to be common knowledge around the WarnerCorp office that Ilona was being blackmailed, but not what the blackmailer was threatening to expose. As Schwartz pointed out, if everyone had already known about the sex club, it would have obviated blackmail, at least so far as the office was concerned, so we would assume that the threat had been to make the facts public, whatever they were. Warner got in one last denial of the sixteen couples and serial-sex scenario before he left, not obviously overjoyed, but not particularly worked up, either.

When I had let Buck out, I came back to clear the coffee things, but Schwartz was already putting cups in the sink.

"Was that a waste of time, or what?" I said, taking a seat on the stool.

"Was it?" Schwartz said. "We need a word with Brandon Wilson, preferably tomorrow morning. There's no great urgency about your return to WarnerCorp. And, come to that, I think I will accompany you."

"True," I said. "I wonder who's right about what went on and with whom. Maybe Ilona gave Buck a reality-lite version of events. I mean, we have only Buck's word that he was putting the moves on his ex-wife's brother's widow, one husband removed. Maybe she thought a story about a little swinging would go down better than the facts."

"Perhaps, but maybe Brandon's version is not in fact the truth. He's talking about his parents, after all, and in particular his mother, and there's bound to be some confusion in his mind."

"But you'd think that would tend to tone it down, in his mind, at least," I said.

"Maybe. But there's no telling what the human mind can do with unpalatable facts. They can be suppressed, they can be exaggerated, or both." He ran water into the sink. "Try to see him soon and see if there is a shred of concrete evidence to clear this up."

He turned the water off. "I am a private detective, Rainer, and so are you. Human behavior, human action, is sometimes seemingly inexplicable, but there's usually a cause to what people get up to. Someone thought black-mailing Ilona Marchand would be profitable, or perhaps the motivation was hatred for her. Someone thought killing her was necessary, or at least expedient. We have to wade through muck on occasion. Let's not forget our waders."

"No, sir," I said.

Chapter Twenty-Four

Friday, April 10

I called Brandon Wilson the next morning. From the way he sounded on the phone, he had not revised his approach to life since I'd brought him home. He wasn't interested in talking about his parents' extracurricular activities, but I kept at it, and for some reason, he didn't hang up on me.

I told him we'd interviewed someone who had given us a different version of events, and I asked him if he could account for the discrepancy. He said he didn't know anything about it except what he'd seen on the DVDs, and I asked him what DVDs? But I had a feeling I knew already. Brandon said, "Look, Dad had a bunch of videotapes—"

"Videotapes?" I said. I don't think I kept the surprise out of my voice. "A bunch of them?"

"Yeah," Brandon said, "he kept them in a 'secret' compartment behind the bookcase in his study, a few dozen of them, but who has a, what's it, a VCR anymore? So I did some checking around, and I found this place locally that would convert tapes to disk, you know, discretion assured and all that."

"You wouldn't happen to remember the name of this place, would you, Brandon?"

"I can look it up," he said. "Look, I'm a little out of it at the moment, so's it okay if I call you back with the name?"

"Sure," I said, "as long as you do remember to call me back." I gave him the number, made a mental note to follow up, and let him go back to sleep.

Schwartz had been listening to my end of the conversation. I looked at him, and he looked at me. Finally, I repeated the whole conversation for him. It was just as well that Josh wasn't around.

"Unbelievable," he said finally. "Everyone seems to have known about this club, and one hopes we're not about to drive up to interview people who were actually members. Good Lord."

"Yes, sir. I think 'discretion' has gotten about as stretched in meaning as it will bear."

"And we have no way of knowing whether Ilona Wilson, as she was then, was even aware that her husband was preserving a record for posterity. Literally for his and her posterity. This must mean that Brandon has viewed them, if he had the tapes converted. Or am I making an unwarranted assumption about this?"

"I doubt it," I said. "Why would Brandon have them converted if he wasn't going to watch them? And if he has watched them, he's seen what was going on, and if he's seen it, then either the gangbang scenario is right, and Buck got a watered-down version from Ilona, or Brandon's just lying to us."

"Why would he choose that particular lie to tell us?"

"Got me, sir."

"Well, please follow up with Brandon. He may well need reminding."

"Sure thing."

We got ready to head up to WarnerCorp. We decided to stick with jackets and neckties rather than trying to blend in, so I put on a nice Harris tweed herringbone and a dark blue rep tie, and he wore a medium gray suit, light blue shirt, and dark gray tie. At least we didn't look like a couple hard-boiled P.I.s as we headed up College. I drove the BMW sedan.

Schwartz avoided the wall of silence on the drive to the office at Keystone at the Crossing. "'The Science of Deduction' is all well and good as a title, I suppose," he said, "but what I find interesting about it is that 'deduction' is the noun form for two different verbs, 'deduce' and 'deduct'; what's less amusing is that some people get them confused, God only knows how. 'To deduce' something or other certainly isn't the same as 'to deduct' something or other, and both verbs are regular, or weak, as the experts would say." Fortunately, we don't have to worry about how big a part of what I get paid for is listening to him talk about things not germane to any case we may have at any given time.

He went on, of course, but I'll spare you the rest of it on "to deduce, deduces, deduced, have deduced" and "to deduct, deducts, deducted, have deducted." It was a slightly drizzly early May morning, so I kept switching back and forth from intermittent wipers to off, and short as the drive was, I was glad to arrive at the WarnerCorp building.

I called, and my friend Appleby met us in the lobby. I introduced him and Schwartz to each other, and he brought us up to the top floor.

Appleby brought us back to Buck Warner's office, and we'd just sat down when my phone rang. Appleby headed back to his office, and I stepped out into the hall to take the call. It was Sergeant Steve Ripley, of all people. I whispered, "Ripley," to Schwartz.

"The inspector thought you and Schwartz would like to know," he said, "that we put a watch on public records down at the City-County Building, and you'll be pleased to know it worked. Medsker came in to inquire about ownership of a certain house and lot in Arden, and, when he found out it had been bought by Seamus Ellenbogen after it was foreclosed on Ms. Jonson, he requested further information about property owned by Ellenbogen. He had no idea we were listening in on the conversation, of course. He and Blessing, it turns out, have been holed up downtown at a no-tell hotel." Actually, he mentioned the name, but they have a tenuous hold on respectability, and they really wouldn't appreciate the publicity, so I'll leave it at that. I'm not just making things up here, although, of course, it would be easy enough to do that, and who would ever know?

"So, anyway," Ripley went on, "our boys have been supporting themselves stealing cars short term so they can get away after sticking up shops with inadequate security cameras, although we did get a couple good views from a 7-Eleven and a liquor store that actually had working cameras pointed in the right direction, if you can believe such a thing. Blessing and Medsker had the sense to spread their hits out geographically, every couple days or so, here and there, one driving and one sticking up, so we just waited for the dime to drop, and it finally did. Blessing showed up yesterday at the Records Office to find out who had owned the house on Delaware after Aunt Janet passed, namely as I said Seamus Ellenbogen, and he found out when it sold, and he found out what Ellenbogen bought next. Probably the best day's work he ever put in.

"Of course, we've had a guy watching the Ellenbogen house in Broad Ripple, and after Blessing visited the Records Office, we added two more, so when they saw the boys letting themselves in the back door about one a.m. this morning, they called it in, and we sent a couple cars to pick them up. They brought tools with them, of course, the kind you use to tear up floorboards and the kind you use to persuade people to tell you which floorboards to tear up. Would you believe they were using a flashlight but didn't have the sense to draw the blinds? We had three men inside the house with them before they figured out they weren't alone. You know, sometimes it does seem just too easy.

"So by three this morning, they were in holding cells at 42nd Street, and they were really singing up a storm. Evan Blessing explains that he was seduced into a life of crime by his acquaintance, not friend, Richard Medsker, and of course, Medsker blaming it all on Blessing, so apparently, all those packages we took out of the septic tank were just the result of some sort of misunderstanding."

Ripley was interrupted by someone at his end, and he told somebody to do something, and they needed further information, and he gave it, and then he got back to me. "Still there?"

"Oh, yeah. By the way, Steve, before I forget it, I want to pass on Mr. Schwartz's appreciation for this call."

"Don't mention it. The Inspector made me do it. On my own, I'd have left you guys out high and dry."

"Yeah, okay, but I owe you lunch or dinner at Harry and Izzy's sometime."

"Sounds good," he said. "I'll see if I can fit it in. So, what it comes down to, we took them red-handed in the Ellenbogen house, and they know they're in for it. Blessing says Medsker did the carving on Eugene and Lawrence

Abernathy, and Medsker is just as clear that Blessing did it, and if either of them had a brain, they'd realize it doesn't matter a damn who did what, they were in it together, and that's all we need to put them away for good, even if they don't get the needle. If they ever see daylight again, it won't be our fault.

"Anyway, the inspector thought, we thought you ought to know. You guys have been all right on this one, and—"

"Stop right there," I said, "or you'll say something we'll both regret. Let's not get soft here."

"Well, the inspector mentioned that Schwartz could have called O'Connell at the *Times,* but he didn't. He played it straight, and so have you. So—"

"Harry and Izzy's, any time, Steve."

"How's Tuesday lunch sound, Rainer?"

"Sounds great to me." We hung up together.

I went into Warner's office, ready to give the good news to Schwartz, but he and Warner were talking cars, which Buck seemed to know a lot about. He was telling Schwartz about the Corvette he'd given Iris for her birthday last June, and Schwartz was holding a magazine, apparently from the bookcase next to Buck's desk, which had a photo of that very model. Schwartz handed me the magazine, saying, "There's a very interesting article about that Corvette here."

They went on talking as I looked at the article, but my attention was attracted by the notation in Schwartz's handwriting, above the headline: "We are under surveillance, audio and visual." I skimmed the article, to play along. I wasn't sure Buck was in on it until Schwartz said, "I wonder if it makes sense to begin the interviews before lunch, Mr. Warner."

Buck said, "Well, I'd think they would keep until we get back from Del Sol, wouldn't you?" Schwartz agreed, and they rose, and I rose.

As we headed toward the elevator, Schwartz asked me what Sergeant Ripley had wanted. I tried to sound offhand, telling him that the perpetrators in the Abernathy case had been captured breaking into the Ellenbogen house. We got in the elevator and headed down. When we got to the parking lot, Schwartz suggested we take his car, and I understood why we'd brought the

BMW. Warner got in the back seat, and Schwartz joined him, "so I won't have to strain my neck, Mr. Warner."

I headed toward the restaurant, and Schwartz apologized to Warner and asked me for a full report of the talk with Steve Ripley: "We can be candid with Mr. Warner, Rainer." I had filled him in by the time we arrived at Del Sol in Carmel.

"Mr. Warner had an idea he wanted to share with us," Schwartz said when we were seated. "However, he confirmed, circumspectly, what you suspected from your first visit on Monday: there is every reason to suspect that the offices are all equipped with hidden microphones and cameras, and there is just no way to communicate without tipping off the listener and watcher that you are on to the surveillance. I apologize, Mr. Warner, for making you carry the conversation earlier, but my knowledge of automobiles is sadly limited."

"Oh, you did all right," Buck said.

"Thank you, sir," Schwartz said. He turned to me. "And I must apologize to you, Rainer, but it's a matter of some urgency to find out where and by whom those video cassettes were converted to disk. Would you mind calling our informant again? Surely by now, he's in a position to be more helpful than he was earlier."

So there were limits to how candid we could be with Buck; he wasn't in our confidence about the nature-study antics. I suggested that I get a separate table, and they were perusing the menu as I sat down at a table for two across the room. I called Brandon, and after four rings, he picked up. He sounded a touch better, and as far as I could tell, he hadn't started drinking, fortunately. He had to go look for the information, but he finally found it.

"It's called A.M.C.E.," he said.

"No, you mean A.C.M.E.," I told him.

"Bullshit, man, I'm reading it off the damn card," Brandon said. "It's like 'am-see,' but all capitals, with periods. Acme would be like in the Road Runner cartoons, the stuff Wile E. Coyote buys to catch him, the rocket sled, and all that. This is A.M.C.E." He gave me the phone number and the street and email addresses. I thanked him and asked him to please keep this to himself. I was tempted to ask him not to get back in touch with A.M.C.E., but decided that might just make him call them up for the hell of it. He asked if we were making progress on catching his mother's murderer. Rather than tell him we leave such matters to the police, I said we were getting close to finding her blackmailer, and that would probably lead to her murderer, and he was being very helpful. I went ahead and emphasized that he could best help now by keeping quiet about what we had just discussed. Sober, he sounded a lot better, I decided.

I called Steve Ripley back. "How would you like to double my debt to you, Steve?"

He said he was doing all right as things stood, but I reminded him that there was another murder case we were staying out of, and I mentioned that Buck Warner was having lunch with Schwartz and me at Del Sol. "There's a company that converts old videotapes and stuff to modern media," I said, "called A.M.C.E., and no, I didn't get Acme wrong; it's the initials A.M.C.E." I gave him the rest of the information. "I could call up the Department of State and find out who owns it, but I have a feeling you'd be better at it than I would."

He said he'd see what he could do, but he'd have to check with the inspector. "Are you and Schwartz going to be up there at Warner's offices?" I said we would probably be there all afternoon or until we got thrown out, God knew which. He seemed concerned about the possibility we might wear out our welcome. "You showed up last Tuesday, and the next thing you know, you're phoning in a dead body for us," he said. "You can see how they might not be so fond of you."

I assured him we had the company CEO in our pocket, but he expressed skepticism about that. "Guys like that," Ripley said, "get used to living by different rules than the rest of us."

"I don't think this one thinks that way," I said.

"Which means you really don't know him that well," he said. "I'll check out A.M.C.E. and get back to you, Rainer." There's nothing like Harry and Izzy's prime rib following their giant shrimp cocktail to promote human fellowship and goodwill to men.

I made do with the chips and salsa and left enough of a tip to head off resentment, and I joined Schwartz and Warner as they finished their lunch. We headed back down Westfield, cut over to Keystone, and made it back to the offices of WarnerCorp. Schwartz filled me in on their lunch conversation on the way, and I reciprocated with an edited update on Brandon and Ripley. Buck's opinion was that every single person at WarnerCorp was technically proficient enough to have bugged everyone's office, including their own, of course. Of course, that meant everyone would be able to detect such bugging, if it had occurred to them to look, but Buck thought most of them were probably relying on overall office security to keep things private. As he put it, people tend to drift into a false sense of security. It was good to learn that Buck Warner was now firmly off our list of suspects. Schwartz would hate the idea of eating with a blackmailer at least as much as eating with a murderer, probably more.

Chapter Twenty-Five

Friday, April 10

When we got back to WarnerCorp, Schwartz and Warner headed for Henry Appleby's office to work out a plan for figuring out the bugs without alarming the bugger, if possible. I headed for the COO's office to talk with Clare Thompson. She had just gotten back from lunch herself, and she asked me to take a seat and gave me her full attention, despite the fullest in-tray I'd seen on anyone's desk at WarnerCorp. I asked if I was keeping her from work, and she said it would keep, just the routine reports that any corporation has to generate.

She was in her late forties, possibly fifty, I estimated, athletic in build, with gray hair cut shorter than mine, and she wore the same not-quite-exactly-like-Buck outfit the others had on. It suited her, in fact. Her dress and person both said no nonsense, loud and clear. I'd like to tell you that I learned a lot from my talk with the corporate COO, but Thompson wasn't gossipy. She told me her job was basically to keep up to date on what was going on in the company, so that she could advise her boss, the CEO, to ensure his decisions were based on day-to-day reality. She was certainly immune to flattery, when I said that Buck Warner must rely on her heavily for understanding what was going on. She said that what was going on was the same thing that had been going on for years, and if something were to happen to her, Warner could get equally valuable advice from anyone else in the company. She was married, had been for almost thirty years, and had two daughters, both married, and three grandchildren. She had a few photos of the family, some good nature landscape photos on the walls, not her own work, she said, but no masterpieces in evidence.

After taking forty minutes of her time I went next door to meet with Lara Collins, Chief Programmer and, of course, CSR. She was ten years younger than Thompson, verging on plump but not really quite there, dark-haired and tanned, married with kids in high school, as devoid of makeup as Clare Thompson, and very fond of her job. She told me that, of the various updates to WarnerCōp in the past decade, almost half had been her responsibility. She talked me through what seemed to be all of them, not that the details really meant much to me, and ten minutes into it, I decided she was trying to convince me she was just as dedicated a computer nerd as any of the others, but more so. After half an hour I decided she wasn't trying to convince me of anything, she was just that way, for real. From the prints on her walls, which seemed to focus on early computing machinery, mechanical calculators and such, I got the impression that she must compartmentalize things, with one personality for the office and a human side for home. I was glad I wasn't married to her, at least at the office.

I had already spoken with Jean Stevens, as Chuck Wood, but I stopped to say hello, and she returned it civilly enough, but didn't invite me in. Iris Warner wasn't at the office, so I made a mental note to call her later. Of course I'd met with Henry Appleby before, and he was still meeting with Schwartz and Warner, so I headed west across the open area to George Kearney's office.

Kearney, Prime Programmer and CSR, was also civil enough, but he gave me the impression that, if he wasn't actually too busy to be wasting time with an outed P.I., he certainly thought he was. Kearney was in his mid-forties, with brown hair and enough gray at the temples to appear distinguished in a mirror. He had photos of himself with wife, sons, and a daughter, but when I asked, he said he was divorced, and his wife and kids lived in Virginia, where his wife had family. His eldest was at Ohio State, and the younger boy and his daughter were in high school. I restrained myself from asking how a Prime Programmer differed in responsibilities from a Head, Chief, or Top Programmer. He answered my questions briefly but, it seemed, directly. Whether he went home to a cold, lonely house or a red-hot girlfriend remained undiscussed by the time I called it quits. We were both relieved when I left him for Geoffrey Parsons.

Parsons, the last on my list, was CFO, which at least I had some inkling of the meaning of. He was forty-some, dark blond with a matching mustache, a few pounds overweight, and friendly as the day is long. He said Buck had asked them all to be as accommodating as possible, and he certainly tried to roll out the red carpet. He gave me the rundown on WarnerCorp from the financial side, and a rosier picture could not have been painted. The company was perfectly situated, with a suite of products that would never go out of style, and everyone in the company was set for life financially, with generous salaries and five percent of the company stock each. He didn't hesitate to explain that Buck Warner owned fifty-five percent of the stock, which was only natural, since WarnerCōp was his brainchild. The nine other members of the company had been with WarnerCorp from its beginning as the corporation that purveyed the product to the customers. Parsons compared the profit-sharing very favorably to the arrangements at Apple and MicroSoft, as well as at several other corporations I'd only vaguely heard of. He seemed to know a lot about the entire universe of software companies, in and out of the health-care field. His desk was completely clear, not even a lamp or a computer on it. I always find that level of neatness unsettling, if not exactly suspicious. His laptop rested on a swing-out tray attached to his chair. The photographs on the walls were all black and white, landscapes with no portraits or still lifes. I asked him if he'd taken them himself, and he said he had. There was a small bookcase with the standard set of binders and a few reference books that didn't look particularly used. I got the impression that he kept his personal life strictly separate from work, and the easiest way to do that was to avoid entanglements with his physical office. But that was really just a guess, and I kept it to myself when I reported to Schwartz later.

By four o'clock I'd made the rounds, so I went by Warner's office to see if he and Schwartz were still in session. Warner was working at the computer on his desk. He said Schwartz had had some more things to go over with Henry Appleby, so I thanked him and went down to Appleby's office.

Schwartz and Appleby were looking at a huge screen on the inside wall of the office, split into nine smaller rectangles, each showing a person sitting at his or her desk, except for Iris Warner's, Jean Stevens's, and Lara Collins's, whose offices were empty when I joined Appleby and Schwartz. Stevens, then Collins, returned to their respective offices from wherever they'd been. Appleby was clicking on one rectangle, then another, to get the sound feed from each office in turn. "Big Brother" was the obvious remark, so I shut up.

Appleby clicked on an icon, and the views of the offices were suddenly gone. In their places were screens, with a line below each identifying the person whose computer screen was shown. He showed us how he could click any of the screens and bring it up to take up his big screen, then go back and full-size another screen. He stacked them, set them side by side, and in turn gave us a full-size view of each of the offices. "Buck expressly tasked me to include his office and computer along with everyone else's," Appleby said. "He's obsessive about not being privileged over anyone else."

I caught a gleam in Schwartz's eye as Henry showed us his surveillance system, so I said nothing about the privilege of holding fifty-five percent of the company's stock. Schwartz asked Appleby a few questions about security. We learned that all the private offices could be locked by the occupant, but apparently, nobody but Appleby was in the habit of locking their doors. Appleby had the sole master key, and everybody knew it, and of course, everybody knew he was in charge of security and knew that he had access to their offices and their computers. To the best of his knowledge, Appleby said, no one seemed bothered by the arrangement, and of course, no one was being forced to stay at WarnerCorp.

Schwartz asked about hiring and firing, specifically firing, which apparently had been part of Ilona Marchand's responsibility. Appleby said he thought it had technically been her responsibility, but he'd been the most recent hire, eighteen years before, and there hadn't been a full-time firing or other departure since he'd joined up. Aside from Ilona's. "Why would anyone leave? You can come and go as you please, stay home if you like, take off any time you want to, and financially you're really set for life. Some people have businesses they run outside WarnerCorp, and the only restriction, obviously, is noncompetition.

"Well, look, why would anyone even want to compete with a company that treats you like this? I mean, even if you stood to make a fortune, you'd be taking it out of your own pocket. Like any group of people, there are some it's easier to get along with than others, but so what? You get that anywhere. I think, hell, I know perfectly well that there have been a couple of interoffice relationships that got closer than they probably should have, but when it came down to it, things ended with minimal hurt feelings. This is really a great bunch of people, and more than that, they're bright enough to know a great thing when it's handed to them. I should have said we're bright enough to know it. I'm one of the crew, too, after all."

"But," Schwartz pointed out, "one of them is almost certainly a blackmailer and a murderer, and by your own account, everyone here knows enough about security to have blinded your system long enough to have killed Ms. Marchand."

"Yes, and they're smart enough to have covered their tracks," Henry said. "I have to admit that the one weakness of the security system is my own damn fault. I simply assumed that any threat would only be external. Everyone here knew the system well enough to know how to defeat it. It's the old story: the castle is safe from outside attack, but one person inside the castle walls can open the drawbridge to the enemy outside."

"Or assassinate the châtelain," Schwartz said. "The walls protect the keeper of the keys, but he—she, in this case—is vulnerable from within. Yes, Mr. Appleby, I believe you are correct that your fault was trusting the loyalties of those within the walls. Everyone in the company has good reason to be grateful for their position, but someone wanted more.

"As you can understand, Mr. Appleby, you were the obvious first suspect in Ms. Marchand's murder, since the security of the company was in your hands. But I've learned to be a bit leery of obvious suspects. It's possible, of course, that you're so fiendishly devious that you have shown me everything to divert suspicion from yourself, but I'm inclined to doubt it.

"So, Mr. Zufahl and I thank you for the tour of the castle's defenses, and we will leave you to strengthen them further. I expect we'll see you again in a day or two." He touched hands with Henry, and then I did, and we went to say goodbye to Buck Warner. He was on his way to Appleby's office, and Schwartz told him he thought we had made progress today. Schwartz said he hoped to have something more substantial to report in a day or two at the latest, and we took our leave from WarnerCorp.

In the elevator, Schwartz headed off conversation, but in the car, he asked what I'd learned of interest. I told him not much, but I could report verbatim when we were back at the office.

As we were about to pull out onto the street, my phone rang, and I parked at the side of the road to answer it and put it on speaker. Steve Ripley said he'd looked up A.M.C.E., which stood for Appleby Media Conversion Enterprise. He had an address and so on, but he said that the name was the only thing I couldn't have googled; it was in the incorporation documents but otherwise was never used. And it was a privately held small business, naturally, with one owner. The connection was pretty obvious at this point. I thanked Steve, rang off, and Schwartz pointed out that it would be only a short distance out of our way home. I turned left rather than right onto 86th, and before long, I spotted it, at the end of a strip mall on the south side of the street, between a nail salon and a check-cashing place.

We parked and went in. The young fellow behind the counter looked a bit annoyed; he was looking forward to closing up for the day. All the same, when Schwartz gave him a line about having a couple dozen old video cassettes to convert to DVDs, he gave us a sheet with prices for various options including DVD, thumb drive, and so on, for various quantities and speeds of recording, and so on. The kid couldn't have been much over sixteen. Schwartz hinted that there might be something of a private nature on some of the cassettes, and the boy gave him the company policy about discretion, respect for privacy, and so on some more.

Schwartz asked if they ever got anything really interesting in that line, and the young man said sure, but he said the company strictly forbade invasion of customers' privacy. Actually, he said clients' privacy, but we let it pass. Schwartz asked whether he'd ever come across anything he was tempted to make a copy of for himself, and the boy got a little indignant, told him they'd never do something like that; their business was based on trust, and they returned people's original materials and one newly converted copy, unless of course, the customer wanted multiple copies, in which case they made however many the customer wanted. If the kid was putting on an act, he had a great future awaiting him on stage.

Schwartz asked whether he was the only employee of the company, and he said no. Another fellow worked mornings, and he himself did afternoons. We got his business card, which he took from a holder on the counter. The card was one of those glossy, over-designed things with funky, hard-to-read typefaces made even harder to read by pointless graphics in too many colors, some of them metallic.

Schwartz asked whether he'd taken an order within the past six months from anyone named Marchand or Wilson, and the kid started to say that telling us would be a violation of company policy or natural law or something, but when Schwartz laid a folded Ben Franklin on the counter, the kid made it disappear and then disappeared himself into the back room. While he was gone, Schwartz snagged another business card from the rack. The kid came back with a big black book, which struck me as pretty old-fashioned for a media-conversion place. He went back through several pages in the book, but came up with nothing, he said. When it was clear we'd learned as much as we were going to, Schwartz thanked the guy, and we took our leave.

On the way home, we talked it over. "I'd trust A.M.C.E. about as far as I can throw a Methodist church," Schwartz said. "That based-on-trust business is ridiculous. It's not a bank or a medical practice, where people come back year after year, after all. Do people bring in their old media batch by batch, one after the other? Nonsense. You gather them all up at once and get them converted, right? God knows what that boy has seen his customers bring in, what he's watched. Good Lord." I had to agree.

We stopped at Sahm's Place for dinner, and the onion rings and fried mushrooms were as good as ever. Schwartz showed me the other card he'd picked up at A.C.M.E., belonging to one Robert Benedict, and the dime finally dropped.

Chapter Twenty-Six

Friday, April 10

When we got back to the office, the landline was ringing. It was Neil Parkinson, who told us he'd had a call that morning from Interpol, after which he'd called the banking people in Chicago who'd inherited the armored-car heist history. He had spent the day in discussions, and the upshot was that Viola Ketchum, having restored almost the entire amount stolen two decades before, shy only twelve or thirteen thousand or so, would eventually be receiving a reward of about ten percent of the total, less what the IRS saw as the due of the U.S. Treasury. Parkinson said the hardest part of the day had been trying to get a straight answer from the IRS about how big a bite they would be taking, which wasn't really surprising. They hate to commit to less than they might eventually feel entitled to. He said he'd informed Ms. Ketchum of the good news, and he wished he were twenty years younger.

That put a smile on Schwartz's face. Parkinson said Ms. Ketchum had seemed "extremely gratified" by the news, and he predicted we'd be hearing from her quite soon. "She seems quite overwhelmed by her good fortune," he said.

"Well, we can count on the Internal Revenue Service to help her get back down to earth," Schwartz said.

"One thing I think I should mention, though, is that she seems eager to share," Parkinson said. "It was all I could do to explain to her that she owes me nothing, legally or morally, since my fee will be included in your invoice for your services, and that includes the trip to Geneva, since, after all, you hired me to—"

"Of course," Schwartz said. "And there will doubtless be further need for you in the tax discussions, although I was thinking of recommending that she seek financial advice independently." He hates discussing money with clients. Or anyone.

"Not a problem at all. It's been a pleasure, I assure you. Such a charming young woman." They chatted for a few more minutes, then rang off.

It wasn't ten minutes later that the phone rang, and of course, it was the client. I stayed on the line as usual. She was bubbly, to put it mildly. Schwartz tried calming her down, but when she suggested forking over ten percent of her ten percent, he jammed the brake down hard.

"Absolutely not. First of all, Ms. Ketchum, we have no idea how rapacious the IRS will be. Mr. Parkinson tells me that the reward, whatever it amounts to finally, will be paid as a lump sum, which maximizes the percentage the IRS will lay claim to. It could be as much as half, although I tend to doubt it will be quite so much. The IRS does, in fact, have what effectively amounts to the capacity for shame, and they don't like to be seen as—"

"But Mr. Schwartz, if you hadn't figured out Uncle Jim's puzzle, and the code and everything, which I still don't understand how you did it, I'd have had nothing, and the police told me about catching those criminals breaking into Uncle Jim's house, and I could have been there, and they'd have killed me if I'd been there, if it hadn't been for you, so I really owe you my life, not just ten percent of the—"

Schwartz hit on the perfect way to stop her, of course. "Viola," he said, "I will send you a bill once we know what you've actually gained from Uncle Jim after the IRS has collected its share. I can assure you that my bill will be closer to one percent of your bounty than to ten."

"You called me Viola," she said. "You actually called me Viola, like we're friends, not just neighbors."

"Of course," he said, "although I would question the validity of 'just neighbors', since good neighbors are among the most precious things in life, when you come down to it." He cleared his throat. "You have been an ideal client, Viola, and it has been a pleasure working for you, in every way."

That got her but good. She still wanted to insist on ten percent of her net reward or even of the pre-IRS amount, but Schwartz said, "Viola, the IRS is not the only entity with self-respect and even a reputation. I have to look in the mirror to shave, and I could not face myself if I knew I had taken unfair advantage of a client, friend, and neighbor." I thought to myself that I hoped he was proud of making a woman cry.

He had had years more practice than she had at insisting, so eventually, she agreed to wait till the smoke cleared when he assured her an invoice would be forthcoming. When we all hung up, he told me, "Make sure we don't exceed one percent of her net, or I'll never sleep again. Freda wouldn't let me." For someone who doesn't believe in an afterlife, he certainly lets his late wife boss him a lot. Or pretends to.

Schwartz went over what we'd learned, and we agreed it looked good for a resolution the next day, if we could arrange to have everyone together. He asked me to get Inspector Mercer on the phone if possible and to stay on the line. It was getting late, but I called and, after a couple transfers, heard that raspy voice, "What do you want?"

Schwartz was at his smoothest. "Inspector, has the murderer of Ilona Marchand been arrested?"

"You know good and well he hasn't," Mercer said, "or she hasn't, for all I know. Why? Are you saying you know who killed her?"

"No, I'm not saying that," Schwartz said, "because I don't, but I have a viable suspicion, and if you would like to join me and Mr. Zufahl at WarnerCorp tomorrow, at ten o'clock, say, I think we might be able to cast some light on the matter."

"On Saturday?"

"Yes, I know it's Saturday."

"Look, Schwartz, if you are withholding evidence in a murder case, I'll have your license—"

"No, Inspector, I have no clear evidence of his guilt, and yes, 'his' is, I believe, the correct pronoun. I have no evidence that you or your men could not have discovered yourself, but I believe that, if properly presented, it will help identify the guilty party, and further investigation of the sort you are far more capable of than I will establish his guilt. No, it wouldn't be sufficient for an arrest now, but if you and perhaps Sergeant Ripley will join us at WarnerCorp tomorrow morning—"

It took quite a while for Schwartz to convince Mercer that the matter would have to wait until the next day, but he finally agreed to be there.

Schwartz hung up, and so did I. He went back to his book. He was rereading *The Seven Pillars of Wisdom,* God knows why. I went back to transcribing notes, but I don't mind telling you my heart wasn't in it.

Schwartz looked up from his book, with a finger marking his place, and said, "Rainer."

I said, "Yes, sir?"

"Call her."

"Beg pardon?"

"Call Ms. Warner, please, and ask her to be sure to be at the company's offices tomorrow. You could let her know that we intend to expose Ms. Marchand's murderer. I'm sure she would appreciate that. Meanwhile, I need to call Mr. Warner to make arrangements for tomorrow."

I thought about it and decided he was right, but I'd rather not call Iris from the office. I said I'd be back in a little while. I left Schwartz dialing Buck Warner and went to my room upstairs to call Iris.

It was pleasant hearing her voice. I filled her in on the matter of what was bugging Buck, or rather what had been bugging him. She didn't sound at all surprised that he'd been attracted to her former sister-in-law. "You know, Rainer, that makes a lot of sense, now that I think about it. They've known each other for years, and why wouldn't he be interested in her? Ilona was one of the best people I've ever—" Suddenly, she was choked up. I waited for her to get control, since I couldn't pat her shoulder over the phone. So Schwartz wasn't the only one.

"I'm sorry," she said after a moment. I heard her blow her nose. Even that sounded nice. I realized this was going to be a hard one to get over, but I'd gotten over things before. I'd manage. As my AA sponsor had put it about reality, the good news is that you don't have to like it.

"Iris," I said, trying out the high road, "have you thought that maybe Buck needs you right now, more than ever?"

"What do you mean, Rainer? Are you saying you'd want me to get back with him?"

"No, no, I mean, you said you and Buck were better friends than you'd ever been before, since the divorce, and now he's dealing with a lot, with Ilona gone, and everyone in the company on the police list of suspects. When Mr. Schwartz and I—"

"Leo," she said.

"When Leo and I talked with him, it was like he'd been waiting for someone to listen to him about her. It was all dammed up inside him, and then it just came pouring out, you know?" I listened, but heard nothing. I wondered what she was thinking. I wished I knew what she was thinking. I wished I knew what I was thinking.

"Rainer," she said, "I can call Buck at any time, but I'm not Ilona, you know? I loved her, not just as a sister-in-law, but as a really close friend, especially after Andrew died, and I know how special a person she was, so I understand quite well what Buck is missing. But I don't think calling him would make it easier for either of us."

"For either of you?"

"Right. He's hurting in his way, and I am in mine, but I don't think we can share all that grief and make it subside."

"Oh," I said. Not too impressively, I'm sure.

"Oh, indeed, Rainer. I need to talk with you, if I can, but not about Buck. There's another matter that, well, that takes precedence, if that makes any sense."

"Well, yes," I said, "and I need to talk with you, although I'm not sure how exactly to go about it. There's so much that needs explaining, and I know Mr. Schwartz wants to go back to WarnerCorp tomorrow, about Ilona, and—"

"I'll be there tomorrow, Rainer." I really liked the way she said my name. I really wished she weren't the owner of five percent of WarnerCorp. I really wished for a lot of things.

"I'll see you there then," I said. "I don't know if we'll have a chance to talk, with everything that needs to be resolved, but maybe afterward we could meet somewhere."

"Is there anything wrong with my house?"

"Not at all, Iris; it's very nice." Oh, yes. Very nice indeed.

"Then let's plan to meet here, tomorrow, after five sometime. Depending on how things go at the office."

"All right," I said. I almost said, "It's a date," but stopped in time.

"Good," she said. "It's a date." We hung up together.

Chapter Twenty-Seven

The next morning Schwartz and I arrived at the WarnerCorp building at the same time as Inspector Mercer and Sergeant Ripley. They brought along a second car, a black and white with two uniformed officers, who stayed behind as the four of us went in. Henry Appleby was at the elevator to bring us up to the offices. Aside from nods and good mornings, there wasn't a lot of chitchat, although we were given to understand that some people weren't thrilled to have had their weekends interrupted.

Henry left us to return to his office, and the four of us visitors headed for Buck Warner's office. He got us as settled as possible, and Schwartz explained how he thought we should proceed. Of course, Mercer didn't like it, but Buck sided with Schwartz, and like it or not, it was his company and his office and his staff that was about to be diminished by one murderer, and that carried the day.

Buck agreed to assemble the staff in the conference room next to his office, and he turned to his laptop and sent out a text summoning everyone to the northwest corner room. We moved there, and Buck took the chair at the end of the long table nearest the door. Schwartz and I stood back as everyone filed in, noticeably less chipper than the last time I'd seen them there, when I was Charles Wood. Inspector Mercer and Sergeant Ripley took positions standing against the wall on either side of the table, not far from Buck Warner's seat.

Iris and Henry Appleby were the last two staff members to join us. I smiled at Iris when I caught her eye, and she tried to smile back, didn't quite make it, but nodded as she took a seat.

I noticed that they'd once again mapped their office locations onto the conference room. Buck Warner was at the head of the table, with Geoff Parsons sitting on his right, then Keith Benedict, George Kearney, and Henry Appleby along that side. Iris sat at the end opposite Buck. Jean Stevens sat on Iris's right, then Lara Collins, and Clare Thomason. The last chair, on Buck's left, where Ilona would have sat, was empty.

Buck Warner thanked everyone for coming, as if they'd really had a choice. Looking at them, I had to admit that one of them was a very cool customer, considering the situation. Buck remarked that it wasn't necessary to introduce Inspector Mercer, Sergeant Ripley, Leo Schwartz, and Rainer Zufahl to the WarnerCorp staff, or vice versa, but he thought the inspector wanted to make a statement.

Mercer took a step forward, cleared his throat, and spoke. He was brief and very much to the point. He said that we were gathered at the request of Leo Schwartz, that this was not an official inquiry, but that the police were present in case they were needed. He didn't say they'd better be needed or Schwartz would have a lot to answer for. "So, you all realize you are here voluntarily, and let's just hear what Schwartz has to say." He stepped back, looked at Schwartz, gave a quick short nod.

Schwartz went to the empty chair on Warner's left. I stood to his left, about midway down the table. Rather than sit, Schwartz held the back of the chair like a lectern. "Good morning," he said. "Most of you are hoping, or expecting, to learn the identity of Ilona Marchand's killer today. One of you, at least, already knows, because he *is* the killer. Looking around the room, I would be—"

Henry Appleby interrupted. "You say 'he,' Schwartz. Are you excluding the women from consideration, or—"

Jean Stevens interrupted Appleby. "Or is your masculine pronoun supposed to include the feminine, as if—"

Kearney and Thomason interrupted in turn, and then more joined in, and there was more talking than listening. Mercer and Ripley looked at Schwartz, and so did Buck and Iris, who seemed to be the only WarnerCorp staff who weren't talking. Faces were getting red with anger or frustration or both.

Schwartz let it go on for a few more seconds, then he suddenly roared, "Shut up!" They shut up. "We'll never get out of here at this rate," he muttered. He took a breath.

"I'll be as brief as possible," he said, "but I'll thank you to listen and wait until I'm finished, and if you still have questions, I'll try to answer them." He paused and looked around the table, from Buck to Clare.

"From the start," Schwartz said, "this has been a matter not of money but of passion. Among the problems wealth brings is the ability to gratify one's appetites, without the limits that are normally imposed by financial considerations. Great wealth means the ability to buy almost anything, but some things are more expensive than others, and some things cannot be bought. At any rate, some things cannot be bought with money."

"Geesh, Schwartz," Henry said from down the table, opposite Schwartz, "are you going to lecture us, of all people, on—"

"Patience, Mr. Appleby, patience," Schwartz said. "I need to establish the stage on which the play was acted out. Buck and Iris Warner were divorced, Ilona Marchand and Keith Benedict were widowed, and the others in the company were in marriages or other relationships or both. People who have worked together for many years, as you all have, come to know each other quite as well, in many ways, as people who have been married for years. In certain ways, often rather better than marriage partners know each other. Hopes and dreams, likes and dislikes, fears and hatreds, all kinds of emotions, are shared, and not always equally, or reciprocally.

"Human beings are, as Aristotle put it, rational animals. That is, we are capable of reason, although, of course, we are not always ruled by it. 'Sometimes rational animals' might put it better, in fact.

"Ms. Marchand, as you all know, was twice widowed, and she was by all accounts an admirable, intelligent, compassionate woman. And she was—" Schwartz looked around the table again. "—a passionate, attractive, desirable woman. I have no idea, to be perfectly honest, how many of you here today found her, on some level at least, desirable."

"Schwartz," Buck said, shifting to look up at him, "do you really have to—"

"Yes, I do," Schwartz snapped. "Ms. Marchand was desired, but being blessed with wealth, she was not influenced by considerations that would have affected most women in this world. She was very much her own person, in every possible way, and her affections could not be bought.

"But, distasteful as it is to have to say it, what cannot be purchased can sometimes be obtained by other means, and this is what led, however indirectly, to her murder." He had their attention now.

"You, Mr. Warner, were attracted to Ms. Marchand, and you pressed your case, unfortunately too soon after her husband's death. However one may feel about Ernest Marchand, who was in certain ways less than ideal as a husband, he enjoyed his wife's affection, whether he deserved it or not. Ms. Marchand was still mourning his death when you spoke to her, and—"

"Damn." Buck looked like he wished he were dead.

"And it was too soon," Schwartz went on, "for her to consider your suit. Being, as you are, sir, an honorable, decent man, you backed away, gave her the space, the time. You gave her the greatest gift you could have given her: you gave her your patience."

"Yes," Iris said from the foot of the table. "You would." She looked then like a woman still in love with her husband.

"This was not really a secret here within the company," Schwartz said. "What some of you here also know is that Ms. Marchand was also being pressured, in a far less decent way, by another person who desired her. She was being threatened with blackmail."

That produced another gender-based dichotomy around the table. The women sat there impassively; this was no news to any of them. Except for Buck, the men looked shocked. One of them was faking it, of course, but, if I hadn't known who he was, it would have taken a better detective than me to have picked him out.

"There were videotapes," Schwartz said, "recording activity that Ms.

Marchand had engaged in, years ago, as Ms. Wilson, recorded by her husband, whether with or without her knowledge and consent, I do not know." That was technically correct, I guess. "There are times, as Inspector Mercer has observed, when human behavior is very difficult to understand, and wealth is no protection from folly, whether it was Mr. Wilson's or his wife's, we have no way of knowing at this time." I thought he was icing the cake a bit thick with possibilities here, but there it was.

"Those videotapes were found by her son, Brandon Wilson, who was led, by curiosity or some other impulse perhaps, to wish to see what was on them. He found an establishment that could convert the decades-old media to a modern format. When questioned by Mr. Zufahl, Brandon Wilson claimed to have forgotten where he had had the videotapes converted.

"I am inclined to believe that Brandon's memory was clearer than it seemed, although as everyone here knows, except perhaps the police, his memory may well be less reliable than it should be. At any rate, after searching for a memorandum of the transaction, or perhaps after soul-searching, Brandon supplied Mr. Zufahl with the name of the company he had used." He paused for another survey of the room.

"The name of the company is A.M.C.E., which stands for Appleby Media Conversion Enterprise." That got their attention. Every pair of eyes but mine shifted to Henry Appleby. Schwartz went on. "Yes, your company, Mr. Appleby. Like several others at WarnerCorp, you have outside interests, outside affairs. No doubt converting media has its interesting aspects, aside from the financial."

Henry was keeping himself under control well. "Now, look, Schwartz, that's just a small business I started to provide—"

"To provide jobs for your son," Schwartz said, "and for your nephew, your late sister's son. When Mr. Zufahl and I visited A.C.M.E. yesterday, your nephew wasn't present, but his business card was." He took a card from his breast pocket and handed it to Inspector Mercer, who showed it to Steve Ripley.

"No doubt your nephew was involved in the conversion of Brandon Wilson's videotapes, and no doubt he was acquainted with Brandon, and with Brandon's mother, as well. Indeed, it's likely that Brandon chose A.M.C.E. because he knew and, unfortunately, trusted Robert and your son. So, when the—" Schwartz paused, and I was sure he was looking for a softened version of 'salacious,' "When the provocative videotapes of Ms. Marchand, formerly Ms. Wilson, were converted, it would not be surprising if Robert mentioned the matter to his father, who worked with her at WarnerCorp."

Of course, they all knew who was related to whom, even if they hadn't known that Keith Benedict's son and Henry Appleby's nephew Robert worked at A.C.M.E., and all eyes had shifted from Appleby to Benedict. Benedict wasn't handling the attention well at all.

"Robert mentioned Ilona's, that is, Brandon's videotapes to you, Mr. Benedict, either as soon as he saw what was on them or shortly thereafter, and this provided a lever, as you thought, to apply to Ms. Marchand. I don't know or care, really, whether you had expressed your desires to her before and had been rebuffed, but you must have been aware of how Mr. Warner felt about her and, perhaps, how she felt about him. Time was not on your side, Mr. Benedict. Nor, of her own free will, was Ilona. In any case, armed with a threat to her respectability, you attempted to compel that which would not be freely given." Benedict seemed to have shrunk a bit. He was shaking his head back and forth, his mouth forming words, but no sound came out.

"How did you approach Ms. Marchand, Mr. Benedict? Did you hint that you knew things she would have preferred to keep private? Or were you more direct? Did you tell her you would keep the matter quiet if she was prepared to acquiesce, or did you tell her you had the digital files on hand, ready to be put on the internet? Did you threaten the object of your desire with worldwide public exposure? Did you let her imagine what it would be like to have those long-ago scenes put out for anyone with a computer to see?"

Benedict was like an insect pinned to a card. "No," he finally managed. "I just told her it would be embarrassing to have that stuff out there, and it would be good to have a friend who could keep that from happening, but she—" He broke off, struggling. "She—" He gave up.

"She defied you, didn't she, Mr. Benedict?" Schwartz said. "She refused your suit. She defied you as you had never expected her to do. You had stolen that stationery, concocted that ridiculous note, and waited for her to crumble. But she didn't crumble, did she? Did you think she would come running to you to save her from blackmail? In any event, she did no such thing." Schwartz paused. The tension in the room was thick enough to cut with a knife.

"She spoke with Mr. Zufahl, a private detective, instead. Were you afraid he would discover that you yourself were the source of the blackmail you had offered to protect her from? You went to her, spoke with her about blackmail, but you miscalculated. It was by no means common knowledge that Ms. Marchand had been threatened, and she was one very perspicacious woman, wasn't she, Mr. Benedict?"

Benedict reached inside his jacket, and the next thing I knew my gun was out, and my arm was extended in his direction, over Clare's head, and I was praying he'd draw on me. Benedict stared at me and very slowly took out a handkerchief, wiped sweat off his face. I thought, who the hell carries a handkerchief in his breast pocket, and lowered the Sig, but it stayed out. Steve Ripley had moved over and was waiting right behind his chair. Schwartz went on.

"She saw through your machinations, didn't she, Mr. Benedict? She saw you for the kind of man you are, sir. I imagine she defied you, told you to get out of her office, and made it clear she intended to tell Mr. Warner, the head of the company, what sort of person he was harboring at WarnerCorp. She turned away from you, Mr. Benedict; she turned her back on you, didn't she?

"And that was Ilona Marchand's big mistake. She saw you for the man you are, but she was too generous a person to imagine that you would strike her from behind. She saw you as a shameless manipulator, but she didn't realize you were a backstabber. She should have. She would be here now, had she realized the true depth of your depravity.

"She turned away, and you snatched one of those polished stones from her desk and struck her on the back of her head. You cut a length of cord from the window shades, and you strangled her as she lay there unconscious. If you couldn't have her, no one could."

"No," Keith Benedict said. "She was going to tell Buck, and he'd have fired me if he'd known about it. I couldn't lose my job. I couldn't...." His voice trailed off into sobs. He buried his face in his hands.

"No," Schwartz said. "You could lose your job. You couldn't bear the thought of being fired from the company you'd worked for for twenty years. You couldn't bear a shadow of the shame you willingly threatened Ms. Marchand with, could you?" He looked up. "Inspector Mercer, he's all yours."

Benedict went quietly, at least, Steve Ripley getting him to his feet and handcuffing him as he informed him that he was under arrest for the murder of Ilona Marchand and gave him the Miranda warning in front of a dozen witnesses. Lara and Clare were crying, but Jean just looked grim as Steve took Benedict away, calling for the two uniforms to meet him at the elevator downstairs. Iris looked sad but calm, not angry.

Schwartz had been on his feet awhile, but he didn't sit in Ilona's chair. Mercer asked Buck whether he needed the police from here on, and Buck said he didn't. Mercer left, with a curt nod to Schwartz on his way out.

Buck said, "Well..." and then he suddenly gave way, his face in his hands, and his friends came up to him, reached out, and patted his shoulders, and Schwartz turned to me, raised an eyebrow. We left the conference room. I glanced back, caught Iris's eye, and she mouthed, "Five." Schwartz and I caught up with Mercer at the elevator. He just shook his head as the elevator took us down to ground level.

Chapter Twenty-Eight

When Schwartz and I got back home, Viola was waiting by the front door. Schwartz got out and went to her while I put the car up. We gathered in the office, and she sat in the red-leather chair. Schwartz brought iced tea himself, the ordinary black oolong. He said the special brew had taken on too many connotations for him for the moment. He repeated what he had said to her earlier, adding that he hoped she wouldn't react like a winner of the lottery, letting the sudden windfall upset her life permanently. "But how—" The client didn't get it all out. She looked at me, saw no help, then back at Schwartz. "It's just overwhelming, Mr. Schwartz."

He doesn't have to like it. "I should hasten to explain," he said. "The legal status of that money is by no means clear at present, but I have to say that I suspect there are clear legal claims on it, so I'm not promising you any amount of dollars or Euros, free and clear.

"In fact," he said, leaning back in his chair, getting comfortable for the long haul, "I believe that the account and the safe-deposit box are connected to a robbery over thirty years ago, a robbery that cost at least five lives at the time and has cost two more lives again quite recently."

"But how could you know all this?" Viola wanted to know. "The files said nothing about money or robbery or, well, anything."

"In fact, you are absolutely right about that," Schwartz said. "But let us consider the files. As I said earlier, we assumed that the corrected files were the ones we were meant to look at. All of us worked from that assumption, until it occurred to me that the seemingly uncorrected files were the key to the puzzle."

I was still catching up at this point. At least Viola had company.

"Looking at the printout of the file-comparison program Rainer had run on the files, I was suddenly struck by an interesting fact about the misspellings. They were all of a kind. There were no transposed letters, no doubled letters, no incorrect letters replacing correct letters.

"In every case, the misspelling consisted of a word with a missing letter. It occurred to me that the missing letters conveyed the message. That is, in fact, your uncle didn't send a message. He sent everything *except* the message. The message was not in the files; rather, the message was what was not in the files."

"Good Lord," I muttered as the lights began to come on, however dimly.

"Now," Schwartz said, "I must admit to a foolish mistake on my part, and I mention this only for the sake of complete honesty. I began reading my hard copy of the Ellenbogen manuscripts, the supposedly 'uncorrected' set, marking omitted letters in the margin, in red ink." He picked it up from a file folder at his elbow on his desk and handed it to Viola. "I was almost finished with the section 'The End of All Things' before I realized how unnecessary it was. I could easily have used Mr. Zufahl's printout of the differences. Out of a sense of completeness, or perhaps just obsession, however, I continued to the end. The message is thus conveyed by my red notations in the hard copy you are now holding."

Viola seemed not to mind when I got up and stood looking over her shoulder. She read the first few letters in red: *"e, r, t, n, u, e, n..."* She looked up. "If that's the message, Mr. Schwartz, I'm still not getting it." Same here, I thought.

Schwartz was trying not to wallow. "Well," he said, "the entire message was easier to deal with when Rainer sent me an electronic copy of the results of the comparison. I simply went through the file and deleted everything except the letter that was missing from the 'uncorrected' file." Which meant he'd figured that part out days ago, and it hadn't occurred to me there was anything suspicious about his asking me for the results in digital form.

"When I was done, I had a vertical column of letters. I ran them in as a single paragraph, and this was the result." He fished a hard copy out of the stack in the file folder on his desk and handed it to Viola. It read:

ertnuenettesfuengtofneufsiartgtnihcstsissudvonfneufnireivnusiortreivfneu

ftiuhllunovonallunnebeisshcessissiortiessudlluneudettesonugtnihcstreivall

unovonfneufreivottoeudthcasnietiuhsudgtoonutpeseudevenegicidodemru

ogeureirtsudniledeevirpessiusknab

"I confess that I didn't see light at this point, and it took some thought, and some staring at the message before I noticed that the word 'neuf,' French for 'new' or 'nine,' occurred four times. This turned out to be the result of happenstance, but a happenstance that, logic aside, tipped me in the direction of understanding. Notice that every time 'neuf' occurs, it is preceded by the letter *f*." He underlined the four instances for her. "This surely could not be coincidence, I thought: 'fneuf' is meaningless, but I was now mentally open to numbers, and I realized that this five-letter sequence was 'fuenf' backwards, that is, the German word for 'five' spelled with following *e* rather than the usual way, with an umlaut, 'fünf.'" On the bottom of the sheet he wrote the word both ways. "By the way, there are only four German words ending in -*nf*, all four letters each, the others being 'Genf', 'Hanf', and 'Senf': 'Geneva,' 'hemp,' and 'mustard.' But that has nothing to do with this. Pardon me." Viola asked him to go on. She seemed no more enlightened than she had been.

"I looked through the paragraph and found that there were other numbers spelled out in reverse. Rather than weary you with all the intermediate steps in my considerations of the text, I decided to reverse the entire paragraph. Seamus must have decided the coded message would be too easy to unravel if he sent it right-reading. Your Uncle Jim was a puzzle-maker, and like many people, he could be a bit obsessive about his specialty. I took a leap of faith and, rather tediously, I may say, keyed the letters from back to front, resulting in this version."

He got another sheet from the folder and handed it to her. I looked at it too:

banksuissepriveedelindustrieruegourmedodicigenevedueseptunootgdushu iteinsachtdueottovierfuenfnovonullaviertschintgunosetteduenulldusseitroi ssissechssiebennullanovonullhuitfuenfviertroisunvierinfuenfnovdussistsch intgtraisfuenfotgneufsetteneuntre

"It begins to become clear at this point, doesn't it?" Schwartz said.

"Well, not particularly," Viola said, "although I see some French at the beginning, a bank, Swiss, private..." She looked up from the sheet. "Mr. Schwartz, I'm afraid you must think I'm really stupid, but I still don't see how this all works out."

By now, Schwartz had long since convinced the client that he was some sort of decoding genius, which of course, was all he'd wanted. "It helps to divide things up a bit, with word spaces. Here." He handed her the next sheet.

bank suisse privee de lindustrie rue gourme dodici geneve due sept uno otg dus huit eins acht due otto vier fuenf novo nulla vier tschintg uno sette due null dus sei trois sis sechs sieben nulla novo null huit fuenf vier trois un vier in fuenf nov dus sis tschintg trais fuenf otg neuf sette neun tre

"What on earth is 'tschintg', and how do you pronounce it?" I asked.

"It's Romansch for 'five,' and I have no idea," Schwartz said.

I didn't find his explanation particularly helpful. "What's Romansch?"

"One of Switzerland's four legal languages," he said. "If you'll restrain your impatience, I'll make it clear in a minute." I shut up and listened.

"How did you know how to break up those words?" the client asked.

Schwartz was smug, but holding it in pretty well. "Since the bank was a Swiss one, I reflected that Switzerland has four legally recognized languages. German is dominant in the north and central regions, French in the west,

Italian in the south, and Romansch, a dialect that, like French and Italian, is descended from Latin, is spoken in relatively few areas, but especially the canton of Grisons, in the east. As you doubtless know, the multiple languages of Switzerland are the reason that the country's name is given as Latin 'Helvetia' on postage stamps, rather than 'Suisse,' 'Schweiz,' 'Svizzera,' and 'Svizra.'

"Seamus used French, German, Italian, and Romansch words for the numbers, but you'll notice, if you look closely, that not all numbers have been used. I had to do a bit of research," he admitted, "because I wasn't familiar with the Romansch numbers, but it wasn't really difficult from this point on." He showed us a table of the numbers zero to nine for French, German, Italian, and Romansch, with some words crossed out. He laid it on the desk rather than handing it over. I retrieved it later:

French	German	Italian	Romansch
zero	null	zero	nulla
un	eins	uno	in
deux	zwei	due	dus
trois	drei	tre	trais
quatre	vier	quattro	quatter
cinq	fuenf	cinque	tschintg
six	sechs	sei	sis
sept	sieben	sette	set
huit	acht	otto	otg
neuf	neun	novo	nov

"Seamus refrained from using the French, Italian, and Romansch words for 'four', namely 'quatre', 'quattro', and 'quatter', and the French and Italian for 'five', 'cinq' and 'cinque', because they contain the letter q; he avoided the French and Italian 'zero' and the German 'zwei' because of the z and the French for 'two' and 'six', 'deux' and 'six', because of the x. Obviously, it would be difficult to find words to insert in his text containing q, x, and z, and omitting those letters would have been unduly conspicuous. This caused, among other things, heavy reliance on the German 'vier' and 'fuenf', without which I'd almost certainly have taken much longer to understand what was going on. Breaking the first few words of the paragraph into lines gives us…." He handed her the next sheet:

bank suisse privee de lindustrie

   rue gourme dodici

   geneve

   due sept uno otg dus huit eins acht due otto vier fuenf novo nulla vier tschintg uno sette due null dus sei trois sis sechs sieben nulla novo null huit fuenf vier trois un vier in fuenf nov dus sis tschintg trais fuenf otg neuf sette neun tre

"Next, I capitalized," he said, "added a missing accent or two, and translated the spelled-out numbers into figures." Another sheet for Viola and me:

Bank Suisse Privée de l'Industrie

   Rue Gourme 12, Genève

   271828182845904517202636670908543141592653589793

"Now, Swiss bank account numbers aren't that long, and so a little experimentation with that string of forty-eight numbers led to three strings of sixteen:

Bank Suisse Privée de l'Industrie

   Rue Gourme 12, Genève

   2718281828459045

   1720263667090854

   3141592653589793

"So there are three account numbers?" I asked.

"No, as a matter of fact, and I'm frankly not sure why exactly Seamus included two dummies into the message, but he did. Ordinary human psychology is murky enough, and the psychology of a puzzle constructor, all the more so. Can you think of any reasons to be suspicious of two of those number strings? Think approximations of irrational numbers—"

"Pi," I said. "Put a decimal point after the three at the start of the last line, and that's pi to, uh, fifteen decimal places." Viola looked up at me, clearly impressed.

"Yes," Schwartz said. "My favorite mnemonic for pi is 'How I want a drink, alcoholic of course, after all these lectures exploring quantum mechanics. Get me one properly aged scotch', which would provide five more digits, not that we need them."

"Beg pardon?" Viola said.

"Count the letters in each word," Schwartz said. "'How,' 3; 'I,' 1; 'want,' 4; and so on."

I started to ask, "Which of the other numbers—"

Viola interrupted, "Damn, yes! Two point seven one eight two eight one eight two eight, etc. is *e*, the base of natural logarithms, Mr. Schwartz."

Schwartz beamed at her. He loves an intelligent client. "So, crossing off the approximations of pi and *e*, we have the real account number and the name and address of the bank." He gave Viola one last sheet.

Bank Suisse Privée de l'Industrie
Rue Gourme 12, Genève
17202636667090854

I admit I was still stewing over the time he'd let me and Viola spend on the damned manuscripts, but after all, he had produced results. Twenty million Euros, or even a tenth of it, less taxes, is not something to be laughed at.

"Mr. Parkinson, as you know, met with the bank officials and the legal authorities, and he will be speaking again with representatives of Interpol tomorrow," Schwartz informed her.

"The robbery took place over thirty years ago, involving men who thought, incorrectly, that they could get away with a considerable sum in bearer securities, bonds, and other documents, as well as a considerable amount of cash. In fact, the criminals barely managed to hide their loot before being captured. The authorities were able to identify one key member of the gang, and to save his own skin, he betrayed his fellow thieves." He leaned back now. The exposition, even with so many visual aids, had been exhausting emotionally and mentally.

"Mr. Parkinson is a man of sense, education, and intelligence, which are not commonly found in a man of his probity. You can rest assured, Ms. Ketchum, that he will represent our interests, yours and ours, with ability and determination."

Viola nodded agreement, then somewhat illogically looked at me, apparently for my opinion. "You can trust Neil Parkinson with your life," I told her. That comment out of my own mouth surprised me. I realized that there was no good reason for me to be standing there, so I went back to my desk.

"I had no idea," Schwartz said, "what amount the reward might be, but I thought ten percent might not be unrealistic. The original loss, of course, was not covered by insurance, so from the Treasury's viewpoint, the recovery of this money is a significant event, and simple public relations should head off any attempts at parsimony."

"Neil said it would be over two million dollars," Viola said. "Damn."

"Indeed," Schwartz said. I knew we were both considering that one word: Neil.

Schwartz once said to me that the frustrating thing about writing fiction would be that it has to be plausible, whereas reality suffers from no such handicap. "Take the year 2016, for example. Great Britain decided, for no obvious reason, to extricate itself from the European Community; Bob Dylan was awarded the Nobel Prize for Literature; the Chicago Cubs won the World Series, and the former star of 'The Apprentice' was elected President of the United States. None of that would be tolerated in a novel without a lot of background preparation to help the reader swallow it, but in the real world, it just happened, all in the space of about half a year. Fiction needs sugar to help the medicine go down, but reality just happens, with no sweetener provided." So, I guess what it comes down to is that, weird as that code was, it really was how Viola ended up with Seamus's inheritance.

Chapter Twenty-Nine

Saturday, April 11

I'd like to be able to tell you Schwartz, and I spent the rest of the day engaged in some intellectual discussion of the human psyche, puzzler or not, but the truth is that I managed to get all my remaining notes transcribed that afternoon, and he spent half the time packing aerial salutes with zinc stars, half with Lawrence of Arabia. I finished on the dot at four-thirty, and I told Schwartz I wanted to change my shirt before I went to see Iris. He asked me to tell her he was looking forward to seeing her at St. Luke's or Orchard Park before long. I said I would.

As it happened, I did deliver the message. Iris and I were having tea, of course, on the patio behind her house, and she began the conversation, "God, I could use a meeting, Rainer."

"Same here, and Mr. Schwartz, I mean, Leo says he's looking forward to seeing you in a meeting soon. I could surely use a meeting myself."

"You know what? I was sort of disappointed this morning. I was, really, I was actually hoping Keith Benedict would pull a gun or something, and you would shoot him dead."

"Really," I said. "That's quite a wish, Iris."

"Yeah, and not exactly in the spirit of AA, I realize. 'Let there be no gossip or criticism of another, but instead let there be love, understanding, and acceptance.'"

"No gossip or criticism or shooting dead of another, but...." I told her how I'd felt when Benedict reached inside his jacket.

"Do you think that's strange, Rainer?" she asked. "That I wanted to see you shoot that son-of-a-bitch Keith Benedict dead? For killing Ilona?" She took a sip of tea, set the cup down. "Do you think I'm hopelessly depraved because I wanted to see you shoot a man?"

"Well, my experience with depravity is pretty much professional," I said. "We've had some interesting cases lately, including finding two men chopped into chunks and dumped into a septic tank and one buried under a deck, and thieves ready to murder to recover their loot, who'll spend the rest of their lives sitting on death row because they killed people for money, lots of money. At least you came by yours, honestly; you didn't steal it or kill anybody for it."

"So," she said, "we come to the real roadblock, Rainer." She smiled the way people smile at funerals. "All my money."

"Well, yes," I said. "All your money." I took another sip of that tea. It tasted good. I thought it might be the best tea I'd ever tasted. "And you call it a roadblock, right?"

"I love it," she said, ignoring my question. "You're not put off by the fact that I wished you'd kill Keith, that I wish you'd killed him, this afternoon, and let me tell you something: I still wish he'd given you the excuse. I still wish I could have seen you shoot that bastard dead. But that doesn't bother you a bit, does it? And we both know why, don't we?"

"Sure. I wish he'd given me the excuse. I wish I could have killed him for what he did to Ilona. He's as rich as you are, and you know as well as I do that his lawyers will fight for him all the way, and he'll never get the death penalty for murdering one of the nicest people I've ever met. I met her only twice, but she deserved better than that."

"Yes, she did. And you're right. Money can help you avoid responsibility, and other things, but it's no good with sobriety."

"No, it's not. But it sure presents a problem when—"

"When you're looking over the high brick wall topped with broken glass?" she said.

"Something like that, yeah."

"Well," she said, "I want you to know I'd really like to get to know you better, and I hope it's possible for you to overlook the inessential things that can get in the way—"

"I would like to get to know you," I said, "but the fact is that there really is a very big problem to deal with. This business, the detective business, introduces you to people who will do anything for money, for love, for revenge, for any number of reasons. It teaches you lessons you'd probably be better off not learning, frankly."

I took her hand, held it in both of mine. "Look," I said, "When I was a uniformed cop, I saw things, heard things, that had a permanent impact on me. I'd like to say it was one-sided, that we were the good guys and they were the bad guys, and it was always clear who was on which side of the line. But even when you think you know people pretty well, they can surprise you." I ran out of words, so I stopped talking.

Iris took up the slack. "You do realize that I've talked with Leo, don't you, about you, I mean? And that he filled me in on your time in uniform?"

"I knew you'd talked, but—"

"So he told me what happened. You didn't go with the flow; you refused to go along with the 'go along to get along' routine; and you paid the price for it. You didn't take money when it was put in your hand, and you got singled out."

"Yes, well," I said, "it turns out it's not hard to arrange a frame when a whole precinct is behind it, and—"

"And you're still paying the lawyer's fees, month after month." She smiled. "And I hereby promise never to offer to take care of it for you."

"Uh, thanks?"

"You're welcome," she said. "You've got your life and your obligations, and I've got mine, and I promise I'll never try to buy you. I hope we're both willing to provisionally overlook the fact that I'm rich, not that I really earned a dime of it." I suddenly realized she had tears in her eyes. She took off her glasses and wiped her eyes with a tissue.

"That's right," I said. I still wasn't sure how this was going.

"So," she said, "the main question is, do you have a dinner jacket?"

"Beg pardon?"

"Do you have a dinner jacket?" she repeated. "And shoes and pants and—"

"Of course," I said, "among other things. A detective has to have a pretty extensive wardrobe, after all, to fit in in a wide variety of settings. Most of mine aren't at the dinner jacket end of the spectrum, but I can avoid standing out on formal occasions. Why, are you planning a party?"

Iris put her glasses back on and smiled, nodded, then looked serious again. "Look, I want you to know, Rainer, that I like what I see and hear and that I definitely want to get to know you better." She paused, and her face came closer to mine. "I want to know you better, Rainer, and I'll never try to buy you, so if that's agreeable to you, maybe you'd consider kissing me, for starters, just to see if it's feasible."

Her smile was irresistible. I leaned toward her, and our lips touched, and I realized that she was a woman I could trust to lead me where she wanted me to go, that I could trust her as I'd never quite been able to trust anyone for years, that she would take me with her where she wanted us both to go, and I could let go and let her lead the way.

It was really late when I put the Prius to bed in the garage, and I was lucky to hear the alarm clock the next morning.

Chapter Thirty

Thursday, April 16

Five days later, a few things had happened, including billing clients and filing income-tax returns, and Schwartz and I were back at the Thursday Night Twelve and Twelve meeting. The topic was the Eleventh Step, which is about seeking through prayer and meditation to improve our conscious contact with God as we understand Him, praying only for knowledge of His will for us and the power to carry that out, and the discussion was going counterclockwise around the room, when Phil came in at about twenty minutes after the hour, wearing a different T-shirt, AC/DC, tail out of course, and with his phone of course. Also, without a canvas bag, which seemed an improvement.

I was wondering just how Phil had managed to get loose but figured his mother had posted bail, and I kept an eye on him just in case. When his neighbor on his left had finished sharing his thoughts about Step Eleven and a couple other matters as well, Phil just muttered, "Pass," without bothering to introduce himself or say why he was there. The woman on Phil's right said her name was Marcia, and she was an alcoholic, and she was just going to listen tonight, and on it went.

When it got to me, I said, "My name's Rainer, and I'm an alcoholic," and I said some not particularly original or insightful things about the step, and when I passed, it was Schwartz's turn.

Schwartz said, "Hello, my name is Leo; I'm an alcoholic," and he glanced over in Phil's direction, but Phil was staring at his phone, probably watching a video, given that he had earbuds in. Schwartz started to go on, but suddenly Phil looked up and said, "And you're still a motherfucker too." He stood up while drawing a pistol from under his shirt, at the back of his belt. This time he'd brought an automatic rather than a revolver, an old, not at all shiny Colt .45. Schwartz's left hand grabbed my right wrist, and he barely whispered, "No," as he stood up.

As Phil came toward Schwartz, he smiled like a kid who has discovered where mom and dad hid the Christmas presents and has just opened every last one. The room was very quiet indeed, and there was a loud snick as Phil thumbed back the hammer, and he smiled even wider, glanced at the cocked hammer, as he brought the Colt up to point at Schwartz's chest. Schwartz stood there waiting, my wrist still in his hand. I thought about trying to use my left hand, then it was too late for trying anything.

"Now dodge this, motherfucker," Phil said, squeezing the trigger. There was a really loud click as the hammer dropped. Phil stared at the gun in his hand as if wondering how it had got there. Schwartz took hold of the front end of the pistol as Phil got the hammer cocked again and clicked it down again. With a sudden wrench, Schwartz tore the gun out of Phil's hand.

The same men as three weeks before grabbed Phil, hauled him back to his chair, and sat him in it, not a bit gently. Tony took his place behind the chair, his hands on Phil's shoulders. I was calling 911 myself as Schwartz pulled a chair over to face Phil. I told Schwartz the cops were on the way.

Schwartz ejected the magazine from the .45 into his left hand, looked at it, and remarked, "Fully loaded." He began thumbing cartridges from the mag, letting them fall to the carpet. He shook his head sadly, holding the unloaded pistol muzzle downward in his right hand, the now-emptied magazine in his left.

Phil seemed even more upset than before. "I cocked the damn gun, motherfucker. Why didn't it fire?" He seemed to feel he'd received inadequate firearms tutelage from Schwartz on top of all those other imagined injuries. "I cocked it. It should have fired, motherfucker."

Schwartz dropped the empty mag among the cartridges on the floor, raised the pistol so he could take hold of the slide. He racked it back, let it snap forward again. He showed Phil how the hammer was now cocked. "You loaded the magazine, but you didn't rack the slide. If there'd been a full mag in there just now, that would have cocked the piece, and then, as the slide moved forward again, it would've stripped the top cartridge from the mag and loaded it into the firing chamber. As it is now, racking the slide back cocked the piece, but there was no cartridge to load." With the pistol still pointing at the floor just in front of Phil, Schwartz pulled the trigger, and the hammer fell with a very loud click indeed. Someone gasped.

"Give 'em back," Phil demanded, trying to move forward under Tony's grasp. He stayed put. I heard the steps of the uniforms out in the hall. So did Phil. "Let me have it," he said.

"No," Schwartz said, laying the .45 down at his feet, with the magazine and the cartridges, "much as I really would like to 'let you have it', that's not what's going to happen, Phil. I don't want to be mean about it, but you've had two chances at me, and I think that's more than enough."

"Motherfucker," Phil said again. "You could have done it for me, motherfucker." It sounded like he meant Schwartz could have loaded the pistol for him, but I realized he probably still meant Schwartz could have done the Fourth Step for him. Marcia, at the door, called, "Down here," to the police. They came into the meeting room, drawn Glocks at their sides.

"No," Schwartz said, "I couldn't have, Phil." Without realizing it, I'd expected it to be the same pair of cops this time. Same shift, same day of the week, and same time of day. But it was Officer Peña with a different, younger partner. "Doing it for you is really just about the one thing I couldn't've, shouldn't've, wouldn't've ever done for you. You still want to do it your way, and your way means you think you're entitled to a free ride." Schwartz turned to Officer Peña. "Same as last time," he said, "just a different gun."

Peña holstered his own sidearm and nodded to his partner, who got the handcuffs on Phil and helped him to his feet. No introductions were made, but I read Kerr on his name tag. I wondered whether he pronounced it 'cur' or 'car'. I wondered if Olson had retired or was on vacation or had just taken the day off. I wondered if maybe my concentration was wandering. Kerr started to head Phil toward the hallway while Peña gathered the evidence. "My fingerprints are all over it," Schwartz said. Peña nodded. He signaled Kerr to wait up.

"Maybe now they'll keep him out of circulation," he said. "Shouldn't've made bail last time. I bet it'll be harder to get this time." He shook his head. "How'd you know he hadn't loaded the piece?" he asked.

"I didn't for sure," Schwartz said, "till I saw he hadn't cocked the hammer. Knowing Phil, I figured that, if he'd managed to rack the slide to load and cock it, he wouldn't have managed to lower the hammer without firing it. If it had been cocked, I'd have known I was in real trouble."

"Damn, you're cocksure, Schwartz." It was hard to tell whether Peña was more impressed or exasperated.

"'Cocksure' is probably the best word for it, all things considered," Schwartz said with a smile.

Officer Peña turned to me. "And you just stood there, Zufahl. You're carrying, of course, and you just let this clown pull the trigger on your boss," he repeated.

"No," Schwartz said. "Mr. Zufahl was in the act of drawing when I stopped him. He was only following orders." I've known Schwartz for ten years, and he can still surprise me with what he considers humor.

Phil chose the moment to contribute yet another totally redundant four syllables. Peña told him he had the right to remain silent and, if he knew what was good for him, he'd better start exercising that right, and did he by God understand these rights as he had explained them to him, and by God, he'd better. Even Phil got the point. He shut up.

Peña turned back to Schwartz. He clearly wasn't amused. "Honest to God, Schwartz, holding Zufahl back just makes no damn sense. This guy puts a gun on you, and you're so damn confident about your judgment of what's his name, Phil, here, you don't even let your man do anything to stop it. That's just crazy." He turned to me again. "Next time, you might consider defending your boss anyway, no matter what his damn orders are. He keeps this up, sooner or later, he's going to stop a bullet, and you're going to look and feel pretty useless just standing there with your piece holstered. I'm sure he pays you enough that you'd miss it if he was dead."

I was almost ready with a suitable comment worthy of that crack, but Schwartz beat me to it. "Now, Mr. Peña," Schwartz said. "As I said, Mr. Zufahl was simply following my instructions, and if I can't expect an employee to follow instructions, I don't—"

"Oh, can it," Peña said. "'Mr. Peña', 'Mr. Zufahl', my ass. It's bad enough having to put up with the pair of you as private dicks, but for God's sake, spare us all the phony formality. And what passes for comedy." He headed for the door, nodded to his partner. "Bring him, Kerr." It was 'car.'

Peña turned back to Schwartz and me. "I need to see you two at the station." He looked around the room, without noticeable enthusiasm. "And anyone else who'd care to make a statement, come on down. Hell, everybody, just consider it a general invitation. Let's make a party of it." Peña turned back to the door, muttering bitterly, "Christ Almighty."

Schwartz turned to me and smiled. He patted me on the shoulder. "Crime in Italy," he said.

Appendix

The Ellenbogen Manuscripts

Note: What follows, through page 304, is based upon an accurate scan of the documents Leo Schwartz found in the patch box of Seamus Ellenbogen's flintlock Kentucky rifle. Certain changes have been made. Specifically, the name and the location of a certain bank have been changed, as has the number of the relevant account, for obvious reasons. I have included this on the chance that you might like to try to solve the code yourself. Please use pen, or bear down hard with pencil. —Rainer Zufahl

What's Wrong with AA

A.A. saved my life. I have been sober now for over two decades, and I owe it all to the program of Alcoholics Anonymous. It's not easy; it's hard. But it's not complicated; it's simple. It's a common misconcption, as Ed L. liked to say, that alcoholics can't drink. "Hell, we all know that trick," he would say. "We can all get that done. The point isn't that we can't, since we obviously can. The point is that we don't have to." Very true. Back then, I had no choice. I was way beyond Isak Dinesen's "What is man, when you come to think upon him, but a minutely set, ingenious machine for turning, with infinite artfulness, the red wine of Shiaz into urine?" I was a by no means ingenious or precisely tuned meat-machine, the principal function of which was to transform, with no particular arfulness, bourbon into urine, dry heaves, hangovers, and blackouts.

Speaking for myself, it seems to me that it comes down to five things, which needn't be numbered, since unlike the Twelve Steps, they are done more or less all at once. The five things I have done and contiue to do are these:

I have a sponsor, and I stay in touch with him.

I work the Twelve Steps with the guidance of my sponsor.

I read the so-called big book, *Alcoholics Anonymous,* the chapters in the front and the stories in the back.

I go to meetings, participate in discssions, and listn to other alcoholics.

I don't drink alcohol.

It took me an incredibly long time to realize that these five items would help me stay sober. If I don't ingest alcohol, I don't get drunk. Who knew? Back when I was drinkig, I was crazy enough to tell myself, night after night, as I poured the first drink, that I would not get drunk that night. One resolvd to stay sober should not be pouring himself a drink.

My first sponsor used to remark that Alcoholics Anonymous was founded by a stock-market speculator and a proctologist, so how prety should we really expect it to be? He would point out that acceptance does not mean approval: The bad news is that reality is not going to transform itself to suit your preferences. The good news is that you don't have to like it.

I won't say that I'm a friend of Bill W., who, from what I've heard and read and been told, was a pretty nasty piece of work. But Bill W. and I have something in common, and so do our wives. Bill and I got beter than we deserved. Lois and Kim deserved better than they got. One of the things wrong with A.A. at the individual level is the attempt to elvate William Griffith Wilson to some sort of pseudo-sainthood.

Bill was a TLC—a thief, a liar, and a cheat—from the get-go. Like many if not most alcoholics, he was an egomaniac with an inferiority complex. His own description of his activities up to the founding of A.A. is honest enough, so far as it goes, sometimes unconsciously so, I believe. To call him a stockbroker would probably be libelous—not against him, but against Wall Street, which one must admit would be quite a feat. His account of the early years of the program minimizes the contributions of others, primarily that of Dr. Robert Holbrook Smith, and he cheerfully takes credit for the work of others. Search in vain for a mention of Henrietta Seiberling or Sister Mary Ignatia. Presuring the A.A. Board into granting him royalties on sales of the "Big Book" and copyrighting the text in his own name as sole author, which he obviously was not, are a couple examples closely afecting the program itself. His carrying on short- and long-term adulterous relationships, including his unfortnate habit of trying to "Thirteenth-Step" attractive female newcomers and, in his will, bequeathing his longtime mistress a share of his fortune, had to have tried Lois's patience to the braking point.

His long-winded preaching in the "Big Book" and in the *12 & 12* about proper sexual conduct was monumetal hypocrisy. What kind of man would take advantage of a newcomer's emotional fragility for his own sexual gratification? "Seduction" is far too kind a word for his cold-hearted use of his exalted position as co-founder. One can't help wondering how many of the women whose vulnerability he exploited stayed sober, once the hard fact of their betrayal sank in. How many of them went back to the bottle to drown the memory of their being used by the self-appointed top man in A.A.?

From Bill's own account in the "Big Book," one can't help suspecting that A.A. itself was intended as just one more money-making scheme, and he may well be the one person who has ever profited financially from the program. (There may be others. I'm a drunk, not a historian. Or an historian either.) He borrowed, without acknowledgment, in Ross Thomas's phrase, elements from the Washintonians, from the Oxford Group, from Reinhold Niebuhr, from … It would be an exaggeration to say that, if some particular though, word, or deed is helpful, useful, valid, then it was lifted from an outside source, and that, if it is original with Bill Wilson, it is harmful, obstructive, and worse than useless. But it would not be a gross exaggeration. For example, in 1950 A.A. finally acknowledged Niebuhr as the author of the Serenity Prayer, which it had been distributing in varius forms since 1941.

This is not intended as an attack on A.A., any more than radiation therapy is an attack on the patient. But what many in the program are looking for is some sort of super-sponsor, some hero or savior whom one may salute, or worship, to whom one can bend the knee. It seems to me, however, that A.A., not being an organization, needs no plaster or plastic saints to bow down to, no superstars to get of on. The Führerprizip is something the fellowship can and should do without.

Let's be specific, then, just as the medical team tries to focus th beam on the malignancy, not on the healthy tissue. Take the *Twelve Steps and Twelve Traditions,* first pblished in 1953, written by Bill W. and edited apparently by no one. Bill's intellectual laziness may be responsible for the most egregious example, in that he may have been indulging in a form of shorthand when he uses "A.A." to mean "alcoholic" or "member of Alcoholics Anonymous" in such passages as "Why must every A.A. hit bottom?" and "… we A.A.'s have known from the very beginning …" It is possible, though I doubt it, that in the first two decades of A.A. some people used "A.A." to reer to a sober drunk, but I have never heard it in the most recent two decade of the program, and I have been listening. In any case, it's not correct, it's not in current usage by even one human being, and it's a scandal to leave such a ludcrous anachronism (to be charitable) in a book intended to help people stay sober. My Grandmother Vaught used to say that she liked the King James Version of the Bible better than the more modern-sounding Revised Standrd Version, "because that's how people talked in them days." Grandma had an excuse, in my fond opinion.

Alcoholics Anonymous, again imo, has no excuse for leaving in the *Twelve Steps and Twelve Taditions* the faulty usage of "A.A." and "A.A.'s" to refer to (a) person(s); minus signs for lines mean "from the foot of the page":

p. 5, l. 10	p. 38, l. −10, −4	p. 98, l. −3	p. 141, l. 13
p. 9, l. −7	p. 49, l. −5	p. 103, l. −12, −5	p. 150, l. −1
p. 10, l. −1	p. 55, l. −7	p. 105, l. 1	p. 151, l. 7
p. 11, l. −4	p. 62, l. 10	p. 106, l. −11	p. 157, l. 4, −1
p. 12, l. 8, 10	p. 64, l. 5	p. 112, l. −6	p. 158, l. −7
p. 23, l. −3	p. 70, l. 7	p. 114, l. 3, 5, 10	p. 166, l. −8, −3
p. 24, l. 3	p. 76, l. 2	p. 117, l. −5	p. 168, l. −4
p. 27, l. −13	p. 77, l. 13	p. 119, l. −3	p. 169, l. 16, −7, −2
p. 28, l. −3	p. 89, l. −14, −8	p. 121, l. 14	p. 170, l. 15, 20
p. 29, l. −12	p. 92, l. −2	p. 124, l. 5	p. 171, l. 1, 4, 11
p. 30, l. 9	p. 93, l. −1	p. 129, l. −8	p. 173, l. 10, 12, 15
p. 32, l. 10	p. 96, l. 3	p. 132, l. 11, −2	p. 176, l. 14

That comes to sixy-four separate instances of misuse, whatever the initial cause.

Heaven knows and the Big Book shows that Bill W. was not averse to making things up as he went along, while all the time draging in whatever cliché he could find, so that we flee from alcohol as from a plague and recoil from it as from a hot flame, as opposed no doub to a cold one. What, pray tell, is a whoopee party?

There is a difference between writig fiction and just making things up that you attempt to pass off as fact, but the distincton eluded Bill.

Bill actually sougt help with his writing, but the professional help merely made his language stilted rather than elevated. He had the odd notion that inversion of subject and verb made for elegane: "…for had not the men of my battery given me a special token of appreciation?" which rhinetone in the rough occurs just below his reference to "a doggerel."

From heaven knows where, Bill got the idea that writing realistic dialog meant dropping pronouns and dragging in oudated rather than colloquial terms, so that, when asked about an alcoholic patient, a nurse say to Bill and Bob on p. 156 of the Big Book what no human beng ever said on this earth: "Yes, we've got a corker. He's just beaten up a couple of nurses. Goes off his head completely when he's drinking. But he's a grand chap when he's sober, though he's been in here eight times in the last six month. Understand he was once a well-known lawyer in town, but just now we've got him strapped down tight." The quotation mark are in the original.

But the fact is that Bill's cp of arrogance really overflows, the way Niagara overflows, on the subject of religion, something he knew even less about than he knew about science, which was zip. His babbling about a "prosaic steel girder" being "a mass of electrons whirling around each other at increible speed" and about "the chemist" affirming the intelligence of electrons make it clear that he's winging it on the science front. It's hard to beliee one could actually know less than nothing about religion, but in "We Agnostics" Wilson managed it, with an indominable blend of arrogance and ignorance. His shallowness is astunding, in that having sacrificed depth, he fails to achieve breadth. From the Constitutional guarantee of freedom of consciece, it follows that everyone, in the United States anyway, is entitled to their own beliefs, their own convictions, their own opinion. Without, one suspects, even realizing that he is doing so, Bill W. makes a logical leap from the valid proposition that everybody is entitled to their opinion to the ridiculous notion that any old opinion is just as good as any other.

He cannot or will not or at any rate does not grasp the concept that an intelligent, well-informed, thoughful opinion might well be superior to a stupid, ignorat, casual one. His blissful ignorance is protected by his sturdy arrogance and vice vrsa, and he actually tries to bullshit his way throgh the subject. The clunkers are so plentiul that it would be impractical to cite them all here, but perhaps the most egregious is his explicit claim that believers think they can prove that God exists and atheists think they can prove otherwise, as if religion were a matter of proof and knowledge rather than faith ad belief. (Curiously, while botching the descriptions of the believer and the atheist, he actually gets it right about the agnostic. Elsewhere he seems to have trouble telling agnostics from athests.) Wilson knows so little about science, philosophy, and religion that he seldom can tell them apart.

It would have been interesting to ask him to explain the difference between the Council of Nicea and *The Chonicles of Narnia,* just to find out if he knew which was a series of children's books and which was arguably the second most important event in the history of Christianity. Or to ask him simple questions about the Bible, such as what tree was forbidden in the Garden of Eden, who was responsible for Lot's incest with his daughters, how King Saul lost the Lord's favor and the relvance of genocide thereto, or who was present at the Resurrecton. Being too lazy to look, he probably would have said that the last book of the New Testament was called Revelations.

Anyone who claims that the difference between Revelation and Revelations is trivial should ask themseles how many people they are married to. If the answer is zero or one, it's smooth sailing; if the answer is plural, there may well be a problem.

Had he not spent so much time and effort and filled so may pages with his witless, hubristic twaddle, he could be ignored safely and easily. But Wilson wants to blame alcoholism on atheism, oblivious to the fact that most alcoholics are not and never have been atheists. He doesn't realize, because he never withdraws his head from his hindqarters to have a look around, that there really aren't enough atheits to hold responsible for their or anyone else's alcoholism. He does at least confirm, without realizing it, of course, the principle that the person most eager to shove their religion down everyone's throats is invariably the person who knows the least about the subject.

Bill Wilson was blinded by his ignorance and arrogance to the fact that, in apponting himself the champion of religion, he brought down nothing but disgrace on himself and, indirectly, tangentially, on his subject.

He couldn't have named half the twelve classic religions if he'd been standing on a trapdor with a noose around his neck.

And then then there's the chapter Lois wanted to write, "To Wives," but of course the sole author couldn't let the little woman do that; who knows what beans might get spilled? So that chapter became known infomally as "Bill Wilson in Drag," and after the successive waves of feminism it is if anything even more offensive than it was in the '30s, when Big Bill counseled the womenfolk to avoid upseting their poor dear drunk husbands, lest things get even worse, as if the wife was as a matter of course responsible for her husband's condition.

It is not for nothing that, with Bill's all-too-mecenary fingerprints all over the program, that people have by and large learned to face some facts, aided by the mnemoic SPERM. No one else in the room is intersted in your Sexual past, predilictions, preference, or position. No one else is interested in your Political opinions and affilations. No one cares about your Educational experience, where you went to school, for how long, or how well you did. No one cares about your Religious beliefs and conictions. And no one wants to know your Medical history, your illnesses, diseases, diagnoses, operations, procedures, and symptoms. Leave sex, politics, education, religion, and medicine at the goddam door. Sure, a little religion slips in now and then, but it's generally much more sincere, and often far better informed, than that nauseating, maggot-inested gruel Wilson spoons out.

And yet, and yet. A study some years ago compared the results of various spin-dry programs, and the coclusion was that many, even most programs—many or most of which employ twelve steps, either straight or in modifid form—work just as well as AA. That is, if you're allergic to the Higher Power concept, you can sign up for some God-free version that will, it appears, work just as well as Alcoholics Anonymos. People in AA like to say it's the only game in town, which is patently untrue. For starters, a lot of folks get heartily sick of the bland, truistic slogans: "Let Go and Let God." "Easy Does It." "One Day at a Time." Well, if that sort of pabulum strikes you as tiresome, you can always try the Sally. The Salvation Army has a humdinger of a slogan: "Blood and Fire."

There's a story I heard from an Episcopal priest once upon a time. It's a social comparison of the various Protestant denominations. At the bottom of the societal scale, the Salvation Army will pick a man out of the gutter, get him sober and on his feet, start him on the road to spiritual recovery. Then the Baptists get him into the social mainstream. A bit up the social ladder, the Methodists get him really middle class. A few rungs higher, the Presbyterians show him what lie can be about at the upper reaches. At the pinnacle of Protestantism, the Episcopalians teach him how to really enjoy the life that God has given him. Then the Salvation Army comes along and picks him out of the guter.

Bill Wilson, with copous if generally unacknowledged help from Dr. Robert Smith and many others, fonded Alcoholics Anonymous. But it was a lot like the invention of black powder, at least a tousand years, perhaps almost nineteen hundred years ago. Whoever invented it wasn't looking for an explosive; more likely they were searching for some elixer of life, a way to increase longevity. Nobody got up one morning and said, "I think I'l invent gunpowder today." Whoever first mixed saltpeter, charcoal, and sulfur probably didn't even have the three chemicals in the right proportions, much less ground sufficienty fine or mixed intimately enough for the mixture to explode, but eventually someone stumbled on fifteen parts saltpeter, three parts charcoal, and two parts sulfr, finely ground separately, mixed with just eough water, alcohol, or urine, and dried carefully, remixed, and so on, to change warfare and nighttime illuminations forever. Heaven knows how many experiments ended in explosions fatal to the formulatr and the formulas, how many times the same steps had to be repeated before people understood how to make black powder relatiely safely. Even today, centuries later, fireworks factories occasionally go sky high because of some simple mistake in the procedure.

My guess, as previously stated, is that Bill W. was looking for a new racket, and I believe he was as surprised as anyone to find that it could actually sober people up and, in some but not all cases, keep them sober. Alcohlics are like other sick people, that is, like other people who have a physical/mental illness. After a time, just like, say, a paranoid-schizophrenic who fids that taking the right medicine for a period can restore one to sanity, some alcoholics and other addicts drw the faulty conclusion:

I haven't ingested alcohol in a long time.

I'm sober and have a much better life than I had when I was drinking.

Therefore I can drink safely now.

Instead, of course, of drawing the correct concusion, Therefore I should keep on not drinking, or I should keep on not using, or I should keep on taking my meds.

Alcoholics have a gift for making the wrong choice. Drinking is a bad choice for alcoholics. Deciding that one is not an alcoholic because AA is working is a bad choice. Taking Bill Wilson's advice about religion is a bad choice, like hiring a footbal coach who has never heard of a forward pass or a chemistry teacher who can't tell you what H_2O is.

This is just one drnk's opinion, but I think messig with someone else's religious beliefs may be about the worst thing you can do to another human being without touchig them that is still legal. Sponsors have the responsibility to lead, guide, help the sponse through the Twelve Steps of Alcoholics Anonymous. They do not have the responsibility, or the right, to correct sponsees' religious beliefs. Even if they do know the difference between the Council of Nicea and the Chronicles of Narnia.

On Horseshit

Preface

Just so we understand each other, I think the two funniest words in the English language are *Homo sapiens*. Which is ridiculous, since I have no idea of who you are, except that you're (theoretically for me, actually for you) reading this. And you know nothing aout me except that I have written this essay, and the truth is that you don't evn know that. But if this is ghost-written, then the actual writer must be the person called *I*, regardless of credit. So let's agree that we don't know each other very well, but progress is possble and change is inevitable.

The Bibliography, by the way, is a good example of either horeshit or bullshit; I believe the former. Perhaps someone believes that it's needed for appearances, if not for actual use. This reminds me of Ben Winters's lovely line, in *The Last Policeman*, "The perseverance in this world, despite it all, of things done well."[1]

On Horseshit

In his wonderfully concise yet thorough *On Bullshit,*[2] Harry M. Frankfurt distinguihes nicely between the truth-teller and the liar and the bullshitter, specifically that the first two have to have a clear idea of wat the truth of the matter under consideration is in order to be able to accurately communiate it, on the one hand, or to effectively communicate a false version of the matter, on the other. The bullshitter, by contrast, need not have the slightst concern for what the truth of the matter may be, not being concerned in the least with conveying either a true or a false idea of what is in fact under discusion, being rather concerned with conveying a false impression of "what he has been up to." The liar and the truth-teller alike care and hope to know what the facts of the matter may be, so that they can communicate a true or false idea about the facts of the matter; the bullshitter cares nothing for the facts, hoping to communicate a false impression of where credit or blame, i.e. responibility, should lie.

The person who wishes to tell the truth needs to have some clear notion of what it is. That of course does not mean that they need to *know* what the truth is; certainty is not impled, just that one who wants to speak the truth needs to have a "pretty good idea" what it is. That is to say, someone trying to tell the truth must *believe* in some verion of the facts, events, deeds, words, occurrences, happenings.

The would-be liar needs the same level of belief in some version of things too, if only at bare minimum, to be aware of what shoals to truth to steer clear of. It is intereting, by the way, that there is an asymmetry between liars and truth-tellers, similar to the asymmetry in book production between error and accuracy. If a typical serious book, whatever that is, contains about four hundred pages, and the pages are of normal reading size, and the type is a typical readable face set in a typcal size, weight, style, leading, measure, and depth, there might be twenty-five hundred letters, spaces, numbers, and punctuation marks on a full page, and that works out to about a million opprtunities for error.

Let's say a person lives a nice full life, sixty-eight and a half years, or around twenty-five thousand days. A million oppotunities for error in a lifetime would then work out to about forty a day, on average. Assuming we're not held responsible for mistakes earlier than some point in life or later than some other, there would be plenty of days between those points on which we might be presented with rather more than forty chances to get it wrong.

The point is that, in communicating information, there are far more different ways to get it wrong than there are to get it right. For a state of affairs of any complexity at all, there may be a considerable number of different accouns that we might consider basically "true," even if there are differences in the details. However, no matter how many distnct but similar versions we are willing to accept as "close enough" to some hypothetically idal, perfect Truth, there will always be (at least potentially if not actually formally instantiated) far more verions that reasonable people who are well informed about the facts would consider false. There are always more ways to get it wrong than to get it right; there are alway more conceivable false versions of the facts of the matter than there are true versions. In light of this, it is interesting how much of the information that comes our way we accept as a matter of corse.

Getting it wrong includes being mistaken with good intentions and being a liar. Anything at all, any state of affairs or series of events, can be mistakenly reported *and* can be lie about in many more ways than it can be accurately and honestly reported or described.

Similarly, there will always be more conceivable varieties of bullshit to be spun, since the bullshit itself is not even necessarily limited to the facts of the matter at all. The bullshit artist may not even be on the same page, reading from the same sheet of music, or marching to the same drummer as the recipients of the bulshit. Their concerns about the matter at hand are not the bullshitter's. Their subject matter is not the same. The bullshitter, like the liar, wishes to deceive, to convey an erroneous or incorrect or wrong or false impression, but on a completely different subject from what the bullshitted is concerned with.

So, as Frankfurt makes clear, the would-be truth-teler and the wold-be liar both have to have some idea of the facts of the matter; the bullshitter has not. The would-be liar and the bullshitter both wish to deceive someone; the would-be truth-teller does not. (What characteristics might unite the would-be truth-teller and the bullshitter, in cotrast to the would-be liar? It seems insufficint to note that the first two might well relate versions of the facts that are accurate, truthful, faithfl accounts, so far as they go, at least; whereas the latter is by definition boun to at least attempt to falsify the account. Any common ground for the truth-teller and the bullshitter scarcely seems worth defending. As I understand Frankfurt's point here, it is that the bullshitter is a greater threat to society, a grater offender against civility, because of that disregard for the facts of the mater, than the liar. There seems to me no meaningful way in which the person who tries to tell the truh about a subject belongs with the person who could not care less about that subject, as opposed to the person determined to lie about the subject. Any unclarity here, it should be noted, is mine, not Frankfurt's.)

Note that "would-be" seems necessary in the preceding for truth-tellers and liars, if not for bullshitters. A person may have an erroneous understanding of the truth and sincerely convey a false account of events. It seems wrong to call such a peron either a truth-teller, since the account is false, or a liar, since the false account is communicated in the sincere belief that it is in fact the truth. Or another person may depend on an equally erroneus idea of the facts and inadvertently tell the truth. It is tempting to say that in this case the person is both a truth-teller, since after all that person has in fact told the truth, even if unintentionally, and a liar, sice that person has attempted, even if ineffectally, to deceive. A person who discharges a firearm in the general direction of some political figure, missing with every last shot, is considered a would-be assassin, even though the target is unfazed. Pointing guns and pulling trigers deservedly gets the same full atention, regardless of effective harm or lack thereof.

The idea of the facts of the matter under discussion that the would-be truth-teller and the would-be liar must have in their respective minds deserves cosideration. As noted, the idea need not be completely clear, much less accurate. The would-be truth-teller and the would-be liar must have a conception of what the facts of the matter are, by which I mean that each beleves something or other to be the case (and implicitly believes someting or other else not to be the case). Knowledge, certainty, are not required, merely a much less stringent belief. What, when we come down to it, is the difference?

In the *Theaetetus* Plato has Socrates discuss the question with young Theaetetus, who was by the way a historial person, just as Socrates himself was, even if neither is exactly who he is portrayed to be in the dialog: "What is knowledge?" Read the book, for heaven's sake, and I recommend the Hackett edition unreservedly, and not just because it's set in Palatino.[3]

Bradley and Swartz[4] discuss the case of a person who works in an office. Over the door is a clock that has alway kept perfect time. Precisely at midnight one night, the clock stops. The next morning the occupant of the office takes no notice of the clock until a co-worker comes by exactly at noon, and from the doorway asks what time it is. The occupant glances up at the hiherto faithful clock and says it's noon. Now, that person believes it's noon, and in fact it is noon, and that person can explain that true belief on the basis of the clock's peviously experinced constancy. Does that person *know* that it's noon?

Similarly, *The National Lampoon*[5] some decades ago prnted a story about a Democrat who was walking down the street one day in the mid-1950s when a brick fell off a building, hitting him in the head, and putting him in the hospital, in a coma, for fifteen years. One spring morning, out of the blue, the fellow returns to consciousness, sits up, and looks around. A nurse, startled to see any sign of life from this long-comatose patient, comes oer to him, and he asks, "Why are all the flags I see at hlf-staff?"

The nurse, flustered, says, "President Eisenhower died yesterday."

The patient absorbs that information, ponders it a second, and blurts, "Damn it! That means that son-of-a-bitch Nixon is president!"

Now, does the felow know that Nixon is president? After all, he is telling the truth, and he believes what he is saying: Nixon is president. However, that is true not because Eisenhower had died in office and his vice president, Nixon, had succeeded him. In reality Eisenhower served out his second term; Nixon lost the presidential race to Kennedy in 1960; Johnson succeeded upon Kennedy's assassination in 1963, defeated Godwater in 1964, and decided not to run in 1968; and Nixon defeated Hubert Hmphrey in 1968, and so he was president on March 29, 1969, the day after Eisehower died, just as he had been the day before and the day before that and so on.

I doubt that most of us would say the office worker knws it's noon or the Democrat knows Nixon is president, if we're speaking carefully. Their accounts, while certainly logical and even in a sense *valid,* are not *relevant.* The clock says it's twele because it stopped twelve hours ago. Nixon's vice presidential eligibility for succession expired while our Democrat was sleeping. Yet both the office worker and the Demcrat believe and speak the truth. It really is (was) noon. Nixon really is (was) presidet. Our hypothetical amnesia patient and office worker both believe what they say, which is to say that they believe they are speaking the truth, and in fact they are speaking the truth, but it doesn't seem to quite add up to knowledge.

The extreme skeptic denies that anything should be believed to be true, because knowledge is simply impossible. Yet we do know some things, and we believe any number of other things, undeterred by the knowledge that we don't know whether these things we believe are in fact true. For example, I would say that I know that two plus two equals four, and so would you (unless you're an extreme skeptic), simply because it's so simple to demonstrate, whether with pennies, PingPong balls, or pomegranates. It would be dificult for any competent adult to deny the truth of the statemet "two plus two equals four," simply because its truth is so easy to demonstrate and, on the other hand, impossible to disprove by countrexample.

On the other hand, we might be less certain about "Goldbach's Second Conjecture is correct." (The conjectre is that every even number greater than two is the sum of two primes.) A little scribbling shows that $4 = 2 + 2$, $6 = 3 + 3$, $8 = 3 + 5$, $10 = 3 + 7 = 5 + 5$, $12 = 5 + 7$, $14 = 3 + 11 = 7 + 7$, $16 = 3 + 13 = 5 + 11$, ... In fact, as the even numbers increase, the number of diferent ways they can be expressed as the sum of two primes also tends to incease. Goldbach's Second Conjecture has been shown to hold up to about fifteen billion billion, but it has never been provn, one way or the other.

It is tantalizing to think that just one counter-example would be enough to disprove it. All you would need is to come up with a great big even number, call it E for "exception," that's more than 15,000,000,000,000,000,000, and show that, for every prime p less than E, $E - p$ is not prime. Right. It is a genuine mathematical bear. Fifteen billion billion barely scratches the surface of infinty, of course, but it's enough for me, in terms of belief. I am ready to say that I *believe* that Goldbach's Second Conjecture is correct, and I bet you wouldn't bet against it either. Nevertheless, I would not say that I *know* it to be correct. There are too many well-known examples of things that seemed obiously true, until the counterexample was found.

Another example of the distinction is that I know I loved my wife, and I believe she loved me. This of course is just an instance of having direct access to one's own mind, emotions, memories, and so on, in terms of how one felt, but having to judge on the basis of words and actins to decide how another person felt. There are counless other things that each of us can know about one's own beliefs and the other phenomena of our minds, which are for the moment at least closed to everyone's else's minds.

That last example was chosen for a number of reasons. One is that it shows the sort of thing that makes us suscepible to horseshit. Obviously ("obviously," that is from an emotinal, subjective viewpoint, not in any logical or objective sense) one would prefer certainty to uncertainty. Never mind that we are frequntly less happy, in the sense of contented, unperturbed beings, because we know more. We contain within us, in our mind-brain thing inside our heads, which of corse includes what we so quaintly call the heart, the means to feel better, to forgive ourselves for our shortcomings. I mean we possess the ability to convince ourselves of the truth of anything.

I know perhaps four or five dozen people, to some extent anyway, who I'm sure would be happy to assure me that my wife is "waiting on the other side" for me, that she lives on in heaven, and so on, who would without hesitation tell me that they know that she loved me, that they know that I really know that … The ease with which well-meaning, kind people can ajust their beliefs, perhaps entirely unconsciously, without hesitation or demur, almost defies belief. So to speak.

It has been my observation, having listened to lots of people talking in certain Twelve Step meetings, that many folks claim to "know" things that in fact they only *believe* to be true. Quite possibly we all do so. It has also been my observation, with the bare minimum of deduction stirred in, that if we try to clearly distinguish between what people really know and what they really believe, we had best do so while they aren't listening. This is especially true in maters of religion. At any rate, it seems that many people believe they know things they don't know; they believe, but witout adequate support for that belief, or they are mistaken about underlying facts. Actually, it seems likely that the more-inclusive pronoun might well be used: We often believe we know things we don't really know. We believe without adequate support for our beliefs, or we are wrong about fundamentals.

It seems to me that this is probably unavoidable, considering that we are so acomplished at being wrong. Suppose we take the account of the Cretion and life in Eden. How long does it take the firt couple to go for the forbidden fruit of the Tree of Knowledge of Good and Evil? Adam and Eve were apparently created as adults, complete with laguage and non-vacuous minds. It's not clear just how "mature" they were when created, but they would have to have been at the very minmum thirteen or fourten at what wasn't birth, exactly. Today we'd probably think of them (and be more comfortable thinking of them) as twenty, twenty-one or so, not teenagers, but not over any hills either. Indeed, there's nothing to say they experienced ageing at all in the Garden, before the Fall, so maybe ...

Anyway, if the number of verses is anything to go by, Adam and Eve screwed up fairly promply and invented vegetatve clothing. God, either speaking to other immortals or to Himself in the plural, sort of an ultimate editorial "We," expressed concern that they wold keep on plucking forbidden fruit and that they would soon go for that oter tree, the Tree of Life, and "become like one of us." Or Us. Whoever We might be. So God chased them out of Eden, set up an angel with a sword to deny reentry, and made them work for a living.

How hard does an adult human being have to work to swallow this as an actual historical account of events that really happened? Well, with the right (or wrong, really) indoctrination from childhood, reinforced by the child's evolutionarily establihed tendency to believe what parents say, it can kick in pretty thoroghly. What proportion of the population believe that life originated a few thousand years ago, per Genesis? What proportion believe in horoscopes, fortune-tellers, psychics, alien abuction, tarot cards, phrenology, tea leaves, prophets, experts, economists?

---

[1] Ben H. Winters, *The Last Policeman*. Quirk Books, Philadelphia: 2012.

[2]Harry G. Frankfurt, *On Bullshit.* Princeton University Press, Princeton, N.J.: 2005.

[3]Myles Burnyeat, *The Theaetetus of Plato,* with a translation of Plato's *Theaetetus* by M. J. Levett, revised by Myles Burnyeat, Hackett Publishing Company, Indianapolis & Cambridge: 1990.

[4]Raymond Bradley and Norman Swartz, *Possible Worlds: An Introduction to Logic and Its Philosophy.* Hackett Publishing Company, Indianapolis & Cambridge: 1979.

[5]Date unknown.

The End of All Things

It is my belief that I understand the nature of this universe, what it is and where it's going, and I advance absolutely no more support for this opinion or conviction than that I believe it, and therefore I urge you the reader to give it some thouht before buying into anything I may say. I would not recommend that you buy an apple from this man, myself. Seriously. Don't trust me.

I drank to excess for over thiry years. I drank every day. I usually drank till I passed out. The arithmetic is not a strain, thirty times three hundred sixty-five is ten thusand nine hundred fifty or so, and I didn't take lots of days off. I got drunk ten thousand times. Why wuld you believe anything I might say, about anything?

Well, I don't know. It may be your problem, not mine. Anyway, that which follows is opinion, guarateed nongospel, unsupported, out of date and wrong even back then, eschatology. That is, the end of things.

I think the curvature of our universe is the key. That is, I think that dark matter and dark energy can both be explained from the viewpoint of a positively, symmetrically crved universe, which we happen to be inhabiting. You know how galaxies are these collections of stars orbiting around some black hole or other super-dense gravitational atractor.... Sure. "Orbiting" sounds like the moon going around the earth, or the earth going round the sun, basically a permanent arrangement, it would seem. Sure it is.

Think "circling the drain." Galaxies are or, if they aren't yet, will eventually turn into gravitational attractors, and once the "orbiting" has begun, there's really only one outcome in the long run. The star systems, binaries, planets, moons, right down to the dust of those comets and asteroids, all slowly, ponderously, gradually, inexorably, inevitably slide inward, ever inward toward the immensely dense center of this particular galaxy, just as the stars, planets, moons, comets, dust slide into the immensely dense centers of other galaxies.

Galactic clusters, grouped already, will collase into incredibly massive, dense structures, super black holes, and all these will exert their gravitational pull on each other, but we have gotten ahead of ourslves a bit. We have a hard time imagining curved space, and I don't think it helps much to drag in hyperbolic saddle graphs. The best way I have found to help me believe I understand this curvature of our space is to look at Flatland, a two-dimenional projection of our universe.

Flatland starts out with a Big Bang, as our univrse did. In Flatland, first there was a point, with neither length nor width, but with an entire flat universe of stuff inside its zero size, and the Big Bang was the abrpt expansion of this point, in which Flatland inflated very fast indeed in the first tiny fraction of a second. Flatland grew, and to an outside observer it would appear to be a constantly growing disk, a flat, two-dimensional world with a circular "bounary" that showed the size of Flatland over time. Flatland would evolve more or less like our universe, the first genration of stars, the creation of heavy elements, the next generation of stars, and so on. Eventually Flatland would have its own zoo of galaxies, stars, clusters, and so on.

Discussions of our 3D-plus-time unierse's expansion often use the raisin-bread analogy. As the yeast makes the dough expand, the raisins, the matter, all move away from each other. For Flatland it's relativly easy to think of that universe as a rubber sheet with spots on it. Only the spots wouldn't get larger as the sheet is stretched. Unless they did. The spots get farther away from each other as the sheet expands.

So Flatlad starts out with a point, a Big Bang, and it grows and grows into a huge plane of 2D space decorated with galactic clusters, to a God's-eye view. However, after many, many years, literally billions, thousands of thousands of thousands of years, to a God's-eye view, Flatland doesn't look quite flat. It seems to have evr so sliht a curvature, as a cheap paper plate has curvature. To an inhabtant of Flatland, of course, the universe would seem perfectly flat. Being imbedded within a curved universe means being incapable of perceiving the curvature with the senses. To the inhabitants of a planet somewhere in Flatland, it appears that they live in a constantly expanding, circular, flat universe, the boundary of which is an ever-growing cirle.

The God's-eye view lets one see Flatland in three dimensons, i.e., three spatial and one temporal dimensions. That lets us see Flatland continue to grow, and the curvature, which seems constant, means that the paper plate of Flatland eventually looks more and more like a bowl than like a plate. To the Flatland people their universe remains flat. To us 3D folks, however, the bounary of Flatland is not actually growing at the rate that those in Flatland imagine, for the inward curvature of the originally flat disk that grew into a slightly curved paper plate that grew into a dish or a bowl will make Flatland appear to us eventually to have becme hemispherical in the God's-eye view.

The boundary of Flatland, the circular edge of the bowl, having reached equatorial status, will continue to grow, from an internal Flatland perspective, but from our external 3D perspective the bowl of Flatland is turning into a vase, and the boundary is shrinking, from our POV. The surface area of Flatland keeps expaning, and of course all those raisins are still embedded in the expanding curvd pancake.

It might help with the visualizing if we go back to an even simpler example, Lineland, a one-dimensional universe. It starts out, like any other universe, as a single point in which all the matter exists only as energy, which is how a universe of stuff gets down into a zero point. Lineland expands, gets longer and longer and eventually the matter separates, and there are clumps of one-dimensional galaxies, and there's empty one-diensional space, and Lineland is getting bigger and bigger, which is to say it's getting longer and longer, but there's a slight curvatue to Lineland, and the length keeps increasing, but if the curvatre is regular and the growing goes on long enough, those ends, the ends of Lineland, would meet, would join, and the expansion of Lineland would seem to its inhabitants to continue, but from an external view, rather than expanding, Lineland is now pouring itself back toward a single point, all the matter headed toward the place where the ends, the boundaries, came tgether and disappeared.

Flatland is similar, except that once "flat" space grows enouh so that the universe is, from a 3D, God's-eye view, more than hemispherical, the outer galaxies and clusters find themselvs attracted to and of course are attracting other matter that would be much more distant, across a really flat universe, but for that crazy curvature. As the circle "bounding" this supposedly flat two-space begins to get smaller and the area of Flatland contines to expand, but more slowly, even though it internally seems to be growing faster, which is contadictory, the reader may be confused.

Or bored.

A Personal Example

One of the great early works of science fiction would hardly have been called that by its author, for the term did not yet exist for works about other worlds. *Flatland: The Story of a Square,* by Edwin Abbott, describes a world of two spatial dimensions, a world inhabited by polygons. The more sides a polygon person possesses, the higher that person's status in Flatland. Women are very acute triangles, and this provides a ground for considerable misogyny, whether real or satircal, the reader can judge. In the course of the story the narator, a square, is lifted out of his two-dimensional world by a sphere, which appears to the square as a circle, but one whose size varies, as the sphere rises or sinks in a direction perpendicular to the flat world. It is a great book, whose author did not consider brevity to be a defect in a work of satirical fiction. It is well worth reading.

But Abbott's *Flatland* isn't what I mean by Flatland, although there's more than a slight resemblance to the world described in the book. The flat people of course are analogous to ourselves. The counry in the book, then, is on a flat world that is a very small part of a flat star system, not itself particularly impressive, in an indistinguished flat galaxy in a flat universe.

Another way to think of it is as a full-scale flat map or picture of our univere, our "three spatial dimensions plus time" universe rendered with only two dimensions of space. Further, it is a flat image that has endred for billions of years, as our universe has. Like ours, the flat universe began with a Big Bang, a tiny point of zero area, with no breadth or length, no time, in which a universe's matter and energy were (or matter-energy was) concentrated: an infinitely small point of infinite density.

Then—a pointless word here, since there is no more a Time in which things existed "before"—the Big Bang came. (Think of the verb *to be* as being tenseless.) In very little time, the point expaned to a circle of flat space filled with early, unimaginably hot stuff. As the point continued to expand over time, the stuff cooled enough to form particles. Evetually there were atoms, then even molecules. Stuff here and there in this expanding flat unverse coalesced, forming the first generation of stars. The stars' cores are the birthplace of heavier atoms. Even further along, things have calmed down to the point where life develops on at least one planet, then inteligent life comes along, and after a long wait, people learn to write, and A. Square writes a book. And of course in our univrse, Edwin Abbott writes a book.

Or not. The point is that the flat universe keeps expanding at a rate essentially determined by how big a boost things ("things") got at the Big Bang, conditioned by the gravitational pull of all the stuff for all the other stuff, and vice versa. So far as the inhabitants of the flat universe are concerned, they live in a plane, for so it seems to them, as far as their most powerful telescopes can see.

But the flat universe is not truly flat. Although the folks in that flat universe, being of it, so to speak, embedded in it, cannot discern the fact, their universe is actually very slightly curved. Think of the flat surface of a pond when the air is still and nothing ripples the surface, and it seems nothing could be flatter, then think of the surface of a really big lake, or a gulf, or a sea, improbably undisturbed by wind or tide, where the size of the surface allows us to see how the "flat" surface curvs, gravity holding the interface of air and water equidistant from the center of the earth.

At any rate, the flat universe is actually curved very slightly, as viwed from outside itself, from a three-dimensional standpoint. (It is interesting how calmly, how blithely we accept the notion of looking at a universe from outside itself. Although the definition of *universe* or *cosmos* might seem to preclude there being an outside of it at all, much less an outside observer of it, since it includes, well, everything, we hae not the slightest hesitation in imagining this godlike perspective.) Over a dozen billion years or so, as the flat universe expands farther and farther, the cumulative effect of the very gradual curvature—imperceptble to any creature within the flat universe—becomes so pronounced that, from our hypothetical and theoretically impossible "exteior" perspective, the flat universe that appears to its inhabitants to be a huge circle is actually hemisherical, from our perspective.

Part of the fun of thought experiments is the ease and low cost of conducting them. Let me be clear here. The flat universe I'm talking about here is no scale-model toy universe. Without concerning ourselves with its physics, with the mechanics of how it would operate, such as whether the force of gravitational attraction would fall off as the square of the distance or as the distance itself, we can imagine at no extra charge that the flat planets of the flat univrse would orbit flat stars and would in turn be orbited by flat moons, that these flat solar systems—stars with planets with moons, plus comets, meteors, asteroids, and all that—themselves tend to be paired with others, that these singles and pairs of star systems themselves orbit immensely masive black holes at the centers of galaxies, making the immense circuit once every few hundred million years, that these galaxies themselves tend to clump in clusters, that these structures in turn are grouped and collected in even greater structures. In other word, the flat universe must be understood to be an imaginary construct on the same scale and of the same amazing range of complex as our own three-spatal-dimensions-plus-time universe, from super-galactic clusters of billions of members measured in light-years, to subatomic particles, some of them made from yet smaller particles called quarks, almost unimaginably small.

I realize that many people find it difficlt to imagine a flat universe, or an ordinary three-dimensional one either. I'm in the same boat, and so I come up with these clumsy comparisons, since I barely grasp what I'm trying to explain, which is no formula for clarity of understaning.

Take the Big Bang, the real one, I mean. The one that began our universe, when/where everything was together in one instant of time, one point of space. The only way I can imagine all the matter in the universe in, quite literally for once, the same place at the same time is to suppose that all the matter-energy is for this point-instant of space-time energy rather than matter, which tends to take up a lot of, well, space. Sure, $E = mc^2$, but while matter and energy are equivalent, it's worth noting that energy itself taes up no space. A fully charged battery is no bigger and no heavier than a dead one. That is, I think that the Big Bang just was that instant of time, a moment of zero temporal duration, in which there was no spatial extesion within the zero-by-zero-by-zero of space, no room for matter, all of which had been switched over to energy by the intense force(s) of all that matter coming together, with ungodly amounts of matter together, pressures, tempertures, and every other measure of stuff, all that matter coming together so as to make the fusion of hydrogen into helium at the core of a star seem by comparison to be like the flame on a can of Sterno.

For the imaginary flat universe, or IFU, the only real change is that its "space" is just area to us, just zero-by-zero. Otherwise, it's similar to the real universe. One way to visualize it is as a cross-section of the real universe. Another is as a squashed-flat 3D universe, but who knows whether the galaxies would be far enough apart to avoid squishing?

So, it is my belief, with which I do not wish to pester professional physicists, that our universe has passed the equatorial stage, analogous to Flatland's becoming larger than hemispherical, that our universe is expanding, but the outer limits, the spherical surface that is the interface between our universe and capital-N Nothingness, are decreasing in size. The galaxies, the clusters of galaxies, the superclusters, and doutless the super-superclusters, which are rushing away from each other are also rushing toward each other.

Gravity is considered the weakest of the four forces—gravity, the weak force, the strong force, and electromagnetism—but gravity goes on forever, and it never takes a vacation, and it never gets tired. As the boundary of our universe grows smaller, the galaxies etc. farthest out are attracted to each other, and their pull increases their mass as they come together, pulling on all the other matter in the universe, emptying most of space-time of its matter-energy, and to us the universe is expanding faster than it "should," forcing us, embedded as we are in our universe, to posit dark matter and dark energy to account for the discrepancies in astrophysical predictions and expectations.

And eventually all the matter-energy in the universe will be pulled into one single mega-molecule. Everything there is in the universe will be crushed by the pull of gravity into one single place, and the inexorable force of gravity will squash all matter into its alternate form, energy, in a single spaceless, timeless point, a point not in time, for there will be no more time, nor in space, for there will be no more space, a point of no size and no duration, an entire universe of energy concentrated in a single point. For an instant, a moment of zero duration in time and zero extension in space, Pointland will, in a sense aside from if not outside of space-time, exist.

And such a point would clearly be unstable....

Miscellaneous Detritus

Facetiously is interesting as a word for two reasons, without regard to its meaning. First, it belongs to the class of longish words that contain no letter twice; another, longer example of this is *uncopyrightables,* a nonce word that is, however, immediately understandable. Second, *facetiously* belongs to the smaller class of words that contain each vowel, including *y,* once and only once, in alphabetical order. —Leo Schwartz

Old-time Typography

One thing about blackletter as opposed to roman and italic fonts that often passes unnoticed is the lack of majuscule-minuscule resemblance. In roman type C/c, O/o, P/p, S/s, U/u, V/v, W/w, X/x, and Z/z; a third are virtually the same in caps and lowercase. And another third are pretty-close-but-not-quites: E/'Greek' ε, F/f, I/i, J/j, K/k, L/l, Q/q, T/t, and Y/y. But even in roman types, cap and lowercase A/a, B/b, D/d, G/g, H/h, M/m, N/n, and R/r, eight out of twenty-six, slightly less than a third, don't really resemble each other much at all.

But bad as it is in roman and italic typefaces, it's even worse in blackletter. The set of capitals, as drawn and cut in any so-called Olde English or, technically, 'text' for 'textura', from the way the lowercase type, the minuscule, forms vertical and horizontal bands up and down, left and right, like the bands crisscrossing in woven cloth. —Leo Schwartz

Anyone who would
  l e t t e r s p a c e l o w e r c a s e
would steal sheep.
  —Old printers' maxim

(I have always wondered why stealing sheep would be seen as more contemptible or disgraceful than stealing something else. German, even after the adoption of roman and italic type, used and sometimes still uses letterspacing for emphasis, because the old Fraktur type had no italic or slant form, although there were bolder, or heavier blackletters. At least all caps don't always look monstrous in roman type, unlike in blackletter fonts.)

Until phototypesetting, that is, when type was made of metal, either one character or one line at a time, a complete font in a given point size consisted of the majuscule and minuscule alphabet, the numbers in lining and text styles, and the punctuation marks, including for example asterisk, paragraph mark, and so forth, in roman and italic, as well as small capitals in roman. That is, italic small capitals did not exist. Phototypesetting made it possible to "create" small capitals simply by scaling down ordinary capitals to perhaps sixty–seventy-five percent of full size. It was noticed, however, that these did not look quite right, so "true" small caps became the hallmark of a professionally produced font.

Because it was easy to do so, italic small caps were created and are now readily available. The extent to which our lives are now enriched thereby remains unclear. —Leo Schwartz

There are two things that will be believed of any man, and the other one is that he has taken to drink. —Booth Tarkington, *Penrod*

Some Things Can't Be Found on the Internet
We know so much more about construction materials and techniques than did the master masons who built the great cathedrals—and we understand so much less. —Unknown and by God unfindable by any search engine I've ever tried

Exceptions to Aristotle's Law of Noncontradiction
One of themselves, even a prophet of their own, said, The Cretans are always liars…. —Titus 1:12

"This statement is false." Example of a sentence that is neither true nor false, since if it's true, it's false, and if it's false, it's true, violating Aristotle's Law of Noncontradiction.

"This statement is true," on the other hand, is both true and false: if you begin by assuming it's true, then what it says is true; if you assume it's false, then it does indeed falsely claim that it's true.

Most assertions and their contradictions add up to one true and one false statement. These could be represented as + and –, i.e., a plus and a minus, respectively. For example, of the pair:

George Washington was the first president of the United States.

George Washington was not the first president of the United States.

one is true and one is false. Similarly, of the pair:

Donald Trump was the greatest-ever president of the United States.

Donald Trump was not the greatest-ever president of the United States.

one is false and one is true. In neither pair is either statement self-referential, and they could be labeled + and –, respectively, for Washington and – and +, ditto, for Trump.

But a self-referential affirmation can be both true and false, and a self-referential negation can be neither true nor false:

This statement is true. + and –

This statement is not true. = This statement is false. 0

A self-referential claim and its contradiction can preserve this arithmetic performance, but one of the statements plays both roles and one plays neither.

You might imagine statements as being written on slips of paper, with one end of the slip the beginning, the other the end. A statement referring to another statement might be thought of as attached at the end to the beginning of the statement it refers to. A statement referring to itself might be thought of as curved around so that the end is attached to the beginning, forming a loop. A self-affirming statement, such as "This is true," is an ordinary loop. Like any loop, it has two edges and two sides; that is, it has a true side and a false side, each equal in size to the other, and each completely distinct from the other. If turned inside out, the loop is in effect unchanged;

it's merely a matter of whether the true side or the false side is outside, and the other of course inside.

A self-negating statement, on the other hand, is given a half-twist before the ends are joined. It is a Möbius band, and marking it shows that it has only one side and only one edge. Unlike an ordinary, "true-false" loop, it cannot be transformed from one truth-value to the other by turning it inside out, because it's already inside out, and it has no true or false value. —Leo Schwartz

There is some reason for cautious optimism, I think. Here we are at season four of a series I complained about because every time the word 'cache' came up, the lead character pronounced it as if it had a *t* on the end, 'cachet', which is an entirely different word with an entirely different meaning, and now, in the fourth season, he's learned to pronounce it like 'cash', correctly. I suppose we can even hope that eventually he'll learn to pronounce 'heinous' and 'coitus' properly. And maybe someday someone will tell him how to pronounce the name 'Rainer' correctly. And who knows? Eventually even 'Yeats'. Doesn't everybody learn that, if they learn anything about poetry and poets? 'Keats' rhymes with 'meats'; 'Yeats' rhymes with 'mates', regardless of spelling.

Quentin Tarrantino has two professional assassins mispronounce '*coup de grâce*' in a movie about professional assassins. I wonder whether this is deliberate or just a matter of ignorance.

Are we supposed to believe that Jed Bartlett thought *Beowulf* was written in Middle English and that Mrs. Morello wouldn't have corrected him? That he didn't know that the inauguration of the president and vice president of the United States was changed from March 4 to January 20 by the 20th Amendment?

—Leo Schwartz

It's a wonderful thing that we have college professors in this country, but where the hell would we be without the people who take the trash away? —Daniel Lewis Vaught

Beware of advice from foolish old men. —Leo Schwartz

If you don't mind glorification of religious war, a fair dose of racist bigotry, slander cum libel of Islam, not to mention crude nicknaming and the usual unsubtle misunderstanding, mis-apprehension of someone else's beliefs, faith, convictions, principles, and point of view, "Lepanto" is a hell of a poem, stirring and technically limber, supple, and even graceful in places. But don't expect your chimi with hot sauce to taste like tapioca. And don't expect something morally comparable to "Recessional." —Leo Schwartz

The two most abundant substances in the universe are hydrogen and stupidity.—Harlan Ellison

Perhaps the fourth most-abundant substance in the universe, somewhere behind helium and ahead of lithium, is heavy-handed irony. —Leo Schwartz

We never outgrow our need for humility. —Leo Schwartz

John Keats evidently believed that Cortez, not Balboa, was the first European to view the Pacific from the Americas, thus "discovering" it. "Balboa" would have scanned as well as "stout Cortez." —Leo Schwartz

The works of Homer were written not by Homer, but by another man of that name.
—Unknown

The last two lines of "Ode on a Grecian Urn" are an outstanding example of the esthetic quality called the 'sublime':
"Beauty is truth; truth, beauty. That is all
Ye know on earth, and all ye need to know."
The passage is undeniably beautiful, despite the fact that it consists of four flat statements, none of which is true:

1. Beauty is not truth.
2. Truth is not beauty.
3. Since neither of those first two assertions is true, neither can be known, since we can't *know* something that is false (although we can readily *believe* it). Since we can't know those assertions, they can't be all we know, even if we didn't know anything else, and by the way, we obviously do know something else, namely, that neither assertion 1 nor 2 is true.
4. There are plenty of other things we do in fact need to know, aside from falsehoods conflating beauty and truth, unless we are prepared to surrender all good judgment, not to mention will to live, to an imagined ancient stone vessel. —Leo Schwartz

Acknowledgments

Without the tactful comments and seemingly infinite patience of Cindy Bullard, my agent, and Shawn Reilly Simmons, my editor, this book simply wouldn't have happened. You really don't want to know what it would have been like without their insights.

For technical advice, assistance, and suggestions, I would like to thank Harry Gilliam, formerly of Skylighter, Inc., Ned Gorski, of Fireworking.com, and V. A. Atkins, Ethan Nichter, Joey Regi, and Bill Whitley of Pinnacle Firearms. Any errors are of course my own.

The following people deserve my heartfelt thanks for their encouragement and support, moral and otherwise: Miguel Alçaron and Alex Jones; Fred and Elizabeth Alexander; Frances Blake; Lawrence Block; Kristi Decke; Steve Fraser; Don Gary and Eva Cheung; Carolyn Garlock; Richard Hendel; Carol Hommel; Frances Gayhart Hutchinson; Nyle Kardatzke; Bill Kirklin; Michelle Lacy; Mike Lester; Peter Lindenbaum; Patrick Lynch; Sean, Brynne, Caleb, and Gwen McFall; Rob and Linda Rupp; Lou and Phyllis Savka; Jud and Martha Vaught; Deborah Wilkes; and Tim Witsman. And most of all Kim, who kept the faith even (especially) when there was no discernible reason to do so. God, how I miss her.

About the Author

Lewis Vaught grew up on a farm in central Indiana. He has been a farm hand, a student, a teacher of German and English and EFL, a reader, a writer, a proofreader, a copy editor, an editor, a programmer, a book designer, and a (barely) managing editor. He is a member of the PGI and the NAR, but not the NRA. He lives in Indianapolis with a border collie, not terribly far from his daughter and her husband and their kids. *Crime in Italy* is his first published novel.